THE SUNDAY MAN

Also by Gavin Robertson

Thousand

THE SUNDAY MAN

Gavin Robertson

Jill
best wishes
Gavin Robertson..

HEADLINE
FEATURE

First published in 1999
by HEADLINE BOOK PUBLISHING

A HEADLINE FEATURE hardback

10 9 8 7 6 5 4 3 2 1

British Library Cataloguing in Publication Data

Robertson, Gavin
The Sunday man
1. Suspense fiction
I. Title
823.9′14[F]

ISBN 0 7472 2206 1 (hb)

Typeset by Palimpsest Book Production Limited,
Polmont, Stirlingshire
Printed and bound in Great Britain by
Mackays of Chatham plc, Chatham, Kent

HEADLINE BOOK PUBLISHING
A division of the Hodder Headline Group
338 Euston Road
London NW1 3BH

www.headline.co.uk
www.hodderheadline.com

for my mother

Chapter One

MONDAY

Atlanta, USA

On what passes for a clear afternoon in Atlanta, the top twenty floors of the Peachtree Plaza Hotel rise above the hazy brown smog that covers the lower fifty floors.

The very top floor houses a restaurant and it was in here that Peter Wilson was sitting, near the glass outer wall looking out over the city. He leant back and ran his fingers through his hair before locking them behind his head and staring back to the table in front of him.

He looked at his watch. She was an hour and a half late and so she should arrive any minute now. He smiled to himself. Just time for a top up.

As if on cue, a waiter approached him with a cordless telephone on a tray.

'Excuse me, sir. Are you Dr Wilson?'

Peter looked up and nodded.

'There's a call for you, sir. But not a very good line, I'm afraid.'

Peter picked up the phone and could hear a hissing and crackling even before he put it to his ear.

'Hello,' he said. 'Is that you, Jaygo?'

'Of course it bloody is. Can you hear me properly?'

'No. Christ, Jaygo. Where are you? It sounds like a Chinese kitchen.'

'Oh, yes, very funny. I'm on a bloody helicopter and they won't turn the sound down for me to make a call. Something about it falling out of the sky.'

He smiled widely. She hadn't changed.

1

'Anyway, Peter, darling,' she went on. 'I'm running a bit late but should be with you in five or ten minutes. Look out your window towards the sun and you'll see me coming in at nine o'clock or something.'

Peter turned to the window and looked towards the gathering sunset. He could just pick out the flashing strobe light of a helicopter about a mile away.

'Got you, Cello One. You are cleared on pad Hotel Hotel.'

'OK. Look, the thing is I'm simply dying to see you. Order me a nice drinkey. Very long and cold with lots of ice but no umbrella.'

'Of course. Shall I come up to the roof to meet you?'

'No. Definitely not. God knows what this thing has done to my hair. I do want to make a proper entrance, you know.'

He smiled again.

'And another thing,' she went on. 'What room are you? I've got the cello with me and it's going to need a nice cool sit down after all this heat.'

'6034.'

'Good. Look, I can hardly hear you in this thing. Five minutes. Ten tops. Love you madly.' And the telephone went quiet.

'If only,' he said to himself as he held out the telephone for the waiter who had been hovering at a discreet distance.

'Thank you,' said Peter. He looked closely at the waiter's name badge. 'Torin?'

'Yes, sir.'

'Well, Torin. I'm going to need a bit of help here. Jocasta Manhattan is going to be here in about five minutes. Yes, *the* Jocasta Manhattan. I want you to call down to the salon and get them to send a hairdresser plus kit up to the roof to meet Miss Manhattan's helicopter. And also send several porters to carry an extremely valuable cello and about a million suitcases to Room 6034. Then come back here with a very long Crème de Menthe Frappée. OK?'

'Hairdresser to the roof, sir?'

Peter pointed with his thumb towards the helicopter. 'That's her, Torin. And take it from me, she does not like to be kept waiting.'

'Yes, sir. A real pleasure.'

When the waiter had left, Peter mused to himself. Meeting Jaygo from a hot and noisy helicopter? Not a *real* pleasure. You'd have to be quite brave really.

His briefcase was open next to him on the table. On the top

2

of a pile of files were three copies of the paper he was due to present at the conference on Tuesday morning. 'Data-handling problems encountered during long-range forecasting of locust swarms.' God, he thought, what a dull title. Right up there with 'Stored maize infestation assessment' and 'The numbers of pests in dry pea silos'.

He smiled when he remembered how he and his student friend David had pinned up dull papers on the laboratory notice board.

'Pete,' he could hear David saying. 'If ever you catch me writing anything really dull, just do the decent thing for me, will you? I'll understand.'

And ten years later, here he was about to give a paper that would have gone straight up on the wall.

It's just that it's got the wrong name, he thought. It should be called, 'Someone's buggered my data about but I don't know why'. Perhaps that would make them sit up. Perhaps not. 'You see, Peter,' Bob Anderson would say, 'messed-up data isn't really interesting until you know why. Give me the how or the who and I'll listen. But, until then, I'm afraid that all you've got is a nice idea that's gone wrong.'

Maybe that's all there was to it. A nice idea that'd gone wrong. No, that was negative thinking. He knew his paper was valid. Someone had got to his data before he could report it. Messing up other people's results was as old as science itself but usually with an identifiable motive. Jealously, religious fervour, or just plain dislike. But his data was hardly likely to invite feelings like that, so what was behind it? Was someone interested in his original idea and just wanted to delay him until they could publish themselves?

He thought the original idea had been good enough. Swarm prediction by tracer-tagging locusts and then tracking their movements by satellite. Peter had been so excited by the first images he had downloaded from the satellites. Clear lines moving in definite directions with a detail not seen before. But then the data had begun to break up. The lines had blurred and become meaningless. Was it just the 'nice idea' not working?

He doubted it. He had run the numbers several times and could clearly see the point where the pattern of results had broken up. But there was absolutely no precursor, no glitch of any kind to set the lines going wrong. It had to be a someone and not a something. Other people's satellite tracking was working and so why not his? Wildebeest, gorillas. Even lions. God, you couldn't move on the

3

Serengeti without running into some animal or other with an aerial sticking out of its head. Yes, he knew that these were big animals with individual transmitters and his were very small and only dusted with tracer but the principle was the same. At least he thought so. It remained to be seen if he could convince the conference. But he knew that scientists liked nothing more than to shake their heads quietly as some new idea took a nose dive.

All he would actually have to show them would be a series of charts and tables getting worse and worse. Not much competition to set against a turtle coming up a beach in the Cayman Islands with a radio glued to its shell.

He took a sip from his drink. Is this my second or third? he asked himself. The trouble with scientists is that they don't know an interesting table of figures when they see one.

He looked back to the helicopter as it began to rise again and approach the roof of the hotel. When it was about a hundred yards away it stopped moving and began to hover. Ah, Peter thought, a delay. This she will definitely *not* appreciate.

Next to his papers was a small gift-wrapped package. He wasn't supposed to remember her birthdays but he always did. He opened the small silvered gift tag 'To Jaygo, The girl who loved the stars. Love from Peter.' He smiled wryly to himself before tucking the package out of sight in the top flap of the case. Perhaps not. Best not.

After all, what could you give a millionaire? She must be that many times over by now. She had taken her cello playing and made it her route to international stardom. Youth concerts and early prizes had been followed by what eventually became a huge music machine. She had popularised the cello the world over. No one had ever played it quite like her. True, others may have been closer to the classical ideal but none of them had her energy and style. International fund-raisers, special appearances for presidents, Hollywood balls. You didn't have to ask – Jocasta Manhattan had done them all. Her CDs jumped to the top of every chart. They said that in her five years at the top she had made more money than Callas and Caruso put together. And she had worked just as hard at her public image. Her flame-red hair and deep green eyes blazed from music-shop windows the world over. Her Belle Epoque Quartet was a household name. Even her more reserved classical colleagues agreed that she had a quite extraordinary talent. Some had said it was her playing alone that had made her the star she was. The jealous said it was her business

4

acumen and flair for self publicity. And people who didn't know music just said it was her looks. Maybe. Her open smile shone out from posters on the walls of people who had never listened to cello music before Jocasta Manhattan. Perhaps the *New York Times* music critic put it best when he wrote, 'For cello lovers there is only time before Jocasta Manhattan and time now.'

Her very public private life had generated as many column inches as her music or her looks. She was a gossip-columnists' dream. So what if her numerous affairs were more imaginary than real? For she was the one who had said, 'I never sue. Print what you want.' She kept to it too. It had made her a lot of enemies and lost her a lot of friends along the way but then, as she had said to Peter once, 'So what? There will always be more people coming to a good party than leaving. That's just the way of it.'

Certainly her refusal ever to sue anyone only increased interest in her life. What was the real Jocasta like? What was she like to know?

She had once dismissed a celebrated series of nude photographs as, 'Mere photomontage. They know they can get away with it because I won't sue.' The result of that particular exercise meant that the photographs (and the name of Jocasta Manhattan) found their way into all sorts of magazines not normally noted for their musical content.

People who had known her before she became famous were frequently quoted without their permission. After one particularly outrageous series of quotes attributed to Peter had appeared in the *Sunday Times*, he had felt obliged to call her and explain that it had been nothing to do with him.

'Don't be ridiculous, Peter, darling,' she had retorted. 'You and I know what's true. If it isn't true, then obviously you didn't say it. It'll soon blow over. I know these people.' She was right. The reporters had eventually grown bored and moved on. More recent stories made better copy. No need to rake over old ground with so much fresh territory to investigate. Even if they weren't going to be any more accurate.

The bar around Peter was filling up fast. Jocasta Manhattan was expected and the word had got out. The circus was coming to town and no one wanted to miss out on a free ringside seat. Peter became aware of people staring at him. Who was the man she had telephoned? Haven't I seen his photograph before? A business partner? A former lover? Wasn't he the man who this? Who that?

He stared uncomfortably into his glass. Never mind, he thought.

They'll soon stop looking at me when she gets here. He had seen it all before.

Suddenly a ripple of spontaneous applause broke out. A camera appeared from nowhere and began flashing. Jocasta Manhattan was making her Entrance.

All eyes turned as she made her way across the crowded room. She waved to people as if she had known them all her life. She even leaned over one of the tables and exchanged a few words. Finally she arrived at Peter's table. 'Peter, darling. Kiss kiss. I hope you don't mind me dropping in on you like this.'

'Hello, Jaygo,' he said. 'What do you want this time?'

'You're *such* a dear, aren't you?' she said, sitting down opposite him. 'I heard you were here too and thought I'd come and see you. That's all.'

'How did you know I was in Atlanta?'

'I spoke to your girlfriend.'

'Aurelia! I hope you bloody didn't!'

'Only joking. Don't worry. But I should have done. Keep her on her toes. Actually I asked your department thingy and they said you would be at some mega conference here so I thought I might as well stop off on my way to Dallas.'

'New York to Dallas by Atlanta? A bit out of your way.'

'Maybe. But I do need to see you about something.'

'Told you.'

'Later. First let's just pretend to be friends and have a drink. Where is my drink by the way? I specifically asked.'

Peter waved at the bar and the same waiter as before weaved his way to the table with the tall green drink on a silver tray.

'Miss Jocasta,' he said as he carefully placed it down in front of her. 'Will there be anything else?'

'For the weekend, Torin? I hardly think so!'

The hapless waiter looked puzzled. 'Miss Jocasta?'

'Nothing now, Torin, darling. I'll wave if I want anything.'

When the waiter had gone, Peter said, 'You're good at names, aren't you? I didn't see you look at his tag.'

'I saw it on the way over. I think of it as part of my job.'

'So,' said Peter, picking up his drink, 'what do we drink to? August 21st? The cusp of Leo on Sagittarius?'

'You remembered. I wondered if you would.'

He smiled at her over his glass. 'Happy Birthday, Jaygo. What is it, twenty-five?'

6

'Sod you, Peter Wilson. You know it's the big Three O. But here's to you, too.'

She took a miniature sip and put the glass down. 'Do you think this is French or Californian?'

'French,' he said without hesitating. 'I don't think they would dare give you of all people Californian. Besides, I don't think they make it over here.'

'Silly drink. But it wouldn't be a proper birthday without one of these from you, would it?'

'Your turn to remember things, I see.'

'We used to think it was such a sophisticated drink.' She smiled to herself. 'It was a good two years. The best.'

'"Items in the rear view mirror",' he began.

'"May appear closer than they are",' she finished for him. 'Meatloaf. I still play it sometimes,' she said. 'You know once I even tried to arrange it for the cello.'

He laughed. 'Even Miss Jocasta has her limits!'

'Don't challenge me. You never know!'

He picked up his glass and looked around the bar. Most people were still looking at them. When he met someone's eye they didn't look away but smiled or just continued to stare.

'I haven't had a drink with you for a couple of years now,' he said. 'I'd forgotten what it was like. Aren't you going to tell me what this is all about?'

'I'm getting round to it,' she said brightly. 'I said "later". Just think of this bit as helping me with my work. I could do with a few column inches in the Bible Belt. So you can tell me all about your conference thing. Your girl said it was at CEC, whatever that is.'

'Centre for Epidemiology Control. It's the most important of its kind. A world thing.'

'Wow,' she said, 'and you giving a paper. Does that make you a "world thing" too?'

'Unfortunately not. My paper was booked in six months ago, when I thought it was going to be a lot better than it is. I counted my chickens I'm afraid.'

'Never mind. I'm sure you'll be your usual winning self. But haven't I heard of CEC? Don't they do Aids and stuff like that? Are you walking your six-legged insect friends into the world of medicine?'

'No. CEC do Epidemiology. How things spread. So Aids is pretty much their thing. I thought it would be interesting to compare the spread of locusts to the spread of disease, just to see if both camps could learn something.'

'And can they?'

'Let's just say that things didn't work out as I planned. But look, I'm much more interested to know why you've come all this way off course. When does "later" come?'

She laughed. 'After a bath, that's when. I was in a scheduled jumbo for a whole hour before the ride in the horrid helicopter. And I've got to fly out again soon, so I thought I might borrow your room for a bit.'

'Of course. They have a swish restaurant on the ground floor. I can book a table for nine o'clock if you like.'

'No. I do not like. I'm going to have a nice long soak and then a room service dinner in Room 6034 if that's all right with you. You always said I looked better with wet hair and I can't eat out looking all stringy, can I?'

Behind them the sinking sun had reached the level of the layer of brown air hanging over the city. As it did so, the sky above it changed to a warm yellow and the buildings that spread away from Peter and Jaygo were diffused with a golden warmth.

These warm colours seemed to take a brittle edge off Jaygo. He sensed her relaxing a little. Her shoulders dropped and she smiled warmly as she put her hands flat on the table and rubbed them gently backwards and forwards.

'So,' she said after a moment, 'tell me about Cambridge. I read that Tom Collis died.'

'Yes. Only sixty. Much too early. But, you know, I think he felt his life was more or less played out when he came back from Kano last spring. It was as if he knew he had done all he could and he only had some details to work out.'

'He must have died disappointed then.'

'How come?'

'Ah,' she began, 'I rather had the idea that you marrying his darling daughter, Aurelia, was one particular detail he wanted sorting out.'

Peter did not reply immediately.

'I mean,' she went on, 'couldn't you two have got a ring and pretended or something? Everyone knew you were his two favourite people. After all, he introduced you in the first place, didn't he? And you both knew almost to the day when he was going. Would it have been so difficult?'

'Everyone?' he said. 'Favourite people? I don't know what you're talking about.'

'Oh, come on, Pete. We may have lost touch a bit but we've hardly lost sight. I know what happens to you and you know what happens to me.'

'But there's a difference,' he countered. 'I just have to pick up a paper to find out about you, but you have to pick up a telephone and actually ask about me. And, that being the case, who have you been ringing up?'

'Never you mind,' she said, putting her head playfully on one side. 'But actually I just read his obituary. Didn't it say "The work of Professor Collis was important not just because he founded the United Nations Institute in Kano but because he has been able to ensure its continued existence by finding such an able successor as Peter Wilson who takes up his new post as Director of the Kano Institute next year"?'

'Except that I won't be.'

'Why on earth not?'

'If anyone was pretending things for the old man it was the British Government. They never intended to continue funding beyond the end of the year and, with no British funding, the Nigerians aren't going to go for a British Director, are they?'

'But who have *they* got?' she asked. 'You told me last time that the others aren't any good. More or less just students, you said.'

'I'm afraid you're right. All the biologists who were any good have left to work in Europe or the States. Following the kudos, it's called. What's left behind is a load of second-raters.'

'And you.'

'And me.'

'Second-rater?' she queried. 'I think not. You took the best first of our year. And you alone among us took a Cambridge Ph.D. And not everyone gets a deputyship at a UN institute by the age of twenty-five. You were the last best hope of our year.'

He sighed.

'Actually,' he began, 'I thought Jackie Morton did rather well. At least when she changed her name to Jocasta Manhattan.'

She was not to be deflected. 'In science I mean. Of the set of us that sat down to finals – what? Twelve of us? Who else made it out of the grey?'

'Laurie. He became science correspondent at ITN, didn't he? Formica-topped science maybe, but still science. I think that counts as getting out of the grey.'

'And,' she said slowly, 'there's always Jack.'

'Ngale?'

9

'Yes.'

'Well, hardly,' Peter said. 'Not by his own efforts anyway. Being the eldest son of one of the richest families in Nigeria doesn't exactly make it difficult to take a plum job if you *do* decide to go and live there.'

'No. Probably not. But he's kept the plot, hasn't he? In ten years of solid mess there and several bloody coups he's never once been in the wrong place at the wrong time. He's slipped sideways or up every time. He's stayed clean. Most West African politicians would be glad just to have kept their heads but he's done a lot better than that. And he's kept in touch with you too. I think he's been pretty supportive of your institute, hasn't he?'

'Within limitations. The last time I saw him he hinted pretty strongly that when the old man died he'd have to back off and put his weight behind a local candidate for top job. After all, he more or less "inherited" Tom Collis but he could hardly have another whitey taking over what is seen to be more or less an ex-pat set-up. And, even though he as good as told me no local candidate would be up to the job, he would still push one for essentially political reasons.'

Peter swilled the ice around in his glass.

'Well, not in so many words. He dressed it up in his silver-tongued way. You know Jack. But yes, that is more or less what he said.'

She was fixing him with a stare he didn't recognise. Worry? 'I know,' she said. 'I know because he told me more or less the same thing.'

'How? I didn't know he still kept in touch with you. Or you with him come to that. I didn't think you ever liked him all that much.'

'I didn't. He always gave me the creeps. A schemer. A plotter. And he still does give me the creeps.'

'Still? You've seen him recently?'

'Oh yes. Our Jack Ngale is moving centre stage for us both. He's the "later" I want to talk about.'

'Well then,' said Peter, 'let the "later" begin.'

He waved at the waiter and the ever-hovering Torin was immediately at his side.

'Yes, Doctor?'

'The bill, please.'

'Of course.'

Peter turned back to Jaygo. 'Times change, don't they? I remember when we had to sit near the door in case we had to make a break for it. And now they hover next to us.'

'I remember the signs,' she said. 'First you would pinch your nose and then your left ear.'

'Like this?' he said. 'First the ear and then the nose?'

'Go, go, go,' she laughed as she stood up quickly and turned to the exit. Peter clicked his case shut and stood up to follow her. But before he could take a step, Torin was at his side.

'I'll put it to your room, sir, no need to sign now.'

'Well done, Torin,' said Jaygo laughing. 'You'll make an honest woman of me yet.'

All eyes followed the two of them as they made for the glass doors at the side of the restaurant. 'Which is more than you ever offered to do.' She added to Peter.

Peter's room was ten floors below the restaurant. So it was still ten floors above the smog and shared the same view of the golden sunset.

The outside wall was made up entirely of glass, which gave the room a rather open if disconcerting feel.

Peter's single suitcase was open on the bed. His unpacking had only got as far as taking out a couple of shirts and putting them next to the case.

Jaygo's cello case and five designer suitcases were stacked neatly against the side wall.

Peter expected her to go straight to the cello to check it but instead she made for the glass wall. She pressed her forehead against the glass and tried to look down. Then she tried to look sideways. 'It's amazing,' she said. 'You can see for miles. We could be floating or anything.'

'This is the highest I could get. Once I had to stay on the tenth floor and I felt quite cheated.'

There was a knock at the door and a porter appeared with another five suitcases.

'Thank you,' said Peter. He turned to Jaygo. 'How the hell did you fit this lot in the helicopter?'

'I didn't,' she laughed. 'These came by land taxi. I could have left the whole lot at the airport but the less time my cases spend in thieving magpie country the better I've found it.'

She pointed at the cases and quickly counted them off. Then, glancing almost imperceptibly at the porter's name tag, 'Well, Victor,' she said, producing a ten-dollar bill from her handbag.

'This is for you and there's another fifty if you can keep the phone from ringing for two hours. OK?'

'Thank you, Miss Manhattan. No problem.' He bowed unnecessarily and was gone.

'Fifty well spent,' she said. 'I know my friends in the travelling circus that passes for the press.'

She went into the bathroom. 'Wow,' she called, 'it's all black marble and gold taps. This may be the Bible Belt but they know all about bathrooms. Look, *two* dressing gowns and simply *loads* of towels. Are you sure you haven't got a Little Missee Secret hidden away in Atlanta?'

'No such luck. It's just a standard double. Lacrima Christi College are picking up the tab.'

'Well then, Mr Deputy Director, they must think very highly of you.'

'Come on, Jaygo. You must have stayed in a million hotels like this. They're all the same.'

She walked past him to the glass wall again. She put her arms out straight and pressed herself to the glass. 'Come on, nothing,' she said. 'It's our little home for a couple of hours. Pretend with me.'

She turned around to face him and put her arms out again as she leant backwards. 'Help, help. I'm falling out. Come and rescue me!'

He laughed. 'Be careful what you wish for. You go ahead and have your bath now. I've a couple of calls to make. Any dinner preferences?'

'I don't know. Something Atlanta. What are they famous for here?'

'Martin Luther King and Coca Cola.'

'Oh. Southern Fried chicken it is then. Or am I getting Martin Luther King and Colonel Saunders mixed up?'

'That's Kentucky. Saunders was the one with the recipe and Martin Luther the one with the dream.'

'Of course.' She smiled at him. 'Silly Old Jaygo.'

'Do you know,' he added, 'they actually have a restaurant here called "I Have a Menu"?'

'No! That's awful! You'll have to take me there one day! Actually I always wondered where he got the idea for that speech from.'

When she had gone into the bathroom he ordered dinner from room service then dialled Aurelia in England.

It did not pick up for six rings. When she answered it was a rather hurt voice that said, 'Peter? Is that you? You were going to ring earlier. Is everything all right?'

He grimaced. 'Sorry. I had to go out to CEC to sort out my slides for tomorrow and the traffic is murder. I've only just got to the hotel.'

'So long as everything is OK.'

'It's fine, sweetie. Don't worry. How are things your end?'

'Fine too. I was with Daddy's bees till midday. There's always something to do and I hate it when you're flying. This afternoon I went into college to sort out one or two things for the reception on Thursday night. Are you sure you'll be back in time?'

'Of course. I'm coming on a flight that gets in about three. Loads of time even if there is a delay.'

'Delay? What delay?'

'No. I said even if there *was* one. I'm sure there won't be.'

'Of course there won't be. Just look after yourself and come back safe.'

'Yes. Thursday then. And after I've been out to Kano to sort things out at the end of the week we'll have a whole month together. Have you had any more ideas about what you want to do?'

'Not really. A week here first getting over everything, I should think. I can't leave the bees too long anyway. But we could have the odd day in London if you like. You said you would take me to the Picasso Exhibition.'

'Of course I will. And why don't we stay late one night and take in a play or something? I think you and I are the only people I know who haven't actually seen *The Mousetrap*.'

'Oh yes. You come up with such good ideas. But I won't keep you on the phone. This must be costing a fortune.'

'OK then, but I'll ring you after the meeting tomorrow and I promise not to be so late.'

'That would be very nice. I love you. Tomorrow then.'

'Talk to you soon, darling. Bye.'

He placed the telephone slowly back on the table by the bed. He could hear Jaygo singing in the bathroom.

The falling sun had reached the edge of the smog and the room became darker. He turned on a lamp on a low glass table and, as he did so, he caught his reflection in the floor-length glass of the window.

Had he changed much since the Jaygo days? Not much, he thought. Still looking OK. Maybe a bit rounder in the middle.

13

Hair still a bit too long but people didn't comment so much now. Perhaps they put it down to him being a scientist.

Jaygo came out of the bathroom wearing a large white towelling dressing-gown. On her head was a towel wrapped like a turban. She sat down opposite him and unwrapped the turban with a flourish and a shake of her head. Her long hair, dark with wetness, spilled free and shook droplets onto the carpet.

'You haven't seen me with wet hair for eight years,' she said. 'No make up and all.'

'You look the same, Jay.'

'Trick of the light.' She relaxed back onto the chair and put her arms over the side so her fingers just trailed the carpet.

'You know,' she said, 'I've been on tour for ten weeks now. Five concerts a week, all in different cities. God knows how many dinners, receptions and parties. And in all that time no one has called me Jaygo. Let alone Jay.'

'No one calls you Jaygo? What about the lovely Hugo, what does he call you?'

'"Jocaaasta". He calls me "Jocaaasta". God I'm so sick of being a "Jocaaasta".'

'That's not very nice. I thought you two were engaged. Or is that rock on your hand just for decoration?'

She held out her left hand and moved a large solitaire diamond back and forward with her thumb. 'You noticed then?'

'I could hardly miss it, could I?'

'It's nice, isn't it?' she said, holding it closer to look at it. 'God knows what it cost him. But I don't know that the whole thing is such a good idea.'

'Oh dear.' Peter walked over to the fridge. 'Drink for madam?'

'Yes, please. Soft. No tray.'

'What's the matter?' said Peter, returning with two tins of fruit juice. 'He sounds all right to me.'

'He is,' she said, taking a can from him. 'Sort of. But,' she said, brightening, 'I don't think I could ever marry a man with such a hairy back! I mean, what if I woke up in the night with my face buried in it! Gawd!' She laughed at Peter as he sat down opposite her.

'Anyway,' she went on, 'he should sound nice. He writes all his own Press Releases.' She put on a stage Spanish accent again. '"Jocaaasta. How does this make me sound? Sympathetic? I want to sound sympathetic, my petal." Bloody creep.'

She put her can down on the table.

'Do you remember a long time ago,' she began, 'you know, at the "end" of us as it were. You said something special to me. Do you remember?'

He stood up. 'I took it pretty hard, you know. People say all sorts of things at a time like that. You were going to New York and we both knew you weren't coming back. Not to me.'

'Yes,' she said, 'but one thing in particular. You said that if ever I needed anything then you would help me. Whatever. Whenever.'

He turned away from her and looked at her pile of suitcases. Then he walked over to the window. Five minutes ago it had been sunset and now it was nearly dark. Cars were moving in slow lines with their headlights on far below. The only sound in the room was the quiet hiss of the air-conditioner.

'People usually say that,' he said eventually. 'It's to do with them pretending it isn't really goodbye. It helps.'

'But if I'd stayed with you,' she said, 'I would never have found out about myself, would I? I had to know if I could make it. You would have done the same if it had been you.'

'Maybe.'

'I offered for you to come too.'

'I know,' he said, 'but we both knew you didn't mean it and we both knew I couldn't go.'

'Well, Peter, what was I supposed to say? I thought you were being oppressive. Trying to hold me. And all the time I could feel myself being sort of pulled away from behind. Upwards and away. I'd have been crazy not to go to New York. You even said so yourself. You said it as well as me.'

'Look, do we have to go over everything?' he asked. 'Jaygo one. Peter nil. It happens. Eight years. It's long enough. We weren't special, just young. A student romance. The world went on spinning.'

'You didn't write,' she said.

'What was I supposed to say? "Come back, Jaygo"? You wouldn't have.'

There was a knock at the door. Dinner had arrived. Jaygo turned to the window and resolutely didn't face the room while the waiter wheeled in a dinner trolley. Peter signed the bill without reading it.

The two began to eat without talking.

After a few mouthfuls, she put down her knife and fork.

'It's "later" now. Can I start?'

'More memories?' he said and immediately regretted it when he saw the expression on her face.

15

'If you're going to be like that you can bugger off.'

'Bit of a waste of your time coming here then, wasn't it? You could have gone straight to Dallas and skipped the helicopter bit. And that might have been better for your cello too. I'm sure it hates lots of temperature changes.' And I wouldn't have forgotten to ring Aurelia, he added to himself.

'I thought I could count on you,' she said.

'Did you now?' he said slightly irritated. 'Call in a few favours? I can't imagine I've got anything you want any more.'

She pushed her plate away and stood up. 'Don't be so bloody, Peter. I'm in the shit and I need some good advice.'

'Then ask Hugo. "Jocaaasta my dear, let me deal with eet".'

'Stop it!'

'Well, honestly, Jaygo. If not him then one of your army. Call an expert in. Buy one. I don't know.'

She turned to face him.

'You forget I know you pretty well, Jay,' he said, pointing his fork at her. 'When you telephoned me yesterday, I knew you weren't just "running into an old friend". Because that's not what you do. You only keep in touch when you want something. You've homed in on me every couple of years or so, decided what you wanted in advance, taken it and then vanished into thin air again.'

He put his knife and fork down on his plate. 'Take last time. You just "happen to be in London" so you phone me and ask to use the Chapel at Lacrima Christi College for some film music recording or other. I agree. Set the chapel up. Line up the choir for you and everything. But do you turn up on the day? No. "Sorry, Peter darling, simple *have* to go to LA. Can't *possibly* make it after all." But you pay everyone anyway so that makes it all right, doesn't it? Did it ever occur to you that those people were not actually doing it for the money? I know them. They were doing it because it was a chance for them to meet the great Jocasta Manhattan, make music with her. They were really looking forward to it. The boys in the choir. Everyone.'

'And you?' she interrupted.

Peter shrugged. 'And what did they get?' he asked. 'A faxed thank you and a cheque signed by your secretary.'

Jaygo rubbed the sides of her neck with both hands and looked at him.

'And the next time,' he went on, 'the College again. You wanted to use the Master's Garden for a photo shoot for the cover of some CD or other. Well, for that one you actually turn up. Even gave a cheque for the Bell Lessing Library Fund to the master's wife. But you come and go within three hours and don't stay to talk to anyone at all. Oh, no, that's not quite right. You manage to give the head porter a kiss to thank him for letting you park on the grass. Turns out to be quite a kiss, I believe. Tongues and all. God, a man of sixty! I'm surprised he didn't die on the spot!'

Jaygo picked up her can of juice. 'Oh, for goodness sake. Just a bit of fun.'

Peter shook his head at her.

She gave a meek smile. 'Sorry,' she said quietly. 'Won't do it again.'

'Oh, well,' sighed Peter looking down at his plate. 'Tell me what it is this time. I can always say no.'

She looked at him carefully before speaking. 'It's not really a favour,' she began. 'Well, that's not the main thing. It's a bit difficult because it's partly to do with us. You and me. Sort of.'

He leaned back in his chair. 'OK then. Fire away.'

'And Africa,' she went on. 'It's to do with Africa and you know all about that. And you know the other person involved pretty well.'

She bit her lip and sat down again. 'Actually, I don't really know where to start. It's a bit of a mess. You see, I've let myself in for something I can't back out of. You might know what to do. It's just a mess really.' She hunched her shoulders and folded her arms.

Peter looked at her and frowned. This wasn't like her. She was always so certain. Brash even. And here she was clearly confused. He felt unnerved.

She began speaking again without looking at him. 'And it's about Jack Ngale. He's the other person involved. I know you can't stand the man and nor can I. But we both have to deal with him and that's that.'

Peter put up his hand. 'Whoa there! Not so fast. I don't like him much but "can't stand" is a bit strong. Jack holds the purse-strings to the Kano Institute so I have to meet him from time to time. We're civil enough. Eat out sometimes. That sort of thing. We were all students together, for God's sake. And that includes you of course. But I didn't know he had any actual dealings with you.'

She dropped her shoulders and turned back to Peter. 'I'm involved now. Too much.'

She took another sip from her drink. 'The thing is he's been sort of following me about for a couple of years by telephone. Always ringing me up on some excuse or other. Wherever I am, he seems

17

able to get my private number. Then he started turning up at my concerts without warning and coming backstage afterwards. And he keeps sending me things. Flowers. Presents.'

'So, he's a fan,' said Peter. 'Put his flowers with the rest, I say. He always fancied you in the old days. Probably still does.'

Suddenly the telephone rang.

'Shit,' she snapped.

Jaygo picked up the phone. 'I told you no bloody calls.'

Peter smiled. This was more the Jaygo he remembered.

'Oh. Sorry,' she was saying. 'Yes. He's here. I'll get him.' She looked up at Peter and put on a polite voice. 'Dr Wilson, it's for you.' She was smiling now.

Peter stood up. 'Who is it?' he mouthed.

Jaygo put her hand over the handset. 'Aurelia,' she whispered.

'Shit,' mouthed Peter as he took the telephone.

'Hello again, darling,' he said brightly. 'Are you all right?'

'Yes,' began Aurelia. 'I'm all right. Who was that?'

'What?'

'That woman on the phone. Is she in your room with you, Peter?'

'It's just someone from the conference, darling, she's brought over the photocopies of the slides for tomorrow.'

'She sounded jolly rude. And why no calls?'

'It's nothing really,' said Peter. 'She'd just dropped some of the papers and they were all out of order. She says she apologises.'

Peter looked up and smiled at Jaygo.

Jaygo opened her mouth wide in surprised amusement. 'Apologises!' she whispered loudly. So saying, she undid her dressing gown, held it wide open with her arms outstretched and said loudly, 'Tell her I'm really sorry, Dr Wilson. Really sorry!' Then she closed the gown and winked at Peter before sitting down again.

'What's going on, Peter?' asked Aurelia. 'Was that her?'

'Yes, darling. She's really sorry. She didn't know it was you, of course,' he said looking over at Jaygo who had picked up her drink and was pretending not to listen.

Peter turned away from Jaygo to listen to Aurelia. 'Oh, well. I suppose it doesn't matter,' she was saying.

Jaygo looked up from her can, made a face at the telephone by the bed and stuck out her tongue.

'I was just going to sleep,' Aurelia went on, 'when I thought about your dinner jacket. I was talking to Lizzie Lessing this afternoon and she says this do on Thursday for the opening of the Bell Library is going to be a formal dinner at high table so it'll be DJs as well as gowns. And I wondered if yours needs cleaning?'

'What? Oh no, it'll be fine.'

'Oh good. And what do you think I should wear? Do you think it needs to be long?'

Jaygo was now playing an imaginary violin and rocking from side to side.

'I don't know,' said Peter. 'Perhaps long would be nice. Maybe the blue one?'

'Oh good. That's just what I was hoping you'd say. Well, I mustn't keep you.'

'Yes,' replied Peter, 'there really is still loads to do.'

'OK then. Bye. Love you.'

'Yes, darling. Bye.' He put the receiver down and sat opposite Jaygo. He smiled at her. 'Well, I liked the apology. But I'm not sure she got all of it.'

'Just a bit of fun,' smiled Jaygo back at him.

The light had almost gone from outside. In the distance another helicopter winked its strobe as it crossed the city. Jaygo sat back and brushed the carpet gently back and forth with her finger tips at either side of her chair.

Eventually she said, 'You haven't seen me without my clothes for eight years. I'm still in quite good shape, aren't I? Not gone all baggy yet.'

He did not reply but stood up and began to pour them coffee. His black. Hers with just a dash of milk and one sugar. He pushed her cup over to her side before taking his own over to the window.

'You were going to tell me about Jack Ngale,' he said.

'Yes,' she began. 'But I've got to go back a couple of steps to tell you how it all started.'

She stood up and walked over to stand next to him as he looked out over the nightscape. 'Do you know a band called Ladysmith Black Mambazo?' she asked.

'South African, I think. World music stuff, gospel chants. They play them a lot on the radio in Kano.'

'That would be them,' she said. 'Well, I had the idea that we, the Belle Epoque, could adapt some of their music. I know it sounds crazy and Hugo didn't think we could do it at all but I made him have a go and it worked out really well. The cello, me, plays the bass voice, the piano plays a drum part and the violin and viola take the other voices. I really liked it the minute we tried it and even boring old Hugo had to admit it worked.'

She held an arm out in front of her and absently traced patterns on the glass with her fingers.

'We tried it out as an encore at a couple of concerts,' she went on. 'It went down quite well and it was at one of these concerts that Jack Ngale turned up and he went a bomb for it. Afterwards, when he came backstage, he couldn't stop talking about it. He wanted us to do a whole album and said we would sell really well all over Africa and probably everywhere else as well. Said it was just what the market wanted. Which was news to me, because I'd never known him buy a single record so I didn't think he knew what he was talking about.'

She dropped her arm back to her side and went back to the trolley to pick up her coffee. 'Well, eventually we agreed we'd release the piece we'd done that evening as a single just in Nigeria to see how it went. And I have to admit he was right. Up to number one in the main charts inside a month,' she took a sip from her coffee. 'Just right, thanks.'

'I don't know that I ever heard it. When was this?'

'About six months ago. Perhaps you missed it. Anyway, Jack wouldn't stop going on about it. Lots of phone calls and faxes so eventually Hugo and I agreed to do a whole album and record it between concerts over a series of months. Frankly, it's not very difficult music and it didn't take much rehearsal.'

She looked down at her engagement ring and began rocking it backwards and forwards again with her thumb.

'So we sent a promo CD of it to Jack and he just sort of hijacked it. Title, cover, the lot.'

'Title?'

'Yes,' she said dropping her hand down again. 'I wanted to call it *Belle Epoque Plays Mambazo* or something like that. But Jack said I looked like a lion and we should call it *The Music of the Lion.*'

He looked at her, puzzled. 'Lion?' he said. 'There haven't been any lions in Nigeria for a long time.'

'I know. Jack said there used to be loads and that was what mattered. Look, I'll show you the cover picture. I've brought a promo in my bag to give you.

'Normally our own company does the artwork,' she went on, walking to the bathroom to collect her bag. 'We do that so we can keep a house style and we do it to a pretty pro standard to help cut down pirate copies.

'But,' she called through from the bathroom, 'Jack bloody steam-rollered that too and then came up with something totally ridiculous.'

She walked back into the room carrying a CD case which she handed to Peter. 'What do you think?'

Peter sat on the bed to examine it more clearly under the light.

The picture showed Jaygo in a short gold lamé dress standing with feet apart and her arms held out so that she made the shape of a large X. She was in the middle of a large bowed gold arch. Her hands were gripping the arch above her and her feet were resting on two stylised jewels at the base of the arch. Around the arch were the words *The Music of the Lion*. The face in the picture was leaning forwards. It was recognisably Jaygo but had been made up to look like a lion as well. The eyes too were half lion, half Jaygo. Her red hair streamed out from her face like a mane towards the gold arch.

Peter looked at it without speaking. He pursed his lips.

'He told me it was a local thing,' she said. 'That gold thing. A torque, he called it. He said that everyone will know what it is and that it will help sales.'

Peter continued looking at the picture.

'Do you know what it is?' she asked. 'Jack said you might recognise it.'

'Oh, yes,' he said quietly to himself. 'I know exactly what it is. And I'll tell you something else,' he said, looking up. 'Your friend Jack Ngale – *the* Ngale to give him his proper name – is a very clever man.'

Peter walked over to Jaygo. 'This thing,' he said, tapping the case, 'this gold arch is more than just a bit recognisable. It's called the Idona Zaki.'

'Is it famous?'

'Oh, yes. I'd say that,' he smiled. 'And there are two things about it that really matter. First, it's a sort of icon, more than that, to Jack Ngale's ancestral tribe, the Ngalese. They sort of worship it. Revere it. It's their symbol of nationhood. It marks them off from the other tribes and, in their view, makes them better, superior. It's the one central thing that binds them together. They call themselves The People of the Lion. And the English name of this thing, the Idona Zaki, is The Eyes of the Lion.'

He paused to look at her.

'But,' he went on and tapped the case again, 'the second important thing is that it's missing. Lost. Gone. And the circumstances of its going do not reflect at all well on the chief who lost it. He disgraced himself in his people's eyes and, by implication, them as well. They say that through his stupidity he lost The Eyes of the Lion and with it went their pride. Actually they cut off his head and threw it in the river to let him know how they felt. But it didn't get The Eyes back and it's been missing ever since.'

Jaygo took the case from Peter and looked at it again. 'The Ngalese, you say? So this torque is to do with Jack?'

'Bit more than that, Jay. He's the Main Man. You remember when he first came to Liverpool he called himself Ole Akin Ngale. Ole means son. Akin means strong, the eldest son. And Ngale is a title more than a name. It means king, chief, head. So the name he used when he came first doesn't mean anything unless you say it all, Ole Akin Ngale. Well, even then he was pretty astute and got tired of explaining all that whenever he met someone so he took up the name Jack to make him sound more European. So he'd fit in better.'

'So Jack's not his real Christian name?'

'Oh no. And as for being Christian, our friend Jack and his people are just about as far from gentle Jesus and the angels as it's possible to get. Anyway, when Jack's father died – he incidentally was the great-great-great-grandson of the one who lost The Eyes – Jack dropped the Ole and Akin parts of his name and became just Ngale. *The* Ngale.'

'But you said they cut the original one's head off . . .'

'Yes, but he had sons. Lots of them. The Ngale is supposed to father as many children as possible. They start at about age twelve and carry on till they die. Thirty or forty children is not uncommon.'

'Wow. That's going some. Lucky old Jack!'

'True,' went on Peter. 'Well, the Ngale after the one who lost his head, swore to make good his father's name by returning The Eyes of the Lion. And each new Ngale takes up the quest. It's become a bit of a pointless ceremonial thing now because they're never going to find it. A bit like looking for the Holy Grail if you like. An honour thing. But they are all expected to do it.'

'Well, if it's all that important, how come the first one lost it? I mean it looks a bit big just to go missing.'

'Bit big?' said Peter. 'Oh, it wasn't as big as this,' he said indicating the CD case. 'It was just a normal torque, to be worn around the neck of the Ngale on ceremonial occasions. It was probably about a foot across. Maybe a bit more. This is just a picture.'

Peter looked at the case again. 'But it's interesting. Some historians think it might have been quite a lot bigger.'

'Don't they know? There must be pictures of it.'

'Yes, there are, but they are all stylised and any records are only oral. Nothing was ever written down in those days. It was all songs, stories, folk tales and so on. Which means they can't be depended on. There will have been all sorts of exaggeration.'

Jaygo shrugged. 'Does it really matter how big it was if it's missing anyway?'

'Yes, it does,' continued Peter. 'Because if it's normal size, about a foot across say, it's just a missing torque. Special to the Ngalese but not of much interest to anyone else. But the point is that, in all the pictures, the two stones, the actual eyes, are always in proportion to the rest of it. At a foot across that means the emeralds, because that's what they are, would be about the size of grapes. Pretty huge but not unheard of. However, if it was this big,' and Peter held his hands out in front of him two feet apart, 'that would make the emeralds the size of eggs. They would be the biggest anywhere. A matched pair that big. Name your price. Millions. God knows how much. At that size they become something in their own right, never mind what the Ngalese think of them.'

'Wow!' said Jaygo. 'Quite a thing then. Naughty old Ngale for losing it. But you never got to that bit. Tell me what he did. You'd think he would have taken better care of it.'

'Oh, he did,' said Peter. 'And he didn't lose it exactly. He swapped it.'

'Eh?'

'Yup. Swapped it. Let me tell you what happened. You have to remember all this took place nearly three hundred years ago. We are talking about the beginning of the slave trade. Which of course meant pretty rich pickings for the Ngale and his ilk.'

'Pickings? I should have thought they kept a bit out of the way in case they were rounded up or something.'

'Ah, ha,' smiled Peter. 'That's the PC version. Heartless white slavers going into the bush to collect hapless villagers? Not really.'

'Go on.'

'The slaver would park his ship offshore, row in with his men and negotiate, place orders if you like, with local chiefs who would then go up country and round up people to fit the slaver's requirements. Whitey would then pay on the nail and sail off into the sunset. There were huge profits all round. The local people had all the beads and mirrors they could handle and the slaver usually arrived in the Caribbean with at least half his cargo still alive.'

'Beads and mirrors? Come on, Pete!'

'Well, the slavers used to bring manufactured things like china, bales of material, knives. They also ran a line in nice plump white prostitutes from the East End lured to sea by a few glasses of gin and a knock on the head. I think you'll find school history books skip the details. Particularly the English ones. England being the home of most self-respecting slave-traders.'

'God,' said Jaygo. 'I never dreamed it was like that.'

'Must have been, if you think about it. There were tens of thousands of slaves shipped altogether. It was a proper trading arrangement with the full connivance of the Africans. People like the then Ngale were particularly successful because he had a big army and imperial guard who could deliver fit young men, which is what the traders most wanted.'

'OK,' she said. 'I'll go with that, but how would the Ngale keep up a supply? He must have used up the people who lived near the coast pretty quickly.'

'He did. But routes were developed to places further up country. It got to the point when he would cordon off the whole area belonging to some smaller tribe. Then he'd gradually tighten the cordon and tell them they could either have their heads cut off on the spot or walk quietly down to the coast and sail away with the nice man in the stovepipe hat.'

'Hat?'

'My favourite thing in this savoury tale. Do you know what a Kindrale is?'

'Nope.'

'It's the name given to one of the Haitian voodoo dance figures. A man with a white painted face in a top hat, he prances about spreading evil and bad charms.'

'What has Haiti got to do with it? That's the other side of the world!'

'A lot of the slaves finished up in the sugar fields of the Caribbean in places like Haiti. It's my guess that the last thing they saw before being ushered to the holds of the slave ships was the great slave-trader himself counting them on board. The very picture of respectability. Frock coat, top hat and white as the devil himself. Just ripe for a voodoo tale, I should say.'

'Did you work that out yourself?'

'It wasn't difficult. I've seen pictures of one of the big slave-traders. He looks like that famous portrait of Brunel standing in front of those ship chains. His name was John Etherington and in the best-known picture of him he's wearing his frock coat and stovepipe hat with the Ngale next to him. Etherington is smoking a long clay pipe and the Ngale is proudly holding up a nice cup and saucer.'

'Cup and saucer!'

'Why not? Good trading stuff. Porcelain was pretty much unknown in West Africa and the going rate for a hundred slaves would have been a couple of crates of Harrods sale china.'

'The whole thing is horrific. I just can't believe it.'

'You don't have to. I'm afraid it's no less true because you don't want to believe it. Don't forget, our John Etherington was not exactly in the Gentle Jesus squad either.'

'OK. But I still don't see what this has to do with that gold torque thing.'

'I'm coming to that. It seems our Ngale friend overstretched himself on one occasion. He rounded up practically a whole tribe, the Bentobese, for the lovely Etherington. He didn't know it at the time but one of the few Bentobese he had *not* managed to grab was the son of the head man, the Ole Akin Bentobe, who was on some foraging expedition of his own. Now, that's crucial, because, when the Ole Akin came back he found that the Ngale had marched off with his father. He was so angry he decided to join forces with another tribe to teach the Ngale a lesson, and probably chop his head off too.'

'Any vodka in the fridge?'

'What?'

'Vodka. I want a vodka.'

'Look, are you listening to me?'

'Of course I am. The Bentobese. But I'm ready for a vodka. Do you want one?'

'No.'

Jaygo opened the mini-bar and looked through the row of miniatures. 'Got one. Now go on about the Bentobe chappie.'

'You have the attention span of a six-year-old.'

Jaygo unscrewed the top of the small bottle and took a swig. 'Ready again.'

Peter sighed. 'By this time the Ngale had struck a deal with Etherington who had taken the men on board. The Ngale is about to head off home with his booty when he hears that the Bentobe Ole Akin and his mates are only a day away from turning up at the coast and wanting his father back.'

'Tricky,' said Jaygo, finishing the vodka in a gulp.

'The Ngale is going to be outnumbered by the approaching Bentobese and his only hope is to enlist the help of Etherington who he knows has magic things called guns that could help him get rid of the Bentobese and still keep his cups and saucers. So the Ngale goes back to Etherington and says how about it?

'Etherington says he would be delighted to help but that such help does not come cheap. Well, says the Ngale, how about some more slaves next trip. Sorry, says Etherington, can't wait that long.

'So, the Ngale is facing the wall, he knows that without Etherington and his muskets he will be pushed into the sea. The Bentobese might not get his father back but it will probably make him feel better to see the Ngale's head rolling down the beach.

'So the Ngale says to Etherington, name your price. Anything.

'Actually, says Etherington, there is something I would quite like. How about that gold thing you carry around with you, what is it? Something ceremonial?'

'Shit,' said Jaygo. 'The torque?'

'Exactly. Of course the Ngale can't possibly part with it but unless he gets the help of Etherington it's not going to be much use to him anyway, is it?

'Impasse. Eventually the two men strike a deal. The Ngale agrees to hand the torque over to a group of local missionaries who agree to act as a third party pending the outcome of the battle. The priests are not at all keen on this but know enough about the Ngale and Etherington not to make waves. So, everyone eventually agrees, if the Bentobese can be seen off, Etherington gets the torque. If Etherington loses then at least he gets to keep the people he already has on board, the Ngale keeps the torque and the two men can begin a fresh set of negotiations when Etherington comes back the next year. It's not much of a deal and neither man has much intention of keeping to their side of it but it is all they can come up with. Meanwhile, the Bentobese are now only half a day away and so the Ngale vanishes off into the bush to await the outcome.

'The next morning, the Bentobese arrive at the coast all fired up, expecting to face the Ngalese for the glorious battle. Instead they find a few rows of funny-looking white men lined up on the beach with what look like miniature spears. No problem, they think and they set to. Now, the Bentobese have never seen guns before and when Etherington's men get down on one knee and start shooting, the Bentobese get the fright of their lives. They have no idea what is happening but soon catch the general idea. Once they realise they can't get near enough the funny-looking men to get in a decent spear throw they turn tail and run. Africa cup early result, Gunpowder one, Bentobese nil.

'So, technically, the torque and the day belong to Etherington and he goes to the mission to recover it. The Ngale turns up, pretending to congratulate Etherington but in reality to try to get hold of the torque before Etherington can get it to the ship.

'But the Ngale and Etherington are not the only ones who can't be trusted because when Etherington arrives at the mission the door is swinging open on its hinges and the torque and the priests have gone.

'Etherington goes berserk and accuses the Ngale of killing the priests and taking back the torque. The Ngale similarly goes ape-shit and accuses Etherington of doing much the same thing. The Ngale says he couldn't possibly have done it as he was further up the coast hiding during the night and Etherington says it wasn't him because he and his men didn't come ashore until just before the Bentobese arrived. They shout at each other for a bit but eventually call it a day. Etherington goes back to his ship and the Ngale goes back to his people and says, "Sorry, chaps, I seem to have temporarily mislaid that gold thing."'

Peter shrugged and blew out his cheeks. 'The rest you know.'

'What happened to the torque? Had it really gone?'

'Well,' said Peter, 'it certainly wasn't at the mission.'

'People must have some idea though. Aren't there any theories?'

'Loads. Some think Etherington killed the priests and stole the torque before the battle. And others say the priests took it themselves and hightailed it into the bush. Perhaps they made their way along the coast to another mission and then took the torque on the next ship back to Rome.'

'Rome?'

'Yes, to use the torque as a sort of present to the blameless Vicar of Christ to encourage him to give them a less miserable posting than West Africa. I think you'll find there are quite a few bits and bobs from around the world stashed away in the Vatican.'

Jaygo stuck out her lower lip. 'But couldn't it still be in Africa? Perhaps the priests never made it home.'

'No, I don't think it's still there. Someone would have come across it and known what it was by now. It may look like wild country but every inch belongs to someone. They know their own bits of land pretty well.'

He took a vodka from the mini-bar and offered her another. She shook her head.

'One thing's for sure. The Ngale didn't have it. Hence the head-rolling game when he got home.'

'Aren't people still looking for it?'

'Not really,' he replied. 'Everyone more or less accepts it's gone for ever. Every now and again the Nigerian Government accuses the British government of having got hold of it via the Etheringtons. A bit like the Elgin Marbles. But the present Etheringtons flatly deny that their family ever had it. But they do point out that, if they did, technically it would belong to them anyway because the Ngale swapped it fair and square. John Etherington kept his side of the bargain and saw off the Bentobese and so title to the torque passed to him according to the agreement witnessed by the priests.'

'Which is true. If it belongs to anyone it belongs to the Etheringtons,' said Jaygo and then added, 'What time is it?'

Peter looked at his watch. 'I don't know. I haven't set this since I arrived. Why?'

'I've got to get organised to go to Dallas,' she said.

'Oh.'

'Sorry. Party nearly over. But I still haven't got around to asking you this massive favour.'

'Which is?'

Jaygo sat down on the bed. 'I've got to meet Jack Ngale in Kano on Saturday to finalise the launch of the album next week.'

'So?'

'So I want you to come with me.' She looked up at him. 'I know you'll be in Kano because I've checked,' she added quickly. 'And I don't want Jack steam-rollering me into anything else. I've told him I'll stay for three days but that's all. Any promo after that they can do themselves. But he wants me to do a tour of the major cities with a whole string of appearances.'

'He'd pay you, presumably. If you can fit it in you might enjoy it. Something a bit new for you.'

'He's offered to pay all right – way over the top in fact. He hasn't even asked me to play or anything. He just wants to parade me around.

'But you know him better than me,' she went on. 'You'd be better at standing up to him when he gets pushy. I mean, you'd know all about that gold thing and I wouldn't.'

She took his hands and gently pulled herself up so that she stood right in front of him. She stood on tip toes and kissed him briefly on the lips before moving away. 'Thank you,' she said. 'I knew you'd say yes.'

Peter ran his fingers over his lips where she had kissed him. 'I haven't said yes.'

Jaygo appeared not to have heard him. 'And you tell me the Kanoites will know all about the torque?'

'Definitely. You'll see it yourself wherever you look in Kano. Posters, T-shirts, that sort of thing. It's the logo on the local beer and I've even seen it on boxes of matches. The Ngalese are still the biggest tribe in Kano and the torque is still very much in their mind.'

'Even though they haven't got it any more?' she said, looking in the fridge again.

'They think they will have it back again one day,' he said, watching her. 'Christians think they'll find the Holy Grail. The Ngalese think they'll find the torque.'

Jaygo took a can of fruit juice and moved over to the window as she pulled the ring on the lid.

'Look,' she said. 'It's completely dark now. But it's still all hazy. Do you think it ever clears down there?'

Peter was slightly annoyed that she was wandering again. 'I haven't said yes. And you didn't have to come all this way to ask me. You could have just telephoned.'

She put the can down and put her arms around him. 'I don't think so. It wouldn't have been quite the same, would it?'

'Jaygo. No,' he said, taking her arms away.

'Don't be like that,' she said. 'You always used to say that you only really understood things when your arms were around me, didn't you?' She put her arms around him again.

This time he did not break away but cupped her face in his hands and kissed her on the top of her head.

'Jaygo. Jay. That's a long time ago. We're not going back. We live in completely different worlds now.'

She squeezed her arms more tightly and rested her head against his chest. 'I'm not sure that I'm understanding things any better but, by Christ, this feels good.'

Peter almost reluctantly put his arms around her.

'See?' she said, looking up at him. 'I told you it felt good.'

He looked down at her. Her eyes seemed very close and very big.

'We were always the wrong height for this, weren't we?' she said, standing on her toes again and kissing him on the lips again.

She ran her tongue over her top lip still looking him straight in the eyes. Then, with her mouth slightly open, she began to kiss him again.

As they kissed, she pressed against him and moved her hands up to the back of his head and moved her fingers backwards and forwards through his hair.

After a long time, she pulled away from him and leant back in his arms as she linked her fingers behind his neck. 'There,' she said quietly. 'I told you.'

They smiled at each other. 'You're a bad woman Jackie Morton,' he told her. 'A very bad woman.'

She gave him another squeeze before breaking away to look at the clock by the bed. 'I don't know about that. I just don't want you making any silly mistakes, that's all.'

She walked past him on her way to the bathroom. As she went by she trailed a hand across his chest. 'Perhaps eight years isn't quite as long as you seem to think.'

She emerged from the bathroom a moment later with a bundle of her clothes which she put on the bed. She reached for a small case from the big pile and took out a jumper and pair of jeans.

'I think I'd better get going now so I'm going to change. Don't look,' she said, dropping the dressing gown to the floor and pulling on a pair of pants.

As she zipped up her jeans she grinned at him. 'I told you not to look, you dirty old man!'

'What time's the Dallas flight?'

'When I get to the airport,' she said, snapping the locks closed on the case. 'It's my jet.'

'Oh,' he said. 'And where are you going after Dallas?'

'Back here,' she said, beginning to brush her hair. 'Tomorrow night's some private do and then it's back home to England at about midnight.'

'Why didn't you wait to see me there? You seem to know my movements pretty much to the hour.'

'Ah,' she said, pulling some loose hairs from the brush, 'but what you call the "army" will be with me then. And I don't think Hugo would like me "apologising" in front of strange scientists he doesn't know.'

Her hair was almost completely dry now and as she pulled the brush through it to arm's length, it fell back to her sides. 'Be a darling and call down for some porters to take this lot down to the foyer so I can get a taxi. I really have to dash.'

Peter made the call. As he put down the phone he asked, 'Where are you playing tomorrow night? I'll still be here and perhaps I could meet the famous Hugo.'

'Actually it's a big political fund-raising dinner at the Governor's place. Tickets only and five hundred dollars at that. But I can get you a freebie, if you like.'

'Oh,' he said. 'Maybe best not then. No DJ and all that.'

Sensing the disappointment in his voice, she added, 'We're going to play the Beethoven Triple Concerto. You remember. It was our music that first winter. We played it when we sat by your lovely open fire in the flat, didn't we?'

'I expect so,' he said quietly. 'But I don't remember there being a cello in it.'

'Well, there is now. You always used to say you thought it would be the music they played in paradise. Do you still think so?'

'I expect so,' he repeated as quietly as before.

He looked at her. 'Jay, what is all this about?'

'All what?'

'You know quite well.' He waved his arm around the room. 'You appear out of the blue, start talking about the old days, kiss me and then ask to see me again. You can't just go back and have a look at the past to see if you really liked it.'

'Is that what you think I'm doing?' she said.

'What then?'

'Look,' she said. 'I'm not trying to do that. You can't turn clocks back. They don't work that way.'

'Well, we can't go forward either, can we? We've completely lost touch. You and your jets, governors' dinners, album launches and so on. I don't live there. I mean, your idea of a working lunch is probably signing some deal, approving a cover design and then racing off to play a concert in some city or other. And my idea of a working lunch is a leisurely wine tasting at the college before going down to Byron's Pool to sleep it off. Our worlds don't touch. And pretending they do isn't . . . isn't . . .'

'Isn't what? Helping? Is that what you're going to say?'

'Well, it isn't is it? I honestly don't know what you feel about

31

me now. And you don't know what I feel, do you? So, what's going on here?'

She was about to answer him when the porters arrived with their trolleys.

There was a flurry of activity as cases were loaded up and sorted. Peter lifted the cello case carefully on to one of the trolleys by itself. 'God,' he said. 'This thing weighs an absolute ton.'

'It has to,' she said. 'It's got its own climate control thingey in the case. Cost a fortune. But then, so did the cello, so I suppose it's worth it. Hugo says so anyway.'

'Good for "Hugo says" then,' said Peter to himself as he placed it on the trolley.

Suddenly the room was quiet again.

Jaygo took his hands in a businesslike manner. 'Lovely to see you, Peter. Simply lovely.' She was back in Jocasta Manhattan mode.

He raised her hands to his lips and kissed them. 'Nice to see you again too. You're looking good.'

She pecked him on the lips. 'Kano it is, then. We'll talk on the phone to fix the details.'

Just as she was leaving she blew him another kiss. 'Keep this for me, Pete.'

Peter closed the door after her and turned back into the room. He looked at his single case still on the bed and then at the place where her ten cases had been piled. He walked over to the table by the bed and picked up the CD case to examine it again. She makes a good lion, he thought. He traced a finger around the line of the torque and smiled. She would make a good anything really, he added to himself. She just has to choose something to be good at it.

He put the CD case down on the table and looked at the telephone.

Aurelia, he thought to himself. Aurelia.

He walked over to the mini-bar and poured two miniatures of Irish whiskey into one glass. He stood by the window.

'Ladies and gentlemen of Atlanta,' he said out loud, raising his glass for a toast. 'I give you Miss Jocasta Manhattan. Jaygo to her friends and Jay to me. I'm not sure where she was yesterday and I don't know where she will be tomorrow but I can tell you, my friends, that it won't be here.'

He was about to drink from the glass when he noticed a full moon appearing between two tall buildings to his left.

32

'Ah,' he continued. 'August. Full moon. Then that must be Jaygo's moon.' He bowed slightly to his imaginary audience. 'Everybody, please, raise your glasses to Jaygo's moon.'

He threw his head back and downed his drink in one.

Chapter Two

TUESDAY

Peter woke up at about nine o'clock the following morning. He was thinking of calling room service for coffee when the telephone rang.

'Hi, Peter. Are you watching the TV?' It was Laurie Miller.

'Laurie! I didn't know you were in town.'

'Never mind that. Just turn on the news. It's wall-to-wall on Channel BG50.'

'What?'

'Just do it. I'll meet you in the coffee shop in twenty minutes.'

'What?'

But Laurie had already hung up. Peter looked at the handset, puzzled, before picking up the TV remote control.

He flicked though what seemed an unnecessary number of channels before he came to BG50. A young woman with a serious expression and shoulder pads was speaking directly to the camera.

'Update. For the latest news on the CEC bombing we are going over live to our reporter, Sarah Furlong.'

The picture changed to another young woman wearing shoulder pads, holding a microphone. Behind her were rows of police cars and fire engines. Behind them again was a large building on fire. Peter realised with horror that it was the main block of the Centre for Epidemiology Control.

'The explosion took place at about five o'clock this morning,' the reporter began. 'It appears to have been a large incendiary device and the seat of the fire is thought to have been in the main lecture theatre where an international conference was due to begin later today. The only person in the building at the time was the night janitor who was on his rounds. He is uninjured but is not available for comment.'

The picture suddenly returned to the studio where shoulder pads number one was saying, 'We interrupt our live coverage to take you directly to police headquarters where Chief Railton is about to make a statement.'

Peter began to dress as the scene changed to a grey-haired man of about sixty on the steps outside police headquarters. He was surrounded by thrusting microphones and cameras. 'I have to tell you that a telephone call was received here at about six o'clock this morning. The caller identified himself as a spokesman of The Brothers of the Lion and claimed responsibility for the CEC bombing. At that time, details had not been released to the media and the caller described enough of the location and nature of the explosion for us to believe that the as-yet-unidentified Brothers of the Lion are indeed responsible or at least closely connected to this event.'

An unseen reporter interrupted. 'Chief Railton, can you elaborate on this group? Are The Brothers of the Lion known to you?'

'Negative. We have no record of any organisation of that name here in Georgia. We are currently checking with both New York and TG in Geneva but it appears at this time that we are dealing with a new organisation.'

'Did the caller give any motivation, Chief?'

'Negative again. But we can assume from the timing and incendiary nature of the bomb that destruction of property rather than hazard to life was the chief purpose of the device. I'm afraid that is all I have for you at this time, people. Now, if you'll excuse me.' He turned to go and was followed by the microphones and cameras but he did not speak again and disappeared into the wooden doors at the top of the steps.

CEC? thought Peter. Who the hell would want to set fire to that place? And what about the conference? Bound to be cancelled. Shit. He reached for the telephone again but it rang before he could pick it up.

'Did that wake you up then?' It was Laurie Miller again.

'Shit, Laurie. What the hell's going on? And what's going to happen to the conference?'

'Good question, and I've a good answer for you. Just get down here.'

'No, Laurie. I've got some calls to make.'

'Do it from down here on my mobile. We have to talk. Shall I order breakfast for you? I think I know what this is about so get yourself in gear.'

'What's what about? The bomb?'

'In one, Peter. Don't forget I've got four hours over you on this one. But if I'm going to stay ahead of the pack I'll need you. Coffee white or black?'

'Laurie, what four hours? What is all this?'

'OK. White. Now shift it.' Click.

Peter finished dressing, watching the television screen. They were showing an aerial view of the CEC complex with a black column of smoke still rising from the main building. 'Fire tenders were on the scene within five minutes,' Shoulder Pads was explaining, 'but due to the intense heat generated by the device, extensive damage had been caused before the crews could gain ingress.

'I spoke a few minutes ago,' she went on, 'to Dr Bob Anderson, Director of the Centre and this is what he had to say.'

A rather tousled Bob Anderson, who appeared to have been called from his bed to make a statement, appeared. His familiar lined face looked stunned and angry.

'I have no idea who would have carried this out,' he said. 'The Centre for Epidemiology Control carries out humanitarian research for clients all over the world. It is inconceivable that any rational organisation should wish us harm.'

'Don't be so bloody naive, Bob,' said Peter to the television. 'The Centre's popular enough but you personally have more people gunning for you than Bonnie and Clyde.' He flicked off the television, picked up his keys and left the room to join Laurie.

When Peter arrived at the coffee shop, Laurie was standing in front of a wall-mounted television smoking a cigarette. He was a short man and seemed to have put on yet another stone since Peter had seen him less than a year ago. He was scratching the top of his head.

'Look at this,' he said, without turning to Peter. 'Chaos. Fire engines and police cars all over the place. Anyone with a fireman's hat could go in or out taking away or planting evidence to their heart's content. Christ, anyone would think they'd never seen a bomb before.'

'Good morning, Laurie. Good to see you too.'

'What? Oh, sorry. Yes, good morning, Peter.' Laurie adjusted his cigarette to the side of his mouth and held out his hand. 'I've got a table over there if you like.'

They collected some coffee from a side counter and sat down.

A waiter in a white jacket appeared with an ash tray. 'I'm sorry, sir, smoking is not permitted in the dining area.'

'Good idea,' said Laurie, stubbing it out in his saucer before turning back to Peter. 'Now, do you know anything at all about this?' he said, waving his hand towards the television.

'Me? No, why should I? Look, can I use your phone?'

'You see,' said Laurie, pointing to his cup. 'Decent coffee. Why can't you get decent coffee in England? Is it the water, do you think?'

'Probably,' said Peter, slightly irritated. 'I said, can I borrow your phone?'

'If you want to ring about the conference, don't bother. It's all sorted out. You're on at three.'

'At three! You mean the conference is still on? I can't believe that!'

'Relax,' smiled Laurie, holding his hands up. 'There is an alternative venue worked out.'

'Alternative venue? Already?'

'Sure. At the university. Don't believe what you see on the television. Bob Anderson got a bomb threat call at ten last night. He told the police and they told him that it was most likely a hoax. Apparently our so-called Brothers of the Lion have been making a whole series of hoax calls over the last week or so. No one has ever heard of them and no bombs have gone off. In fact, the police were so convinced it was a hoax that they didn't even plan to go and check the place out until later today. Meanwhile they said to seal the building off and set up an alternative venue for the meeting until it was all sorted out.'

'Move the conference, Laurie? You can't just "move" a whole conference.'

'Why not? It's only bums on seats,' replied Laurie who was by now looking towards the food counter. 'Are you up for some beef hash? Pancakes perhaps?'

'What?'

'Bums on seats. It can take place anywhere. I think I'll go for some sunny side up on toast. Come on.'

Peter shook his head and drank some coffee. But Laurie was making his way to the food counter. He looked over at the television where they were playing the Bob Anderson interview again.

Laurie returned to the table with his plate piled high with a substantial meal.

'That looks disgusting,' said Peter.

'Relax,' said Laurie. 'You're just jet-lagged. Be fine in a couple of hours.'

'Now, Laurie. You can start by telling me what you're doing here in the first place. Surely the conference isn't worth ITV sending a correspondent?'

'Ah, ITV. Sad story there. I'm afraid I don't work for them any more.'

'Oh? Sad story?'

'Yes. Their idea, not mine,' he said vaguely. 'Something to do with hotel expenses and hotel bills.'

'Oh.' Peter smiled.

'Yes. Quite a few actually. I'm afraid I rather overstepped the ten percent rule. Silly me. But the upshot was that I could either go quickly and quietly or go quickly and quietly. So basically I was out on my ear. That wouldn't have been so bad except I lost my ITV press pass and official contacts. It's no joke being a freelance you know.'

'You must have landed on your feet. Atlanta. This hotel. That's quite an outlay.'

Laurie looked down at his meal and began cutting it up. 'Actually, the air fare is a loan from my mother and, as for this hotel, no way. I'm in the airport Howard Johnson. It's officially "Laurie on his uppers week" sorry to say. But,' he said, brightening, 'this very nice breakfast is courtesy of my old friend, Peter Wilson.'

'Thanks.'

'No. Thank you, old man. But I'm only partly here for the conference. I'm trying to follow up on a story.'

'Oh?'

'Yes. Let me start at the beginning.'

'About time.'

Laurie ignored him and went on, 'I'm coming to it from the pharmaceutical industry side. Do you know what a Laboratory Re-agent Pack is, LRP for short?'

Peter shook his head and went on drinking his coffee.

'Thought not. Well, an LRP is a set of stuff, solvents, re-agents, glassware and so on. The big pharmaceutical companies put special ones together for different customers. Giant medical kits if you like. Big enough to set up a whole laboratory from scratch in some cases. Everything you need. And then you can top yourself up with smaller packs as you need them. With me so far?'

'More or less. Sounds pretty logical.'

'It is. And it's good business. But tell me, Mr Scientist, what is the most common sort of laboratory in the world? You know, for a Laboratory Re-agent Pack?'

'I don't know,' said Peter. 'Pathology perhaps? Histology?'

'Nope.'

'What then?'

'Give up?'

'Give up.'

'Your actual gruesome twosome, Morphine and Heroin.'

'What!'

'Absolutely. Think about it. The world's top-selling drug after aspirin is street heroin and all its derivatives. And someone has to actually make them from raw opium. It's the same basic process all over the world. Colombia, Vietnam, Thailand. Wherever. Frankly it's an LRP market just too big for the drug companies to ignore.'

'Come off it, Laurie. You're off your rocker!'

'No. No, I'm not. Look, once one company started doing it they all had to follow suit. You can't just hand a huge slice of business to a competitor because you don't like the flavour. Oh well, I'll grant you they don't call the Packs "Drug Baron Starter Set" or "Morphine Motherfucker Kit". No, they call them things like "Field Analysis Laboratory Set No. 3" or something. And they don't advertise them of course. Don't have to. And they don't tell anyone who doesn't have to know. But believe me they are all at it like rabbits in sacks. All the big companies and half the small ones too, probably.'

'You're being ridiculous,' said Peter. 'And even if it were half true, the police would be on to them by now.'

'Of course they are. But why should it bother them?'

'Why?' said Peter. 'Because it's what they do. They go around kicking laboratory doors down all the time. "Right, you lot" they say. "Making drugs? Under arrest the lot of you!"'

'Now who's being ridiculous? It's not in their interest to do anything major.'

'Of course it is. It's what they *do*. It's what they're *for*, for God's sake.'

'Don't be so bloody naive, Peter. Look. The customs people here make two percent on every shipment and the police make five. The US market is worth hundreds of millions alone. They're not going to rock the boat, are they? Besides if they tacitly support the big companies at least the druggies get reasonable quality re-agents, which helps keep the products of reasonable quality. And clean drugs mean fewer deaths. Looks better.'

'Fewer deaths! God, Laurie, there's dozens of drug-related deaths every week. Look in any paper.'

'Yes, but that's just gang action. Shootings and so on. Not much from the stuff itself except for a few first time ODs. Bottom people. A few small-time pushers perhaps. And they're all replaceable anyway. Street drugs is one market where all the customers want to grow up to be retailers, isn't it?'

Peter waved at the waiter to bring him some more coffee.

As he poured it, Laurie asked him, 'Could you bring me a local paper please? The *Atlanta Courier*, I think.'

'Of course, sir, shall I charge it to your room number, sir?'

Laurie looked quizzically at Peter.

'All this on one bill, please. Room 6034.'

'Of course, sir,' said the waiter, gliding away.

Laurie put down his knife and fork and turned his attention to his coffee. 'Where were we?'

'I think you were about to be carted off to the funny farm.'

Laurie turned suddenly serious and jabbed a finger towards Peter.

'Listen to me, Pete,' he said angrily. 'I'm not pissing about. It's not a conversational game. That bomb was not a game.' He waved toward the television set. 'Do *you* know what that's about? Do you?'

'No. Of course not. And nor do you.'

Laurie turned his finger towards himself. 'Well, I—' he said, tapping his chest. 'I think I do.'

'What then?' said Peter. 'And don't be so uptight,' he added, putting down his coffee cup. 'All you've told me so far is this drugs story. You haven't even mentioned the bloody bomb.'

Laurie appeared to calm down. 'OK,' he said, holding up his hands. 'Sorry. But what I've told you isn't speculation. I've got it all documented. Photocopies. Transcripts. The lot. You see, when I started on this story a couple of months ago it was just the usual run-of-the-mill drugs baron stuff. But the deeper I went the bigger it got. It snowballed. And these people are making a lot of money. Millions. Tens of.' He put his head to one side. 'Hundreds probably. And now this.' He waved his hand towards the television again.

Peter put his cup down. 'OK, Laurie. I don't buy what you say but let's suppose for a moment that I do. And if only a quarter of what you say is true, you had better shut up. I don't know what the people you are talking about will do if you decide to publish. No, I've *no* idea what they'll do but I'm sure it will be more than just leave a message on your answering machine asking you to call it off. And if what you say *isn't* true they'll be just as pissed off. You can't go around slagging everyone off. Customs. Police. Transnationals. At the very least they'll sue you for every penny you've got.'

'What? Both pennies?'

The two men smiled.

Peter looked at his watch. 'Five?' he said. 'Can't be right.'

'No, Mr Jet Lag. It's ten.'

'Shit. Then I'm supposed to have called Aurelia by now. Bugger it.'

'Never mind her for a moment. I was going to tell you about the bomb.'

'I suppose you're right. She can wait. Tell me what you were going to say.'

'Well,' said Laurie, 'Bob's the key. Bob Anderson.'

Peter looked surprised. 'You sure?'

'He's the one definite link connecting the drugs and the bomb. But we'd better get over to the university. With your help I might be able to get an interview with Anderson this morning. Have you got any wheels?'

'A car? Yes, I've hired one. But I've got stuff to do first. And anyway,' he said, calling for the bill, 'nobody calls cars "wheels" any more.'

'We do,' smiled Laurie.

The white-coated waiter appeared with the bill already made out and set it down for Peter to sign.

Peter glanced at it. 'It says two cooked breakfasts here. We only had one.'

'Well, actually,' said Laurie, 'I had a little bite before you came down. I hope you don't mind.'

'Christ, Laurie. It's no wonder you look like a bloody football,' muttered Peter as he signed the bill.

Laurie appeared not to have heard but turned to the waiter. 'Good man this,' he said. 'Good Wheels man. If you need a Wheels man you can't do better.'

'Thank you,' said the waiter, taking the bill without any expression on his face.

As they left, Laurie turned to Peter. 'I hope you didn't tip him.'

'Of course I tipped him. Why not?'

'He never brought the paper, did he?'

'Oh, well.'

'Oh, well nothing. I wanted to show you the photo on the society page.'

'What was it?'

'The caption read, "Jocasta Manhattan dined last night at the Peachtree Plaza Restaurant in the Sky with Dr Peter Wilson, the distinguished British scientist. It is rumoured they are renewing their one-time affair although neither was prepared to comment."'

'Shit. Did it really say that?'

'Scout's honour. Words to that effect anyway. But no one will take it seriously. The only person who could possibly object is your lovely Aurelia and she's hardly likely to see it.'

'Suppose not. But it's not very nice, is it? Anyway, it wasn't dinner. Just a drink. She was passing through Atlanta and just dropped by.'

'I think not, Peter,' said Laurie. 'Jaygo never just "drops by". You know perfectly well that every move that woman makes is planned a long way in advance.'

Peter collected the car keys from the front desk before the two men made their way down to the basement car park.

'It's a cheat you know,' said Laurie when the lift reached level minus four.

'What is?'

'This place. It claims to be the world's tallest hotel, or did. But they only got away with it by simply counting the number of floors and adding on these below ground ones. The real winner was in Manila all along.'

'What are you going to do then? Write an exposé?'

'No. But I just like to keep you informed.'

'Thanks, but I was looking for something about this bomb thing and its link to Bob Anderson.'

Peter drove up the ramp into a hot Atlanta morning with the haze already beginning to build.

'Where's the air-conditioning?' asked Laurie.

'Open the window.'

'Shit. I thought you were on expenses.'

'I am. Mine. And so are you, Mr Double Breakfast. So tell me about Bob.'

Laurie rubbed his face. 'Well,' he began, 'who has our esteemed friend and Director of CEC managed to upset most in the past five years?'

'You mean apart from his friends, his colleagues and probably his family? Well, I'd go along and say probably the big pharmaceutical companies, from what I read.'

'That's right,' replied Laurie. 'But I don't know what made him think he could get away with it.'

'I don't think he did it to get away with anything. He just said things he thought needed to be said. He wanted to do the right thing.'

'Right thing?' questioned Laurie. 'He should have thought more about what he was doing. Look, he more or less lined up four of the biggest companies in the world and told them, their customers and anyone else who would listen, that they were a bunch of money-grubbing shits using vast profits from dollar-a-drum pills to finance dodgy research into even more dollar-a-drum pills.'

'Hold on, Laurie. I don't think he ever went quite that far.'

'But he did,' countered Laurie, 'at least here in the States. I read he actually sued one of them in a test case over some particularly suspect test results for some Aids drug or other.'

'And who won?'

'The company, of course. AbChem in that instance. Better lawyers got them off on a technicality. But everyone got to see what had been going on. It gave our Bob guru status with every crackpot group in the consumer field. A sort of Ralph Nader for the new millennium. Only it wasn't the car companies everyone was suddenly gunning for, it was the pharms boys.'

'It would have happened one day anyway the way they carry on. Bob just happened to be the main man at the time.'

The car stopped at traffic lights. 'Rush hour,' added Peter. 'Great time to drive anywhere. And I still don't see why I've got to go now if I'm not due on till three.'

'People to see. Things to do,' replied Laurie. 'Pull in over there and I'll buy that paper.'

'Things and people for you maybe,' said Peter looking in the wrong wing mirror.

A car blared its horn as it went past. The driver was looking straight ahead but his arm was stuck resolutely out of the side window with his middle finger raised.

'See?' said Laurie. 'He can't afford air-conditioning either. Bound to lead to stress.'

Peter shook his head and pulled in to the side of the road next to a drug store and drummed his fingers on top of the wheel while Laurie went to buy a paper.

Laurie was already turning the pages as he walked back. 'Ah,' he said, getting into the car. 'Here we are. Nice picture of Jaygo. Not so good of you.'

Peter pulled out again into the traffic.

'It says here,' continued Laurie, 'that international celebrity and cellist Miss Jocasta Manhattan last night dined in the Restaurant in the Sky with her ex-lover Dr Peter Wilson. Miss Manhattan exclusively told our reporter, Hannah Mears, that she and Dr Wilson had been seeing each other as regularly as her busy schedule allowed and that he would be joining her on her upcoming visit of African States to promote her controversial new album, *The Music of the Lion*. Well,' concluded Laurie, 'lucky old Dr Wilson.'

'Shit,' said Peter irritated. 'That's total crap. She didn't speak to anyone and we didn't have dinner at all.'

'Mmm,' went Laurie. 'Not in the restaurant maybe, but one can only speculate what went on behind the closed doors of Room 6034.'

'It was just supper, for God's sake!'

'Glad to hear it,' said Laurie smiling.

'How do you know about the room anyway?' asked Peter.

'I'm a journalist. I have to know things.'

Another car passed with its horn full on but this time the finger gesture came from behind a wound-up window.

'I can see why they all drive automatics now,' said Peter. 'They need to keep one hand free the entire time. And what's everyone on about anyway?'

'You're supposed to go at the same speed as everyone else,' said Laurie. 'But don't worry. They're excellent drivers and won't bang into you.'

'And your mother!' shouted Peter as a pick-up truck swerved in front of him.

'Take it easy, Pete! Do you want me to drive?'

'No. I do *not* want you to drive. I'm the "Wheels Man", remember?'

'OK. But do you want me to go on reading this or not?'

'No.'

'Good. The next bit is about your African itinerary. Et cetera. Et cetera. Ah, here we are. This is the bit I heard on the news. "Amid mounting speculation on the current status of the relationship between Jocasta Manhattan and Dr Wilson, Miss Aurelia Collis, demure current fiancée of Dr Wilson, was unavailable for comment at her home in England last night".'

'Christ! Let me see that,' said Peter, grabbing for the paper.

'No!' said Laurie, pulling it away. 'And don't worry, Pete. It's all just lifted from Jaygo's web pages. She's got more than three hundred by now.'

'I know that. But I didn't know I was on them. Let alone Aurelia.'

'Oh, come off it, Peter, Jaygo's worth half a page of any paper's money. She doesn't care what they write.'

'But, Aurelia – how do they know about her, for God's sake?'

'I don't know,' shrugged Laurie. 'But I told you, don't worry. She's not going to read the *Atlanta Courier*, let alone plough through Jaygo's unofficial web sites.'

'Thank God for that. I've told Aurelia before what Jaygo's like but she won't listen.'

As they approached the university, they found themselves in a slow-moving lane of traffic turning off to the main car parks. A temporary road block had been set up at the entrance and a policeman was checking conference name-badges before waving people through and ticking off names on a list.

'My badge is in the case on the back seat, Laurie. Could you be a sweetie and grab it for me, please?' said Peter. 'And how are you going to get in, by the way?'

'Press Pass at the ready, courtesy of Bob Anderson,' said Laurie reaching behind him to open Peter's briefcase.

As he opened the lid, Peter's present for Jaygo fell out of the flap. Laurie surreptitiously opened the gift tag and read the message before folding it shut again. He turned to the front and passed Peter his badge.

When they had been checked by the policeman and were looking for somewhere to park, Laurie said, 'Pathetic really. I mean was that supposed to be some sort of security check or what?'

'It was a gesture,' said Peter. 'At least they'll know who has come in and out.'

'Huh. They didn't even look in the boot. Maybe an exchange visit to Belfast or Tel Aviv wouldn't go amiss.'

'They're not looking for anything,' said Peter. 'Just watching who goes in. That thing last night was an incendiary device designed to go off when nobody was there just to set the place on fire.'

'Is that right, Peter?' said Laurie looking absently at the sports page of the paper. 'I don't remember seeing you in Belfast when I did my stint there.'

'OK. OK. But they've got your name so you had better behave yourself.'

'Silly game, baseball,' said Laurie, looking at a photograph in the paper. 'Girl's game really.'

'Why don't you help me look for a parking space instead of being an expert on everything,' said Peter.

Laurie looked up and saw a space. 'Just there, old man, to your left.'

'Yes, I saw it too,' said Peter.

'Anyway,' said Laurie, folding the paper away, 'what does Aurelia know about Jaygo? You and Jaygo, that is.'

'Nothing,' said Peter, reversing into the space. 'These cars are very wide, aren't they? There's nothing to know anyway. I told Aurelia that we went out for a while when we were students. And Jaygo turns up in Cambridge from time to time so she's seen her a couple of times. But there isn't much else to know, is there?'

Peter pulled forward and tried to reverse into the space again. 'There's no feel to this wheel,' he complained. 'Power setting's all wrong. How am I supposed to know what direction it's pointing? And if you ever tell Aurelia that Jaygo came to Atlanta I will personally wring your neck.'

'Now, would I do that!'

'Good,' said Peter, turning off the ignition and reaching for his case. 'Good.'

As they walked away from the car, Laurie pointed at it. 'Long as well as wide, isn't it?'

'Sorry?'

'Long. The car. I mean it sticks out from the others by about two feet, doesn't it?'

'Shut up.'

'I've never understood,' continued Laurie. 'You tell me you can fly a helicopter all round your patch in Kano but you can't drive a car properly, let alone park one.'

'Jet-lag,' explained Peter. 'And when you fly a helicopter you get to wear headphones so you don't have to listen to inane passengers and their paper reviews.'

They followed a series of blackboard signs that directed them to the main lecture block and up the wide steps to the tall entrance doors.

Just inside, a woman was sitting at a trestle table ticking off names and handing out photocopies of the revised timetable.

'There's a refectory upstairs,' she said. 'Coffee is served all day and there's a lunch for delegates at one. There's a diagram on your schedule showing you where everything is.'

'Thank you,' said Peter, 'but I've been here before. I know where everything is.'

Laurie was peering at a group of delegates gathered at the opposite side of the wide hall.

'He's not here yet. Let's go upstairs.'

'Who's not here?' asked Peter.

'I told you. "People to see." One in particular actually but I don't see him yet. Fancy a doughnut?'

'We can't really see everyone from here.'

'No. He's not here. Let's just say he rather stands out from a crowd.'

The woman looked up from her list. 'Dr Wilson? Do you have any slides for your lecture? I'm afraid any sent ahead were lost last night. I don't have a record of who sent what.'

'I have them with me,' said Peter.

'You can hand them in to the conference office we've set up next to the eating hall. We haven't got a projectionist or anything but they can copy them onto transparencies and then you can work them from the podium, if that's all right?'

'That's fine by me,' smiled Peter and turned to follow Laurie who was already heading to the side of the hall towards the stairs.

Peter handed his slides in at the office and found Laurie sitting in front of a plate of mini doughnuts and two plastic cups of coffee.

'Feeling better yet?' said Laurie. 'I thought you might be up to some breakfast by now.'

'Do you ever stop eating?' asked Peter. 'Is your man in here by the way?'

'No. And no,' said Laurie, choosing a doughnut.

Peter looked distastefully at his coffee, took a tentative sip and grimaced. 'The water, you said? And now we're sitting comfortably you can continue with your conspiracy theory about the fire bombs of Atlanta.'

Laurie looked serious. 'OK,' he sighed. 'It's a flyer but here goes. First, do you know that Bob Anderson's written a new book about his beloved pharmaceutical industry?'

'He's written loads of books. He's an Institute Director. Par for the course.'

'Yes. Regular stuff. But this latest one is a bit different. It was due out next month but his publishers have suddenly got cold feet and pulled it. AbChem and Geneva pharmaceuticals threatened to sue them to the hilt if as much as one page got out.'

'What was in it?'

Laurie took another doughnut. 'His original title was *Dream Companies – Nightmare Crops*. It's to do with his Broken Circle theory. Do you know it?'

'He mentioned it to me once. It's a re-run of his old TTPC thing isn't it?'

'That's right. Tobacco, Tea, Palm Oil and Cocoa. TTPC. He used to maintain that those four crops were the corner stones of colonial power. He said TTPC was the backbone of the whole expansion bit and that it wasn't anything to do with Union Jacks, Queen Vic, the missionary position or anything else. He always said whoever controlled the TTPC crops could rule the roost.'

'They did,' said Peter, trying his coffee again.

'Yes. And it worked perfectly well. Those four crops still account for three-quarters of all Third World cash crop exports. You can leave out food crops like rice and wheat because you don't have to process them and they'll grow anywhere you like. But the TTPC group *have* to be grown in the tropics and you need a partner who can manufacture a finished product from them, or at least package and market it right. Now, you can't eat any of them so they have to be sold to your partner for them to be of any use if you want to buy the food you should have been growing yourself in the first place. And so, once you get an economy dependent on one or more of them, you have to go on producing them ad nauseam just to eat. Right?'

'So Bob used to rattle on.'

'And he was right,' continued Laurie. 'But there is more to it than that. Because if you control the manufacture and distribution of the finished product, you effectively control the two key prices. The price you pay the producer and the price you put the stuff on the world market, don't you? But bringing in all this lovely money also brings in the banks, who in their turn control the price of money. So, we have a nice little circle building up.'

As he spoke, Laurie took several doughnuts and arranged them in a three-quarter circle on the table between them. He then pointed to them in turn.

'Farmer. Shipper. Buyer. Manufacturer. Market. That's the way the money flows.' He followed the three-quarter circle around with his finger. 'Only I don't see this particular circle going all the way round, do I? Not much money making its way back to Johnny Farmer, is there?'

'They got some,' said Peter. 'They still ate and you said it was cash for crops.'

'Maybe a bit,' said Laurie, 'but nothing compared to everyone else in the chain.'

'So Bob always used to say. But I think he was way out of date even ten years ago. When the Third World nationalised everything in sight back in the sixties the producer prices went up. If they hadn't been so bloody inefficient it might even have worked.'

'But it didn't work. The money never got back to the farmers, did it?'

'No,' said Peter, looking closely at the doughnuts still on the plate. 'It didn't work because the governments were no keener to hand the money back down the chain than anyone else. Human nature.'

'So what happened to the money?' asked Laurie.

'Well. The governments spent it. Or, more accurately, the people who ran the governments spent it.'

'Yes,' said Laurie triumphantly. 'And what did the lovely government people spend the lovely money on if they didn't give it to the farmers?'

Peter lifted his arms up. 'You tell me? What do governments ever spend spare money on? Armies. Airlines. Even the odd navy.'

'Yes, but these new countries had no idea of the going rate for ships and aircraft. Pretty soon they had to borrow to be able to afford what they were told they wanted. They began to compete with each other to see who could have the longest row of second-hand jets. And pretty soon our friend Mr Third World Debt was knocking at the door.'

Laurie picked up more doughnuts from the plate and put them in the middle of his three-quarter circle. 'The Banks. Private. National. International. Banks. Banks. Banks. Different names, same game. Lend high, lend long and every now and then up the interest rate by a quarter of one percent. And, so sorry, didn't I explain how compound interest works?'

'Laurie, this is old hat. First-year economics stuff. Even Bob Anderson doesn't see it in such simple terms any more.'

'True enough,' said Laurie, picking up one of the banks and eating it. 'He doesn't. But let me finish. Conventional wisdom has it that the banks, and I'm including the World Bank in this, have pretty much taken over the role of Empire Bogey Man. They control the Third World interest rates and can squeeze as hard as they like. The poor keep poor, the rich keep rich and the banks keep the rest.'

'So?'

'Well, Bob takes it a stage further now. He may be a prickly old bugger but he's as clever as all hell. In *Nightmare Crops* he argues that this banks thing is not a status quo. Not stable as in the old Empire days or even as stable when the Third Word debts were quietly building up. And that's because that very stability depended on the Third World countries having fuck-all choice. The good old TTPC lock in. They had to go on growing them or they didn't eat at all.'

'Actually,' said Peter, 'not all of them eat anyway. You may account for fifty doughnuts every breakfast but one out of four people in Africa didn't eat at all yesterday.'

Laurie ignored him. 'So Bob's new point is this. He says the set-up becomes unstable if the Third World farmers can grow another cash crop outside the TTPC set. Get out of them and you can rock the boat. And he says they *can* do it. Or at least some of them can.'

'Oh, yes? By growing what?'

'The Nightmare Crops – opium poppies and coca, for cocaine. Perfect, my friend. Easy to grow. Exclusive to the tropics. High value. Low bulk. Distribution chain already in place and customers quite literally whacking each other over the head to get hold of the stuff. And even if the total annual turnover doesn't reach the TTPC crops it doesn't really matter because you knock out so many of the parasites in the chain.' Laurie picked up several of the doughnuts from the table and put them back on the plate. 'Oh, look. No Mr Bank and his chums any more. How sad. Who knows, there might even be some left for the farmers but don't hold your breath. But, by heck, a hell of a lot for Mr Shipper and Mr Distributor and, how handy, they are already nationalised.'

Peter leaned back and considered Laurie carefully. 'OK,' he said eventually. 'I'll give that a maybe. But what's Bob's problem in publishing that? It's a theory. It can be aired.'

'Because of this,' said Laurie, pointing at one of the remaining doughnuts. 'The manufacturer. You still have to process raw opium into heroin and morphine. And our Bob says that the big pharmaceutical companies are hand in glove with the shippers and suppliers. Those giant laboratory kits I was telling you about earlier. Bob did his research pretty carefully, that's his bag after all. He followed one of the chains of production all the way from a farm in Nigeria to a New York street-dealer. And he calculated that ten cents on every retail dollar went the way of AbChem. He did it again in Ghana and got the same figure, ten percent, but this time it was Geneva Pharmaceuticals. Every plank in his story is solid four-inch oak. You can't get a razor between them. Solid. Frankly, he's got them bang to rights.

'Now,' went on Laurie, 'God knows how, but the companies got hold of a draft of his book. They told him they'd sue him to hell. Fine, he said, go ahead. They told him they'd cut all their industrial grants to CEC. Fine, he said, go ahead. Take our sponsored students away too, they said. Go for it, he told them. I told you he was a prickly bugger. So they did all this and Bob didn't even blink. Well, money talked in the end of course, and AbChem and Geneva leant so hard on the publishers that they pulled the book. No one will touch it now and Bob is well and truly stuffed. Up the creek without a platform so to speak.'

'But *you* know about the book, so others must. Why can't it go out into the press or TV?'

'Of course we know about it. Quite a lot of people do. And you would too if you'd come down from your ivory tower every now and again. But the point is that, without Bob's hard documentary evidence, it's all just rumour. Hearsay. We *have* to chapter and verse it.'

'Why won't Bob back you?'

'He says that without a proper book no one will take it seriously. He thinks it'll become just another press exposé and run into the long grass of the libel courts. That or the companies will lean on the papers or TV the way they did with the publishers.'

'Mmm. Another maybe. But how does that get us here?'

'OK,' continued Laurie, 'he can't publish an ordinary book and so the only guaranteed publication route he sees left to him is directly to the scientific community worldwide. So he calls the biggest conference he can afford, gets as many top names here as he can. And then, hey what's this? What do you know, the key-note conference speech is a two-hour knock-out from our friend Mr Director of CEC. And what is the title of this long speech he wants to make? "Dream Companies – Nightmare Crops." I tell you, Peter, I've seen a draft of the speech. It's the real McCoy top to bottom. The lot. And the conference proceedings will be winging their way around the world the day after tomorrow in the little black briefcases of two hundred delegates and visitors, you included.'

Peter folded his arms and rocked slowly backwards and forwards in his seat. 'Wow.'

'Except that it won't,' said Laurie, 'because, oh dear, the conference's proceedings, packed up and ready to go, went up in smoke last night at a tragic fire started by some cranks no one has ever heard of. What a coincidence. What a shame.'

'But the conference *is* still going ahead,' said Peter, leaning forwards. 'We are all still here. If anything there will be more publicity than ever. It's still a go.'

'Only half true I'm afraid,' said Laurie. 'You see, he's not going to be able to give the speech here. It's a university and they are shit scared because they are not headed up by someone like Bob. They've told him, no. They won't risk it and, frankly, I can see their point.'

'But they can't stop him making his speech, can they?'

'The only way they'd let him use this place was on the condition that he kept his big trap shut.'

Laurie looked down at his empty coffee cup. 'I spoke to the university just before I called you this morning,' he added. 'They said they had come to an agreement with Bob. Conference without the speech or no conference at all. Bob had no choice but to fold. At least he gets his conference and maybe even a few more converts when people get to hear about it. Better than nothing.'

'But look,' said Peter, 'if this stuff is half as solid as you say it is, you could still go with it yourself. Deep-Throat it, if necessary. It's been done before, it works.'

'I've just told you we can't do that. Our papers, stations or whatever, won't touch the story without the published speech. And, anyway, Bob doesn't want it all to go off half cock. He's the Ralph Nader man. Up front. On the table. In the open.'

'You're stuffed then, aren't you?' said Peter finally. 'One bomb and you chicken out. It looks like your Brothers of the Lion, or whoever they are, have won the day. Which brings me to another thing about the bomb. The pharmaceutical companies. Dodgy dealings and even those chemical pack things I can just about believe. Wide boys, they may well be. But bombers? Absolutely not. No way at all. Get real, Laurie.'

Laurie shrugged in reply. 'OK. Then who?'

'I don't know. But nor do you. I say Bob's speech and the bomb are separate things. Not linked.'

'Perhaps one of AbChem's druggy customers could have been paid to plant the bomb,' said Laurie hopefully.

'Is that your best shot, Laurie? Forget it.'

Laurie moved a doughnut absently around the table with his finger. 'I still say the two are linked.'

'And I say they're not,' said Peter.

'A fiver says they are.'

'Tenner.'

'Done.'

The two men smiled at each other and shook on the bet.

'Tell you what,' said Laurie after a pause, 'you hang on here and I'll mosey around and see if I can find my man. Perhaps he can shed some light on this for us.'

'OK,' said Peter, picking up the doughnuts on the table and putting them back on the plate. 'But who is he?'

'Ah,' said Laurie, 'I'm not exactly sure. I only know his name and what he does and I really want to find out what he's doing here. He's Foreign Office, you see, and he's obviously here in some official capacity or other because he's on the conference list as "invited visitor" which really means "here to get a good look at someone". People like him are always turning up at trade fairs, export shindigs or whatever. Usually to see that some Honest Johnny doesn't take too much of a back-hander. That's where I first came across him,' he went on, carefully selecting a final doughnut. 'That "New Trade for Nigeria" bash in London last summer. At the Ritz actually.'

'Bit off your line,' said Peter. 'I thought you were still Mr Science then.'

'I was. But it was all about oil. Frightfully hi-tech and *Tomorrow's World*. Besides, they do an excellent buffet at the Ritz.'

'I see,' said Peter, smiling. 'I'll wait here and guard the doughnuts for you.'

'No. No,' said Laurie standing up. 'No more for me. You tuck in.'

When Laurie had gone, Peter looked down at the table and absently ran his fingers through the grains of sugar left by the doughnuts. Almost without thinking about it, he found himself making the shape of the torque. He ran his finger backwards and forwards around the bowed arch. Then he tapped his finger at either end. 'The Eyes of the Lion,' he said quietly to himself. He tapped the point again. 'Eyes. Twins. Brothers. Shit! "Brothers of the Lion"!'

Peter looked up to call after Laurie but could not see him. He looked down again at the pattern he had made in the sugar. No. Just a coincidence. He lifted his finger and licked the sugar off it. Silly. Just a coincidence.

He picked up his plastic cup and drank the last of his coffee. Besides, the eyes the emeralds reminded him of didn't belong to any lion. They belonged to Jaygo. Now, there really *was* a pair of green eyes. He remembered how he had felt looking into them just before kissing her last night. Or the very first time all those years ago. Something between jumping and falling. She had told him a year later she had felt the same and had even used the same words, 'between jumping and falling'.

But, if she had felt that way, why had she left him? What could ever be more important than that feeling? Did getting rich and being famous really mean more?

In the pit of his stomach he suddenly felt that old sensation of being lifted up and swept away. The 'Bad Jaygo Day' feeling he used to call it to himself. Yes, she had felt the same. Yes, it had meant a lot. But moving on and up had meant more.

'There is more to life than being between jumping and falling,' he had once dreamt her saying. 'Sorry, Peter darling, that is just the way it is.'

He became aware he was rubbing the flat of his hand so hard over the sugar on the table that it was beginning to hurt. Damn, he thought angrily to himself. Can she still do that to me after all this time? No. I won't let her. Go away, Jaygo, with your big green eyes. Your promises and your goodbyes.

Peter puffed out his cheeks and sat back in his chair. Wow. I haven't felt like that for a long time, he thought. Years. He didn't miss her at all now. Hardly at all. Ever.

He let his breath out slowly. 'Damn you, Jocasta Manhattan,' he said quietly. 'Damn you.'

Peter looked up to see Laurie hurrying between the tables towards him. 'Come on, Peter, I've seen him. He's down in the hall.'

'Right,' said Peter briskly.

'Stop,' said Laurie, pointing at Peter. 'I know that expression on your face. Jaygo hasn't got to you again, has she?'

'No, Lol. I'm fine,' said Peter, standing up. 'Just the jet lag.'

'Good,' said Laurie. 'Come on.'

Peter dutifully followed the slightly waddling figure of his old friend. You've been good to me, Laurie Miller, he said to himself. You were there when I needed you that first year after she went. And I've never really done much for you, have I? Maybe one day.

Laurie was almost halfway down the corridor to the top of the stairs before Peter caught him up. 'What does he look like? How will we know him?' he asked.

'Easy,' said Laurie, standing at the top of the stairs and looking down into the big hall. 'He's six foot seven.'

'What!'

'You heard. So you'll spot him all right. But I guarantee it's not his height you'll remember but his face. Hard as fucking nails. No, I'm too kind. He looks nastier than that. And now look, the bugger's gone. Perhaps he's gone into the lecture theatre. Let's go back along the corridor to the top entrance and see if we can spot him.'

Just inside the door to the lecture theatre a pretty young woman in jeans and special Conference T-shirt was sitting by a table ticking off names of people as they came in.

'Are you a delegate, sir?' she asked Laurie.

He held up his hand to her. 'Not stopping. Just having a look-see.'

'I'm sorry, sir,' she smiled politely, 'but I need your name to cross you off.'

Peter smiled at her. 'He's Laurie Miller, press. And I'm Peter Wilson, delegate. And he's right, we haven't come to sit down but only to see if a friend is here. If he's not, we'll be back later.'

'Thank you, sir,' she said. 'In that case I'll tick you as in *and* out!' she added brightly and grinned up at Peter.

'Good idea,' smiled Peter.

'Lost him. Let's try downstairs again,' Laurie said as he pushed past Peter. 'Come on, old man.'

Peter shrugged at the girl. 'Like you said. In *and* out.'

Their second visit to the top of the stairs was no more fruitful than the first. 'Damn,' Laurie muttered, 'I could have sworn it was him. I mean he's six foot million, you can't exactly miss him.'

'If you say so. But we have,' Peter replied as the smaller man headed towards the top doors again.

Just as he spoke, the tall wooden doors to the upper hall blew across the corridor. Immediately through the open space flew the girl and the desk to slam against the opposite wall. Followed by more furniture and an enormous roaring, crunching noise. All the fire alarms in the building went off and the fire sprinklers came on. Then came a high-pitched shouting noise, almost like a football crowd. Later Peter would come to realise it was screaming. The second Atlanta bomb had gone off.

Peter and Laurie were knocked off their feet, blown back along the corridor. Peter was unhurt and sat up to see Laurie lying on his back, shouting, 'Jesus, Mother of God, what was that?'

'It's a bomb, Laurie. Another bomb.'

The two men climbed to their feet and picked their way towards where the doors had been and where the noise was coming from.

The body of the girl was lying across the broken remains of her desk. She was on her back and her neck was almost at right angles to her body. Her eyes looked as though they had been pushed in by two heavy thumbs, the sockets filled with red. Her mouth was open and blood was trickling from the side. She was completely still.

Water splashed onto her face from an overhead sprinkler, washing the blood away as Peter watched. Then no more blood came from her mouth. She was bleeding, Peter thought dumbly, and now she isn't. Another splash of water from overhead and her face was clean. There's no expression, thought Peter. Not pain, not shock, nothing. He turned towards Laurie who was going into the empty space left by the doors.

'Oh, my God,' he was saying. 'Oh my Living God.'

The next five minutes were as near hell, as near madness as Peter had ever known.

The screaming was replaced by a low moaning as they made their way down to the middle of the lecture theatre. Everyone seemed to be dead or nearly so. Everything was broken.

Peter walked to the front of the theatre and looked back. Most of the seats and the people had been blown away from a central area about ten square yards in diameter. Beyond that the debris was piled up in blackened clumps of smashed furniture. He and Laurie appeared to be the only two people standing.

Peter watched as Laurie climbed the concrete steps to one side of the theatre. At first Peter thought Laurie was hurt because he was holding both hands to one side of his head but, as Peter approached, he realised Laurie was using his mobile phone with one hand and sheltering it from the sprinklers with the other.

'Having dinner! I don't care if he's having a baby,' Laurie was shouting. 'Get him on this bloody number and tell me how much he'll pay for an on-the-spot exclusive. Yes, on the spot. Just do it will you, woman!'

Laurie took the phone from his ear and held it in front of him to dial another number.

'What are you doing?' asked Peter.

'Trying to make a bloody living. What are you doing?'

'At a time like this? We have to help.'

'Oh, yes?' said Laurie, putting the phone to his ear again. 'A bit past help most of this lot, I should say. You can start ringing their families if you like.'

'What!'

But Laurie was talking into the telephone again. 'Hello? Yes. *Standard*? Put me through to the news editor. Get him off the sodding phone then. Just do it.' He shook his head and listened again. 'OK, I'll hold for thirty seconds. Tell him now that it's Laurie Miller on site at the Atlanta bombing. Yes, bombing. I want his best price, no pissing about, for an on-the-spot. Yes. Now.' He shook his head again and looked up at Peter.

'I'm sorry,' he said. 'But this is what I do. I know it's a bomb and a lot of people are dead but it's also news. And if I move, it can be my news. Tide in the affairs of man, OK?'

He turned his attention back to the telephone. 'Bob? Yes, Laurie Miller. Can you put on CNN? Good. They'll be here in about ten minutes. Big bomb. University. About a hundred dead. Yes, Bob. Believe me, CNN will be here before the fire brigades but I'm here for you now. I was less than fifteen feet from a door in line with the blast and I'm at the seat of the explosion now.' Laurie gave an angry expression and shook the phone. 'Yes, lousy line. So what are you offering? No. Start again, Bob. No. Better. Better. OK, I'll go with that. Yes, I do appreciate it, you old skinflint. So put me through direct to news dictation. I've got two-fifty words ready and I'll do the header at the end.' He looked up again at Peter and put his hand over the phone. 'Look, I'm sorry if you don't like it but it's too big a chance to miss. This is the *Evening Standard*,' he said, holding up the telephone. 'They'll give me three grand on the nail for two hundred and fifty words. You may have that millionaire witch in your private box but I'm grubbing around in the stalls.'

He turned his attention back to the telephone. 'Yes. Starts. A second bomb went off in Atlanta, Georgia, six o'clock this afternoon London time. It was a high explosive device planted in a busy lecture theatre at the university just as a major international conference was due to begin at eleven local time.'

Peter turned away and walked towards one of the piles of broken furniture. He could immediately see several bodies. One man had his face turned upwards, like the girl, with his eyes pressed in and his mouth open. The sprinkler had washed his face but the water around his head was pink. He, too, had stopped bleeding. Peter knelt down next to the dead man and reached out to touch the face. It just felt wet. Not like a person at all. Peter looked towards Laurie who was still talking into his telephone.

Peter stood up and walked slowly to the next mound of wood. He remembered later not being surprised that the debris had landed in piles rather than being scattered around. It just seemed that was the way it had landed. Almost tidy. And the only sound was the hissing of the sprinklers and the moaning of the injured.

He came across four more bodies, this time all face down. He knelt down and stood up again without touching anyone. He put his hands on the top of his head. I don't have any idea what I am supposed to do, he thought. No idea at all. He bent down again and put his hand on the shoulder of one of the bodies and began rubbing it gently.

Then he was aware of Laurie tapping him on the back. 'Come on, Peter, old man, time to go. Now.'

Peter stood up. 'No, Laurie. I think we have to stay. Help. Rescue people will be here soon. We can tell them what happened. We were here.'

'Yes, Peter, but not now. What will you say anyway? "I was here. A bomb went off"? I think you'll find they know that already.

'Look,' Laurie went on, putting his arms out and gripping Peter by the elbows. 'I worked in Belfast for four years. There are two types of bomb. Building bombs and people bombs. This was a people bomb. End of story. There is absolutely nothing you can tell them they can't see for themselves. They'll just sit you down, give you loads of water to drink and make you repeat everything six times over. Now, you're not hurt, I'm not hurt. We have to go now while we can. Get yourself together. We go and collect our things and go back to the hotel. We can do anything you want from there. OK?'

'No, Laurie, not OK. We have to stay.'

'Yes, Peter, yes OK. Now do what I tell you for once in your life. Come on.'

Laurie climbed quickly up the concrete stairs, stepping around the face-down body of a blonde woman, to the top entrance where the doors had been.

Peter looked around him again before slowly following.

By the time Peter had reached the top, Laurie was already emerging from the cafeteria with their briefcases.

'Where is everyone?' asked Peter.

'They've run away. They always do. It's natural.'

'We stayed.'

'Yes, but I'm a journalist and you're probably in shock. Is there a back way out? Because I'd rather ask questions than answer them right now.'

'The other end of the corridor,' answered Peter. 'Some stairs go down to the gardens for the summer.'

Laurie made his way in the direction Peter had indicated. He stepped around the dead girl without looking at her. Peter followed.

Once outside, they made their way around to the front of the building and the car park. Groups of delegates and staff were standing back from the building just looking at it. High above them the first news helicopters were glinting in the sun and the wail of sirens heralded the imminent arrival of the fire engines and ambulances.

'Laurie, I won't go,' said Peter suddenly. 'At least we can tell them we are all right. They'll have to count everyone.'

'They won't even think of that until half of this lot have gone,' said Laurie. 'You're going to have to trust me on this one, Peter. I was in Belfast in the bombings and, believe me, even there hardly anyone knew what to do after a mega blast like this. And you saw these clowns on TV this morning. A Jam Stall would be too much for them. I tell you, if we can do anything useful we can do it back at the hotel and get some dry clothes while we are at it.'

'We can't go there looking like this,' said Peter, indicating his soaked jacket. 'Anyway, your clothes aren't there.'

'Yes, they are. Didn't I tell you I'd checked out of the Ho Jo?'

'No. And why my hotel?'

'Because you're on expenses and I'm out of money. Is that your car sticking out over there, old boy? Are you fit to drive or do you want me to have a go?'

'No,' said Peter firmly, walking around to the driver's side.

As they drove out of the car park past the now-deserted checkpoint, Laurie began his telephoning again.

'Bob?' began Laurie again. 'I'm making my way to a landline right now. I'll be in the Peachtree Plaza Hotel in about ten minutes. I think it's on 34th and Main. Why not see if you can open a broadcast-quality hook from their conference suite or whatever. Get it to Room 6034, name of Wilson. I'll be ready for a full interview about two minutes after we get in. I can do about ten minutes straight in for background, description and motivation. I'll feed you the questions before we start. And I'll have Dr Peter Wilson with me. He's one of the senior bods who was going to address the conference. He should be good for a few lines of quotes but I don't want to run him live unless I have to.'

Laurie paused and nodded his head several times as he listened to the reply.

'Fine. Fine,' he began again. 'We can broad-brush the money numbers now and talk details later. You're good for it, I know you. And you can feed it out if you like. Eighty-twenty to me sound good? What? Fifty! Bob, you're going to kill me. I say seventy-thirty. OK, sixty-forty. Done deal.' He flipped the telephone shut and looked at his watch.

'After the bomb,' said Peter quietly, 'you clicked into gear, didn't you? I don't think I've seen you like that before.'

'I told you,' said Laurie, opening his telephone again, 'it's what I do.'

'But I think it was more than that,' went on Peter. 'A lot more.'

'Bugger!' said Laurie. 'Batteries going. Can you go any faster?'

'No.'

Laurie looked at the unresponsive telephone in his hand. 'Bloody thing.

'You're right,' he went on. 'It was the real me for a change. I was there and I suddenly had something to do I knew I was good at. It doesn't happen very often for a two-bit journalist like me so I have to make the best of it. I think the first time was another bomb do in Belfast. A pub bomb. Not big by this standard and only one person killed. But I suddenly saw everyone else just milling about and thought, "Hey, I know what to do here." I phoned all the right people, set up the story, did a couple of interviews with survivors. I kept the wrong photographers away till my boys arrived. Did a thirty-second feed for local TV. All that sort of thing. I think it was like a performance. Suddenly the focus was on me and I knew I wasn't going to put a foot wrong.'

He opened his telephone and tried dialling again before flipping it shut with a grimace.

'I'm sorry if I was a bit pushy back there, Pete. But, as I said, it doesn't happen very often.'

'Just at explosions then?'

'No, no. That's not it at all,' said Laurie. 'It happens at the very moment any story breaks. It *can* be a bomb like this, but it could be something quite different. Once I was doing a fill-in interview at the Stock Exchange when a big Japanese bank crashed. It was just the same. I knew who to call, how much to ask and who to ring next. It wasn't really just the excitement of being there, it was actually being the important person in the middle. Love of the limelight, I suppose.'

'And it's not just me,' he went on. 'You can see it in anyone when they get on real home ground. Take old Jaygo, for instance. You must have seen her when she walks on stage.'

'Jay?'

'She clicks in. Takes over. You can see immediately she is doing what she's best at. You don't have to worry about mistakes because she isn't going to make any.'

'I suppose so,' said Peter. 'I don't think I've ever really thought about it.'

'And you? What clicks you on, Peter?'

'Something, I suppose. As I say, I've never really thought about it.'

'Well, it's about time you started. Ah, is that us up ahead?' Laurie pointed at a tall glass skyscraper.

'Yes. Five minutes.'

When they had reached Peter's room, Laurie slipped into journalist mode again and conducted his operations lying on the bed with the house telephone clamped to the side of his head for the next two hours.

Peter sat at the other end of the room watching the television with the sound turned down. He flicked disinterestedly through the channels.

About five of them were devoted entirely to the bombing. Coverage seemed to consist mainly of aerial views from the helicopters and short interviews with delegates who had been too far away from the building to have seen anything very interesting. There were no shots from inside the building. Presumably because they were still taking away the bodies, thought Peter.

There was much speculation in the studios as to who had set the bomb off. It seemed no warning telephone call had been made but suspicion naturally fell on the mysterious Brothers of the Lion who had claimed the first bomb.

'These people must be tracked down wherever they are,' said one local politician. He raised his finger in general warning. 'This is America and we will not tolerate the wanton taking of life and destruction of property.'

Nods of agreement followed from everyone in the studio, including the anchorman.

Nice sentiment, thought Peter. Shame about Vietnam.

To Peter's eye, most of the other channels seemed to be devoted either to enormously fat people on chat shows or to advertisements interrupted by brief coverage of sports such as basketball, which were themselves further interrupted by endless changes of players and obscure penalty pauses.

Peter became aware that Laurie was calling him. 'It's her majesty, Peter. She wants to talk to you.'

'Who?'

'Jaygo. She's heard about the bomb.'

Peter took the phone.

'Peter, darling. Are you all right?'

'Fine. We weren't near. Did you see it on the television?'

'No. It was on the radio thingy. We were nearly diverted.'

'Sorry?'

'From the airport. We were coming in to land back in Atlanta and they nearly diverted us to Alaska or somewhere.'

'I thought you were in Dallas for a concert.'

'No. Just a recording. Of course nobody, least of all Hairy Hugo, saw fit to tell me it started at eight o'clock in the morning. So I told them at ten that enough was enough and we left.'

'Oh.'

'Yes, I'm not going to break my fingers for anyone at that time of the morning.'

'Break your fingers?'

'Concert talk, darling. It means playing too much. Anyway the good news is that the Governor's thing tonight is bound to be cancelled because of the bomb thing and so we'll all be able to have a proper dinner together. You know, you, me, Laurie, Hugo and one or two others.'

'One or two?' asked Peter.

'Well, ten actually. Can you choose somewhere for us? What was that place you mentioned – "I have a Dream"?'

'"Menu",' corrected Peter, smiling. 'But I think it's more of a Diner. Anyway, Jay, I think you had better count me out. I think I'm pretty dazed.'

'Don't give me that crap, Peter. If anyone's dazed it's me. I've just done ten weeks on the road with bloody Hugo pawing me at every turn. One of these fine days I'm going to stick my bow right up him!'

Peter laughed. 'Concert term? Means playing too much?'

She laughed in return. 'God, it's good to be finished this tour,' she said. 'Nothing now for three weeks.'

'What about Nigeria?'

'I don't count that as work,' she said. 'I'm going with you.'

'Mmm,' went Peter uncertainly.

'Don't be so awful! It's going to be fun. And I've hardly asked you anything yet about Africa. You'll have to tell me loads more on the way back to England.'

'How? Are we on the same flight?'

'Ah, I had a mini idea about that. I got them to phone your hotel about your flight and they thought about ten tomorrow because you've booked a taxi, right?'

'You nosy bugger!'

'Well, why don't you cancel it and come back to England on the Lear with me and the Belle Epoque at about ten? You can bring Laurie and we can all have a jolly time.'

'I don't know,' said Peter. 'I've got a paid-up return ticket and I'm sure Laurie will have too.'

'Well, you'll get your money back then, won't you? A bonus from Auntie Jaygo.'

'I suppose we could. I'll ask Laurie. Are you sure you've got room?'

'Simply loads, of course. And you know Lol will say yes so don't bother to ask him. Promise him an exclusive interview or something.'

Laurie was tapping Peter on the shoulder and waving his hand to indicate he wanted the telephone back.

'OK, fine,' said Peter. 'Look I've got to go now. If I change my mind about dinner, what time shall we see you?'

'Eight sharp, darling. And don't bother choosing a restaurant. I'll get one of the local PR people to fix it. Wear a tie and tell Laurie to practise his table manners beforehand.'

'Eight o'clock then. Bye.'

Peter handed the telephone back to Laurie. 'Lucky day for Mr Football,' he said. 'Din-dins with Jaygo at eight and a free flight home on her executive jet tomorrow morning. And she says if you eat your greens she'll give you an exclusive interview.'

'Wow! Good old Jay! Will we get our money back on our proper tickets?'

'Bound to. Or a credit. Can't be bad.'

'Sounds great,' grinned Laurie, dialling a number. 'I'm going to be finished here in about half an hour. Do you want to pop out for lunch or shall we order a trolley?'

'Do you never stop?' smiled Peter. 'Sandwiches will be fine by me.'

But Laurie was already turning back to his notes and talking down the telephone.

Peter went back to the television by the window. Lear Jet eh!

Ten minutes later Laurie decided he had milked his story for all he could get and called to Peter, 'The phone's free now, Pete, if you want to make that call.'

'What call?'

'*That* call.'

'I didn't say I wanted to make a call.'

'Well, I think you should, old boy.'

'Who to?' said Peter. 'Oh Christ. Aurelia!'

'The very lady.'

Peter dialled the number. While it was connecting, he asked Laurie, 'What time is it over there now?'

Laurie looked at his watch. 'Early evening. Eight or nine.'

'Hello, darling? Is that you?' began Peter.

'Yes. Are you all right?'

'Did you see it on the news?'

'What news?'

'About the bomb,' he said. 'There's been a bomb here.'

'In Atlanta? My God, no. I haven't heard. I was at college.'

'Yes,' went on Peter, 'at the university where the conference was. I'm afraid some people are dead.'

'Dead? But I thought your meeting was at CEC.'

'Yes, but they moved the meeting to the university because of the bomb there.'

'At CEC?' Aurelia was clearly confused. 'I thought you said the bomb was at the university?'

'Yes. Another one. Two bombs.'

'Two bombs? I don't understand.'

'Yes, two,' went on Peter. 'But it's over now. Laurie and I weren't anywhere near either of them. We were very lucky.'

'Laurie? Who's Laurie? Do I know him?'

'Laurie Miller. I think you've met him. He's an old friend. He was at university with me and Jaygo.'

'Jaygo! Is she there?'

'Of course not,' said Peter quickly. 'It's just where I met him. At Liverpool. He's here with something else. He's a journalist.'

'Journalist? Bomb? What are you talking about?'

'He was with me, looking for a contact when the bomb went off. We weren't hurt. I'm just ringing in case you saw it on the news and were worried. Everything's fine.'

'And the woman?'

'What woman?'

'The one in your room last night. You said she was from the conference but I thought she was English.'

Peter thought quickly. 'Oh, her. One of the secretaries. The one who came for the slides. No, I'm sure she's OK.'

'Thank goodness for that,' said Aurelia. 'I mean I don't know her or anything but when it's someone you've actually spoken to . . .'

Suddenly a picture of the girl by the door came into Peter's mind as she lay there with her eyes pushed in. 'Yes,' he said dumbly. 'I'm sure she's all right.'

'It's too awful,' said Aurelia.

'We're all a bit shocked here. People we knew. That sort of thing.'

'Well, if you're not hurt. That's the main thing.'

'Yes, darling. Laurie wants to call his mother now. But I'll see you tomorrow. I have to go. But I'm fine. Really.'

'I love you, Peter. Take special care.'

'Yes, sweetie, till tomorrow then. Bye.'

Peter handed the telephone back to Laurie.

'Went all right, did it?' asked Laurie, smiling. 'Put her mind at rest, did you?'

'Piss off.'

'Of course,' said Laurie, 'I'm not sure it was a *frightfully* good idea to mention dear Jaygo.'

Peter put his hands up. 'Christ, it just sort of slipped out.'

'Anyway,' continued Laurie, dialling his number. 'I couldn't but notice a teeny bit of a contrast between your two calls.'

'What?'

'Well,' said Laurie, putting the phone to his ear, 'to the lovely Miss Aurelia you were the repressed Englishman making a fuck-up of a phone call. But to our Jaygo a few minutes ago, you were quite different. I thought for a moment there I actually saw you smile.'

'What's that supposed to mean?'

But Laurie held up his hand and began to talk into the telephone. 'Yes, it's me again. I've spoken to Nick at the *Mail* and he's happy to run the same lines if you'll go halves for me. OK? Yes. Sure. Well, that just about wraps it up for us. I'll call you if I get anything on the bombers but the locals are sitting pretty hard on the police here so don't hold your breath.'

Laurie put the telephone back on the side table and looked up at Peter. 'Lunch now.'

They opted for some sandwiches in the room and sat down by the window with some beers from the refrigerator.

Laurie sipped appreciatively. 'Nice beer,' he said. 'Definitely the water.'

He considered his drink for a few more moments before putting the can down and looking at Peter.

'Have you thought who was in the lecture theatre at all? You might have known some of them.'

'One for sure,' replied Peter.

'Bob?'

'Yes,' said Peter thoughtfully. 'He was a great one for hanging about before things. He was bound to have been there. And, anyway, he was on first.'

'How well did you know him?'

Peter sighed. 'Not all that well. We were on first name terms and probably met two or three time a year. Over six or seven years that's something. He kept up with what I was doing. Enough to ask me to speak. What I do is a bit outside his line but he liked different disciplines to share results. "Linked science" he called it. And I was one of his "links" and so he produced me from time to time to talk to mainstream epidemiologists.'

'What were you going to speak about?'

'My locusts. How they spread. Why they go in the directions they do. How to stop them.'

'Go on,' said Laurie.

'Are you sure you want to hear? Today I mean?'

'It might be relevant.'

'To the bomb? Not really.'

'You don't know that. Try me.'

Peter gave a slight shrug. 'OK. Well, the thing about locust swarms is that they exist in two forms. Phases. First of all, they're on the ground as young forms without wings. Individually they're called hoppers but when you get millions of them it's called a blanket.'

'Millions?'

'Oh yes. Locust swarms comprise millions. Anyway, as hoppers they don't move very fast because they haven't got any wings, but they do a lot of damage. And they're not actually very difficult to control at this stage because they are very vulnerable to DDT.'

'DDT? I thought that stuff was banned.'

Peter smiled and picked up his beer. 'Banned?' he said almost as much to himself as Laurie.

He looked at Laurie and raised his can in a toast. 'Only in theory.

Oh, I know it's the big bad wolf of the environmentalists. But it's got four big aces going for it.'

He put his can down and counted them off on his fingers. 'It's cheap. It works. It's not poisonous and you can make it in Africa.'

Laurie did not reply but looked at Peter with a slight frown.

'Yes, cheap,' said Peter counting on his fingers again. 'Ten, maybe twenty times as cheap as the next best thing. And it does work. OK, maybe not on flies or boll-weevils in California any more but it's a winner for African locusts every time. As for three, not poisonous, did you know it's the only insecticide never to have actually killed anyone outright? And you can't even say that about petrol. And as far as "made in Africa" goes, number four, that really is important because it cuts out expensive borrowing from European banks who probably wouldn't give credit anyway.'

Laurie scratched his chin.

'OK,' went on Peter, 'so you can control the young stage locusts, the hoppers, with DDT but when the adults are flying it's another matter. You can drop stuff from helicopters but it spreads out too much vertically to be much use. And a big swarm could be ten miles across. More. They land every night when it's too cold to fly but you can't do helicopters at night. The adults take off again the next day,' he lifted his hand above his head, 'then come down to feed again that evening.' He brought his hands down and then rubbed the sides of his neck. 'Frankly, controlling the adults is a bitch.'

Peter began walking up and down by the window wall.

'And they really eat everything,' he continued. 'If you go where they've been, it's like a desert. No grass. No leaves on the trees. And definitely no crops.'

He ran his fingers through his hair. 'You know, I went to Gombe once after a swarm. It's quite a big town about a hundred miles or so from Kano. It looked as though a fire had been through the place. I hardly recognised it. Even the grass in the gardens was all gone. And yet, ten miles outside town everything was normal. Green as ever.'

Peter drank from his can and shook it to check it was empty. 'And that was quite a small swarm,' he said. 'God knows what a big one would be like.'

'Haven't you ever seen a big one then?' asked Laurie, slightly surprised.

Peter took two more beers from the mini-bar and handed one to Laurie.

'No,' he said, 'no one has. You see, large swarms are pretty rare. They only happen every fifty years or so, maybe less often. But really big ones, Lion Swarms they're called, are even rarer, one maybe every two or three hundred years. That'd be a sight, wouldn't it, Lol? Fifty square miles of locusts. Like one huge animal moving over the country.' He spread his hands out slowly. 'Can you imagine it?'

Peter drank from his can and looked down at Laurie. 'Thing is,' he went on, 'you only get Lion Swarms if six or seven ordinary swarms come together. The last time even three looked like combining was back in 1963 when the controls were all in place. It wasn't going to be a Lion but everyone panicked and sprayed in time.

'You see,' he continued, 'back then, in the sixties, West Africa was still being run properly. The new states were still reasonably efficient and they all had anti-locust set-ups who knew what to do and how to work together. It was all run by ex-pats anyway so the swarms never really built up to danger levels and they dealt with the blankets pretty well. I'm afraid it's a different story now.'

'Oh?'

'Yes, the Brits have gone now. Along with most of the French and Germans. In fact there's hardly a decent Locust man left on the West Coast.'

'Can't the local people do it?' asked Laurie.

'If only,' said Peter. 'There just aren't enough decent scientists to do anything. I mean, would you stay there if you could get a better job in England?'

Laurie shrugged.

'Anyway, there isn't anyone who really knows how to coordinate things on that scale. It needs armies and masses of helicopters. And West African armies don't exactly work hand in hand, do they?'

Laurie shrugged again. 'If you say so.'

'I do,' said Peter, beginning to pace up and down again. 'These Lion Swarms take quite a while to build up. About eighteen months or so. You see several big blanket swarms first. They have to be at the same stage, which might happen after a good rainy season. Then you get the adults, then the hoppers again and so on. The thing is, the adults fly but have to go pretty much with the prevailing wind. So if you get several fair-sized swarms flying in different parts of one big weather pattern, an anti-cyclone in fact, then they swirl around in decreasing circles, rather like water around a plug hole in a bath. OK. So let's say they all drop to earth about the same time to breed again and the weather pattern moves on. But the hoppers don't fly so they don't go with it. But then they become adults again and take off. Now, just say they are all still in synch and another anti-cyclone turns up. They all start swirling around each other and getting closer to the centre. If this repeats enough times, say three or four, they all speed up like water near the plug hole. I have to say, the chances are pretty remote but, if it *does* happen, you might suddenly get six or even seven big swarms all coming together in one place at one time. And *voilà!* A Lion is born!'

'Then?'

'Then the wind moves on and the locusts eat everything in sight for miles. Everything that grows. And if the wind doesn't come back they start dying off for lack of food. Millions and millions of them. And it's really hot, don't forget, so they go off pretty fast, start to rot. All these millions of dead locusts, right? Which suits the flies just fine.'

'What flies?' asked Laurie. 'You didn't say anything about flies.'

'Ordinary flies. They love it. Miles and miles of rotting locusts to feed and breed on. Must really stink. But, of course, where the flies go, your normal fly-type diseases go too. Cholera, typhoid. polio, you name it. So you've suddenly got a nice little plague of flies going. And then, after six months or so the rats start to catch up. There are always a lot of rats about but with so much food they build up pretty fast too. And when the rats really get going, there's a good chance you're going to get all the diseases *they* cart about with them too. And then we are talking a proper plague. Plague plague. Takes about a year. The locusts may be long eaten up and gone but you don't have time to be grateful because the whole place is crawling with rats. I tell you, Laurie, it's the old sequence. It can still happen.'

'What "sequence" would that be, old boy?'

Peter was now walking quickly to and fro, waving his arms excitedly. 'The Plagues of Egypt I mean.

'Definitely the same sequence,' he went on, almost to himself. 'It must have been the same thing. And I had the bloody thing there,' he said, holding a hand in front of his face. 'I had it. And then some bastard blew my numbers away!'

Peter held up a finger and thumb an inch apart. 'I was that close.'

He stopped talking and blew his cheeks out before letting a long breath go.

'Look, I think it was the same thing,' he began again. 'It's in the Bible, for Christ's sake. The seven plagues of Egypt. They thought it was some punishment for knocking the Jews about but it wasn't. Just the consequences of a Lion Swarm. God, they must have been *so* scared. And do you know what? The people then, they couldn't help themselves it was all so massive. They had no food left to eat and no clean water and half of them were dying anyway from God knows what.'

He held his hand out. 'And what did the rest do? Most of them just sat down and died too. No one was going to come to their aid and they couldn't help themselves, so they just sat down and cried. I mean, we are talking the Waters of Babylon here.'

He shrugged. 'OK, so the Bible version is a bit stylised and the timing isn't accurate. They weren't exactly writing it down as they went along. But it's the best historical description of a complete bio-failure we have. And, what's more, we know people today react the same way to total fuck-ups. Take Hiroshima,' he said, beginning to pace again. 'What did the survivors do? Organise themselves? Help each other out? No. They just sat down and cried. And the people just outside the disaster area, what did they do? They didn't go in to help, did they?

'I tell you, Laurie, they all just ran away. Just like your people today. An ever-widening circle of people shouting, "Christ, man, don't go back there. That's Hell on Earth."'

He moved his hands down slowly to his sides. 'Hell on Earth,' he repeated quietly.

Peter drew in his breath and suddenly pointed at Laurie. 'And it's going to happen again. This year some time. I'm not quite sure where but *some*where in West Africa. Next month or so. Next week even.'

'What? Hiroshima?'

'No, idiot. A Lion Swarm. There's been six or seven fair-sized swarms there for about eighteen months or so. You can see them from the satellites. If you know what to look for. Well, some of them. I thought so anyway,' he ended rather lamely.

'And you were going to tell them all that today at the conference?'

'Sort of,' Peter replied, beginning to smile. 'But maybe with a bit less shouting and a few graphs to back me up.' He held up his hands again. 'I'm sorry,' he went on. 'This isn't what you really wanted to talk about, was it? I just get carried away, that's all.'

'It's fine by me, old man. If it takes your mind off today, that's OK with me. I'm afraid we saw some pretty grisly things back there. Your first bomb and all that.'

Peter looked out of the window. 'My first bomb,' he said absently, thinking of the dead girl again. 'Do you mean it gets easier?'

'Yes, actually. When you know what to expect.'

'Oh, good,' said Peter. 'I can't wait for my next one then. Perhaps after a few more, I'll be able to call up my mates and flog them the story.'

Laurie did not reply and Peter immediately regretted what he had said. 'Sorry,' he said, turning to face his friend. 'Bad taste.'

Laurie smiled. 'Don't mention it, Pete. Perhaps it's time for another beer?'

Peter shook his head. 'No. But you go ahead.'

'Don't mind if I do,' said Laurie.

'Anyway,' said Peter. 'The police.'

'What about them?' asked Laurie, peering into the mini-bar and carefully selecting a can.

'Well,' said Peter, 'they must know we were there because we were checked in at the car park. They'll want to contact us. Witness statements and all that.'

'Possibly,' said Laurie. 'Probably, even. But we're easily traceable and we're still in Atlanta so we won't be suspects. My guess is that even if the local lot don't know what to do, some national squad or other will hot-foot it here and take over. In fact, they were probably on their way here following the first bomb last night. And what *they* will do is count and identify all the people who went in, subtract the rips inside and that leaves them with the people they have to talk to.'

'Rips?'

'The bodies. The dead bods.'

'Rips?'

'RIPs. Sorry. Belfast term. Not very nice.'

'Jesus.'

'I said I'm sorry. Anyway, you're right. They will want to talk to us. But we haven't got much to tell them, have we? We arrived. Had a coffee. Walked about a bit. And then, bang. We didn't even talk to anyone we knew.'

'The girl. She ticked us off on her list.'

'What girl? Oh, her. Well, I think her list got a bit smudged, don't you?'

Peter breathed in and out slowly. What an epitaph, he thought. Pretty girl, but got her list a bit smudged at the end.

As if on cue, the telephone rang. 'Perhaps that's them now,' said Laurie, going over to pick it up.

Peter changed his mind about the beer and went to collect one from the fridge. By the time he was opening the can, Laurie was putting the receiver down.

'Well,' said Laurie, 'I was partly right and partly wrong. It seems that the winners of this month's unlikely combination competition are in the lobby and are about to join us. Two of Atlanta's finest accompanied by a certain Miss Jocasta Manhattan.'

'Shit,' said Peter. 'Do you think we had better put some kind of story together?'

'No. Not really. We just say we ran away. Leave the police to me and I'll leave you to deal with Jaygo.'

'Great. But she wasn't coming here until eight. What do you think she wants?'

'Maybe she just wants to see if her beloved is unharmed.'

'You're joking,' said Peter. 'At least I hope you are.'

'Why's that?'

'Oh, you know her,' continued Peter. 'No one really knows what she's up to. I mean, did I tell you she wants to come with me to Kano this week?'

'Does she now? I knew you were going but I didn't know it was à deux.'

'Yes, unfortunately. Hang on, how did you know I was going?'

Laurie playfully tapped the side of his nose. 'Lauro El Journalisto,' he smiled.

Peter sighed briefly. 'Oh. Well, anyway, it seems she's got involved in some music thing out there and wants me in on her meeting with Jack Ngale because she thinks he wants to pull a fast one or something.'

Laurie's expression had immediately become serious. 'Jack Ngale?' he asked.

But Peter was on his way to the door and hadn't seen Laurie's face.

'Yes,' he said. 'You remember Jack. He was at Liverpool with us. He's quite a big wig now.'

'That's putting it mildly,' said Laurie almost to himself.

Peter went out into the corridor. 'They'll be here soon,' he called.

73

'Peter, come back. They'll be a few minutes yet.'

Peter returned but left the door ajar. 'Yes,' he went on. 'Our Jack's gone up in the world. Politics. Business. Farming. And now music. Did you know he was *the* Ngale now, by the way?'

'Yes. I know all about him actually. And I know what he does best – what his main game is.'

'Oh?' said Peter, sensing something in Laurie's voice.

'Heroin. He's the biggest shipper on the West Coast.'

'What! Jack? No way. And anyway they don't grow heroin on the West Coast.'

'I only wish that was true,' said Laurie. 'But I'm not wrong. Young Jack is in it up to his elbows. He's one of the Nightmare Crop men Bob was going to talk about. I tell you, Jack Ngale, *the* Ngale if you insist, is one of the new breed of drug barons.'

Peter looked more closely at Laurie. 'Are you sure?'

'Absolutely, old boy. But, more important, have you seen him lately?'

'I see him quite a lot actually. Every couple of weeks or so when I'm out there. He's a sort of honorary president for our Research Institute.'

'Is he now? Now that's a thing.'

'He's all right,' said Peter. 'Slippery bugger but he always was. He's a legit businessman.'

'Oh no he's not,' replied Laurie. 'Bob Anderson's got, or rather had, chapter and verse on him. Look, tell me quickly before the others get here, did Bob know exactly what you were going to talk about today?'

But Peter was heading towards the door again.

'Peter, I'm serious for God's sake! Get Jay to back out. That Jack is really bad news.'

'It's a bit late frankly. Can we talk about it later? I think I hear our guests arriving.'

The door flew open and Jaygo marched into the room waving her arms theatrically above her head. 'My God,' she cried, 'I told them you were in no fit state to go with them and that you hardly knew the bloody woman.'

She marched straight over to the window, hunched her shoulders and folded her arms.

Behind her followed two rather ordinary-looking patrolmen with their peaked caps held politely under their arms.

'I'm Officer Heap and this is Officer Small,' began one. 'Which of you two gentlemen is Peter Wilton?'

'I am,' said Peter. 'I am Peter Wilson.'

The patrolman consulted his notebook. 'Wilson. Yes, sir. I understand you were close to the explosion at the university this morning.'

'Yes,' said Peter. 'Just inside the building. We thought there was a risk of fire so we ran out, I'm afraid. We stayed for about a quarter of an hour and then came back here.'

'I see,' continued the policeman. 'And you, sir,' he said, turning to Laurie, 'would you be Mr Miller?'

'Yes,' said Laurie. 'We might have stayed but my friend here felt unwell and I thought we should come back here and talk to you later.'

'That's quite all right, Mr Miller. But I'm afraid I've come about a different matter. Dr Wilson,' he said turning to Peter, 'I believe you might be able to help us with the formal identification of one of the unfortunate victims.'

'Oh?' said Peter. 'Dr Anderson? But surely his family are in Atlanta? I mean, his wife?'

'No, sir. I'm sorry, but I believe you knew a Margaret Carslake? Professor Carslake?'

'Oh no.' Peter sat down heavily on the edge of the bed. 'I didn't know she was here. Margaret? Are you sure it's her?'

'I'm afraid so, sir. We have initial identification from her conference identity badge and her passport photograph.'

'Oh no,' repeated Peter to himself. 'Not Margaret.' He rubbed his hands over his face.

The older of the two policemen sat down on the bed next to Peter. 'I'm very sorry for your loss, sir. We have spoken to the Professor's relatives in Britain and they have told us you knew the deceased sufficiently well to make a formal identification.'

'John and Betty?' said Peter. 'You've told her parents? What did they say?'

'I don't know, sir,' continued Officer Heap. 'We faxed your British police with the details and they called on Mr and Mrs Carslake personally and informed them.'

'Informed,' said Peter almost to himself.

'Yes, sir. I'm very sorry but I have to ask you formally at this time if you feel you knew the deceased well enough to make a positive identification.'

'Margaret?' said Peter, cupping his face with his hands. 'Yes. We worked together at the Institute for a year.'

'Institute, sir?' said the policeman, consulting his notebook again.

'Where I work,' continued Peter. 'In Kano. She came there to do research. Look, officer, is she . . . I mean . . . was she badly injured? I mean, of course she was badly injured but . . .' His voice tailed off as he looked down to the floor.

The policeman spoke quietly. 'I understand she died from internal injuries sustained from debris. But I have been told her face is not marked. She was apparently climbing the stairs towards the rear of the hall when the explosion took place.'

Peter looked over at Laurie. 'She must have seen us,' he said. 'She was coming to see us. Another four seconds and she would have been out of there.'

'Look, Officer Heap, or whatever your name is,' said Laurie irritably. 'It's quite obvious that this man isn't going anywhere today. Can't this wait until tomorrow?'

'I'm afraid not, sir,' said the other policeman, speaking for the first time. 'The nature of the inquiry requires formal identification be made today before a post mortem examination can be commenced.'

'Good God!' said Jaygo. 'What the hell are you on about?'

'I'm sorry, ma'am,' continued the policeman in a level voice. 'This is a very serious incident and procedures have to be expedited to establish the type of explosive used.'

'Well, pick up bits of furniture then,' replied Jaygo. 'Leave the people alone.'

'I'm afraid we do need to carry out certain tests. It was a very unusual explosion.'

'Oh, bang bang,' said Jaygo sarcastically. 'How many sorts of bang are there?'

'Let it go, Jay,' said Laurie walking over to her. 'They are just doing their job.' He put his hand on her arm.

'Don't touch me!' she said sharply and turned away to resume her hunched stance by the window.

Laurie shrugged at the policeman.

'I'm sorry,' said Peter standing up. 'Of course I'll come with you. Do I have to bring anything?'

When Peter and the policemen had left, the room seemed suddenly quiet. Neither Laurie nor Jaygo spoke. Eventually Jaygo took a small bottle of wine from the mini-bar and poured two generous glasses. She took one over to Laurie who was sitting in the armchair.

'What was it like?' she asked. 'I can't imagine it.'

'We weren't near,' said Laurie. 'We weren't near enough to see anything.'

She looked at him over her glass quizzically. 'Oh? I heard one of your reports. It sounded to me as though you had been pretty close. You made me feel I was there.'

'Well, you don't need to hear it all again then, do you?'

'Don't you want to talk about it? It might help.'

Laurie shrugged. 'It's not that,' he said. 'Reporting it and telling a friend about it are different things.' He stood up and walked past Jaygo to where she had been standing by the window.

'It was awful really,' he began. 'I've never seen so many dead people. I mean, in ordinary life you never see a body, do you? Ask people when they last saw a dead person and they say it was when their granny died. At a funeral or something. Just one person pretending to be asleep. Not like today at all. Suddenly to see sixty or a hundred people dead all at once and it's too much. You can't cope in a normal way because it isn't normal at all. And then suddenly I thought, they're not just dead. They're murdered. Somebody did this on purpose. Who could do this?'

He drank from his glass.

Jaygo began to speak but he held up his hand.

'And suddenly,' he went on, 'you find you are not thinking about the dead people at all, but the people who did it. Who they are, how to find them, where they might be. You see, that's normal thinking. Your mind doesn't let you think about the unbearable so you send yourself down a safer route. One you can deal with that doesn't involve all the dead people.'

He took another drink. 'I suppose one day you have to go back and confront what it was like but I think you can make excuses to yourself for quite a while. I hope so, for Peter's sake.'

'And you?' said Jaygo. 'How are you?'

'After today?' he asked. 'Not so bad. I was in Belfast so I saw one or two things. But nothing on this scale. At least I knew a little of what to expect when we went in.'

'I didn't really mean that,' she said.

'What then?'

'You,' she said. 'I meant how are *you*?'

He looked into his glass and swilled the wine around a few times.

'That sounds like a pretty direct sort of question,' he said looking up at her. 'But I'm fine. Really I'm fine.'

She did not answer him and he looked down again. 'For now,' he said. 'For now,' he repeated, looking back at her.

'You know, don't you?' he asked.

'Yes. I'm so very sorry. I heard.'

'No need to be. I don't think about it most of the time. It's like seeing the bomb. Something in you blocks it out. They call it a coping mechanism, don't they? Perhaps that's why I did OK today.'

'I'm sure you'll be fine,' she said.

'Well, no actually. That isn't going to be the case really. And they don't tell you much at the beginning. You have to work it out of them. And when you finally get the facts from them you don't like it much but at least you know where you stand.'

Laurie looked up at her and smiled. 'You want to ask when, don't you?'

'No. Of course not.'

'Some people are too polite to ask but you can tell they want to know. Perhaps they ask each other. But it's the one thing no one can really know. And if you've heard any different, then it's made up.'

'Of course I haven't asked anyone,' she said. 'I wouldn't.'

He appeared not to have heard. 'I know the *how* but not the *when*. Actually it's not as bad as you think. Most people know what the matter with them is some time before they die. I just know a bit sooner, that's all. And most people don't know the when until it's pretty close so I'm not all that different from other people really.'

Neither spoke for a while. Eventually she said, 'You're good at explaining things. I've read dozens of articles about HIV and Aids but no one has ever put it quite like that. I think I understand more now.'

'Perhaps I should write it down then. Be a real pro journalist.'

'Well, why not?'

'Because frankly, Jay, it's incidental. I want to write about a lot of things. Do a lot of things. Pack a lot into whatever is left without having to write about the clock all the bloody time.'

He walked over to refill his glass. 'Writing about yourself isn't very satisfying really. I'd much rather crack one really big story and throw myself into it. Kick the top off some big wasp's nest or other. Something other people might be too scared to do because of consequences that might turn up. Well, there can't be any consequences for me because I won't be around. I think it gives me a bit of an edge and I ought to use it.'

'Consequences? How do you mean?'

'Take the example of the Mafia in Italy. Look what happened to that magistrate who decided to go after them. They just started taking out his family one by one until he broke and stopped investigating them.'

'I remember that. He didn't stop. I'm sure some leading family member or other was sent to prison. Ten years for fraud if I remember rightly.'

'Ten years, was it?' said Laurie. 'Fraud? Was that it? Does ten years, five with good behaviour, seem a fitting sentence for supplying half of Southern Italy with heroin for ten years with nothing off for good behaviour? Enough for a middle man perhaps, which is all he was. No, Jay, big fish swim in deep waters. You don't catch them in hand nets. And I'll bet you there was hardly a hiccup in the whole heroin supply chain. Our magistrate lost all his family and the Mafia didn't even blink.'

'So?' she began. 'Are you going to take up where he left off? Go to Naples or somewhere and set up shop?'

'No. Of course not. I don't know anything about Italy. That was just an example.'

'What then? Oh, Laurie, are you sure you're not just looking for a windmill to tilt at? You're a journalist, for God's sake. Not some mad white knight charging about putting the world to rights. I told you, you're good at explaining difficult things. Concentrate on that if you want.'

'You're missing the point,' he said. 'If I had twenty years ahead of me then I could go on "explaining things" as you call it. And if I was any good, I'd finish up with my photograph on top of some column in a heavy Sunday newspaper pontificating away. No thank you.'

'What then?'

'Well, there is one story. It's what I came to Atlanta for. But things have gone a bit off course and the man I wanted to talk to has left the scene, as it were.'

She looked puzzled.

'Bob Anderson,' he said. 'One of the people killed this morning.'

'Go on,' she said.

'He was going to give a paper at the conference,' began Laurie. 'And there were about three thousand copies ready to go out but they went up in smoke just before he followed them. I think consequences is the word we were using.'

79

Jaygo continued to look puzzled. 'Maybe I'm being thick or something,' she said, 'but I don't follow you. You say you came here on some story or other. And someone else, who isn't a journalist, can help you. And then a couple of bombs go off. What's the connection?'

'No, he wasn't a journalist of course and it isn't really a "story" yet in that sense of the word. Parts of a jig-saw waiting to be put together really. Bob Anderson was one piece and the conference was going to be another. It was a start. All I had really.'

'Not much of a jig-saw puzzle now. You only had two pieces and they have both fallen off the table.'

She smiled at him and offered to pour him some more wine. 'Perhaps you need another of these.'

'Thanks,' he said, taking the glass. 'Well, in a funny way the bombs prove there really is something big worth writing about. While I've been backgrounding this over the last six months or so I've sometimes thought I was imagining it all. Then today happened and I suddenly know I'm bang on target.'

'You and everyone else in town, I should have thought,' said Jaygo. 'Bombs in America are pretty big news. You didn't get to talk to your man Bob Anderson, so I guess you're back in the peleton with all the other scribblers now.'

'Perhaps,' he said thoughtfully. 'My main man has gone, it's true. But I've got a couple of back-up people I can still talk to. One of them was at the conference as a sort of delegate. I know he wasn't in the hall when the bomb went off so maybe he's still around.'

'A colleague of Bob Anderson's?' she asked.

'Hardly,' smiled Laurie. 'Peter and I were looking for him when the bomb went off. I wanted Peter to meet him because they both know about Africa in their own ways.'

'Africa?' said Jaygo. 'You want to write about Africa?'

Laurie smiled again. 'It's to do with Africa but not exactly *about* Africa, if you see what I mean.'

'No, I don't see what you mean. But if you didn't see him to talk to I'd say that was another blow for you.'

'Possibly,' said Laurie rather wearily. 'I think I'll check the airline lists and see if he's gone back to the UK yet. I think I can still get to see him one way or another.'

'What do you mean "check the airline lists"?'

'Manifests. The list of who is on what flight.'

'How will you get hold of those?'

'It's not hard. They're available all over the world at travel agents and so on on a computer system called Galileo. It's not particularly difficult to access.'

'Wow,' said Jaygo. 'Sounds as though investigative journalism has moved on a bit since Woodward and Bernstein.'

'Just a bit,' agreed Laurie. 'Actually I think I'd better do it now in case he goes back today. They archive some lists once the flights are over and they're much harder to get then.'

Laurie took out a laptop, sat on the edge of the bed and began tapping away at the keys.

Jaygo looked on, impressed. 'Don't you have to plug it in or something?'

'No,' said Laurie, squinting slightly at the screen. 'It's got a modem link and you just have to hook into the local phone network in the usual way.'

Jaygo pulled a face. 'Usual way?' she said.

But Laurie was concentrating on the screen and did not hear her. After about a minute he said, 'Ah, here we are! In!

'Well,' he said, looking up at Jaygo. 'Welcome to the travel agents, madam. What flight would madam like to check?'

'Just like that?' she said.

'Of course.'

'OK then. Give it me.'

'Certainly, madam. And what name will you be using today?'

'My own. Jackie Morton.'

'Ah yes,' said Laurie, tapping it in. 'I remember her.

'Here we are,' he said shortly. 'Morton, Jackie. Arrived Atlanta from Dallas today at 1330 hours on PP 164, due to depart for London Heathrow on PP 951 tomorrow morning. Yes, madam, everything seems to be in order.'

'Impressive.'

'Next question please.'

'What about your man then?'

'OK,' said Laurie, returning to the keyboard again. 'Here he is. Arrived flight BA 505 two days ago at New York. On to Atlanta this morning at 0630. And, hello, what's this? Departed Atlanta already? And not to London either? Well, I'll be buggered, PP 101 to Kano of all places! Well, that is good news. Very good news indeed.'

'What is? Show me,' said Jaygo trying to see over his shoulder.

'Look,' said Laurie, tapping the screen. 'He's changed from a BA flight to a PP flight.'

'PP?' queried Jaygo. 'You said I was on a PP. Anyway, I can't see anything.'

'That's right,' said Laurie. 'PP means Private Flight. Like your jet. But my man hasn't got his own plane, so who the hell is he flying with?'

'I can't see anything at all,' said Jaygo.

'It's the screen on this thing. There, is that better?' he said, folding the lid flat. 'Look, there he is. Etherington, John.'

'What!' cried Jaygo. 'It can't be! It's too much of a coincidence.'

'You know him?' said Laurie, surprised. 'He's Foreign Office. Hardly your type I would have thought.'

'Well,' began Jaygo.

'Jesus! Bingo!' Laurie shouted, staring at the screen. 'Look whose plane he's on. Jack bloody Ngale! No wonder he made such a quick exit.'

'Laurie, you're not listening,' said Jaygo. 'That name – Etherington. Peter knows that name. It must be the same one.'

Laurie looked up at her. 'Peter? Peter knows John Etherington?'

'No. But the name. And the link with Jack. It must be the same family or something. It couldn't just be a coincidence.'

The computer suddenly beeped loudly and the screen went blank.

'Damn!' said Laurie. 'They must have seen the hack and shut me out. Anyone would think it was illegal.'

He pushed the lid shut. 'So,' he said, looking up at Jaygo again, 'tell me about Peter and John Etherington.'

Jaygo sat down next to Laurie on the bed. 'Well,' she began, 'I think you had better ask Peter yourself. It might be nothing at all. I could have got the name wrong but he was telling me about someone called John Etherington and a previous Ngale. It's very complicated and so you'll really have to ask him.'

Laurie scratched the top of his head. 'I don't think he's ever mentioned that name to me.'

'Well, he wouldn't, would he? It's a historical thing. Something to do with a gold thingy.'

'Thingy?'

'You know,' she said, making a circle shape in front of her with her hands. 'A torque. A gold necklace thing. A sort of treasure.'

'Gold?' said Laurie looking confused. 'But this isn't anything to do with gold,' he added, tapping the computer. 'I'm talking about drugs. Shipping drugs.'

'Well,' she said, standing up and walking away. 'Whatever it's about, I think you've just found a few more pieces of that jig-saw you've been so careless with. And, unless I'm much mistaken, Laurie Miller is going to get his little story after all.'

'Mmm,' went Laurie. 'Could be interesting. The sooner Peter gets back the better. Did they say how long he was going to be, by the way? I don't remember them saying.'

'An hour or two, I should think. Do you know anything about this woman he's gone to identify?'

'That depends what you mean by "anything".'

'You know exactly what I mean.'

'Do I?' said Laurie. 'Well in that case, yes, I should say he did know her pretty well. She worked with him for about a year when he first went to Africa. He was getting over you at the time and he sort of fell right into her big blue eyes.'

'Oh?' said Jaygo, trying to sound neutral. 'And what happened to her?'

'I'm not sure exactly,' replied Laurie. 'I only met her a few times. They spent a lot of time together, I know that. When they came to the UK, I mean. I thought she was rather nice in a bookish sort of way.'

'Clever, was she?'

'Pretty much. She went to take a chair in Philadelphia when she left Peter.'

'Oh dear, another career girl up and leaving Peter for the bright lights of America?'

'It wasn't like that at all,' said Laurie with slight irritation. 'I gather she wanted to seal the thing properly and get married but Peter didn't feel much like it just then. Eventually she said to him, "Me. Or I go." He called her bluff and off she went. Tears before bedtime all round, I expect.'

Jaygo thought for a moment. 'He's going to be terribly upset when he sees her.'

'I think so. But it was a while back now. Must be six years at least. And he's been with Aurelia for the last five.'

'I thought she'd only been on the scene for a couple of years.'

'Depends what you mean,' said Laurie. 'He's known her quite a long time. She's the daughter of the ex-director of Peter's institute. In fact, thinking about it, he may even have met her before he met Margaret.'

'And are they happy? In love?'

'They're engaged if that's what you mean.'

Jaygo looked thoughtful.

'What's it to you anyway?' said Laurie carefully. Then he pointed his finger at Jaygo. 'Leave him alone Jay, he doesn't need you now.'

'What's that supposed to mean?'

'It means he's settled. Calm. He doesn't need you marching back into his life and knocking things over.'

'Oh?' she said irritably. 'You speak for him, do you? Make his mind up for him, do you?'

'Now you leave him alone, Jaygo.'

'Don't tell me what to do, Laurie Miller. The way you talk anyone would think you were still in bloody love with him yourself!'

She suddenly put her hand over her mouth when she realised what she had said.

'Ah,' said Laurie slowly, standing up and taking his computer back to his case. 'That's got that little thing out into the open then, hasn't it?'

'I'm sorry, Laurie. I shouldn't have said that. I didn't mean it.'

Laurie shrugged as he put the computer away. 'Well, it's true I suppose. But I don't think he ever knew. In fact, I don't think he even knew I was, well, you know . . .'

'Gay?'

'If that's the word. I don't know if I thought of it in those terms. Yes, I did fall for Peter and he just happened to be a man.'

He looked at her but she did not respond so he continued, 'It was ridiculous of course. He was in love with you at the time so I don't think he noticed anything at all and I quietly put the lid on the whole thing. I didn't come out till years later. Long after we'd all gone our separate ways.'

She smiled at him kindly. 'Long after we'd all fallen out of love with each other?'

He clicked the case shut. 'Is that what happens? Feelings just go away, do they?'

'You tell me,' she said. 'People change if they don't see each other for long enough. If you leave a baby in the rain for long enough, it dies.'

'"Baby in the rain." That's a Peter expression, isn't it?'

'Yes,' she said. 'He used to say it about us.'

Laurie absently picked up the room service menu on the top of the refrigerator and looked at it.

'You won't tell him, will you?' he said at last.

'About you being gay, you mean? Or the HIV thing?'

'About then, I mean. I suppose he'll know the HIV thing when it turns into Aids or whatever it does.'

'I won't tell him about anything.'

'Thanks,' said Laurie, putting the menu down again. 'I wouldn't want him to think, well, less of me.'

'Oh, Laurie,' she said. 'He wouldn't think any the less of you at all. You know that. He's always liked you and he will whatever happens.'

'I hope so,' said Laurie, turning to her and smiling. 'I'll tell you one thing. It's really nice to see him again, isn't it?'

'Oh, yes,' she said, smiling back. 'I'll drink to that. Where's your glass got to?'

As Jaygo and Laurie discussed him, Peter was standing in the main refrigeration room at the city mortuary.

A man from the National Bomb Squad stood next to him while a technician pulled a large steel drawer out from the wall. On it was the body of Margaret Carslake in a white linen gown with only her face showing. Over her eyes was a strip of white gauze.

The Bomb Squad man read from a clip-board. 'Do you, Peter Wilson, truthfully testify that this is the body of the person known to you as Margaret Hazel Carslake?'

'Yes,' Peter replied almost inaudibly. 'That is Margaret.' He turned away. What had he expected? That it wouldn't be her? That there had been some horrible mix up and that Margaret would not be there? Be safe?

The man nodded to the technician, who slid the large drawer back into the wall. He waited a few moments before saying, 'I'm sorry for your loss, sir. I am afraid there are some papers to sign.'

Peter looked briefly at the wall of drawers. Which one had been Margaret?

Five minutes later, Peter was sitting in a small interview room with the officer from the Bomb Squad who was passing Peter sheets of paper from his clip-board and indicating where he should sign.

'I can go over what each of these are if you like, sir. State, Federal, British Airways and so on, they all say pretty much the same. That the person you saw is the person you said. They authorise the next procedures to be expedited.'

Peter looked up. 'And if I wasn't here? If there was no one to sign?'

The man smiled, not unkindly. 'In normal circumstances we

would hold the deceased until there was someone who could sign. But on this occasion I have jurisdiction as to procedures.'

'Procedures?' queried Peter.

The man shifted uncomfortably in his chair before replying. 'The post mortem, sir. You see, we believe this was a very special explosive device but we need to characterise the injuries to confirm our initial findings.'

Peter looked puzzled.

'It's to do with the nature of the explosion. We think it was a high-pressure device with a relatively thin shock wall and no incendiary component.'

'You've lost me there,' said Peter. He leaned forward to read the man's identification badge. 'Mr . . . ? I'm afraid I can't read your name tag.'

'Gawne.'

'Thank you,' said Peter. 'You were saying?'

'Yes, a high-pressure device. I'd say about five kilos of Semtex Seven. Ever heard of it?'

Peter shook his head. 'Semtex yes. But I didn't know there was more than one kind.'

'It's special stuff,' continued Gawne. 'It's made for use in stun grenades for aircraft anti-hijack work. Makes a hell of a crack and anyone near enough gets soft tissue damage – killed even. But the blast is what we call thin and short and will not damage structures. Hence its aircraft use.'

'But there was damage,' said Peter. 'Benches, desks. All the furniture was broken.' He looked immediately down at his hands when he realised what he had said.

After a long pause he looked up to meet Officer Gawne's stare. The earlier friendly expression was gone.

Gawne sighed and referred to the clip-board. 'The statement you gave states that you were at the entrance of the building at the time of the blast and that you did not enter it again.'

Peter lifted his hands from the desk before dropping them back again.

'OK,' he said. 'We were inside the building. And we went into the hall after the explosion to see if we could do anything. We didn't stay. We didn't see anything.'

Gawne leaned back in his chair and took out a packet of cigarettes and offered one to Peter. Peter shook his head.

Gawne took one for himself and lit it without saying anything.

'Am I being interviewed or something?' said Peter. 'I thought

I was here to identify a body. If you want to interview me then someone else should be here.'

Gawne blew smoke above their heads and held up his hand.

'Look,' he said, 'if I thought you were anything to do with this bomb I'd have ten men in here and so would you. I've told you it was a pretty special bomb and frankly, Mr Wilson, you just don't look special enough to me.'

Peter looked up at him.

'No,' continued Gawne. 'That baby was the most special device I have ever seen. And expensive. Fifteen to twenty grand a kilo and we are looking at about five. I'd give the whole thing a street price of two hundred thousand. And Semtex Seven is batch-traceable even after use. Very easy to trace. No, our man will not have stayed around afterwards. Up. Out. Gone.'

'But a bluff?' said Peter. 'He might have stayed to bluff you.' And he immediately regretted saying such a frivolous thing.

Gawne stood up slowly. 'Do me a fucking favour, Wilson. Save the wise-cracks. I just said this stuff was traceable. By tomorrow morning we will know where the Seven was bought, who bought it from the supplier, who he sold it on to and the size of the diaphragm of the mother of the guy who set it off.'

'I don't understand,' said Peter. 'Who would use a bomb that could be traced?'

'You tell me,' said Gawne. He sat down again and tapped the sheaf of papers on the clip-board. 'Whoever it was,' he went on, 'wanted to kill someone in that room pretty badly and pretty quickly. Could have used a handgun and made a run for it, but that would be risky so he killed the lot of them just to be sure and made off in the confusion.'

'I hardly think so,' said Peter. 'Why kill so many people?'

'Got a better idea?'

'Well,' began Peter, 'a bomb is not a murder weapon – it's a statement. Like the first one at the original conference venue.'

Gawne blew out a plume of smoke. 'Bomb School,' he said. 'Day One. Lecture One. Nine o'clock. If it's a property bomb it's a statement and if it's a people bomb it's homicide. It's called "victim certainty". And this was a people bomb. That device was placed to kill one or more of the people in that room. Take it from me.'

He stood up and stubbed out his cigarette on the floor. He turned back to Peter and leant over the table.

'The delegates at the conference – were they all known to each other?'

Peter shrugged. 'Pretty much. Some people like going to conferences. They work the circuit and go to as many as they can. If you go to three or four a year in your subject you get to know people. Yes, I'd say most of them knew each other.'

'And does that include you? Did you know them all?'

'Not at all,' said Peter. 'First, it wasn't really my subject area and, second, I'm afraid that I don't like going to conferences very much.'

'Then why are you here?'

'The man who organised it, Dr Anderson, invited me. I work in a slightly different field to him but he thought what I was doing would be of interest.'

'And what field would that be?'

'I'm an entomologist. Insects. I work on locusts. How they swarm and things like that. This conference was about the spread of infectious diseases. Epidemics. There are quite a lot of features in common actually. They set up mathematical models of how pathogens move in space and time and I do the same thing with my locusts.'

Gawne sat down again without taking much interest in what Peter was saying. He turned a few pages of his papers over. Peter could see he was looking at a list of names, most of which had a small pencil tick against them.

Gawne looked up and saw Peter looking at the list.

'Look,' said Peter, 'I don't think I can be much help. And, if I'm not being questioned, am I free to go please?'

'Free to go? Well, I guess you are. But you're lucky, aren't you?'

Gawne tapped the list.

'There were eighty people in that hall this morning. Sixty of them are dead and the rest will be by tomorrow. You knew some of them. One of them well enough for her parents to let you make formal identification. And you tell me you don't want to help. That you want to go.'

'I didn't say that,' began Peter. 'I just said I didn't think I could be much use, that's all.'

Gawne did not reply but tapped the list again.

'Are you planning to stay in Atlanta?' he said at length.

'No,' replied Peter. 'I was going home tomorrow. Is that still OK?'

Gawne leaned back and put his hands behind his head. 'I'll be honest with you, Wilson. I don't think you had anything to do with this. It was a special thing. So, no, you're not even on the list of people we need to talk to. Someone will want a statement from you but I guess that can be done by your British police. You are free to go.'

Peter stood up. 'Thank you.'

'Just one more thing though,' said Gawne. 'Do you know if all the delegates to the conference were scientists?'

Peter stood and thought for a moment. 'No,' he said. 'There would be one or two other people as well. For instance, the man I went with was a journalist.'

Then Peter remembered the Foreign Office man he and Laurie had been looking for. 'And at least one person from the British Government, so there could have been others from other countries. I think they come as a sort of courtesy. You see, they ultimately fund a lot of the research. The governments, that is. So they come to see how the money is being spent I suppose.'

'Are you sure they're not just along for the ride?'

Peter shrugged. 'You'll really have to ask someone else that question.'

The telephone rang and Gawne answered. 'Yes? Where is he? Then hold him. And don't let anyone talk to him until I get there. No one. Five minutes.

'Well, well,' he said replacing the receiver. 'It seems the local boys have been getting on with things after all. They've done a pull already.'

'What?'

'Pulled a suspect. I think I'll go and have a little chat.'

'But you said your man wouldn't have stayed in Atlanta.'

'One of them.'

'Oh. Good,' said Peter. 'That's good, isn't it?'

Gawne shrugged. 'Maybe. But if they were as smart as I think they are, they won't have left anyone around who knows anything worthwhile. It could just be a crank but I have to go check.'

Five minutes later Peter was in the back of a police car being driven to his hotel. He had said he would rather walk but they had laughed and said a car would be better.

He realised he had not been 'interviewed' in any real sense of the word but was aware he had not conducted himself very well. Gawne had obviously been fishing for something. Peter wondered if he had said anything he shouldn't have. Only that he and Laurie had been nearer the blast than they had told the policemen at the hotel. Well, there was no real harm in that because they would find out soon enough if any of them read Laurie's reports and they were bound to do that sooner or later. But, if that was the case, why had Laurie pretended otherwise? It was Laurie who was acting strangely, not Gawne.

The only reason Peter could come up with was that Laurie didn't want to explain what they had been doing wandering around the building, rather than sitting in the hall with the other delegates. Peter reminded himself to ask Laurie about this. Perhaps Laurie didn't want them to start looking for the tall man, whoever he was.

Then Peter found the picture of the dead girl with her red eyes coming into his mind. And then there was Margaret. He hadn't needed to ask why her eyes had been covered with that strip of gauze. What were the words Gawne had used? 'High-pressure device, with a relatively thin shock wall'. Yes, that was it. Just enough to push people's eyes in but not enough to knock the wall down.

Peter smiled ruefully to himself. Actually, Margaret's eyes had been her best feature. A deep blue that became even deeper when they had been making love.

Except for those times, and maybe not even then, Peter reminded himself, he had never been very good at reading the thoughts that lay behind those eyes.

They had met during one of Peter's first visits to Kano when Margaret was being interviewed for the visiting fellowship with Tom Collis. He had never thought much about where their relationship might lead. He had had his Jaygo problems to work through and perhaps she had something similar to get over. He thought perhaps they had just been swept up in the excitement of discovering Kano together. They revelled in being in one of the oldest cities in the world, one that predated anything even in the Middle East by several thousand years. It was the point where the Sahara to the north and the forests to the south met. Some people said it was the oldest of all trading cities where barter was woven into the very fabric of the thick mud walls of the old part of the city. Walls that had been rebuilt and strengthened every year after the rains from a time before Europeans were living in stick huts.

He remembered how he and Margaret had spent hours together at the old dye pits just outside the oldest part of the city walls. They would watch as men with long poles lifted swirls of almost black wet cloth from the deep pits and hung them out to dry on high wooden racks. The black of the wet cloth drying to the deep maroons and blues the city was famous for. He smiled as he remembered how one of the old men at the dye pits had nick-named her 'Tuareg', because the deep blue of her eyes perfectly matched the cloth so beloved of the Tuareg Arabs. They would travel hundreds of miles south to the Kano dye pits to buy or trade for the heavy blue cotton. How that same old man had toothlessly insisted she accept a narrow strip of the Tuareg cloth to wear as a band around her wide-brimmed straw hat. How every time they had gone to the dye pits after that the old man had shouted up to them from his work 'Hey, Sunday Man! Tuareg Lady! Come to buy cloth today?'

Sometimes they had taken a picnic to eat in the shadow of the abandoned chapel of Santa Maria next to the cloth market. They would sit under the chipped statue of the Virgin Mary that stood in a niche halfway up the wall. The chapel was used to store the drying racks during the rainy season and sometimes the children would run up and try to touch Peter, before running away calling out, 'Sunday Man! Sunday Man!'

Sunday Man. Another reason to remember his times with Margaret. Peter had been puzzled by the name at first and when he asked people what it meant they pretended not to understand. Eventually he found out from a slightly embarrassed Tijja, his driver. 'It's old talk, sah. Old talk. When white men first come here they come as priests and so every Sunday dress up in white and sing-song. People think they sing for birthday. Sunday born, Sunday man. They think all white people born on Sunday.

'And when you go sit by church under Virgin Lady, they think you Sunday Man too. They know church special place for white people so children try to touch you for good luck. But it is only a children's thing now. Old talk.'

Stretching away from the dye pits to the north of the city was the place that Margaret had loved the best. It was the vast sprawling market area called simply 'Sabon Gari', The Place of Strangers. As Peter sat in the back of the police car that evening he could almost smell again the sacks of open spices, hear the call of the boys with baskets of kola nuts on their heads and feel Margaret's hand in his.

Sabon Gari never closed. No matter when he and Margaret visited it was always teeming with life. Sometimes they would go early in the morning to buy heavy giant yams, sweet potatoes or red-veined water yams. And if there were no paw-paws on the trees at the Institute, there were certain to be plenty at Sabon Gari. Or they would visit in the evening to haggle endlessly over rugs or the beaded and mirrored shawls she collected, the air heavy with the smell of wood fires and oil lamps.

After Margaret had left Kano, Peter would still go and be asked after 'Tuareg'. He would say, 'she's coming back' long after he knew she never would. At first he thought she might come back but she never even wrote to him. Eventually he saw that she, like Jaygo before her, had decided that Peter was not a good bet in the long term.

And then had come Aurelia. She was completely unlike either Jaygo or Margaret. Passive. Completely undemanding. Happy to tag along with what he wanted to do and when he wanted to do it. She wanted nothing more, it seemed, but for Peter to come home from Africa for good and take up a full-time fellowship at Lacrima Christi. But she seemed in no hurry to make him. Perhaps she was quietly confident that he would come around to her way of thinking sooner or later. And perhaps she was right. Jaygo and Margaret were gone. Aurelia remained.

Well, probably 'gone' wasn't the right word to use for Jaygo. She could never really be 'gone', could she? He couldn't simply pretend that someone who had been so important for so long had simply vanished. Besides, they were still 'friends', that incident last night apart, and saw each other from time to time. And that's how it should be. Just 'friends'. Aurelia would understand.

Just as he realised he was thinking about Jaygo again, the police car arrived at the hotel.

Peter was quite pleased that Laurie was out when he reached the room. There was a note on the bed. He picked it up and read it as he poured himself a beer.

'Gone to see a man about a bomb,' it read. 'Don't wait up. Bags I the side nearest the window. L.'

Peter put the note down and caught his reflection in the long windows. Standing there with a glass in his hand, he reminded himself of yesterday and his little toast to Jaygo. But no toast to anyone yet tonight. There was something to do first.

He collected his Filofax from his briefcase and picked up the telephone. The switchboard answered. 'I need the dialling code to call Manchester, England.'

'One moment please.'

When she had given him the sequence he replaced the receiver and took another drink from his glass before picking up the receiver again and dialling.

A few seconds later he heard the reassuring double ring of an English telephone. The line was picked up.

'John Carslake here.' Peter recognised the voice but it sounded much older than he remembered.

'John, it's Peter Wilson. I'm calling from Atlanta.'

Chapter Three

WEDNESDAY

At eight o'clock on Wednesday morning Peter was leaning on the hotel reception counter going through his bill. Laurie was standing next to him smoking a cigarette under the disdainful stare of the concierge.

'Don't check everything, Peter. It looks so common.'

'I have to justify this when I get home,' said Peter. 'Judging by this lot, they'll think I've been on some monster piss-up instead of a conference that didn't actually take place.'

'Well, it wasn't all me,' said Laurie, flicking his cigarette into an ornate display of greenery. 'The DD knocked back a few as well, you know.'

'DD?'

'The Devil's Daughter.'

'Jaygo?' asked Peter

'He only has the one. Speaking of which, I think that's her carriage now.' Laurie pointed to a long white limousine drawing up outside.

Peter sighed and signed the slip of paper and looked up to see the little man swaying towards the entrance carrying his briefcase.

'She didn't say she was coming herself,' said Peter, catching up with his friend. 'Just that she was sending a taxi for us.'

'She thinks these things are taxis,' said Laurie as the electric door of the hotel glided back in front of him.

By the time Peter had seen the luggage into the boot, Laurie had already found the bar, opened a fruit juice and was pouring it into a crystal tumbler.

'Not such a bad life is it, old boy?' said Laurie. 'A stretch. The only way to leave the city.'

'Yes, Lol,' said Peter. 'But it's her life, not ours. A yellow cab would have done.'

'Lighten up, you old fart,' said Laurie. 'Enjoy yourself. I mean, how many times have *you* been in one of these?'

'Well, actually . . .' began Peter.

'That's what I thought,' said Laurie. 'Never. Well, I'm going to enjoy it. You can shut up and watch telly.'

Peter shook his head. 'Is there any coffee?'

Laurie investigated the bar that ran along one side of the car and pointed triumphantly at a gold-coloured vacuum jug. 'I think so, sir. Black or white, sir?'

Peter poured himself a cup of coffee and then sat back on the long seat that ran along the opposite side from the bar.

'What time did you get in last night? I must have crashed out.'

'About three,' said Laurie. 'You snore, you know.'

Peter ignored the remark. 'Who did you go and see?'

'A policeman I know,' replied Laurie. 'Well, half know. But I couldn't find him and ended up talking to your friend, Mr Gawne.'

'The bomb man?'

'Yes. He was pretty pissed off by the time I got to him actually.'

'Oh?' said Peter. 'He was OK when I left. He was going into his "I have a suspect" speech.'

'I know about that,' replied Laurie. 'But he turned out to be a nutter. And so did the next two. So you can imagine he was almost glad to see little old me.'

Laurie gestured out at the traffic. 'Look,' he said, 'a different set of people today. Completely different.'

'What?'

'Look at the cars. Yesterday everyone was shouting and sticking fingers up. But today? Nothing. Why do you think that is?'

'Very funny,' said Peter.

'Do you think we can smoke in here?' went on Laurie, taking out a pack of cigarettes.

'No,' said Peter, pointing at a sign.

Laurie ignored him and lit his cigarette. 'They found the man who really did it about an hour after I arrived.'

'Yes?' said Peter.

'Well, when I say "found" that's not strictly accurate, because he's jumped ship as they thought he would. You'd have seen him, too, if you hadn't been married to that plate of dough-nuts.'

Laurie lowered the window an inch and watched as the draught pulled out the plume of smoke he exhaled.

'If you want to tell me,' said Peter, 'just get on with it.' He reached over to lower the window and allow more of the smoke to escape.

'Don't do that,' said Laurie. 'People will see in. Recognise us.'

Peter did not reply but leant back, sipping his coffee.

'That man I was looking for before the bomb went off. He was from the Foreign Office, right?'

'You said so,' said Peter. 'I don't know who he was.'

'Well, according to his visa, he wasn't primarily in the States to go to the conference. He was actually running an errand. To collect something special for HMG and courier it back home in person.'

Peter frowned.

'Ever heard of Semtex Seven?' asked Laurie.

'Not till yesterday. Gawne said it was what they used for the bomb. "Special" he called it.'

'Not only special,' said Laurie. 'Very difficult to get hold of. You need all sorts of permits. You have to be military to even get on the waiting list. But our man jumped the queue.'

'You said he was Foreign Office,' said Peter. 'So what was he doing with this Semtex stuff? You're not saying he was the bomber, are you?'

'Well,' said Laurie, rubbing the tips of his fingers together. 'The old embossed crown and portcullis cuts a lot of weight, you know. Let's just say he turns up in New York, where they store the stuff, with a pukka purchase order signed by the appropriate Ministerial whatever. Maybe even signed by the Minister himself. And the bit of paper says, "I say, Uncle Sam, let old HMG have a few kilos of your special Semtex for a bit of a prob that's just come up. Can't haggle with a staff discount, just give it to the bod you see in front of you who will personally bring it to London and hand it straight over to our MI5 chaps or whatever."'

'No way!' said Peter. 'I've no idea how they trade in stuff like that but I'm damn sure it's not done on a note and a promise. There'd be confirmation, for one thing.'

'True,' said Laurie. 'But if he can do a Ministerial signature, a dodgy fax or two wouldn't be a problem.'

Peter shook his head. 'No way, Lol, no way.'

'It's a planned sequence,' said Laurie. 'Each step is a bit out of line, but not quite out enough to trigger any panic buttons. And each time someone has had time to wonder what's going on and do some checking, your man has jumped to the next stage. He had to gamble on the loose ends not coming together for a few hours on each occasion. He gambled, no, calculated, they would take about twelve hours to rumble him but by then he was sipping his champagne on the way to the bank.'

'Lost me,' said Peter.

'OK. I'll walk you through it. Monday noon he arrives Stateside. Goes straight to New York with his "high priority" paperwork to pick up the stuff. Gets it. Flies straight to Atlanta. Does his bang and immediately leaves the country.'

'What does he do then? Vanish? Gawne and co. could follow him. Gawne looked like an ends-of-the-earth type to me. And anyway, you said yourself, Semtex Seven is "special". I don't think you could just "do a bang" with it.'

'Why not?' said Laurie. 'It's only special if you want to do something "special" with it. Basically it's like all other Semtex, if you put a detonator in it, it goes off. Put in a simple timer and you've a common or garden bomb with the added benefit that it'll go off with a hell of a crack because it's still Seven even if it's just stuffed into a briefcase. OK, if you want to make fancy stun grenades for anti-hijack use, you have to have a special casing, fuse and so on, but our man doesn't need any of that. He knows that if he lets enough of it off at once it will do the trick. A proper Seven stun-grenade will contain about fifty grams of Seven. Our man went down the five-kilo route. Not exactly the acme of your bomb maker's art but enough to take out a roomful of delegates sitting in rows.'

Laurie flicked his cigarette out of the window.

'Anyway, I'll come back to the bomb in a minute. Let's follow your man.'

'He's not my man.'

'Figure of speech, old boy, figure of speech.'

'So Gawne and his boys follow him. What then?' asked Peter.

Laurie raised his finger. 'Gawne's not in it yet. He's still about six hours behind.'

'OK, but the man's plane has to land somewhere. They can call ahead and get him picked off when he puts a foot on the tarmac. Get him arrested locally.'

'But what if he's got diplomatic immunity? I told you he was Foreign Office.'

'Oh, come on,' said Peter. 'The British Government don't like bombers any more than anyone else. He'd at least be held for questioning wherever he went.'

Laurie leaned back in his seat and put his hands behind his head. 'Ah. I can see your man, our man if you like, is too clever for you. I'll tell you what he did. And you'll like this bit. He flies direct to Nigeria. As soon as he lands, he renounces his UK citizenship and becomes a citizen of the Nigerian Republic. Then, and this is the best bit, he is suddenly promoted through the ranks to High Commissioner, no less. And as such he has absolute and full diplomatic immunity. Can't be touched. Anywhere. *Voilà!*'

'That's ridiculous!' said Peter.

'OK,' said Laurie, looking pleased with himself. 'Pick holes in it.'

Peter thought for a moment.

'What would be the point anyway? He'd be marked. The British would think of something. Take him when he came home.'

'The point is money,' said Laurie. 'A lot of money. Promise people enough money and they'll do anything. And why should he come home anyway. I mean, half the people in Britain plan to leave the place and go and live permanently in Spain or somewhere awful when they get some money. I think it's called the lottery.'

'How much are we talking about then?'

'Well, name your price,' said Laurie. 'And I presume that in this case, the price suited the paymaster just fine. Anyway, a few million here or there is nothing to this particular paymaster if I know anything about him.'

Laurie grinned mischievously at Peter.

'Ah! Here we are,' said Laurie, suddenly looking out of the window.

'Wait a minute,' said Peter. 'You're saying now that you know, or think you know, who's behind this thing.'

'Oh, yes.'

'Who?'

'Well. You know him too.'

'Come on Laurie, what are you on about?'

'OK,' said Laurie. 'In the ordinary way of things, who is the richest person you know? Then multiply what they've got by some large number.'

'Rich?' said Peter puzzled. 'I don't know any rich people.'

Laurie theatrically gestured around the inside of the limousine and then pointed carefully out of the window to the jet the limousine was drawing up next to.

'Jay! What the hell could she have to do with it?'

'Nothing, old boy. I didn't say she did. I just said, multiply her money up and who do you get?'

Peter thought for a moment. 'Jack? Do you mean Jack?'

'I do indeed. And, oh look, unless I'm very much mistaken, the light of his life is here to greet us in person. I do hope he knows who her father is.'

Then Laurie leant forwards and put his hands on Peter's shoulders. 'Guessing game over for now. And not a word of this to her majesty until we're thirty thousand feet up and I've got a G and T in my hand.'

The door was opened from the outside and Jaygo stuck her head in. 'Where the hell have you been? We're just about to miss our slot.'

'Good morning, my darling,' said Laurie, stepping out.

'What have you two been up to?' she said to Peter as he climbed out behind Laurie.

'Well, you sent the car. We came as soon as it arrived.'

'Bloody Hugo,' she said. 'I bet he sent it late deliberately so I'd have to go without you. He doesn't like you, you know.'

Peter went around to the back of the car to collect the cases that were being unloaded by the driver.

'I've never even met Hugo,' he said. 'How can he like me or not?'

'Don't worry,' said Jaygo, 'I've told him all about you.'

Peter shook his head and picked up the cases and began to walk toward the aeroplane. 'I presume this is it,' he said, nodding towards the plane.

'Of course it is. Look at the side.'

Peter read the name of Jaygo's record company painted in red and smiled. 'Why isn't there anyone to carry the cases then?'

'Just leave them by the steps and someone will put them in the hold.'

'What about passports and so on?'

'Don't worry. Auntie has it all worked out. We taxi to the holding area near the terminal and the nice little men come to see us before we go.'

Peter put the cases down at the bottom of the steps. 'Are the others here yet?' he asked.

'What others?'

'Hugo and co, the Belle Epoque itself.'

'Ah,' said Jaygo. 'They're not coming.'

'Why? Isn't there room?'

'Of course, there's bags of room. Anyway they are all very small, including Hugo. No. It's just that they have a recording to do.'

'Without you? Setting up on their own, are they?'

'No. We're doing the music for some silly film or other and we lay down loads of tracks for each bit. My session was fine but theirs was awful and they have to do it again.'

'Says who?'

'Me, actually. And don't worry about them, they're going to follow on First Virgin. This little flight is just for the three of us, so jump on.'

Peter smiled again before climbing the steps behind Jaygo.

Laurie was already sitting in one of the wide seats with his arms outstretched when they went into the cabin.

'Peel me a grape will you,' he said.

Peter shook his head before taking the seat next to him.

'Just off to see a man,' called Jaygo, disappearing towards the front of the aeroplane.

She returned a few moments later with a tall fair-haired man in a white T-shirt, carrying the cases. 'This is Sven,' she announced. 'He's Swedish and doesn't speak much English but is frightfully pretty.

'He says your cases can't go in the hold. The customs men have already sealed it up because of the complicated bits of paper that go with the cello, so these will have to go in here. Anyone would think the cello was a John Grisham protection witness judging by the amount of paper that has to go with it.'

The man in the T-shirt put the cases at the side of the cabin and secured them with straps before going forward again.

'He doesn't look very old,' said Laurie.

'Oh, Sven just reads the maps,' said Jaygo, sitting down next to Peter. 'The other two are much older.'

'Crew of three,' mused Peter. 'Passenger list of three. Seems a bit extravagant.'

Jaygo shrugged. 'Belts on. Off to control.'

'A lot of airlines give you a drink at this stage,' said Laurie.

'Later,' said Jaygo. 'You can't have anything till we get to cruising height. This thing goes up like a lift and you'd be lucky not to spill a boiled sweet when Biggles puts his foot down or whatever he does.'

'Great,' said Peter. 'Thanks for the calming talk. What about exits and stuff like that?'

Jaygo did up her seat belt. 'Look to your left,' she said. 'And look to your right. If we come down then the whole thing opens up like a banana and you can just walk out.'

'Oh good.'

'Or swim out. I can never remember which it is. Anyway, don't worry. Biggles is frightfully good.'

The Lear taxied over to the holding area and waited while the officials came on board.

'You know,' said Laurie, while one of the officials looked over his passport, 'you can tell if a country is worth living in by its airport officials. If a place is easy to get into then it's not worth living there and if it's hard to get out of then you wouldn't want to live there in the first place.'

'I came out of Wales once,' said Peter. 'They just let me go straight over the bridge without any checks at all so that's *that* theory out of the window.'

'Lands of Song are special cases,' replied Laurie.

When the official had gone, the Lear joined the queue for the runway.

'Tighten up, boys,' said Jaygo. 'This is the big one.'

Sure enough, after a short take-off run, the aeroplane lifted clear and threw them back in their seats and went up at an angle of forty-five degrees.

'Shit!' called Laurie above the scream of the engines. 'Is it like this every time?'

'Only after you've bought it,' called back Jaygo. 'Before that they make it go along like a roller skate.'

Two minutes later the engine noise died back to a quiet whistle and the aeroplane levelled out.

Jaygo undid her belt and stood up. 'All right. You've earned your boiled sweets now.'

'Mine's with ice and lemon please, miss,' said Laurie.

'And you, Peter?'

'The same please.'

'Good, three coffees it is,' Jaygo said with a smile and went to a door at the back of the cabin.

A few minutes later she returned with a cafetiere of coffee and three cups. 'The real thing,' she said pouring it out. 'Nothing but the best for my boys.

'We'll drink later,' she said. 'But first I want to ask you properly about Jack. If I'm going to see him on Thursday I want to know what you think he's up to.'

'I told you last night,' said Peter. 'Laurie is the one you need to ask.'

She passed a cup to Laurie. 'Thank you,' he said. 'I'm afraid you're not going to like it much. So first I think you'd better tell me what *you* think he's up to.'

'I don't know really,' said Jaygo, sitting down again. 'He comes to see me from time to time. We talk on the telephone. He's a businessman, I suppose. And I remember he owns a lot of farms in Northern Nigeria. And he's into politics. Pretty influential by now, I think. And I know he owns a TV station. Yes, he's a pretty big wheel in Nigeria, but basically he's just a successful businessman with his eye on the main chance.'

Peter and Laurie looked at each other without speaking.

Eventually Peter said, 'But that's not the main thing is it, sweetie? You forgot to mention that he is the Ngale.'

'Yes, that too,' said Jaygo. 'I know that. He always used to say he would inherit that when his father died. It's titular thing, isn't it? A bit like the House of Lords.'

'I think we know it's rather more than that, Jay,' said Peter quietly.

'What?' she said. 'Yes, well he's inherited a lot of money along with the name. So, he's rich. So what? I'm rich too. It does happen, you know. Money doesn't make him special.'

'His does,' said Laurie, sipping from his cup.

'The thing is, Jay,' began Peter, 'he's not just rich like you. He's above rich. Money simply isn't an issue for him. He doesn't think about money any more than you think about paying for lunch. It's not a thing for him. So you have to ask yourself, if he wants to do business with you, what's he doing it for? Because it's not for the money, take it from me.'

'Are you talking about the CD?' she asked.

'That. And all that goes with it. Tell me, how much does he stand to make from it. A million? Two?'

Jaygo shrugged. 'Maybe.'

'Small change for him, Jaygo. I tell you, he's not doing it for the money.'

'You're just saying that because you don't want me to go to Kano,' she said.

'Yes,' he said. 'I am.'

'And now you're being silly,' she said, slightly irritated. 'A million pounds is a lot of money even for someone like Jack. And it's a lot of money for someone like me too. Someone has to pay for this thing, you know,' she went on, briskly tapping the side of her seat. 'Some of us actually have to get up in the mornings and go to work.'

'Hey! Calm down, Jaygo,' said Laurie. 'Peter's only telling it as he sees it.'

'Don't you tell me to calm down, Laurie Miller,' she said sharply. 'If Jack Ngale thinks he can make a million from the CD, then he probably can and I probably can too.'

'OK, Laurie,' she went on. 'St Peter here doesn't like Jack and never gets tired of telling me. So how is that new? Now you tell me what it is I'm not going to like so I can feel thoroughly miserable about the whole thing. But, just remember, I play the cello for a living and if I don't go, Jack will use that fat Frenchman Dolly Whatshisname and I'm buggered if he's going to play my Black Mambazo Music.'

An awkward silence followed Jaygo's outburst.

Eventually Peter spoke. 'Jaygo darling, yesterday I got the distinct impression that you half wished you didn't have to go. You were even less keen when I told you about the torque on the CD picture. And now you seem all for it. What's changed?'

Jaygo hunched her shoulders and looked away from the two men.

'He rang,' she said. 'That's all.'

'Jack?' said Peter.

'Yes, he rang me this morning,' she went on. 'He wanted to see if you were all right actually. He'd seen about the bomb on CNN, or one of his people had, so he rang me to see if you were all right.'

'Why the hell should Jack think I was in Atlanta?'

'Well . . .' she said. 'Well . . .'

'You told him I would be here, didn't you?'

Jaygo became irritated again. 'I might have, that's all. Well, yes, I told him a few days ago. Look, I told you I'd tried to ring you in Cambridge to ask you about this CD thing. And the dippy I spoke to said she thought you were in Kano. So I rang Jack there to ask if he'd seen you and he asked the Institute and *they* said you were here. And he rang me again. Satisfied?'

Peter shrugged.

'You're supposed to be his friend, for God's sake,' she said. 'What's the big deal? And he knew you would be in Kano at the end of this week again so he said why didn't the three of us all meet up for a do?'

'A "do"?'

'Dinner. I don't know.'

'Well, that's nice, isn't it? Last night you weren't even sure if you really wanted to go. And now it turns out you've been planning some weepy get-together all along.'

'I more or less told you what was going on, and don't pretend I didn't. It's going to be a lot of money for not much work and if you were going to back me up it wasn't going to be so bad.'

Peter sighed. 'That's the thing with you, isn't it? Half the bloody story all the bloody time. Then the other half when you're good and ready.'

She looked at him angrily and was about to say something when Laurie cut in.

'Hold it! Hold it! You two can hammer and tongs it like the good old days later on. I think you had both better listen to me before you go on your reunion jaunt to Kano. I know a great deal more about Jack Ngale than either of you seem to. And I've barely spoken to the guy since we left university ten years ago.'

'So what makes you an Africa expert all of a sudden?'

'Not Africa,' said Laurie patiently, 'just Jack.'

Peter poured himself some more coffee.

'And I'm not an expert anyway,' said Laurie. 'I'm putting some material together for something and everywhere I look Jack appears.

'You see,' he went on, 'most journalists actually don't want to be journalists at all. They fancy themselves as writers. Books. Plays. All that.

'Authors.' He held up his fingers to indicate inverted commas. 'They want to be authors.

'I think most of them find out early on that people like what they write well enough to read it. They find they've got a knack of stringing the right words together. They do school magazines, university things, local stuff. And when they find they can make a living at it, they go for it full time. They take a job doing features or news or anything that comes across their editors' desks. I told them I had a First in Zoology so they made me a science correspondent but it could have been cookery as far as I was concerned. Anyway, my degree was good enough for me to be able to talk to research people without making a monkey of myself. I suppose I was lucky, had a few breaks and finished up on the ITN team. It was TV but still essentially writing. I enjoyed it and the money looked pretty good to me then.'

He paused and put his cup down.

'Then it went a bit pear-shaped. Like me.'

Peter was about to speak but Laurie put up his hand. 'No. Wait,' he said. 'I had a few tiffs with the producers. A few problems shall we say and basically they shipped me off to Northern Ireland to become a Farming Correspondent with Ulster TV.'

'I don't remember that,' said Jaygo.

'No,' said Laurie. 'It was hardly a major career move and I didn't make a thing of it. I thought if I ate shit in Belfast for a year or two until things calmed down I could come back to London.'

'Until what had calmed down?' asked Peter.

Laurie looked at Jaygo and smiled before turning back to Peter.

'Not important,' he said. 'But the upshot was that I was sitting in Belfast pubs all day trying to think up interesting things to write about bacon prices and EC subsidies. Of course this was at the height of the Troubles and bacon prices were pretty small potatoes, even by Ulster TV standards.

'I didn't know anything about Northern Ireland politics when I first went. I tried to read up on it but it was like reading about two different countries. I soon realised there wasn't anything to know really. The Republicans wanted the British out. And the Ulster lot, who have never so much as looked at an atlas, thought they were British and said, "No. We live here. *You* get out." Politicians fiffed and faffed but nothing ever changed the lines that had been drawn up God knows how long ago. It was like two drunks in a bar shouting at each other. Eventually they lost their tempers entirely, pushed back the tables and chairs and began to slug it out. Bombings. Shootings. Beatings.

'Most people in Northern Ireland had never seen a war before but that is pretty much what it was becoming. A drunken war. And never mind about truth being the first casualty of war, the first thing either side actually ran out of was money.

'The IRA were all right at first because they could get money from America and the Loyalists started creaming off "development projects" funded by the British Government.

'And despite what they said about each other's funding, it didn't take long for the British and American governments to cotton on and they choked the supplies off as much as they could by tighter banking and better housekeeping. But by then the sides on the ground were in an escalating war which they suddenly found was a great deal more expensive than they had bargained for. They needed money fast and started getting it in the age-old way. Through crime. Selling drugs.'

106

'Oh, come on!' said Peter. 'I've heard some crap about Northern Ireland in my time but that about takes the biscuit! Drugs?'

Laurie looked at him, rather surprised. 'What? If you want to raise money fast you can't just set up Tupperware parties. Drugs are big, fast, easy business. And cash too.'

'Hang on,' interrupted Jaygo. 'I don't remember it being an actual war. Just bombs.'

'Bombs *are* war,' said Laurie. 'OK, if you just want to leave a shoe box of nails and quarry explosive in a pub it only takes a few quid but to keep ahead of the Bomb Squad you soon need expensive kit. Timing devices. Transmitters, frequency blockers, plastic explosive. And if you're talking about a bombing campaign on the mainland, you can throw in training, travel, safe houses, false papers and so on. Not much by NATO standards but quite a few hundred thousand nonetheless.'

Jaygo put her head on one side. 'And you say they could make that much just from selling drugs?'

'Oh, yes. It depends on how long the chain of supply is and the first thing to know is that neither Belfast nor Dublin were established drug cities at that time, like Liverpool or Amsterdam. And that's a good comparison, too, because in places like Liverpool the people who sell the stuff to the local dealers are only importers who buy the drugs from the original producers. There's about a seven hundred percent mark-up at each stage but only two or three hundred to the street people. That's OK, but guess who comes to Belfast and says, "Hey, guys, I actually grow the stuff and can sell it to you at less than any regular supplier. Tell you what, I'll give you the supplier-to-importer price and you sell on from there at regular street prices. Nice deal huh?"'

'What "stuff"?' said Jaygo. 'Hash?'

'A bit. But the money's in heroin. No point selling something the punter might like when you can sell him something he will definitely want more of, is there?'

'No,' said Peter. 'The two are completely different. Hash you just have to grow. Heroin you actually have to manufacture.'

Laurie pointed his finger at Peter. 'Yes. And that takes us back to where we were yesterday morning. The drugs, heroin and morphine, are not all *that* difficult to make. No more than failed graduate-level knowledge required. Most people could churn it out with the helpful kits supplied by those nice people at AbChem or Geneva Pharms.'

Laurie put his cup down. 'And finally, the other thing you need for a nice tidy drugs chain, is people on the ground to look after your people. And in this case there were ready-made gangs. On top of that, was a police force who thought they had better things to do than worry about drugs – which they knew absolutely nothing about anyway.'

'I still think you're being too simplistic,' said Peter. 'Yes, the Troubles escalated as you said, yes, there were some drugs and yes, there were street gangs. But you don't show me a link. Or if you do, it's pretty tenuous.'

'Depends how you look at it,' replied Laurie. 'Go from the Northern Ireland end and I agree it's hopelessly complicated, go at it from a military end and it's still iffy. But go at it from Jack's end and it's straightforward. He saw a market, he had a way of satisfying it and he knew he wouldn't have much competition. So in he went.'

'But Jack would only be about twenty-five at that time,' said Jaygo. 'How would he know how to go about it all? Manufacturing, shipping and all that.'

'Frankly, I don't think he did know all that much when he started out,' said Laurie. 'It was all pretty new to him and I think he looked on Ireland as a sort of training ground for what he had in mind for later. He really wanted to move into bigger markets but couldn't take on established players till he had earned his spurs. Liverpool and Amsterdam are rough places for new boys.'

'If Jack was only twenty-five,' said Peter, 'so were you. I don't go along with most of what you've said but even if I did, I don't think the Laurie I knew then would have seen what was going on. You were a born again farming correspondent, not some super hack delving into God knows what.'

'Thanks for the compliment,' said Laurie.

'You know what I mean,' said Peter. 'I knew you then and you didn't know any more about drugs than I did. You were still an anorak.'

'No, you didn't know me then,' replied Laurie. 'You were off in Africa at your Institute counting locust legs. We only met sometimes when you came to London. You were taking off into what you were doing and, frankly, I thought a decent book would help me take off too. I wanted a ticket out and I wanted to make my name. A book about Jack and his tricks seemed just the thing.'

'But you didn't write a book, did you? I'd have seen it if you had. Where is it?'

'No,' said Laurie quietly. 'I didn't write a book. Or perhaps I should say, *we* didn't write a book. I was doing it with Christopher Iltan. It was going to be a joint thing.'

'Iltan?' said Peter. 'Do I know him?'

'No,' said Laurie. 'He was the person who started me off on the whole idea and I'm sorry to say he's also the reason that the book wasn't written.

'He . . .' began Laurie again, looking for the right word. 'I . . . We were very good friends. He was a line reporter for Associated Press, an American with a degree in Journalism from San Francisco, a few years younger than me. AP had put him into Belfast as a "career move" to boost their team covering the Troubles. The other two APs were much more experienced and had it pretty much sewn up. They didn't want to "babysit", as they put it, some new guy. So Chris spent his time making tea and minding the telephone.

'We got to know each other and spent a lot of time sitting around in bars in the evenings. God, there isn't much else to do in Belfast. He was pretty bright, much too good to be an AP line man, in fact. And the two of us put our heads together and came up with the idea that if we could write a decent book together then it might get us our tickets home. Him back to the States. Me back to London.'

He glanced up at Jaygo. 'Or whatever,' he added.

'So, we moved out of the hotel our people had put us in and took a flat together in central Belfast.

'Funny really, looking back,' he went on. 'We found people really willing to talk about it. Older people, and anyone over thirty looked "older" to us, were appalled by the drugs culture that was springing up around them. Sensible people on both sides, and there still were some then, couldn't get anyone in authority to listen to them about drugs. So when they heard we wanted to write a book about it, they practically fell over themselves to talk. Chris did all the main interviewing because his accent was "neutral", I did the background research and started putting it into book form. I would tell him what we wanted next, who we needed to talk to and he would go off and do it. He was really good. He was so natural. Funny too. He went down really well. He was a nice guy. Special.'

'Was?' asked Jaygo.

Laurie did not reply immediately but looked away, searching for the right words.

'They . . .' he looked up directly at Jaygo. 'They shot him. They walked into a pub at lunchtime and shot him where he sat.'

'Who is "they"?' asked Peter quietly.

'Who do you think? It was Jack's lot. I mean, for God's sake, he was an American in a Catholic bar, among his friends. Two black men came in, shot him and walked out again. God, the only two black gunmen seen in Belfast in twelve years.

'I was at the flat at the time and someone from the pub who knew me rang. I went immediately of course. I was out about four or five hours I suppose. At the pub, the hospital, the police station. Though I don't know why, the poor man was dead before he hit the floor.'

Laurie shut his eyes and slowly shook his head before continuing, 'Anyway, when I came home the flat was wrecked. Most of the furniture kicked to bits or pissed on. Shit everywhere. And then I saw that everything to do with the book was gone. Chris's notebooks, typed stuff, everything. Bloody gone and nothing else missing at all.' He looked over at Jaygo. 'I think they call it "consequences", don't they?'

'What did the police do?' said Peter.

Laurie took out a cigarette and lit it before replying.

'Ten o'clock that night the IRA did one of their nail bombs at a youth club. Ten kids killed, thirty injured. It wasn't a very good time to be going up to Plod and saying, "Please, sir, my friend was shot at lunchtime."' He put on an Irish accent, "Sorry, sonny, busy just now."'

Jaygo stood up and started collecting the cups. 'You didn't tell us, Laurie. We didn't know.'

'I wasn't sure what to do at first,' said Laurie. 'I thought it was going to be me next.

'I should have run away to London but there didn't seem much point. I wasn't ever going to be difficult to find. But, as days went by, I saw it was the book they wanted stopped, not me. I suppose I could have started it again on my own but all the best contacts were Chris's and people were not going to be so cooperative next time around when they had seen what happened. I sort of went into a funk and gave up. Turned the handle on a few bacon stories and quietly watched my career go down the tubes for six months.'

Laurie stood up and went to look out of one of the small windows, squinting against the bright morning sun.

'London said I could come home after about another year and I started again at the ITN Science section.

'So,' he said, sitting down again. 'Now, you tell me what a nice guy Jack Ngale really is.'

'I never said he was a nice guy,' said Peter. 'But I don't

think he'd do a thing like that. You must have made some mistake.'

'Oh,' said Laurie, feigning surprise. 'Silly old Laurie, only twenty-five. Must have got it wrong. What a chump.

'Peter,' Laurie went on in a normal voice, 'Chris and I had discovered enough to know it was Jack bringing the stuff into Belfast and on to Dublin too. It wasn't a mistake and we had it backed up three storeys deep.'

'And is he still at it?' asked Jaygo.

'In Belfast? I doubt it. Some into Dublin probably. But, as I said, it was just a testing ground to him and he's gone on to bigger places now. There were new markets opening up, potentially much bigger, and he wanted to get into them before the competition.'

'You make it sound as if he were selling cans of paint,' said Jaygo.

'There's no difference,' said Laurie. 'If you don't mind what you sell or who you sell it to, then drugs is the best thing to be in. Profits are fantastic, no tax, lots of cash and,' he said, raising a finger, 'I think you'll find that your customers are only too keen to come back for more so you don't have all that consumer loyalty to worry about. So? Ready for a new market? How about one of those nice new Eastern European places? Ideal as far as I can see. Crap police and lots of young people with no work and looking for a bit of Western style excitement in their lives. Sounds good to me. Czecho? East Germany? Mmm.'

'And you think that's what Jack's been doing, do you?' said Jaygo.

'I know damn well he has.'

'So what's made you take an interest in him again? You just said he pretty much frightened you off.'

'Things change,' said Laurie, getting up again. 'Attitudes change. I watched him from the sidelines as a sort of hobby for a bit. Chris and I always speculated that Jack would go into South Africa when it opened up and I wanted to see if it would happen. It did, by the way. But nobody seemed to care much and no one tried to stop him. If the narcotic squads knew what he was doing, and they must have, they just treated him like the other drugs barons. Picked up one or two of his little people but left him to get on with it. Policemen have friends and family just like anyone else. And I suppose Jack paid a few sweeteners as par for the course. But, whatever the reason, he just got on with things and grew up to be a major player inside five years.'

He peered out of the window again before turning back to Peter and Jaygo again.

'I think what swung it for me was him deciding to set up in London. His heroin started appearing about twelve months ago. The British knew it but just treated the matter as a local skirmish between drug barons and left it to sort itself out.'

'But you just said that's what he is, a drug baron,' said Jaygo. 'But, more to the point, are you ready for your boiled sweet with ice and lemon yet?'

'Oh yes. That sounds very nice,' said Laurie, sitting down. 'I'm sorry, you two, I'm being a bit of a bore, aren't I?'

Jaygo went to fetch the drinks.

Peter was still looking thoughtful. 'You were about to say why you thought Jack wasn't just another drug baron. Which I'm not yet convinced he is, by the way.'

'Well,' said Laurie, sitting back and blowing out a long breath. 'It's a question of degree. Competitive drugging, which is what he found himself getting into, is pretty nasty. Beatings, setting fire to people and property – that sort of thing. Now, the main players in London are the Chinese and the South Americans. The Chinese also do a lot of the restaurants and sex clubs and the South Americans do the ordinary clubs and the street prostitution. It's a bit blurred at the edges but they pretty much stick to their own territory or at least operate in slightly different areas. But our Jack just does drugs. Only drugs. He's got this amazingly short supply line and just bludgeons anyone out of the way. If he starts a club fire, he doesn't worry if it's full of people at the time or not. If he wants to put a restaurant out of business because its owner is selling drugs on a patch that Jack wants, he just burns the whole place down. And, if it happens to be a busy Saturday night – well, that's just too bad.

'I tell you, Peter,' said Laurie, leaning forwards. 'He just doesn't care about people at all. Take that bomb yesterday at the university. A penny to a pound he didn't do it to kill everyone. Gawne agrees on that. It's just that a bomb was going to be the most effective way of taking out the person he wanted. The other people weren't even in the way. They simply weren't in the equation at all.'

Peter looked at Laurie carefully without replying before standing up. 'I'll go and give Jaygo a hand with the drinks,' he said and went through the door at the back of the cabin.

'Have you got a better idea then?' Laurie called after him.

In the kitchen, Jaygo was putting some glasses on a tray.

'Lost it a bit, hasn't he?' said Peter.

'What?'

'Laurie. What's got into him?'

'I don't know what you mean,' said Jaygo, opening a small cupboard, peering in and closing it again.

'I've never heard so much unconnected rubbish. Belfast, Jack, drugs. I don't think I believe any of it. He's just fitting a story around what's happened to him.'

She stopped what she was doing and looked at him. 'Were you in Belfast?'

'No.'

'Well, he was. And was your friend shot? No? I didn't think so. So don't just say "what happened to him". Don't patronise him.'

'I'm not.'

'You are.'

'Look. Ireland is a complicated place. And I'm not saying Jack never sells drugs. Of course he ships a bit of hash. Christ, he was even at it a bit when we were at university. But all this gang stuff. It's just not his way.'

'Well someone was.'

'Were they?'

'Of course they were. If you actually read about anything before making up your mind, you'd know the drug situation in Ireland is pretty terrible. Look in the bloody papers.'

'OK, OK,' backtracked Peter. 'But that's now and that's Dublin. Not Belfast five years ago.'

'Well, I believe him,' she said, taking an ice bucket from a shelf. 'And, seeing as how we both agree he was actually there, I think you'll find I've made the right judgment.'

'I'm not saying there's nothing to it. I'm just saying he's over the top.'

'Let's read his book and make our minds up then, shall we?' she said, putting out some peanuts.

'What's it to you anyway?' said Peter, reaching over for a peanut. 'Why are you taking him under your wing all of a sudden?'

'I'm not,' she said, picking up the tray and waiting for Peter to stand aside. 'I thought he had something interesting to say so I listened to him. You thought you knew better so you didn't. Now, can I get by, please?'

Laurie looked up approvingly at the drinks tray. 'Ah. That's what I *call* a boiled sweet.'

Jaygo put the tray down and poured them all very large gin and tonics.

'What do we drink to?' said Laurie, picking up his glass.

'Wednesday,' said Jaygo. 'Wednesday in a busy week.'

The three of them smiled. Jaygo took a long sip and leaned back in her chair. 'At least we can agree on something then.'

'Lots of things,' said Peter, offering the dish of nuts to Laurie.

As they were beginning their drinks, a mobile telephone rang from Jaygo's bag by her chair.

'Guess who this is,' she said, taking it from the bag. 'Hugo darling! What a lovely surprise!'

With her free hand she made the gesture of someone putting a gun to her head and pulling the trigger.

'We're simply wonderful, darling. How did the recording go?'

Instead of listening she gradually moved the telephone away from her ear until it was at arm's length.

'I can hardly hear you, darling. Can you still hear me?'

She picked up her gin and took a sip.

'No. No. Can't hear a thing,' she went on. 'We must be too high. All breaking up. I'll call you back later.'

She pressed the 'off' button and slipped the telephone back in her bag.

'Well,' she said sweetly. 'Where were we?'

'Wait a minute,' said Laurie, pointing to her bag. 'If that's a mobile phone, how come it's working up here?'

'It's not *just* a mobile phone. It's a special satellite thingy. Meant to work everywhere but the South Pole.'

'Quite a "thingy",' said Peter.

'Yes, terribly expensive and a frightful waste of money,' she said. 'But Hugo insists I carry it with me in case he suddenly needs to be in touch. Which actually turns out to be every couple of hours.'

'Very touching,' said Laurie, almost laughing.

'Very,' she said, smiling back at him 'He's *such* a darling.

'And talking of darlings,' she went on, 'Peter, you simply have to tell us all about your fiancée. I feel I hardly know her at all.'

'Aurelia?' said Peter. 'She's all right.'

'Mmm,' said Jaygo. 'I was hoping for a bit more info than that.'

'She's an artist, isn't she?' asked Laurie helpfully.

'Yes, she went to art school in Leeds.'

'Leeds?' said Jaygo. 'I did a concert there once. It seemed a pretty dreary place to me. I can't imagine they can get enough people to go there to run an art school.'

Peter ignored her. 'Her father introduced us when I joined Lacrima Christi. I think it was at the Fellows' Christmas party, actually.'

'Love at first sight, was it?' asked Jaygo crisply.

Peter smiled. 'Hardly. I thought she was a bit quiet. And besides, I was with Margaret at the time.'

Nobody said anything.

'Anyway,' said Peter at length. 'I didn't see her again for a year or so. Then Tom had a bout of malaria and took leave to recover and I saw Aurelia at their house when I was visiting him back in Cambridge. We got on well enough.

'Then he became ill properly about four years later. I went to the house quite a lot. There wasn't anything they could do for him of course and he went slowly down hill and died about six months ago.'

'What of?' asked Laurie. 'Cancer?'

'Not strictly speaking.' Peter picked up his glass and watched the bubbles for a moment before continuing. 'He died of "Slim".'

'What on earth is that?' said Jaygo.

'"Slim"?' said Peter. 'It's what they call Aids in Africa. The old boy died of Aids.'

'Aids!' exclaimed Jaygo. 'Was he gay?'

'No,' said Peter, smiling to himself. 'Straight as a die. Aids isn't a gay thing in Africa. It's pretty much an anyone thing. We never knew of course, but we think he picked it up on one of his trips to Gombe.'

'What a thing! The housekeeper,' said Jaygo.

Peter looked at her disapprovingly. 'Look, does it matter how he contracted it? It didn't matter to Aurelia and it certainly didn't matter to me. He was just ill and so we looked after him. Aids is Aids and it doesn't matter how you get it. The end result is the same.'

Peter did not notice the exchange of glances between Laurie and Jaygo.

'It was pretty slow for him,' continued Peter, still looking at his glass. 'He was at home for most of the last year with Aurelia in Cambridge and I was there when I wasn't out at the Institute in Kano.

'We got to know each other pretty well in that year. I suppose it seemed to our friends that we just sort of drifted together. Maybe we did. We just knew we would get married eventually. I don't think I even asked her.'

115

'What then?' asked Jaygo. 'You just woke up next to each other one Sunday morning, did you?'

Peter ignored her again.

'We made a formal thing of it one day when Tom was having one of his bouts in hospital. He said it was what he had always wanted and by then we wanted it too and so we became "engaged" for him. It wasn't a turning point or anything like that but it made him happier and that was important to us.'

Peter finished his drink and put the glass down.

'He was pretty ill by then. But our wedding was something for him to look forward to, although all three of us knew he wouldn't live to see it. Parents like to see their children married off. Grandchildren, that sort of thing.

'I thought at one stage he might want to go back to Kano at the end. He always used to say that you had to leave your bones in Africa to do any good there. But then, about six months before the end, he told Aurelia privately that he'd settle for her taking his ashes out there.'

'I think that's a bit grisly,' said Jaygo.

'Perhaps,' said Peter. 'But actually he'd become a bit disillusioned with it all over the last four years or so. You see, he'd spent most of his life building the Institute up and it broke his heart seeing it taken apart in front of him.'

'How so?' asked Laurie.

'Your friend Jack, I'm afraid,' explained Peter. 'Jack thought the place was too "European" and wasn't "African" enough. So he set about redressing the balance.'

'I thought it had a pretty good reputation,' said Jaygo. 'Tom's work, your work – it put Kano University on the map, a nice link with Cambridge. Didn't Jack see it as a feather in the cap for his people?'

'Apparently not. He wasn't going to be happy until his people were running it. He appointed himself Chairman of the Trustees or whatever they are called. Then he started filling the top jobs with his appointees even if they weren't as good as the people we wanted.'

'Not just a teeny bit jealous about losing control, are we?' asked Jaygo.

'Perhaps,' sighed Peter. 'But it was more than that. Tom had put his life into that place and knew how to attract the right people and keep them. He went out there when it was nothing. He took his wife there and Aurelia was born there. He turned his

116

department at the new university into an Institute. Attracted top-flight visiting Fellows and built up an international reputation as good as anything in the tropics, let alone Africa.

'Looking back on it, I suppose he should have seen the writing on the wall in 1975 when the Brits pulled out half of their money during the oil crisis on the grounds that the Nigerians could fund it from their recently nationalised oil industry profits. But of course they never did and, one by one, he lost his best people to other institutes around the tropics in more attractive places. I mean, you choose, Kano and Jack's hand on the purse or Hawaii and Uncle Sam?'

'But you stayed,' said Jaygo.

'Yes. It still looked reasonable. He and I did some interesting stuff in those days. And anyway we both worked on locusts so we had to be in Africa. We had some really good results and I took up his enthusiasm as his was beginning to run down. I knew Jack better than anyone and thought I'd be able to convince him to fund the place properly.'

'Well,' said Jaygo. 'It sounds as though Tom kept up a head of stream for twenty years but yours ran down after only five.'

'Maybe,' said Peter reflectively. 'Maybe he was just a better man. But when he started he had a wife and a fair-sized ex-pat community for support all over Kano and not just at the Institute. It was a better way of life then than it is now.'

'You could have had a wife if you'd wanted one,' said Jaygo. 'Laurie says that woman yesterday wanted to marry you.'

Peter looked from Jaygo to Laurie. 'Well, I didn't marry her, did I?' he said, standing up. 'Is there any juice in your little kitchen?'

'Probably,' said Jaygo. 'Look in the fridge.'

When he had left, Laurie said, 'Thank you for not telling him.'

'None of his bloody business, is it? Anyway, he was so busy talking about the Archangel Aurelia, he wouldn't have noticed.'

She wiped some condensation from her glass and licked her finger. 'And he didn't even mention the bomb woman,' she added.

'Margaret?' asked Laurie.

'Yes. What sort of artist is Aurelia anyway? Not a piss artist by any chance, is she?'

Peter came back with a carton of juice and sat down again. 'Actually, Aurelia doesn't like Kano very much. I think we'll probably go somewhere else eventually.'

'"Insect Boffin Gives Up Locusts For Love",' said Jaygo.

Peter poured himself a juice without replying. 'Well,' he said

117

eventually, 'if we're going to be married we may as well be happy where we live, don't you think?'

Jaygo pursed her lips.

'Aurelia illustrates children's books,' said Peter. 'She can do that anywhere. And I could find something else to work on. Leaf-hoppers or something like that. I've always fancied Australia actually.'

'You can take it from me that Australia is a very boring place,' said Jaygo. 'Very hot and they don't know when to clap at concerts.'

'Oh, I don't know,' said Laurie. 'I went there on leave a couple of years back and rather liked the place.'

'Well, Peter wouldn't like it,' said Jaygo, pouring out some juice. 'I know him and all there is to do, is drink lager and be sick on the beach. He'd soon tire of that.'

She began drumming her fingers on the side of the carton.

The telephone in Jaygo's bag rang again.

'God Almighty!' she said, rolling her eyes upwards.

Peter looked at Laurie and smiled.

Jaygo lifted out the telephone and began talking into it. 'Hugo, darling. We're just starting lunch so I can't stay on,' she began. Then: 'Oh, Maisie, it's you. What do you want?' She screwed up her face and pressed the telephone against her ear.

'What? Yes of course I'm staying in London. Yes. The others are too. I told you yesterday. Yes, darling, all at Browns. What? Who? No, I definitely will not do an interview for them. And not for any of his other papers either. They can make it up as usual if they want an exclusive. And no, I don't know about tomorrow yet. It's another day, remember. Call me at about eleven and ask me then. Jesus, yes of course tomorrow at eleven, not in the middle of the bloody night! What? No, I don't know what time we land. Just send a car now and tell it to wait. What? No, I can't ask the pilot. He's on the lavatory. Yes, yes. Love you too, darling. See you tomorrow.'

She flicked the phone off and put it back in her bag.

'It's your fault anyway,' she said, looking at Laurie.

'What is?' he said, rather startled.

'Going on about Jack like that. You've quite upset us.'

'Sod off,' he said playfully. 'I was just letting you know that he's not quite the genial impresario you seem to think he is.'

'I still have to go,' she said. 'And so does Peter.'

'Well, that makes me the lucky one then, doesn't it?' said Laurie. 'Just London for me.'

'Mmm,' said Jaygo. 'We'll see about that.'

'Meaning what?' said Laurie.

'Meaning nothing,' said Jaygo.

'Good,' replied Laurie. 'Don't get any funny ideas. And what time's lunch up here?' he added, looking at his watch. 'I make it about eleven.'

'It's six o'clock,' said Peter, looking at his own watch. 'Or is that London time?'

'He's *so* conservative,' said Jaygo to Laurie. 'You can come and help me get it ready.'

'What is it?' asked Laurie.

'I don't know. Sven chooses it. Reindeer balls in runny sauce I expect.'

Six o'clock in London was six o'clock in Kano too.

The Ngale was enjoying the sunset from the long terrace outside his house.

He was sitting alone in a high-backed cane chair. Down from the terrace in front of him a wide lawn swept away to a row of citrus trees on one side and a swimming pool on the other. A man in a blue T-shirt and matching shorts was quietly sweeping leaves and insects from the surface of the water with a small net on the end of a long bamboo pole.

Beyond the pool, the lawn rose again to a thick thorn hedge. Above the hedge could be seen four strands of razor wire tightly stretched between steel posts and running over white porcelain insulators.

An elderly man wearing a white jacket came through the french windows onto the terrace. He was carrying a silver tray bearing a blue plastic bottle of mineral water and a single glass.

He placed the tray on a small table next to the Ngale who reached over to the bottle and unscrewed the cap just far enough to break the seal before nodding to the man in the jacket. The old man picked up the bottle, removed the cap and poured a glass of water that he passed to the Ngale. The Ngale took a small sip from the glass before putting it down on the table next to him. Then he nodded to the old man who took a step backwards and made a half bow and touched his knee with his hand before turning to go.

Night falls quickly in Kano and, within ten minutes, the sunset had given way to twilight. As it became darker, the Ngale stood up and walked slowly backward and forward along the length of the terrace. The tiles felt cool under his bare feet. He heard

119

a mosquito buzzing near his ear, brushed it away and turned to walk into the house.

The long room behind the terrace was simply furnished with low white chairs that contrasted with the grey polished marble floor. On the wall hung heavy rugs suspended from wooden poles.

He walked over to a long teak table in the centre of the room. At one end was a pile of Jaygo's CDs and a large poster version of the cover picture of her standing in the torque. He picked up one of the CDs and took it to an alcove containing a very large stereo system. With his big hands he carefully took the disc from its case and placed it in the drawer of the CD player on the top of the system. A moment later the room was filled with the haunting sound of the Belle Epoque playing Ladysmith Black Mambazo.

He smiled at the picture of Jaygo on the case as he went back to the table and placed it down next to the poster. He stood looking at the poster and listening to the music.

The old man with the white jacket came quietly into the room and waited until the Ngale looked up before speaking.

'Ngale, sah, Mr Etherington is here.'

The Ngale nodded. 'Thank you, Habu. Show him in and bring me a telephone.'

'Yes, Ngale.' The old man touched his knee and turned to go and the Ngale turned back to the poster.

The Ngale looked up as Habu brought John Etherington into the room. The Englishman towered above the old man by at least two feet. The Ngale himself was six foot but even he scarcely came up to Etherington's shoulder.

The two men shook hands without smiling. It was a handshake of recognition rather than of friendship.

'Good evening, John,' said the Ngale. 'Or perhaps I should say, "Good evening, Your Excellency".'

'John will do,' replied Etherington. 'And you? Now we are in Kano, what do I call you? Ngale?'

'Jack, I think. I trust the rest house is comfortable? Everything you need?'

'It's fine, thank you. You are very hospitable.'

'It's the least I could do. You did very well in Atlanta. Can I offer you a beer?'

'Thank you, it's a very hot evening.'

'Welcome to Africa,' said the Ngale, almost to himself. Then he gestured at Habu who left to collect the beer.

'But I think you have been to Kano before, John?' continued the Ngale.

'Not for quite a few years now. Long before we met, of course.'

'Of course.' The Ngale turned and walked over to the long windows that ran the length of the wall that gave onto the terrace. He looked out beyond the garden over Kano. There was just a thin purple line left of the sunset on the horizon.

'Yes,' he said, still looking out over the city. 'But not all that long ago. Five years, if I remember rightly.'

Etherington looked with some surprise at the back of the Ngale. 'You knew I was here?'

'Oh, yes,' said the Ngale without turning around. 'One of the advantages of being the Ngale is that not much happens in Kano that I don't hear about.'

He turned into the room. 'But where are my manners? Please take a seat.'

John Etherington sat down awkwardly on one of the low white sofas as Habu returned with a tray holding a bottle of Star beer, a tall glass next to a bottle opener and a portable satellite telephone.

Habu placed the tray down on a small table next to Etherington and stood back.

Etherington looked at the bottle and up at Habu.

The Ngale smiled to himself. 'He is waiting for you to open it,' he said.

'I'm sorry?' asked Etherington.

'The beer,' continued the Ngale. 'He is waiting for you to open it. Take it as a compliment. He thinks you are important enough to have enemies. It wouldn't do for Habu to offer you anything that someone had had an opportunity to interfere with, would it?'

Etherington looked rather surprised but leaned across and opened the bottle. Habu immediately stepped forward again and poured the beer into the glass. He then took a step back again, touched his knee with his right hand and turned to go.

'And he touched his knee at you as well,' the Ngale went on. 'That's like a bow for him. You have obviously made a good impression on Habu.'

Etherington smiled politely and took a sip of his beer. 'Star,' he said appreciatively. 'I miss this when I'm in England, you know.'

'Well,' said the Ngale, walking towards the table, 'I always say the British left us two worthwhile things – Star beer and, of course, a sense of fair play.' And then he added more seriously, 'I'm afraid they didn't leave us much else.'

Etherington smiled politely again and put his glass down on the small table next to him.

'I could have saved you the trouble of your last visit to Kano,' went on the Ngale. 'It was never in Kano. If it had been I should have found it by now.'

'Yes,' said Etherington, looking up at him, 'I know that now. But I had to check just as I am sure you did.'

The Ngale shrugged slightly. 'Oh yes. I checked too. I presume you were following the Spanish lead about the priests bringing it north in the very beginning rather than taking it back to Rome?'

Etherington nodded.

'But you forgot something,' continued the Ngale. 'And perhaps I did too. You see, the Kano they would have come to then, even supposing they *had* made it this far north, would have been a very different place to the modern city you see in front of you today. It was a walled city, a fortress against the Tuaregs as much as anything. Not at all the sort of place strangers would have been welcomed, least of all by the Emir.'

'But they did come,' said Etherington. 'Maybe later, but they did come. There are the churches and they are definitely Spanish.'

'Like Santa Maria?' questioned the Ngale. 'Yes, they did build Santa Maria. But you know as well as I do that is no more than a hundred and fifty years old. A good two hundred years after the torque went missing. No, John, if the torque is hidden in Africa it is somewhere much older than Santa Maria.'

'I know,' said Etherington. 'But I wanted to check. And you would have done the same if you had been me. The text is not clear on exactly how long they took to reach Kano.'

'Well, perhaps you are right, John. The text is not clear because it is not complete. Yes, it does suggest Kano. But it also mentions other places the priests visited on the way. Two more places in Spain and, of course, Rome itself. And, John, unless I'm very much mistaken, it was your own grandfather who spent his life getting permission to conduct a series of digs all over Nigeria and still he came up with nothing.'

'But he never dug in Kano,' said Etherington.

'No,' said the Ngale. 'He never did come to Kano to dig. But *my* grandfather did. He took the Spanish churches to bits, brick by brick. Nothing, of course.'

'Well why not Santa Maria then?' asked Etherington.

'Because, my dear John, it's not there. I told you the church is just too recent and technically not even *in* Kano. You've been to the church, it's in the market which is outside the old walls. It was built by local people. There would have been no opportunity to hide the torque, even in the foundations. I tell you, John, it's not in Kano. If it *were*, then one Ngale or another would have found it by now. As I said, nothing much happens in Kano that the Ngale does not hear about.' He smiled and added, 'And that includes the hiding and finding of torques.'

'But weren't you ever tempted to look under Santa Maria yourself?' asked Etherington. 'Just to be sure? It's not used as a church now and I don't see that anyone would object.'

'Perhaps,' said the Ngale. 'But enough Ngales have made themselves look foolish in their people's eyes without me adding to the list. And I think we both know that.'

Etherington nodded and picked up his drink.

'Besides,' said the Ngale, 'in the light of what arrived in Kano earlier this week, I think we can both safely call a halt to this ridiculous searching.'

Etherington looked up at the Ngale with sudden interest.

'Has it come? The new torque?'

'Oh yes. I have it.'

Etherington put his glass down. 'Can I see it?'

'Yes,' said the Ngale. 'I think it is important that you do see it. Come with me.'

The Ngale walked over to a door on the far wall from the garden. He unlocked it and stood aside to let Etherington enter the room beyond.

It was a small room, perhaps only a quarter of the size of the room they had just been in. It was similarly furnished but up against the far wall was a large mahogany desk. Upon it was a flat wooden box about two feet square.

'That's it?' said Etherington. 'Is it safe like that?'

'Yes, John,' said the Ngale politely. 'I can assure you it is perfectly safe. I think you will find that the Ngale's house is immune from burglary.

'Besides,' he went on, taking a small key from his pocket, 'it is of no real use to anyone but me. I am the Ngale.'

He opened the box. The inside was lined with black velvet and the torque lay in the middle. It was eighteen inches across and exactly the same design as the one in the CD picture. The green stones at either end of the torque were the size of large grapes.

'Jack,' said Etherington in admiration, 'it's quite magnificent. May I?' he added, reaching out.

'Of course,' said the Ngale.

Etherington picked up the torque and held it in front of him to admire it.

'My God, it's heavy!' he said. 'Is it solid?'

'Solid but unfortunately not solid gold.'

'And the stones?' went on Etherington. 'Are they real?'

'Real enough.'

'It's amazing. All you described and more. You must be very pleased.'

'Oh, I am.' The Ngale took the torque from Etherington and placed it carefully back in its box.

'You are very privileged,' he continued, closing the box. 'You and I are the only ones who know it is here.'

'But the people who brought it? Your servants?' asked Etherington.

The Ngale smiled as he locked the box. 'Only Habu comes in here and he knows better than to notice anything. Besides, he is not strictly speaking a servant. More of a relative.'

Etherington looked puzzled.

The Ngale walked towards the door. 'Come and finish your beer.' He held the door open for Etherington and locked it again behind them both.

'No, John,' he went on, 'Habu is my grandfather's second cousin. I'm afraid I don't know what that makes him to me.

'I can see that you don't understand,' the Ngale went on as they walked back across the main room. 'The Ngales have large families,' he said by way of explanation. 'They look after their own.'

John Etherington sat down again. 'But the people who made it for you? What about them?'

'Unfortunately they are no longer with us,' the Ngale said absently, moving over to the big table in the middle of the room.

'So, John,' he continued, 'have you decided how you are going to spend your newfound wealth?'

'"Early retirement" I think it's called,' said Etherington. 'I shall probably settle somewhere quiet. Goa perhaps. You were very generous.'

'*Too* generous, do you think?'

Etherington was about to reply when the Ngale put up his hand. 'Four million for a relatively simple job? Is that what you think? Come, come,' he went on. 'You must have wondered why I didn't get someone else, someone local to do it?'

Etherington did not reply.

'The reason is simple, my dear John,' continued the Ngale. 'You see, I might want to use your particular talents again at some stage.'

'You didn't mention that before,' replied Etherington after a short pause.

The Ngale smiled. 'Don't worry. I am not going to ask you to do anything like Atlanta again. You can rest assured that your "Action Man" days are over.'

'More than that, Jack. My British days are over too.'

'Possibly,' said the Ngale thoughtfully, 'but you worked in your Foreign Office for a number of years. You know how things are conducted. And you are a clever man too. An educated man. Someone with, how shall I say it? Someone with perspective.'

The Ngale walked over to the window again before turning around into the room again.

'I have plans, John. You could fit into them.'

Etherington did not respond and so the Ngale continued, 'Tell me, do you know the French word *matériel*?'

Etherington looked up surprised. '*Matériel*,' he said. 'Of course. It's a warfare term – it means munitions, weaponry. Literally, I think, the "materials" for conducting war. But surely you're not contemplating a war, are you?'

The Ngale laughed. 'No, of course not. But bear with me for a moment. Tell me what you need in a war apart from *matériel*?'

Etherington thought for a moment. 'An army to use it, I suppose. But what's your point?'

'Exactly,' said the Ngale. 'One is no good without the other.' He held his hands apart in front of him and then clenched them together. 'With both you have a "defence capability". A prerequisite of a nation state.'

'A state? What state?'

'And a state needs other things,' went on the Ngale. 'A strong government and a sense of national identity, wouldn't you say?'

Etherington looked puzzled.

'So,' continued the Ngale, 'put those things together and what do you have?'

'But Jack, this is Nigeria. I don't understand what you are saying.'

'Nigeria? Ah, "Nigeria". Where is that then?' The Ngale made the shape of a square in front of him. 'It is a box drawn somewhere in Africa by the British. A convenience. Just boarders drawn up in London.

'Oh, it's a big country, I'll grant you that,' continued the Ngale putting his hands down. 'Very wealthy even. I'll grant you that too. But it is not *one* country, is it? The Ibo in the East, the Yoruba in the South and the Hausa up here in the North. That's three groups at least who want nothing more than to be in their *own* country.

'Look,' he said, 'your Nigeria nearly split apart in the Civil War back in the sixties. Next time it will. In five years? Ten perhaps. Not longer than that, I think. Read your history, John. Read your history.'

'I've seen that theory,' said Etherington. 'But the groups you mention, Ibos, Yorubas, Hausas. They are big players.'

'And I'm not a big player? Is that what you mean? Jack Ngale and his *matériel* against the rest? No, of course not. I'm not a fool. But look what happened in the Saudi peninsula after the First World War. The people there split up into separate countries as soon as they could. The Saudis took the lion's share. Oman and Kuwait are fair-sized states too. But there are others. Abu Dhabi. The UAE. They are their own countries and they have their own international voice. And when Nigeria breaks up, we shall have ours.'

'Hang on, Jack,' said Etherington. 'They had oil.'

The Ngale wagged his finger. 'Not then, they didn't,' he said. 'Not to start with. And I'm going to put things in place here that will be as good for us as oil was for them.' The Ngale clenched his hands together again. 'A state in waiting. A Ngale in waiting. A people in waiting.'

Etherington did not speak.

'What am I to say to my people when the federation breaks up then?' said the Ngale. 'That I am *not* the Ngale? That five hundred years of history simply do not matter? That we suddenly should become Hausa? Yoruba?

'I hardly think so. This is *my* country. Much of what I want is already in place. I can tell you that Africa will be a very different place in five years' time to today. New states. New wealth. New men. Things move fast. History accelerates. Take the Far East for instance. Malaysia, Indonesia, Singapore – Japan even. From nothing to everything in fifty years. Yes. But they are all collapsing like skittles now. They had it there in their hand and they let it go. Tiger economies? Paper tigers, more like.'

The Ngale was becoming excited and banged his large hands

together. 'It will be different here. We are African. The next century belongs to us.'

Etherington looked down at his feet without answering straight away. He reached for his glass and took a sip before speaking.

'Jack,' he began, 'Jack, my friend, and I hope I can call you that. You and I have worked together on and off for nearly ten years. I think I have been useful to you. I have opened many doors for you. I have introduced you to trading partners both in America and the New Europe. You have prospered, I have no doubt, and you have paid me well.

'The business in Atlanta? Well, frankly you had to use me. You wanted a reliable explosion and a reliable person. And for that you knew you needed Semtex Seven and me. Local people could not have got the Seven and you don't know anyone there you can trust as well as me. And in exchange you paid me exceptionally well and have guaranteed that I won't be prosecuted. But it was a straight business deal for me just like all the others we have done. Now, you may well have other interests. Politics. This "state" you talk about. But I am not a politician. I am a businessman. My job at the Foreign Office facilitated that. But I have left the Foreign Office now, for which I offer you hearty thanks. So now I am free to follow up other business interests that I couldn't before. If I had a use to you it was because I worked for the British Foreign Service. That is over now and you knew that the moment I agreed to do Atlanta.

'I'm sure you and I will do business from time to time in the future but it will be new business. I wish you well in what you want to do but I do not really think I have a role to play.'

'Oh, John, John,' began the Ngale, 'you underestimate yourself. And you underestimate your history. Africa has been running like a spine through your family since the first John Etherington dealt with my forefathers on the beaches of Apapa Bay. Africa is in your blood as much as it is in my skin. Stay in Kano for a few weeks. Be my guest. Reconsider.'

The Ngale stood up and reached for the satellite telephone on the table. 'Here, take one of these. Call me any time.'

Etherington took the telephone. 'A mobile?'

'Yes. You will still find our land lines are not quite up to your European standards but that will work anywhere. It uses ordinary batteries if you need a recharge. If there aren't any batteries at the house, send your driver to Sabon Gari. They will have them there.'

'Sabon Gari?'

'Yes. The big market. I thought you knew it. Near the church of Santa Maria.'

'Oh yes, I do know it. I thought it was just called the Santa Maria market.'

The Ngale smiled. 'Ring me,' he said.

'Thank you,' said Etherington standing up. 'Perhaps I will.' He turned to go. 'By the way,' he added, 'what do you want me to do with the rest of the Semtex Seven? I have put it in the freezer at the house for safe keeping and it should last for about six months if you can find a use for it. After that it will become unstable but still just about usable if you are careful.'

The Ngale looked slightly disconcerted. 'Only six months? You didn't tell me that.'

'Well,' said Etherington, noting his expression, 'it has twenty percent of conventional explosive in it to make it behave the way it does. I've put the detonator in the freezer too so it doesn't get lost. I am sure you know what to do. Just push the ends of the cable into the timer, switch it on and set the timer.'

'Is that all?' said the Ngale. 'Is that enough?'

'It was enough for Atlanta. If you want to make proper stun grenades you'll need to ask someone else. I don't know enough about them.'

Etherington held up the phone. 'Just ring me if you don't know anyone. I can find someone for you.'

Back on the Lear Jet, Jaygo was gathering up the plates after lunch.

Laurie was leaning back in his seat, eyes closed and head lolling, his mouth open.

Peter was finishing his glass of wine.

'Come on,' said Jaygo. 'Make yourself useful, Wilson. You can bring the empties.'

Peter stood up to collect the glasses and followed Jaygo through to the kitchen.

She put the tray down and began scraping the leftovers into a cardboard box next to the small sink.

'You see,' she said. 'Not really so glam, is it? You buy your own plane and choose your own food but you just can't get decent kitchen staff.'

'I should have thought that would make a nice little job for Hugo Says,' said Peter.

She smiled at him. 'That's what I thought,' she said, 'but lately he's been following Laurie's liquid-lunch theory and generally falls asleep when it comes to the clearing-away stage.'

She took the glasses from Peter, making sure they brushed hands as she did so. She looked up and smiled again and put the glasses away in another cardboard box by the sink.

'No actual washing up then?' said Peter.

'I draw the line at some things,' she said, closing the lid of the box. 'Do you think I was rude to Maisie?' she added.

'Who?'

'Maisie. My secretary. The one who rang before lunch.'

Peter shrugged. 'Probably. But I think she got off more lightly than Hugo.'

Before she could answer, the sound of the telephone ringing came from the cabin again.

'Do you want me to answer it for you?' asked Peter.

'No,' said Jaygo. 'Let it ring. It'll only be Hugo again. Or Maisie.'

The telephone continued to ring.

'Or Jack,' said Peter quietly.

She looked at her watch. 'Yes,' she said. 'Or Jack. In which case, if he has something important to say, he can always ring again, can't he?'

The telephone stopped ringing and Jaygo shrugged. 'See? It can't have been all that important. Anyway, coffee time. Shall I make some for Laurie too?'

'No,' said Peter, looking over his shoulder. 'Let him sleep.'

Jaygo began to make the coffee. 'I was right to come and see you, wasn't I?' she said.

'What about?'

'Jack. This Nigeria thing.'

'Well, you know a whole lot more than you did before and that's for sure,' said Peter.

'And not all of it's good, is it?'

'Nope,' said Peter. 'But you always knew Jack wasn't an angel. Still, it's only a one-off. And you don't really have to spend more than a few days there, do you? I think we can get away with you going out there, walking you around a bit and then coming home.'

'Home?' she said, putting her head on one side. 'That sounds nice.'

'Home as in UK. Not home as in home and dry,' he said.

'Well, at least you know what I mean,' she smiled.

Peter blew his cheeks out slightly. 'I'm not sure that I do,' he said. 'I'm not sure that I ever did.'

'Not even before? Before I went to America?'

'No,' he said. 'I don't think even then. I mean there we were one day, planning ahead, and the next you were packing up to go. What sort of "home" is that? Frankly, you must have known what you were going to do for ages before you got around to telling me.'

'Not really. A chance came. I took it. And, anyway, I don't know why we are talking about that now.'

'You raised it.'

'Yes,' she said slightly awkwardly. 'I did. And I get the impression because of that I don't have any right to come back after all this time and ask you for help.'

'I don't know,' he shrugged. 'You came and asked anyway. And, more fool me, I seem to have agreed. But I really mean it when I say it's a one-off. Just Nigeria. No more.'

'Then back to our own little worlds afterwards?' she said. 'Not speaking any more. Not even Christmas cards?'

Peter held his hands palm upwards. 'For Christ's sake, Jay. You've got one world and I've got another. Yes, it's lovely to see you, God knows. And it probably always will be. But that didn't get me very far the first time around and there's no saying it ever would. I don't need all that again. I don't.'

'Look,' she began, 'I'm not asking you to "go round again" or anything. We haven't seen each other properly for simply ages but I think you know as well as I do neither of us has ever met anyone remotely comparable. There. Said it.'

'No,' he said quietly, 'I haven't anyway. But, for whatever reason, it didn't work out last time and it wouldn't again. Another chance might come along and you'd be off again.'

'Do you really think so?'

'Don't you?'

'I might have learnt my lesson,' she said.

He smiled at her. 'Jay, there are a lot of chances left in the sea for someone like you. And besides, it's not just "us" any more. We're both supposed to be nicely paired off.'

Jaygo picked up her two cardboard boxes and put them in a cupboard under the sink.

'Hugo?' she said standing up again. 'Hugo's a businessman. He likes money. And,' she added smiling, 'he likes to goose the goose that lays the golden egg.'

Peter laughed. 'Well, that too.'

'He thinks he's a bit of a Paganini there,' she said.

'And?'

'He's more of a Mantovani on a slipping cassette.'

Peter laughed again.

'You see,' she said. 'I can still make you laugh. Can Aurelia do that?'

'Maybe,' said Peter. 'Given a bit of time. I've only known her for five years.'

She smiled at him.

'I shouldn't knock Hugo,' she said. 'If it wasn't for him the Belle Epoque would never have got going on the money scene. We were doing OK-ish before he came along but you have to know all about contracts and tours and the other two are just musicians.'

Peter looked a little puzzled.

'You see,' she went on, 'there are only two sorts of people in music today. Those in it for the money and those in it for the music and Hugo's very much the first type. He makes us the money and we make him the music.'

'But he's a pretty good violinist. I've heard him play.'

'He practises a lot. Ask Daniel.'

'The viola man?'

'Yes. You know, it's funny, but most violists only take it up because they know they won't ever make first violin but Daniel really likes the viola. Hardly any decent music for it but he just likes it. I think that makes him a bit special,' she continued. 'If it wasn't for the Belle, Daniel would just be a school teacher but I don't think he'd notice the difference. He once told me the only thing he really liked about being in the Belle was that he got to play a Strad.'

'But *you'd* notice if the money wasn't there, wouldn't you?' Peter said. 'You may have to scrape the odd plate while Mantovani slumbers but at least you get your own plane to do it in.'

'I suppose so. The money's all right but being recognised every-where you go isn't so much fun.'

'Look, Jay. I saw you walk into the restaurant the other night. You loved it.'

'Well, that was work,' she said. 'But most places I go, I have to take a plain-clothes type with a .45 under his arm in case someone wants to get famous.'

Peter pursed his lips. 'I read that about you,' he said. 'I thought it was just publicity.'

'That's what John Lennon's friends thought.'

131

'Oh come off it. You're pretty well known but hardly a John Lennon.'

'I'm serious,' she said. 'Go and get my bag and I'll show you.'

Peter fetched the bag. 'Your own .45?' he said.

'Not quite,' she said, taking out the satellite telephone. 'See? One phone.'

She looked up and gave a tight smile. 'And for my next trick,' she said, reaching into the bag again. 'Another telephone.' She looked up and placed the second handset next to the first. 'Only this one isn't a phone. Look.'

She picked the second one up and passed it to him.

He did not take it. 'What is it then?' he asked.

'Watch.' She pressed the side of the handset and a shutter clicked open to reveal a red trigger. 'Not quite your actual .45,' she said, 'but it'll fire four shots. Quite enough for a ten-foot phone call.'

'Christ, Jaygo! Is that thing loaded?'

'Probably. Hugo said I should carry it all the time in case one of the stalkers gets nasty.'

She clicked the compartment shut again. 'Off now,' she said. 'Oh yes, and there's a Mace spray in the bag too if you want to see that. Both thoughtful presents from Hugo in the same week he bought me the ring.'

Peter leant back against the counter. 'Shit, Jay. I'm not sure I know what to say.'

She picked both handsets up and put them back into the bag. 'Well, you don't have to say anything, do you? After all, it's "another world", isn't it? Nothing to do with anyone you might happen to know.'

Peter looked at her before speaking. 'Do you know how to use it?' he asked.

'Oh yes,' she went on, putting the bag on the floor by her feet. 'It comes with half a day's training. You have to remember to shut your eyes and mouth before using it. Or perhaps that's the Mace spray. And kicking people in the balls is another good trick – only I knew that one before.' She looked at him without smiling.

He was about to say something when the telephone rang again.

She let it ring three times before reaching down into the bag. 'I hope I pick the right one,' she said.

Jaygo took out the telephone and put it to her ear.

'Jack! Hi! What a nice surprise. Yes, all fine this end. How are things with you?'

She looked at Peter and raised her eyes to the ceiling and made a winding motion with her free hand.

'Yup. Fine,' she went on. 'Peter wasn't anywhere near. We'll all meet up in Kano later in the week. He said he was going out anyway so I've persuaded him to fly with me on my plane which makes everything easier. And don't fix me up with a hotel or anything because Pete says I can stay at his place which I'd much prefer.'

Peter was waving his hands at her. 'No, no,' he mouthed.

She stuck her tongue out at him and spoke into the telephone again.

'Oh yes, and another thing, Jack. I ran into Laurie Miller in Atlanta too. You remember him, little fat chap who went on to ITV. Yes. Well, he's a big fat chap now and quite an important free-lancer and he says he can get us into the London glossies if I give him an exclusive on the launch. That'd be fabulous, wouldn't it? Then we can push in the UK too. OK?'

She leant forwards slightly at Peter and grimaced.

'What's that?' she said into the telephone. 'Not a good idea? Why not? No, I didn't know you didn't like him. He's all right. Really. Yes, yes. Of course you get to vet everything. No, I can't say no to him now because he's cancelled some Canadian thing just to come with me. It's really no problem, Jack. It's me he's going to write about. Yes. He'll stay with us the whole time. No, no wandering off on his own. I'm sure you'll get on fine. Really. Good. Super. Yes, of course I'll call you again when we get to London. OK. Byeee.'

She shut the telephone off and put it down without looking at Peter.

'Jaygo,' he said angrily, 'what the hell was that about? I haven't agreed to any of that. Flying out with you? You staying with me? A total no-no. Yes, I'll go to Jack with you and help if I can but that's it. And as for that Laurie business, you must be off your rocker. Didn't you listen to a single thing he was saying back there? Are you out of your tiny mind or what? Laurie's not going to go within a million miles of Jack, is he?'

Jaygo put the phone in the bag at her feet.

'You heard Laurie,' she said. 'He thinks that Jack probably didn't know about him in Belfast and so that's not a problem. You heard him say that if Jack *had* known about him he would have done something and not just killed his friend. And anyway, *you* said that *you* didn't believe him anyway so I don't know why you're getting so funny about it.'

'I'm not getting funny about it at all,' said Peter. 'Laurie is quite capable of making up his own mind about things without any help from you. And you can take it from me that it won't include a desire to go and see Jack Ngale.'

'Of course he's capable of making up his own mind,' she said. 'But you've got to admit it's a good idea for you to come to Jack with me. *And* Laurie would get a better chance to to see things for himself first hand. You two just need a little push, that's all.'

'Jesus! Little push?' said Peter. 'And I wonder who that suits then? Me? No. Laurie? No. Miss Jocasta Manhattan? Well, yes. She gets me to help her keep Jack at bay while Laurie gets her some nice coverage. Anyone else? Well, not exactly. So there we have it. All for one and one for one.'

'Why don't you sit down and shut up then, Peter? As you say, Laurie's quite capable of making up his own mind and you're going to Kano anyway, so you don't have to do much more than chink glasses with Jack, if that's all you're up to.'

Peter shook his head at her before going to sit down.

Laurie was waking up. 'Must have dozed off. The altitude, I expect.'

'Something like that,' said Peter.

The two sat without talking until Jaygo came in a few minutes later with a cafetière of coffee.

'Black, I'm afraid,' she announced. 'Unless you want to wait until Sven gets back with the milk.'

'Fine by me,' said Laurie. 'Peter?'

'I'll wait for Sven.'

'Shouldn't be more than a few minutes,' said Jaygo, pouring three black coffees.

'So, Mr Bernstein,' she went on, 'when are we going to see your latest book?'

'I'm not really sure,' said Laurie. 'I've got most of what I want, I think. A couple of leads to follow up in London and the typing time. Spring maybe.'

'Do you think Jack knows anything about it at all?' asked Jaygo innocently.

'Hell, no,' said Laurie. 'It's not even coming out under my own name. I've learnt something since Belfast.'

'Well, if that's the case,' said Jaygo carefully, 'why not come to Kano with me and Pete and see things for yourself?'

Peter shut his eyes and put his head back.

'It could work out very well,' Jaygo went on before Laurie could

134

answer. 'You could see things first hand. And maybe Peter could take you out to where the poppies grow. You could take loads of photos to back your story up.'

Peter opened his eyes and looked at Laurie.

'Thanks, Jay. But no thanks,' said Laurie. 'I've got my head in the lion's mouth as it is. Telling him his breath smells would be a stunt too far.'

'It would be a better book for it though, wouldn't it?' she said. 'You could come as Press for me. Do a feature on the visit. I'd give you an exclusive. Two birds.'

Laurie considered for a minute. 'Exclusive with Jocasta Manhattan? I'm afraid I've only got to surf the web to get one of those, haven't I? Anyway there's something I have to do in London that won't wait.'

'Such as what?' asked Jaygo, looking slightly peeved.

'Such as another Jack thing,' replied Laurie. 'Before the bomb, a guy I know in Atlanta told me Jack's getting a warehouse in London to bring in stuff for processing. He said it's not fully set up yet. I might be able to get a look at it before it's finished.'

'What, go in with a hard hat and a plank on your shoulder?' asked Jaygo.

'Not quite,' said Laurie patiently. 'But if his other places are anything to go by, when it's finished it'll be like Fort Knox. I want to get some pictures before then if it's at all possible.'

'There you are then,' said Jaygo. 'You do need pictures.'

'If you'll let me finish,' said Laurie, slightly irritated.

Jaygo sat back.

'Brent, this American, says Jack's setting up a processing plant under the guise of an importing business. It's already being used as a legit warehouse to bring in stuff from Nigeria and has been going for a couple of years. It's an ordinary warehouse on an ordinary industrial estate but Brent says that's exactly what happened in New York when Jack set up there.'

'How does your friend Brent know all this?' asked Peter.

'Because he uses the telephone,' said Laurie patiently. 'Just like you.'

Peter picked up his coffee. 'Is there really no milk?' he asked. 'We had some before.'

Jaygo shrugged. 'I threw away what we didn't use,' she said, 'and I couldn't find any more. Black's better for you anyway.'

Peter stood up and walked towards the kitchen. 'I'll go and look.'

Jaygo picked up a magazine and flicked through it while Laurie sat back and closed his eyes again.

Peter returned a couple of minutes later with a handful of small milk portions.

He put them on the table without saying anything.

Jaygo put her magazine aside and took a milk. 'Resourceful,' she said. 'Just what we need for a trip to Africa. A knowledgeable guide for my first trip to the dark continent.'

'It wasn't very difficult,' said Peter. 'They were in the cupboard in a box marked "Milk".

'Anyway,' he went on, 'you must have been to Africa before.'

'Actually, no,' said Jaygo.

'Not even South Africa?' said Peter, rather surprised.

'Especially not there,' she said. 'Most self-respecting musicians wouldn't go there during apartheid and now they can't afford us.'

'I think Dusty Springfield went there,' said Laurie helpfully. 'I quite liked her.'

'I saw her in Harrods,' said Peter. 'Very small. But really, Jay, I should have thought you must have been at least once.'

'I told you no,' she said. 'And from what you tell me, I'm not going to like it all that much so I don't plan to make it a regular thing.'

'I didn't say you wouldn't like it. I just said I didn't think you knew much about it,' said Peter.

'Well you'd better give me a reading list before we go then, hadn't you?' said Jaygo, pushing her magazine aside.

'You once told me there weren't any good books about Africa,' said Laurie.

'Not quite,' said Peter. 'I said it was the stories that mattered and you didn't need books for them.'

'Story list then,' said Jaygo, 'that might suit me better. Short attention-span and all that.'

'People in England don't understand about the stories,' said Peter. 'They're not stories about what has happened but about how things are the way they are. Answers to questions really. I mean, here we are discussing Jack Ngale. I've been trying to tell you how he's different from us because he's African, Ngalese, and nothing to do with him being brutal and ruthless to boot.'

'African. Ngalese. The next thing you'll be telling me is he's different because he's black.'

'No,' said Peter. 'The fact that he's black is neither here nor there. He's different because he's African. And trying to explain that without a story is like trying to describe an elephant without moving your hands.'

'That's easy,' said Jaygo. 'Long thing at the front for picking up buns and one foot at each corner for making umbrella stands.'

Laurie laughed. 'That's good,' he said. 'Could you do Nuclear Physics for me? I've always wanted to know about that.'

Jaygo smiled towards Peter. 'His turn.'

'I don't know about that,' he said. 'But I could tell you one about Jack.'

'Well, I think we're all sitting comfortably,' said Jaygo, 'so you'd better begin. And you in the back row, Miller,' she added, 'stop playing with yourself.'

'OK,' began Peter, 'but like a lot of these stories, it starts off by being about something else. In this case, a man called Mungo Park.'

'On the Northern Line?' asked Jaygo.

'He was a Scottish doctor,' began Peter again, ignoring her. 'God knows why he got it into his head to leave Peebles and head off up the Niger River but he did. I suppose we are talking 1800 or thereabouts.

'The first thing that happened is that about half his people caught malaria and died. Park also caught malaria and because he didn't die he took it as a good omen and decided to press on. He must have taken a wrong turning because his particular branch of the Niger soon gave out to swamp and they had to go on by foot. Now, there are perfectly good routes through the forest but apparently Park never found them and had to pretty much hack his way through step by step.'

'Didn't he have guides?' asked Jaygo. 'Coolies?'

'No,' said Peter, 'the guides, as you call them, were people he had recruited from where he landed, mainly fishermen, and had never been up country. They knew as little of forest paths as he did. So, after about a month, they were all well and truly lost. He knew he was heading north but that was about all.

'That part of Africa was pretty heavily populated then but the locals kept well out of the way of the strange people who were trying to cut a track through their territory.

'Park didn't go very fast and never went to the left or right and so they could keep an eye on him quite easily I don't know the names of the areas he went through but they must have belonged to very peaceable people because nobody hindered him and he just went slowly further and further north. I've read his journal and he was convinced he was in some vast primitive wilderness. There were no roads and no towns. If he came across villages they were always abandoned to his eyes. What happened, of course, is that people simply moved out of the way while he went through and then moved back afterwards.

'I suppose people were a bit frightened of him initially because slavery was still about and they might have thought he was on some kind of people hunt. However, one of the chiefs whose land he passed through, thought he should, perhaps out of courtesy, make some sort of contact. The details of what happened next are a bit uncertain, because Park's journal doesn't tally with the version the locals tell, but it seems they sent a delegation of about ten men or so, all dressed up in tribal ceremonial clothes and painted accordingly.

'Park had never seen anything like it. He claims he met them in a clearing and they claim he met them by a river but, whatever the truth, the two groups suddenly came face to face with about fifty feet between them.

'Neither side knew what to do and apparently they just stood there looking at each other for about ten minutes. Then the delegation began to move towards Park's group.

'Park says they charged at him and he thought he was being attacked. There was only Park and about seven others by this stage but one of them had a rifle ready for hunting and so he dropped to one knee and fired in true British style at the approaching delegation. One of them was hit and went down. The delegation didn't understand what had happened and kept coming and so the man fired again and another delegate went down.

'The Africans suddenly saw what was happening and were naturally terrified. They turned and ran back into the forest, taking the wounded men with them. Park thought he would be attacked again and retreated back down the path he had cut and made a fortified camp.

'Well, absolutely nothing happened for three days. Eventually Park decided he had "won" whatever sort of skirmish he thought he had had. He felt he should move on again in the direction he had been heading.

'The local chief decided that discretion was the better part of valour and kept well out of the way until Park and his men had passed out of their territory. The chief may well have sent word ahead because Park does not report seeing anyone at all after that.

'Two more of Park's expedition fell ill and died and the survivors thought they should call it a day and head back. But Park wanted to go on because he didn't feel he had actually achieved anything thus far. He told his men that they had to go forward and that it wouldn't be long before they broke through to easier country and then they could claim to have crossed the forest belt. He said if they did that it would, in the eyes of the people at home, be a significant achievement.

'His people were right of course and he was wrong. They had only gone about a quarter of the way into the forest but they had no way of knowing that. If they *had* gone on I am sure they would have all died eventually and no one would have ever heard of them again. There were dozens of expeditions like his from Europe and there is no reason to think Park's was special in any way. We only know about him because his journal survived.

'So,' said Peter finishing his coffee, 'the group eventually persuaded Park and they turned back. Park's disappointment comes through very clearly in his journal and he really *was* convinced they had been about to make some sort of breakthrough and he blames the other members of the expedition for his failure.'

'On the contrary,' said Jaygo. 'They seem very sensible to me. What was the point in hacking a way on only to finish further up the back of beyond than they already were?'

'That's just the point though,' said Peter. 'They weren't in the back of beyond at all. From the day they had left the coast they were going through country that had been inhabited for thousands of years. Longer than most of Europe. OK, so the people who lived there had never built any cities or roads but they had never needed to. They didn't even need to have farms. The forest was all they needed but their society was just as complicated as Park's ever was. There were territories, hierarchies, alliances and disputes just like anywhere else. It was only because Park couldn't *see* anything he could relate to that he thought he was in unexplored jungle.'

'Really!' exclaimed Jaygo. 'You make it sound like something from *The Boy's Own Paper*. "White explorer meets the Noble Savage".'

'Shut up, Jay,' said Laurie. 'Let him finish.'

'But he hadn't met them, had he?' said Peter. 'When they approached him, he just shot at them. It wasn't exploration at all. It was bungling.'

Peter sat back.

139

'Is that it?' asked Jaygo. 'I thought this was going to be a story with a point.'

'I haven't finished,' said Peter.

'Get on with it,' said Jaygo. 'You're well past your six minutes, you know. And that boy Miller at the back of the class will be up to his old tricks unless you get a move on.'

'Look at it from the Africans' point of view,' went on Peter. 'Here was this strange group of people who seemed to have arrived from nowhere and who had started to make a new path through the forest when there were perfectly good paths already. They had a way of killing animals without catching them first. Not only that, but they ate whatever they caught without regard to the fact that some animals were much better to eat than others. Moreover, the strange people travelled without women or children and there didn't seem to be any point to what they were doing.

'Well, as they went south again, Mungo again passed through the area belonging to the chief who had sent the delegation. The chief thought he should prepare a more elaborate reception this time to show the visitors who he was and what his people were like.

'The chief had his men enlarge the clearing by the river to about four hundred yards square. He set up a wooden throne for himself in the middle and surrounded himself with about a thousand of his army and sent others to follow about a mile behind Park with the aim of completely surrounding Park and his people when they reached the clearing so they could have a proper meeting.

'Park must have been terrified. He was down to four men by this time and suddenly he was confronted by more people than he had ever seen since he arrived in Africa. Shooting his way out this time was clearly out of the question and, to give him credit, he didn't try. They put down on the ground everything they were still carrying, guns included and put their arms up in the air.

'This meant nothing to the chief. Forget universal sign language, the chief simply did not know what Park was doing. If he was trying to communicate, what was he saying?

'Nothing happened for about five minutes. Park and his men eventually put their arms down but still didn't pick their things up. Eventually the chief stood up from his throne and stepped up to about twenty yards from Park's group and began to speak. Park naturally didn't know what was being said and so just stood there.

'The chief finished his little speech and went back to sit on his throne. Perhaps he was expecting a response of some kind but, when none came, he moved on to the next part of the demonstration he had planned.

'He waved his right arm in the air and four of his entourage stepped forwards and stood between Park and the chief's throne. Still no response from Park. The chief waved his arm again and another group of four men came and knelt down in front of the first lot. The chief waved his arm again and the first four produced long machetes and swiped off the heads of the four men kneeling in front of them. Not all at once but one at a time and each with a single swing. No one else in the clearing moved or made a sound.

'Then the chief stood up and approached Mungo Park again to make another speech, completely ignoring the four dead men. When he had finished he went to sit down again. The people either side of him picked up the throne with the chief on it and marched away. When they had left the clearing, the rest of the army simply turned and melted into the surrounding forest.

'Mungo Park and his men were left alone in the clearing with the four headless corpses.'

Peter looked first at Laurie and then at Jaygo. 'End of story,' he said.

'That's a perfectly disgusting story,' said Jaygo. 'I liked mine about the elephant much better.'

Peter shrugged.

'Wait on,' said Laurie. 'That can't be the end. What happened next?'

Peter shrugged again. 'It is the end of the story. Park and his men eventually continued south. He was drowned later but one of his men made it home with the journal. But that's by the bye. What matters to the story is what happened in the clearing.'

'Well, I don't see the point of it,' said Jaygo. 'I thought you were going to come out with a pithy moral or something.'

'It's an African story,' said Peter. 'It doesn't need a moral.'

'Well, I'm not African,' said Jaygo. 'I don't see the point.'

Peter looked inquiringly at Laurie.

'Sorry, old man,' said Laurie, 'I'm afraid I don't see it either. The chief was clearly making some sort of statement to your man but I don't see what.'

'OK then,' said Peter. 'The chief was saying "I don't know who you are or where you come from but I live here. This is my country and I am important. These are my people and they do what I say."'

'I knew that,' said Jaygo. 'I just thought there would be more to it.'

She picked up the magazine 'And I still think it's a disgusting story. You said you were going to tell us about Jack and I don't see what chopping off people's heads has got to do with him.'

'Well, you'd better wake your ideas up then, hadn't you?' said Peter, clearly irritated. 'You're going out to visit Jack this week. On his patch. Where he is important. You have no idea what he wants or what sort of man he is. Wise up.'

'I know exactly what he wants,' said Jaygo, equally sharply. 'He is going to make a lot of money, just like me. I think you are the one who has to wise up.'

'I told you it's not the money,' rounded Peter. 'A million or two is small change for him. He doesn't get out of bed for a million pounds. The torque. The picture of you. There has to be a whole lot more to it than just money.'

'What then?' she asked crossly.

Peter leaned back and put his hands behind his neck before speaking again. 'I don't know. Perhaps *you*.'

'Me?' said Jaygo, shocked. 'You think he wants me?'

'Probably not in the way you mean,' said Peter. 'But he wants you there. You're reasonably famous. Perhaps he wants to be seen with you. Friend of the stars and all that. And you look a bit like a lion and so all to the better. You suit the picture.'

'What picture?' said Laurie.

'The one on the CD,' said Peter. 'Have you got one to show Laurie in your bag, Jay?'

'No,' said Jaygo quietly. 'I haven't. It's just a silly painting of me standing like a tart in a gold ring.'

'Gold ring?' frowned Laurie.

'I told you it wasn't just a "gold ring",' said Peter.

'All right then,' she said. 'A gold torque with green ping-pong balls at either end.'

'*The* gold torque?' asked Laurie. 'The Idona Zaki?'

'Yes,' said Jaygo. 'Something like that. Don't tell me you've actually heard of it?'

'Of course I have,' said Laurie. 'You don't have to do much backgrounding on Jack before you come across it. I mean he's not actually *found* it, has he?'

Peter smiled. 'Not as far as I know.'

'You told me it was lost,' said Jaygo. 'That no one knew where it was.'

'I did,' said Peter. 'And I also said I didn't know what Jack was up to. Maybe he hasn't found it but I can tell you it's no mistake it's in the picture.'

'It would be quite a coup if he *had* found it,' said Laurie thoughtfully. 'I know he's a pretty popular guy out there as it is. With the Idona Zaki he'd be pretty much unstoppable.'

'What would he do with it anyway?' asked Jaygo. 'Wear it to go shopping?'

'What's it like in the picture?' asked Laurie.

Jaygo shrugged. 'Big.'

'He could have had another one made,' said Laurie. 'To look like the original.'

'I don't think he'd do that, 'said Peter. 'He couldn't risk someone finding the original one later.'

'Oh, for God's sake,' said Jaygo. 'It's just a picture on a CD cover. Stop going on about it. A promo thing. If it was all that important, Jack would have said so and he's never even mentioned it. Besides, if you're so fascinated by it, Laurie, that's another good reason for you to come with us. See for yourself if he's got the bloody thing.'

Laurie thought for a while.

'Yes,' she continued. 'The eyes of the silly lion. Only it's lost and Mr Africa here says there aren't any lions in Nigeria anyway.'

'But she's right, Laurie,' said Peter. 'Perhaps you should come out for yourself and see what Jack's up to.'

'No way,' said Laurie finally.

He looked at his watch.

'I've got some things to set up,' he said. 'Can I borrow your magic phone?'

'Be my guest,' said Jaygo, reaching into her bag and passing him the telephone. 'There's a cabin beyond the kitchen if you want to be private.'

'Thanks,' said Laurie. 'I might just do that. Can I take a beer while I'm at it?'

She waved her hand. 'Help yourself.'

'Jay?' said Peter when Laurie had gone. 'Can I ask you something?'

She looked up from her magazine.

'Sorry,' she said. 'I'm already engaged.'

'Seriously.'

'Oh dear,' she said, putting the magazine down. 'What does "seriously" mean?'

Peter thought for a moment before speaking. 'It's about Jack,' he began. 'I mean, Laurie and I have both given you reasons not to see him but you still want to go ahead. Has he got something over you we don't know about? If it's just the record then you don't really need me along and you certainly don't need Laurie. You're not taking the Belle Epoque with you which is pretty odd. And you've got your own Press people but apparently they're not going either. When you came to Cambridge there were at least a dozen people in tow and this CD launch has to be bigger than that, so why were you going by yourself?'

'I'm not going by myself. You're coming with me now.'

'I might have said no.'

'I didn't think you would say no. I was counting on you.'

'But if I had said no?'

'Then I probably wouldn't go,' she said. 'In which case there'd be all shit to pay because there's a contract and I signed it. I agreed to go.'

'Not the Belle Epoque and everyone else?'

'That's right.'

'You mean it's in the contract that they don't go? That's crazy.'

'Yes. But I'm a crazy woman, aren't I? You're always saying so.'

'Look,' said Peter. 'Just what is going on? What haven't you told me?'

'It's just the money,' she said.

'No it isn't, Jaygo. Tell me.'

She looked at him for a few moments before replying.

'It wasn't anything to start with,' she began. 'He rang me up and asked me for a sort of holiday really. He said why not come to Kano because I'd never been. He said I'd really like it there and he was going to show me everything and there would be lots of parties and so on.

'Well, I was pretty fed up with Hugo that particular day for some reason so I told Hugo I was going just to piss him off. I knew the CD was coming out a couple of days after the end of the States tour so I thought it would be a nice break and a chance to get away from everything. Then Jack said you would be there at the same time so we could probably all meet up for dinner or something.

'I didn't think any more about it when a whacking great contract arrived by fax for me to sign. It was like a proper tour contract with dates for appearances, photo shoots, interviews and all that garbage. I rang him up to ask what was going on. I said I thought it was just a couple of parties and a chance to look around.

'He wasn't there that day so I had to leave a message with some snotty woman. Four hours later he was on the phone, as sweet as ever, and said sending the contract had been a mistake and that it had been sent without his approval by the record people but why didn't I sign it anyway to keep them quiet and fax it back to him?'

'And did you?' asked Peter.

'No. I showed the fax to Hugo and he practically hit the roof. He was pissed off enough about how the CD was being released by Jack's company and not ours anyway. And he didn't like the cover picture because it didn't show all the Belle Epoque which made it look like a solo album which it wasn't. Hugo said it was interfering with our corporate image and wasn't part of his strategy.

'I'm afraid I lost it a bit and told him he could play about with his strategy and image all he liked but he knew full well that, as far as most people were concerned, Belle Epoque meant Jocasta Manhattan and that was why I was on the cover. And then I said if he didn't like the picture he should put his own picture on the next CD and then see how many *that* sold.'

'Oh dear,' said Peter. 'How did he react to that?'

'He folded, of course. Because it's true. I suppose I was a bit unfair but I'd had enough of him that day so I just signed the contract and faxed it back to Jack without telling Hugo. The next day I rang around and found you were going to be in Atlanta.'

'So all this was just a couple of days ago?' said Peter.

'A week, actually. I got Hugo to calm down a bit and said I'd meet up with him afterwards for a few days in Martinique or something.'

She stood up. 'That's it really. Jack hasn't got anything "over me" apart from the contract. But it's not something I can really get out of.'

'Mmm,' went Peter thoughtfully. 'And Laurie? Why do you want him along?'

'I like him,' she said. 'He's good company. And if you go on being a misery guts it'd be as well to have him along. Plus he's doing this book on Jack. So it's a chance for me to do something for him.'

'You're not in charge of him, Jaygo.'

'No,' she said. 'I'm not but I am his friend. And you can be too. Be nice to him.'

145

'How do you mean "be nice"? I've known him a long time and I think I know him pretty well. So yes, I'm his friend as you put it but that doesn't mean he's got to go traipsing after us. He can find out his own stuff for his book. He can do it by himself and doesn't need us to help him.'

'Maybe,' she said. 'It's not worth you and I fighting over. We can all talk about it when we get to London.'

'I'm not going to London,' he said. 'I'm going to Cambridge.'

'But I've booked us in,' she said. 'You heard me.'

'I may have heard you,' he said, 'but I'm due in Cambridge tonight. I imagine we'll get to Heathrow about eight so I can be home by ten.'

'Ah,' she said. 'Slight problem there.'

'Shit,' he said. 'We're not going to bloody Gatwick, are we? I never thought.'

'No,' she said. 'Not there either. We're going to City.'

'City? Where the hell is that?'

'City Airport. Docklands.'

'Why on earth are we going there? My car's at Heathrow.'

'We're going to City because I always go there and this thing lives there. If you want, I'll send Maisie to get your precious car and drive it to London. She can leave it at the hotel and you can pick it up after dinner.'

'I'm not going to dinner,' he said impatiently. 'I'm going to Cambridge. This "thing" as you call it, may live in Docklands but I live in Cambridge. And I'm quite capable of getting a taxi to Heathrow so that's what I'll do if you don't mind.'

'What about the booking?'

'Unbook it.'

'And Laurie?'

'Well,' he said. 'I haven't asked him, have I? And nor have you. He's got a home to go to even if you don't.'

She looked at him for a moment without speaking and then went into the kitchen. 'Thank you for that, Peter,' she said as she went. 'Thank you very much.'

'I didn't mean that,' he called after her.

In the back cabin, Laurie was sitting in a large seat by a window with the telephone on the seat next to him.

'You two scrapping again?' he asked flatly when Jaygo came in. 'I could hear you from here. You shouldn't fight, you know. Not you two.'

She picked up the telephone and looked at it. 'Oh well,' she said, 'perhaps not very much changes.'

She sat down opposite him and put the telephone down.

They looked at each other for a while without speaking. 'It was just an idea,' she said at last. 'You know, I thought I would forget him, the way you do with most people. But what I felt about him never got any smaller or further away. So I thought I'd come back and see. I thought if I could get him away from Cambridge for a few days, we would both have a chance to think about each other. But . . . I'm afraid he doesn't like me very much now. As you heard, all we seem to do is squabble and pick at each other.'

'You were always like that,' said Laurie. 'You just said so.'

She smiled at him. 'Maybe. But as soon as he thinks of something, he just comes out and says it and if I answer back he just whacks the ball over the net again. I respond and the next thing you know, it's an argument and someone goes too far.'

She picked up the telephone and began playing with the aerial. 'Sorry.' she said. 'I didn't come to talk about me. I just came in to see if this thing was working all right.'

'Oh, yes,' he said, glad to be back on safer ground. 'It's an impressive bit of kit. The satellite phones I've seen before need a whole briefcase of gizmos and a dish aerial.'

She looked at the phone. 'Well, I guess ten thousand pounds buys you a lot of shrinkage.'

'Jesus! Ten grand. Are you serious?'

She nodded and smiled at him. 'So I hope you told whoever you were calling that you were on your satellite the way people do when they are on their mobiles.'

'No,' he said. 'I should have, shouldn't I? But perhaps pleading poverty to my publisher was not quite the right time to say I was calling by satellite from a private Lear.'

She smiled. 'Probably not. What did you want from them?'

'A teeny bit more of an advance on my book. A smidgen.'

'And?'

'I must have caught him on a bad hair day. He told me to get stuffed.'

'Never mind,' she said. 'Come back and join the party.'

'Yes, I will, but there's one more call to make, if that's all right?'

'Of course. But you looked as though you'd finished.'

'Perhaps I can leave it till we get there. Someone has to be umpire for you and Pete.'

*　　*　　*

In Kano, John Etherington was feeling rather pleased with himself. He had returned to the house that the Ngale had arranged for him and had just enjoyed supper in his room.

He was sitting at a small table near the foot of his bed setting up the plate-sized aerial for his own satellite telephone, next to the case that held the electronics. He didn't doubt that the one Jack had given him would work but he thought it best to use one that he knew used an encryption circuit in case anyone was listening in.

First he called his bank in Switzerland. Yes, Mr Etherington, the funds had arrived that afternoon and had already been redirected into another account as he had asked. And yes, the original account had been closed and, for that small additional fee, had been deleted from the bank's records.

Etherington replaced the handset. Jack was a nice enough chap but better to put a firewall between them. After all, he had come this far by being cautious and, just because things had gone without a hitch, there was no reason to be careless now.

Next he called a number in Kano. Could he speak to Mr O'Leary please? Never mind if Mr O'Leary was in a meeting, he was sure it would be all right. Just tell him it was the Englishman.

In front of Etherington was a small glass of Irish whiskey. Why did people continue to drink Scotch when Irish was so much smoother?

He heard the line being picked up at the other end.

'Good evening, Frank,' he began. 'I am sorry to disturb you but I thought you would want to hear everything is set for tomorrow night. Have your people standing by. I will call you at lunchtime to tell you where to send them. We will not have much time so make sure your pilot knows exactly what he has to do in advance.'

He carefully replaced the handset and turned the telephone off.

From a briefcase next to the telephone he picked up a faded Polaroid photograph and looked at it closely. He smiled with satisfaction before putting it back in the case and taking up a large manila envelope. From this he took several sheets of yellowing paper that seemed to have been torn from a book.

He looked briefly at the pages of closely written handwriting before placing the old paper back in the envelope and taking out a large black-and-white photograph. It showed the statue at the Santa Maria Church.

He ran his fingers around the bowed arms in the photograph

148

Next he took a small magnifying glass from the case and carefully examined the slightly faded inscription on the wall above the statue. *Descansa seguro en los brazos de la madre de Dios* it read. He translated it quietly to himself under his breath. 'Safe in the arms of the mother of God.'

He smiled.

'And mine,' he added softly to himself.

An hour's delay in an aircraft holding-pattern to the west of London had done little to amuse Jaygo and it was nearly ten o'clock by the time the Belle Epoque jet landed at the City Airport in East London.

Fifteen minutes later, Jaygo was supervising the unloading from a large hold under the main cabin. A large metal box about three feet wide by six feet long was visible inside.

'What the hell is that?' asked Peter.

'The cello,' Jaygo answered. 'It has to travel by air in that coffin. Hugo calls it an Environmental Chamber but I call it a padded box. The insurance people won't let the cello travel without it but it's a complete waste of time because the bloody thing would be perfectly all right in the cabin. *And* I could sit next to it instead of Hugo.

'Watch it!' she shouted to a man who was pulling the box out on metal rollers. 'That thing's fucking irreplaceable so just wait until the fork lift gets here.'

'Now, now,' said Laurie. 'Just because we're in Docklands doesn't mean you have to pretend to work here.'

'Shut up,' she snapped. 'And put that cigarette out while you're at it.'

'Sorree,' said Laurie, going to sit in the large black car that had arrived to take them into London.

'I didn't see that thing in Atlanta,' said Peter.

'No,' she said vaguely. 'I left it at the airport by mistake. And anyway, I was in a hurry.'

'Oh,' he said. 'Is it going to Nigeria?'

'Yes,' she said, 'but not this cello. That one's a Strad and is worth God-knows-what so the insurance people will only let me take it to Europe and the States. Everyone else has to make do with a Japanese thing that squawks like a cat but I can't see Jack knowing the difference if it turns up in the coffin thing.'

'But how does it fit in the car?'

'It doesn't. Well, it will with the back seat down but then my

149

cases don't fit in so it goes in a van so we can travel in relative comfort.

'Careful, you idiot!' she shouted at the man unloading the cello again. 'Why I didn't take up the piccolo I'll never know.'

Peter smiled and thought it best to join Laurie in the back of the car.

When the cello, and those of Jaygo's cases that would not fit in the boot, had been safely loaded in the van, she joined them in the car and slid into the driver's seat.

'Are you going to drive?' asked a slightly surprised Peter.

'Yes,' she replied. 'Sven only does planes and the real driver's gone home to watch television so you've got me.'

'I can drive if you like,' volunteered Laurie.

'No,' she said. 'A treat from Auntie Jaygo.'

Laurie had happily accepted her invitation to stay at Browns Hotel with her because, as he explained, he was 'between flats' and thought it was 'a bit late' to turn up at friends'.

Peter had again refused to stay in London and said he would take a taxi from the hotel out to Heathrow even though Jaygo pointed out to him he would not be in Cambridge much before one o'clock.

As Jaygo drove west towards Central London, the tall tower of Canary Wharf with its flashing red beacon loomed ahead of them. Laurie tapped the window. 'I nearly took a job there once,' he said, 'but the editor explained at the end of the interview that it was the paper's policy never to accept any freebies so I had to turn them down.'

'Thank God for standards,' said Jaygo.

'Jack's warehouse is down there on the Isle of Dogs Enterprise Zone,' continued Laurie.

'The one you told us about?' asked Petter with interest.

'Yes, it's on one of the new developments on Heron's Quay. Do you want to see it?'

'Another time, Lol,' said Peter. 'I think we really should get back.'

'Of course we want to see it,' said Jaygo. 'Come on, give me directions.'

Laurie directed the car down the bright underpass under Canary Wharf and, as they emerged into the dark again, he peered out of the window looking for street names.

'Slow down,' he said. 'I think we're nearly there.'

Jaygo drove slowly on.

'I think we must have passed it,' he said. 'Why isn't there anyone to ask the way?'

'Because it's late,' said Peter. 'Who would be wandering about an industrial area at this time?'

'Wait,' said Jaygo. 'There's someone. We can ask him.'

'I don't think that's a very good idea,' said Peter. 'He looks like a drunk.'

The figure approaching them was a short man, swinging his arms backwards and forwards in an exaggerated manner and singing loudly up at the sky. When he was about ten yards from the car he stopped and leant forwards peering intently at the headlights. He stood up again and began a stage military march up to the car and halted. He bowed elaborately and saluted.

Peter could see his face clearly by the lights of the car. He had the wide face and upwardly sloping eyes of someone with Down's Syndrome.

The man drew himself to attention and set off at the march again past the car.

'Oh,' said Jaygo. 'Shouldn't he be at home or something?'

'Yes,' said Peter, 'and so should we. I said I'd be home an hour ago.'

Jaygo was about to reply when she was cut short by Laurie. 'That's it!' he cried excitedly. 'Heron's Quay.'

Jaygo swung the car into Heron's Quay and stopped in front of a large map showing the units on the development.

'Ah ha!' said Laurie. 'Number Five. Kano Imports. That's the baby!'

'Good,' said Peter. 'Can we go now?'

'No, we can't,' said Jaygo. 'Don't be so bloody boring. I'm going to drive past it and get a good look.

'There!' she said as they approached. 'There's a light on. I think I'll go and look.'

She stopped the car ten yards beyond number five. 'Well?' she asked. 'Who's coming?'

Neither Peter nor Laurie showed any sign of moving.

'I mean,' she said with an edge to her voice, 'why doesn't one of you heroes come with me?

'Look,' she went on. 'If there's a light on there is somebody there. We could go in and pretend we were lost and wanted to ask the way.'

'No,' said Peter firmly. 'No.'

'Well, you can stay in the car then, can't you, Mr Chicken? Are you up for it, Lol?'

'I don't know, Jay,' said Laurie. 'It's frightfully late you know, just to walk in. I mean, is it worth it?'

'Let's go back, Jaygo,' said Peter quietly.

'If you're worried about being late back for Miss Cambridge, take the phone and call her. She'll be asleep by now but you can wake her up and say you're going to be even later than you said. Then she can reset the Teasmade for an hour later and go back to sleep again.' She took out the telephone and passed it to him.

'Don't be ridiculous,' he said, taking the handset and looking at it. 'And this is the wrong one anyway. There's no light on the front of it and I don't want to blow my brains out.'

'Eh?' said Laurie.

'What do you mean?' she said, taking it from him and pressing a button on it. 'Shit. Battery's dead. Who left it on?'

'You probably did,' said Peter.

'I did not,' she snapped. 'And this is the right one. The brains-out one, as you call it, lives in a special compartment by the handle. I'm not a complete idiot, you know.'

'What brains-out one?' asked Laurie.

'Well, you can always call her later, can't you?' said Jaygo, ignoring Laurie and putting the telephone back in the bag and hoisting it on to her shoulder. 'Are you coming or not?'

'No.'

'Good. Follow me then,' said Jaygo, opening the car door and stepping out.

'Christ almighty!' said Peter under his breath and going after her. 'You stay here and watch the car.'

'Good idea,' said Laurie, watching Peter hurry after Jaygo.

He caught up with her just as she was standing on tip toe, trying to see through a small window set in the metal door. 'I can't see much,' she said. 'There's an office in a box thing inside but I can't see anyone.'

Peter stood behind her and peered over her shoulder.

He could see that the warehouse stretched back perhaps thirty yards from the road under a high corrugated roof. To the left was the Portakabin office Jaygo had described and there seemed to be another one at the far end of the warehouse but not enough lights were switched on to be sure. Jaygo was right. There was no one to be seen.

'Why are the lights on if there's no one there?' she asked.

152

'There will be someone,' Peter said. 'A night watchman on patrol or something.'

'Do you think there's another way in?' she went on. 'At the back or at the side?'

'We're not going in, Jaygo. We only came to look.'

'Hey! This door isn't locked. I can push it!'

'No, Jay!' Peter said quickly but she was already opening the door open and stepping in.

'Come on, Peter. We can say we're lost, they'll ask us to go and that's all.'

'There could be a dog,' he said stepping inside.

Jaygo was about ten feet inside the door. 'Hello!' she called. 'Anyone at home?' she called again, walking over to the Portakabin.

'You can't go there!' Peter called after her. 'Come back.'

But she was already climbing the three steps up to the office door and going in.

The sound of a flushing lavatory came from the corner of the warehouse behind Peter.

'Oi!' a loud voice called out. 'What do you think you're doing!'

From the shadow beyond the door appeared a very large man in a blue serge uniform doing up his flies.

'Oi, you!' he shouted at Jaygo. 'Come back. And you,' he said, grabbing Peter by the shoulder, 'what the fuck are you doing?'

'Watch it!' said Peter, shaking himself free.

'No, mate. You watch it,' said the man, catching his shoulder again. 'How did you get in here?'

The man started pushing Peter roughly towards the office where Jaygo could be seen through the windows of the cabin.

She stuck her head out of the door. 'Hello. Can we use your telephone, please?'

'No, you can't!' said the man. 'Get out the pair of you! Come on. Out!'

'Look, I'm frightfully sorry,' said Peter. 'We were lost and we saw a light on and just came to use your phone.'

'There's no phone,' said the man gruffly. 'Now get out both of you before Mr Akey sees you. And you take it from me, you don't want to see 'im at all.'

Suddenly there was a voice from the far end of the warehouse. 'What is it? What is happening?'

'You're for it now,' said the guard. 'He's as high as a bloody kite tonight.'

'What is it? Who is it?' said the man, coming down the warehouse.

He was a short black man wearing a business suit and carrying a large white handkerchief in his hand with which he repeatedly wiped his profusely sweating face. 'Who is it, Hogan?'

'Mr Akey, sir,' said the guard. 'These two. I caught them breaking in.'

'We weren't breaking in,' said Peter. 'The door was open.'

'Who are you?' said the African, coming right up to Peter.

'We were lost,' said Jaygo from the office door. 'We came to ask the way.'

'Bring him for me to see, Hogan,' said the African turning and walking quickly towards Jaygo and the office door.

'You're bloody for it now,' said Hogan pushing Peter by the shoulder. 'He's bloody wild is this one.'

The African was standing inside the office. 'Come in so I can see you!' he called to Peter.

Peter climbed up the steps into the cabin and stood next to Jaygo on the opposite side of a large central table to the African.

The man was sweating and wiped his face with the handkerchief as he spoke in an angry voice. 'What do you want here? I will know it!'

'Please don't raise your voice at us,' said Jaygo. 'The door was open and we just came in to ask the way.'

'No, Mr Akey,' the guard cut in. 'The door was locked.'

'Key?' shouted the man. 'You have a key?'

'No,' said Peter. 'The door was not locked.'

'Key!' shouted the man again. 'Give me the key!'

'Look,' repeated Peter. 'We haven't got a key. The door was not locked.'

'Show me the key!'

'There is no key. I keep telling you.'

The man reached into his jacket and produced a large black pistol. He waved it between them and then pointed it directly at Jaygo's face.

'I don't have time!' he shouted. 'Give it to me!'

Peter and Jaygo froze.

'I will shoot you! I will have it!'

'Please, please,' said Peter, putting his hands up. 'We can explain.'

'I will shoot you,' repeated the man. 'Now start talking to me.'

He rubbed the handkerchief over his face with his free hand. His breath was shallow and very fast.

Without taking his eyes off Jaygo, the man moved his outstretched hand around to his right until the pistol was pointing directly at the security guard. He pulled the trigger and the guard's throat exploded as he was thrown backwards against the wall and fell in a heap.

With one movement the African moved his arm forwards and pointed the pistol at Jaygo again.

'Tell me!' he shrieked. 'Tell me!'

Jaygo spoke. 'The Ngale,' she said. 'The Ngale sent us.'

'Oh, shit,' said Peter under his breath.

'Yes,' went on Jaygo almost in a babble. 'He said to come here. The Ngale said we had to see you.'

'You know Ngale?' said the man, suddenly uncertain. 'But you do not know Ngale. He is not here.'

'He said. He called,' went on Jaygo. 'Let me talk to him. He said to come.'

'You cannot talk to him,' said the African regaining his confidence. 'Ngale is not here.'

'Telephone. I can telephone him,' said Jaygo with her voice beginning to waver.

'I have a telephone here. In my bag,' she went on. 'Please let us telephone him. Peter, get the telephone. Now, Peter.'

She took her bag from her shoulder and put it on the table in front of her.

'You cannot call Ngale! He is in Nigeria!' said the man wiping his face again. 'You are deceiving me!'

'No, I can,' said Jaygo, slowly reaching into her bag and bringing out a satellite telephone and holding it carefully in front of her with both hands for him to see.

'Put it down!' the man shouted. 'Now put it down!'

Jaygo took a breath and with one movement flicked open the cover over the trigger, pushed a finger inside and fired the gun.

She hit the man in the hand that was holding his pistol. He screamed with the sudden pain and his pistol fell onto the table in front of him.

He held his injured hand in front of his face for a moment before lunging for his pistol again with the other hand.

Jaygo was standing motionless with her arms outstretched in front of her holding her pistol.

'Fire again, Jaygo!' shouted Peter as the man scrabbled for his gun, but Jaygo did not move.

Peter suddenly reached over and took the telephone pistol from her, turned towards the man and fired the remaining three shots.

The first shot missed altogether. The second hit the man in his

155

chest, throwing him backwards. The final round hit him again just below his throat.

The African made as if to grab at the table, his head shaking violently from side to side and his arms jerking. But he was no more than halfway when he suddenly fell again and lay completely still.

Jaygo was still standing with her hands out in front of her. Slowly she turned her head towards Peter, her face devoid of expression.

Peter put the gun down and reached out his arms.

She took a step towards Peter. He put his arms around her as she began to sob. He held her close and turned his head to look at the two dead men. The blood. Blood everywhere.

Peter gradually became aware of the sound of footsteps running towards them from outside the office. Laurie burst into the room.

'I heard bangs,' Laurie began, 'I thought I'd better come and see . . .' His voice trailed off as he took in the scene inside the office. 'Oh my Christ. What's happened?'

'He shot him,' said Peter emptily. 'He was going to shoot us too. He was going to shoot.'

'Are you hit, Peter?' said Laurie quickly. 'Is Jaygo hit?'

'No,' continued Peter flatly. 'We shot him. Jaygo and I shot him. What do we do, Laurie?'

'Out,' Laurie said. 'Bring Jaygo with you, Peter.'

Laurie dropped to one knee and looked at the men. 'They're dead,' he said. 'Both dead.'

Jaygo had stopped sobbing, now she was breathing in and out with shallow breaths as she clung to Peter.

'Peter,' she said. 'I have to sit down. Let me sit down.'

Peter walked her slowly down the three steps into the warehouse and helped her sit on a wooden box by the door.

He sat next to her and put an arm around her. 'Yes, this is fine.' she said. 'I just had to sit down.'

Peter looked back to the door and could see Laurie inside with his hands on top of his head trying to think what to do next.

'I have to go to Laurie,' said Peter. 'Can you sit here till I get back?'

'Yes,' she said taking a deep breath. 'I'll be all right now. You go and help Laurie. I'll be fine, really I will.'

Peter walked the few steps back to the cabin.

Inside Laurie had begun to pace backwards and forwards.

'We have to call the police, Laurie,' said Peter.

'No!' said Laurie suddenly. 'That is exactly what we must not do.' He held his free hand out at Peter. 'You say he was going to shoot you and so you shot him. How did you do that?'

'Jaygo had a gun in her bag. Like a telephone. We shot him with that.'

Laurie dropped his hands to his side and looked at Peter. 'Jesus. I didn't know she had a gun.'

'Hugo makes her carry it,' said Peter. 'We'd both be dead if we hadn't shot him, I think.'

Laurie put his hands to his face.

'We have to tell the police,' Peter repeated.

'No,' said Laurie, suddenly decisive. 'What you say is good enough for me but it won't be good enough for them. Think, Peter, you're not thinking.'

'What then? We have to say we shot him.'

'No,' said Laurie again. 'Look,' he went on, counting off on his fingers, 'one – who owns this place? Jack Ngale. Two – do you know him? Yes. And three,' he said, pointing out of the door, 'who is *she?*'

Peter did not answer.

'Shall I go on?' said Laurie. 'Like, what the hell are *any* of us doing here in the middle of the night.'

Peter opened his mouth to speak but Laurie cut him off. 'No, Peter,' he said, 'we do *not* go to the police.'

Peter looked down at the two men and the splatters of blood on the walls and floor.

'What then?' he said weakly. 'It's like Atlanta all over again. The police will come.'

'No,' said Laurie, 'the police will *not* come here. Go and put Jaygo in the car. Do what I say.'

'But we shot someone,' said Peter.

'For Christ's sake,' Laurie said, raising his voice. 'It may be a fucking mess but don't make it worse. Just go and put Jaygo in the fucking car and come back here!'

'What for?' said Peter. 'What are you going to do?'

'Just do it,' said Laurie sharply.

'All right,' said Peter quietly. He turned to look again at the two bodies before going out.

Jaygo was sitting up with her head bent forwards. Peter sat next to her.

157

She lifted her head and looked at him. 'I'm sorry,' she said. 'I went to pieces, didn't I?'

'Hardly,' he said gently. 'If it wasn't for you, I think we'd both be dead.'

'Yes,' she said. 'He was going to shoot us. I see it going over and over again in my head. His arm swinging out and shooting that poor man. And then him swinging back again at us. I was so frightened.'

'But you did something, didn't you?' he said. 'I'm afraid it was me that wasn't much use.'

She drew in a deep breath and let it out again slowly. 'That poor man. It wasn't anything to do with him, was it?'

Peter did not say anything.

'You know,' she said, 'it's funny, but I understand your story now. I mean, that man didn't shoot the guard because he wanted to kill him. He was just making a point to us, wasn't he? He wasn't thinking of the guard at all.'

'No,' said Peter, putting his arm around her again. 'But I think he was going to shoot us whatever we said. Come on. I'll take you to the car. Do you think you can walk all right?'

She stood up and looked towards the cabin where Laurie had appeared at the door. 'You all right, Jay?' he called.

'I'm fine now. What are you going to do?'

'I'm afraid we must do what Jack would do in these circumstances.'

'I'm not sure I know what you mean,' said Peter.

'We set fire to the place.'

'What!' said Peter. 'Are you crazy?'

'If we do that,' said Laurie, 'it makes it look as if someone else did it. It's just an ordinary shooting.

'Think about it,' he went on before Peter could say anything. 'We know about this place and what it's used for. Or soon will be if it's not already. And Jack's rivals will know what Jack is up to. We can make it look like one of them.'

'But the two men?' said Peter. 'What do we do about them?'

'You didn't shoot the guard,' said Laurie, 'and you say you only shot the other one because he was going to shoot you. Now, I reckon that makes your conscience as clean as it's going to get. The best thing we can do is to get you two as far away from here as fast as possible.'

'But the police will find us in the end,' said Peter.

'Not necessarily, Peter,' replied Laurie. 'If they think it's a drugland thing, they won't look for anyone else, let alone bother very much. And if the place is burned down they won't have much to go on anyway, will they?'

Peter looked at Jaygo.

'Well?' said Laurie after a pause. 'Have you got a better idea?'

'I don't know,' said Peter.

'Jaygo?' asked Laurie.

She looked at Laurie and then at Peter. 'He's right, Peter. It was an accident. And if we do what Laurie says, it can stay that way.'

'Christ,' said Peter, 'you two are a pair. In case you haven't noticed there are two people in there who were alive ten minutes ago. One of them just an ordinary person who is nothing to do with "drugland", whatever that is. And what do we actually know about the other one? Nothing. And so we just send them up in smoke and walk off?'

'Peter,' said Jaygo, taking his hand. 'Listen to Laurie. He's right. We can't really do anything about what happened. Whatever we do, it isn't going to make a difference to what's happened back there. Let's just do what Laurie says and go.'

Peter let go her hand.

'Maybe,' he said. 'But how? Do we just drop a match on our way out or what?'

'Not quite,' said Laurie. 'We have to find something that will burn easily and pile it up near the office and make sure it's burning properly before we go. So let's stop talking and start looking around.'

Peter sighed. 'It's easier than that,' he said. 'If this place is going to be used to process heroin, then they'll need a laboratory of some kind and that means there will be solvents. Perhaps that's what the other Portakabin is.'

'How do you know?' said Jaygo. 'Shouldn't we just use a lot of paper?'

'I run a laboratory. Believe me, there will be solvents. You go and sit in the car, Jay, Laurie and I can do this.'

'No,' she said. 'I got us in and I can help get us out.'

'Please yourself,' said Peter, setting off to the far end of the warehouse. 'I'll start at the back.'

'What are we looking for?' said Jaygo, catching him up. 'Will it be in bottles?'

'Yes,' he said, 'in Winchesters. Do you know what a Winchester is?'

'No.'

'I do,' said Laurie, coming up behind them. 'Big bottles with little necks.'

'That's right,' said Peter. 'They live in metal cabinets. Or they should do anyway.'

By now Peter had reached the Portakabin at the back of the warehouse and was opening the door. It was smaller than the one at the front and laid out as an office and not a laboratory.

'Shit,' said Peter as Jaygo came in after him. 'So much for my little theory.'

A desk in the middle was covered with brightly coloured brochures with a picture of a black woman making a rug outside a hut. Next to the brochures lay a neat pile of brown envelopes and a sheet of first class stamps.

Peter looked in a box next to the desk. More brochures. He picked one up and looked at it.

'Christ, he was doing a mailing, Jay. Just a fucking clerk.'

'He had a gun,' she said. 'He was going to shoot us.'

Peter dropped the brochure back into the box.

'They'll burn, won't they?' asked Jaygo helpfully.

'Hey!' called Laurie from outside the cabin. 'I think I've found something, Pete. What are these?'

Jaygo and Peter found Laurie looking at a row of three-foot-high metal drums at the side of the cabin.

Peter dropped to one knee to try to read the paper label on the side. 'It's just a shipping label,' he said. 'It doesn't say what's inside. Could be anything.'

'This next one's got a proper label on top,' said Jaygo. 'How's your German?'

Peter stood up and looked at the label Jaygo had found. 'Christ!' he said. 'It's alcohol. Ninety-eight percent.'

'That'd burn, wouldn't it?' said Jaygo. 'Brandy burns on puddings and that's only seventy percent.'

Peter stood back and counted the drums. 'Six,' he said to himself.

'Well?' said Jaygo. 'Will it burn or not?'

He turned to Laurie. 'It wasn't going to be a laboratory, Lol. It was going to be a fucking factory.'

'Well?' Jaygo repeated.

Peter turned to her. 'Oh, yes. It'll burn. But it won't be like a Christmas pudding. If this lot goes, it'll be like a row of bombs.'

'So?' she said. 'You're a doctor. Is this what you ordered or not?'

'I'm afraid not,' he said. 'We just need a few gallons to start a fire. This is something else. But there's far too much for one set-up. They must be shipping it on to God knows how many other places.'

Peter stood back again and looked at the drums. 'And if there's this much alcohol, there'll be ether and acetone somewhere as well.'

'They'll burn too, won't they?' asked Laurie.

'Ether will do a lot more than just burn,' said Peter. 'It'll take the roof off.'

'OK,' said Laurie, 'chemistry lesson over. If we've found what we came for, what do we do next?'

'That's the problem,' said Peter. 'If there wasn't so much, we could just spill a bit, light the blue touch-paper and retire. I don't know about this much. We only want one drum. Not even that really.'

'Well,' said Jaygo, 'why don't we roll one right down to the other end. Open it. Tip it over and roll it away? The stuff'll come out as it goes along. When it's a safe distance from us, we light it and run.'

Peter looked at Laurie questioningly.

'Sounds good to me, Pete. Better than just slopping a bit around.'

'I don't know,' said Peter. 'I still think that's too risky. What if it goes wrong?'

Laurie looked at his watch. 'Make your mind up then. This is not a very good place to be.'

'Let's think,' said Peter. 'We've got time.'

'No,' said Jaygo decisively. 'Laurie found these and I came up with something. Now you help us get one of these down to the other end and if you come up with a better idea on the way, you can let us hear about it.'

The blue drums turned out to be very heavy and it was only with great difficulty that they managed to push one on to its side. They then had to point it in the right direction and roll it down to the other end.

Peter then decided they must stand it up again before they tried to open it. 'We won't have any control if we open it on its side,' he explained. 'We have to stand it up, find something to open the screw plug and then tip it over again.'

Jaygo and Laurie, both already out of breath, only helped Peter right the drum with great reluctance and much swearing.

'All right,' said Peter when the drum was standing up again at last. 'Now we have to find the thing to open it with.'

161

Jaygo leaned over and looked at the orange plastic plug cover on the top, set about four inches from the side of the drum.

'Can't we just pull it off? It looks like a big plastic bottle top.'

'No,' said Peter. 'That's just the cover. Underneath the plastic is a three-inch nut and we have to find the special tool or a very big spanner.'

'Now he tells us,' said Jaygo. 'Great.'

'There might be one in the office,' said Peter. 'We'll go and look.'

'I'm not going in there again,' said Jaygo.

'Well, you look down by the other drums,' said Peter. 'Are you coming, Laurie?'

Peter began to walk towards the cabin.

'How am I supposed to know what I'm looking for?' called Jaygo after him.

Peter did not reply but continued towards the office.

'Come on, old thing,' said Laurie to Jaygo. 'I'll help you look.'

Peter pushed open the door of the office and went in. As soon as he entered, he could smell the blood and traces of cordite from the gunshots. He looked briefly at the two bodies lying slumped in their separate pools of blood before beginning his search.

The single filing-cabinet was locked and he could see nowhere else a set of tools might be. He decided to look outside the office in the main part of the warehouse.

First he looked in the wooden box that Jaygo had been sitting on. Inside it was only a plastic carrier bag. He lifted it up and opened the bag. It contained a small green sandwich box and a Thermos flask. He shut the box and sat down, pressing his hands to his temples. This simply cannot be happening to me, he thought as he clenched his eyes tight shut.

'Hey! No slouching!' he heard Jaygo calling.

He opened his eyes and looked up to see her emerging from the shadows waving a blue ring spanner about a foot long.

'They were in a case next to the drums,' she said. 'I tried it on one of the other drums and it fits.'

'Yes,' said Peter, standing up. 'That's it. Let's do it then.'

The screw plug under the seal was very tight. It took the combined strengths of Peter and Laurie to remove it, even with the spanner.

The three of them again pushed the drum on to its side and immediately the alcohol began pouring out.

'Right,' said Laurie, taking his lighter from his pocket. 'Roll her away.'

Peter leant down and gave the drum a push.

It went about two feet and stopped.

'Christ, that's not a push,' cried Jaygo. 'This is a push.' She stepped forward, brought up her knee and pushed it with her foot as hard as she could.

The drum moved about four feet before stopping again with the opening still continuing to gush alcohol onto the floor.

'That'll have to do,' said Peter. 'Now, give me the lighter, Laurie, and everyone get to the door.'

'No way,' said Laurie. 'I'm not lending you my Zippo. I'll do it,' he said, flipping the top open with his thumb.

'No!' shouted Peter. 'Not from here! That stuff will go up like God knows what. We'll have to throw it from the door.'

'But won't it go out if we do that?' said Jaygo.

'No, no,' said Laurie, 'Zippos don't go out. Steve McQueen used one all through *The Great Escape* and it never went out once.'

'Another time, Laurie,' said Peter. 'Let's just get to the door,' he added, propelling Jaygo to the entrance.

Laurie followed them out, closing the door behind them and looking at Peter.

Peter tuned back and looked through the window in the door.

'It's gone out,' he said.

'I haven't thrown it yet,' said Laurie. 'I was waiting for your say so.'

'Jesus, Laurie, just throw the bloody thing!' He walked towards the car. 'I'll drive,' he added.

Laurie shrugged at Jaygo. 'I didn't want to throw it until Teacher said, did I?'

'Don't piss about, Lol. Just throw it in.'

'Here goes then,' he said, opening the Zippo again and lighting it. 'Goodbye, old girl.'

He opened the door and threw it in. 'Come on, Jay. Let's scarper.'

Laurie and Jaygo scrambled into the back of the car while Peter started the engine and waited.

'It hasn't worked,' he said after about twenty seconds. 'I can't hear anything. We should hear it if that much solvent caught light.'

He opened the car door and peered towards the warehouse. 'And I can't see anything.'

Suddenly there was a loud *woomp* and the door of the warehouse blew open followed by a fifteen-foot gush of blue flame.

'Go! Go! Go!' shouted Jaygo. 'Go, Peter!'

Peter pulled away with a squeal of tyres towards the end of the side road and swerved right back into the main part of Heron's Quay.

As the car straightened out again, they could see the Down's Syndrome man approaching them at a military march some twenty yards away. When he saw the headlights of the car, he came to a halt, stood to attention and saluted as the car sped past him. Laurie looked at Peter questioningly. 'What about him?' Peter shook his head.

Peter slowed down as they approached Canary Wharf and they passed through the bright underpass without speaking.

Coming up on the other side, Peter turned left towards Central London onto a slightly raised section of road. He pulled over, stopped the car and got out, walking around the front of the car and looking back.

The burning warehouse could easily be seen. Already the roof had opened and in several places columns of sparks and flames were rising a hundred feet up into the dark sky.

Jaygo opened her door and went to stand next to Peter.

In the distance they could hear fire-engine sirens approaching.

'Didn't take them long,' she said. 'Quite a fire.'

'From their point of view, the bigger the better. If it's too hot to go near, at least they'll be a safe distance away when the other drums go up.'

'When will that be?' she asked.

'When the pressure inside them builds up enough to blow the lids off. They'll throw stuff up like volcanoes and it will still be burning as it comes down.'

He looked at his watch. 'How long have we been gone? Five minutes?'

'Not as much as that,' she said.

Peter had scarcely looked up at the warehouse when the first of the drums exploded.

There was a flash of blue flame two hundred feet up through the roof of the warehouse. This spread out into a burning umbrella that cascaded down to the fire again. A second later the sound of the explosion reached them. Another plume of burning alcohol followed the first, followed again by the sound of an explosion.

'I should never have let us do it,' said Peter. 'All the other businesses around will be burnt out too.'

'It wasn't just you,' she said taking his arm. 'We all did it.'

He looked down at her and smiled. 'Maybe,' he said. 'But we've destroyed a dozen businesses. Just so we could get away.'

She turned back to look at the fire. 'Do you think that funny little man is all right?'

He took her arms from his and walked around to his door again. 'Maybe,' he said, 'if he knew which way to run.'

Jaygo climbed back into the car and shut the door behind her. 'Do you know the way from here? I can drive if you like.'

'Off Oxford Street, isn't it?' he said. 'I know it.'

No one spoke until Peter was parking the car under the hotel.

Jaygo directed him to a reserved space next to the van that had brought the cello and the cases. Peter recognised his own car in the next bay.

'I'd like to get straight home,' he said. 'I don't think I'll come in.'

'I think you should have a coffee or something first,' said Jaygo. 'It won't take more than a minute.'

'No, really,' he said. 'I'd like to go.'

Jaygo leaned forward from the back seat and put a hand on his shoulder. 'You weren't the only one back there, you know. Please come in for a minute.'

He put his own hand briefly over hers. 'It was pretty terrible for us all. I'm sorry,' he said, 'of course.'

A minute later, Jaygo, Peter and Laurie emerged into the carpeted luxury of the ground floor of the hotel. The concierge was waiting for them.

'Good evening, Miss Manhattan, I am sorry your flight was so delayed.'

'Thank you, John,' she said. 'Has everything been taken to our rooms?'

'Yes indeed. Your staff took the cello case from its travelling box and I carried it to your room myself.'

'Thank you, John. You are very helpful.'

'The night bar is open of course,' continued the concierge, 'if you would like a drink before you go up.'

Jaygo smiled at the concierge. 'Thank you,' she said, 'but I think we'll go straight up.'

'I could have done with a sandwich or something,' said Laurie on the way up in the lift. 'How about you, Peter?'

165

Peter shook his head. 'You can call down for something.'

'Good thinking.'

'We'll all go into my room,' said Jaygo. 'I don't feel as if I've eaten for ages. You ought to eat something, you know, Peter.'

The lift door opened and they stepped out to be met by the floor porter.

'Good evening, Miss Manhattan,' he said with a brief bow.

'Thank you, Malcolm,' she said. 'Thank you for waiting for us.'

'Not at all,' he said. 'You have your usual suite, Miss Manhattan. The gentlemen's rooms are next door and the keys are in the locks.'

'Thank you,' she said again. 'I think that's everything.'

Jaygo's suite door was open. 'This is me,' she said. 'Come on in.'

'Actually, Jay,' said Laurie. 'I think that I'm pretty tired after all. I'll call for something from my room, if that's all right.'

She leant forward and kissed him lightly on the cheek. 'Of course,' she said, 'see you in the morning.'

Laurie turned to Peter. 'You drive carefully now, Wheels Man.'

Laurie turned and walked towards his room.

'And then there were two,' said Jaygo.

'I don't know,' he said. 'Perhaps I really ought to be getting back straight away. Aurelia will be waiting up. You don't know her.'

She took his hand and pulled him gently to the door next to hers. 'No, I don't know her. But I know you and I know it's really late. You've had a hell of a night, you must be exhausted and you'd be simply crazy to drive back tonight.'

He looked in at the open door of the room set aside for him. It did look very inviting.

'Maybe,' he said. 'I could set off early.'

'And I'd like to know you were only next door,' she said. 'Will you stay?'

He looked into the room again. 'All right,' he said. 'I'll give her a ring and go back first thing.'

'Thank you,' she said, stepping up on her toes and kissing him briefly on the lips. 'Give me a ring when you get to Cambridge.'

'Of course,' he said. 'Good night, Jay.'

Peter smiled at her as she walked away. He went into his room and closed the door.

He walked directly over to the telephone by the bed, picked it up and dialled Aurelia's number. She answered on the first ring.

'Hello, sweetie. Are you still up?'

'Oh, thank goodness it's you. Yes, of course I'm still up darling. I though you'd be home ages ago.'

'I'm really sorry,' he said. 'They held us up for simply ages before we could land and then again for ages in customs.'

'What happened?' she said. 'Are you all right?'

'Fine,' he said. 'Absolutely fine. But I'm completely worn out so I think I'll stay the night at Laurie's and get a few hours' sleep before I drive back.'

'Oh,' she said, clearly disappointed.

'It's best,' he went on. 'I really am much too tired to drive all that way.'

'Oh,' she said again. 'Has he got a spare room and everything?'

'Just a sofa,' said Peter. 'But I think I could sleep anywhere just now. Look,' he went on, 'I should be back about ten, OK?'

'Of course,' she said.

'Are you OK?'

'Oh, yes, Lizzie and I have been busy all day getting things ready in college for tomorrow night. I'll have to go in at about twelve tomorrow, but you'll be back by then.'

'I'll see you in the morning then, darling.'

'Good night. Take care.'

'You too,' he said, putting the telephone down.

'Bugger it,' he said to himself. 'What was I supposed to tell her?'

Next he telephoned downstairs for some sandwiches and coffee before looking around his room.

It was much bigger than the one in Atlanta. There was a large sofa and chairs set near a low glass-topped table over by the drawn curtains of the window. On the top of the table was a sizable bunch of flowers set in a pink vase next to a matching bowl of fruit.

'What *was* I supposed to say?' he repeated. '"Sorry, sweetie, but Jaygo and I had to shoot someone and then set fire to a warehouse. And, by the way I'm spending the night in a hotel and Jay is in the next room because she doesn't want me to be too far away. But there's nothing to worry about and I'll be home in time for coffee".'

He lay down on the bed and closed his eyes to wait for the sandwiches.

He was almost asleep when there was a knock at the door.

'Hold on,' he called. 'I'll be with you.'

He went over to open the door. But it was not the sandwiches. It was Jaygo.

Chapter Four

THURSDAY

London, England

Jaygo was gone by the time Peter woke up. He had showered, dressed and packed before he noticed the note from her on the table.

> Peter, darling
>   Not quite what we planned, was it? But thank you for staying in London.
>   Bizi Whiz day for me so I have left you in slumberland.
>   Ring me after ten, 077998–45–77–2183
>   Love,
>   Your Jaygo
>   P.S. Do you think we could fix up a love match between Hugo and Aurelia?

'No,' he said to himself, smiling as he folded the note and put it in his pocket before telephoning downstairs for Laurie's room number.

'I'm afraid Mr Miller has already checked out for the day, Dr Wilson. Would you like some breakfast in your room, sir?'

'No, thank you. But do you have my car keys?'

'Yes, sir. Would you like your car brought to the front for you, sir?'

'Yes, thank you. I'll be right down.'

He took an apple from the bowl before picking up his case and going downstairs.

'Do I need to sign anything?' he asked as he collected his keys from the front desk.

'No, sir. Miss Manhattan has an account.'

And a lot of other things, he thought as he went out to his car.

Peter drove up the Edgware Road under a bright and cloudless sky. There were probably better routes out of London but this was the one he had always used.

He stopped at a kiosk near Lords cricket ground and bought several newspapers.

The fire had made page five of the *Independent*. 'Paint fire on the Isle of Dogs' read the headline.

'A fire broke out in a warehouse on the prestigious Heron's Quay last night,' began the story.

'The blaze is thought to have started in a unit belonging to Kano Imports, a firm specialising in Nigerian rugs and handicrafts. The fire rapidly spread to an adjacent unit which was being used for the storage of paint products. The resulting conflagration and intense heat meant that the fire services were unable to bring the fire under control for several hours. The damage was extensive and eight adjoining units were also partly destroyed.

'A spokesman for Kano Imports said that the warehouse met all current fire regulations but that some electrical contractors had been installing new lighting last week and it is possible that faulty wiring was to blame.

'The London fire service would not comment on this when they issued a statement in the early hours of this morning but a full investigation is thought likely owing to the extensive damage caused by the fire. Large insurance claims are expected.

'A spokesman for the Metropolitan Police said that they would be conducting their own investigation and the possibility of arson could not be ruled out at this stage.

'A man found in the vicinity of Heron's Quay shortly after the fire was taken to Tower Hamlets police station. He was later released without charge.'

Peter put the paper down next to him on the car seat and drove on.

The traffic was heavier than he had expected and it was gone ten o'clock before he turned into the service station at South Mimms for petrol and coffee.

He walked first to the row of telephones in the main entrance to call Jaygo.

He knew a call to a mobile would be expensive, so he lined

up several pound coins on the shelf next to the telephone before dialling the number she had given him.

There was a buzz on the line for about fifteen seconds but no ringing tone. He was about to hang up when a man's voice came on the line.

'International Operator, Toby speaking, how may I help you?'

'I'm sorry,' said Peter, 'I thought I had dialled a direct number.'

'Yes, sir, but you have called a satellite number from a pay phone and you cannot be connected. You need to use a credit card call phone or a standard subscription line.'

'Why?' said Peter. 'I've called mobiles from pay phones before.'

'Yes, sir,' went on the voice, 'but the charging bands for satellite connections are not appropriate for coin call phones.'

'Why not?' persisted Peter. 'I know it will be more than a regular call but I've a fistful of coins ready.'

'Calls to satellite numbers are charged at one hundred pounds for the first three minutes and one hundred and fifty pounds for each subsequent minute up to one hour.'

'Jesus!'

'Yes, sir. That is why a charge line is better.'

'Thank you,' said Peter, hanging up the receiver and putting the change back in his pocket. Jaygo could wait, he thought.

In Kano, John Etherington had no compunction about using a satellite phone. He was making a morning call to Jack Ngale on the telephone he had been given.

'Good morning, Jack. I trust you slept well?'

'Thank you, yes. What can I do for you?'

'Oh,' said Etherington, rather taken aback by the Ngale's crisp tone.

'Well,' he continued, 'I was wondering if I could have the use of a car and driver for couple of hours.'

'Of course,' said the Ngale. 'That is what they are there for. Is there anything else you need?'

'No. Thank you. Look, Jack, is everything all right?'

'Something has come up that needs my urgent attention. Come round this evening and I'll talk to you then.'

'Thank you,' said Etherington. But the Ngale had already broken the connection.

Funny, thought Etherington, Jack was normally so chatty. He shrugged before putting on a light linen jacket and going downstairs to the car.

'I want to buy some presents for my family,' he said to the driver. 'I'm told there's a big market on the edge of the city.'

'Oh, yes, sah, Sabon Gari.'

'That's the name, I think,' said Etherington, settling into his seat. 'Is it far?'

'Other side, sah,' said the driver, taking his seat. 'Not far, you can find what you want at Sabon Gari.'

'Yes,' said Etherington almost to himself as he leaned back and closed his eyes. 'I believe I can.'

Across town, the Ngale was speaking angrily into a satellite telephone to London. 'Who was it?' he demanded.

'I don't know, Ngale,' said the voice on the other end. 'But it was not an accident. Adi Akin was there and the night watch.'

'Of course it wasn't an accident, you fool. I want to know who did it. What does Akin say?'

'No Akin, Ngale. I cannot find him. He was in the fire.'

'And the guard? The shipments?'

'It was a big fire, our father. Everything is gone.'

'What do you mean "everything"?' demanded the Ngale. 'What have you seen?'

'I can't go by, sah. But I can see. All warehouse is gone.'

The Ngale pursed his lips and thought for a moment before speaking again.

'Find who did it,' he said firmly. 'They will pay to me.'

'Yes, Ngale.'

'Send a good man to the China people and one to the South Americans. Ask them until they tell you. Do you understand?'

'Yes, Ngale, they will tell us.'

'Good. And you. Go to Manchester. I will send the Sunday shipment to you there. Can you be ready in time?'

'No, Ngale. All we needed was in the fire.'

The Ngale paused again. 'Are you sure?'

'Yes, our father. I have seen it. It is all gone.'

'Very well,' said the Ngale. 'Go to the Swiss and replace it. Pay cash if you have to. I will not be stopped.'

'No, Ngale. No one can stop you.'

'Good. Find the people who did the fire and tell me.'

'Yes, Ngale. I will do it.'

Tom Collis had bought his house near Cambridge with a view to living in it when he retired. He had found a small farmer's cottage outside Stapleford, some five miles south of the city. He and Aurelia had moved into it together and she looked after it on her own when he was in Africa.

Peter owned a small flat in Cambridge and had rooms in Lacrima Christi as well, but he had more or less lived at the cottage since he and Aurelia had been caring for her father in his last illness.

After Tom Collis died and Aurelia inherited the cottage, she and Peter continued to live there. Once they were married, they intended to find somewhere nearer Cambridge, perhaps in Newnham, with room for children.

They expected that the combined money from the flat and the cottage would buy them the size of house they would be looking for. Indeed, Aurelia had already secretly been checking out which streets in Newnham she liked the look of and had seen one or two houses that she hoped would come up.

The cottage itself was at the end of an unmade track on the brow of a hill that overlooked Cambridge from the south.

That Thursday it was nearly midday before Peter turned off the main road and bumped up the lane. The yellow fields of oilseed rape flowers had been replaced by the darker blue-green of the ripening crop. They seemed to stretch away to the horizon and the heavy, familiar smell of the oilseed blew into the car through the open windows. Peter was very tired and glad to be coming home.

Aurelia's car was not in the drive as he parked next to the house, and he assumed she must still be at the college.

Peter set his case down in the kitchen, before walking into the hall and calling Lacrima Christi.

'Yes, Dr Wilson,' the porter explained. 'Miss Collis is with Mrs Lessing in the new library arranging things for this evening. I'm afraid there's no telephone in there yet but I can walk across and ask her to call you back if you would like.'

'No thank you,' said Peter. 'I expect she'll be finished soon but you might tell her I'm at home if you see her.'

'Yes, sir.'

'By the way,' added Peter, 'do you know how many people are due this evening?'

'Fifty-seven, sir. That is including the Vice Chancellor's party, although I understand they will not be staying for dinner.'

'Thank you. And any word on the benefactor yet?'

'No, sir.'

'Come on, Charlie,' said Peter. 'Someone must have an idea.'

173

'Well, sir,' said the porter on the telephone, lowering his voice, 'I do hear they were in touch with the Master yesterday but only to say they would not be coming this evening after all.'

'Anonymous to the end then?'

'Yes, sir.'

'OK,' said Peter. 'Thanks. Just tell Aurelia I'm here if you see her on her way out.'

He put the kettle on and was just looking through the refrigerator when the telephone in the hall rang.

'Hello, darling,' he said. 'I've just rung you.'

'Oh?' came Jaygo's voice. 'Have you?'

'Jaygo! How the hell did you get this number?'

'I rang the college and they said you'd just rung from there.'

'Oh.'

'Problem?' she asked.

'It's Aurelia's house.'

'So? Well, I won't ring it again then. But I thought you were going to call me earlier on the satellite number.'

'Sorry,' he said. 'But I haven't been near a phone till now.'

'Mmm. Well, I'm only ringing to say that it's all set for tomorrow. Get to City by about half past eleven and that will give Sven enough time to weigh you and put you in the hold.'

'But I've got a Kano ticket from Heathrow.'

'Oh, you and your Heathrow,' she said. 'Cancel it and come with me and Laurie just like yesterday.'

'I suppose so,' he sighed.

'You don't sound frightfully keen.'

'Well,' he began.

'Well what?'

'I'm not sure it's such a good idea, Jay.'

'Why? Are you worried about last night?'

'Which bit? The warehouse?'

'No, that's not the bit I mean and you know that. Look, it just happened, OK? If you want to say it never happened, then you can, but it did. And I'm glad even if you're not.'

'It's not that,' he said.

'It is.'

'Jay, sweetie, it's just not that bloody simple and you know it isn't.'

She did not reply.

'Are you still there?' he said.

'Yes,' she relied. 'Just thinking.'

174

'We can't sort this out over the phone,' he said. 'And it hasn't exactly been a normal sort of week, has it?'

'No,' she said. 'And it isn't finished yet either.'

'Look,' he said, 'I can see Aurelia just coming back. Can I ring you at the hotel tonight?'

'Yes, I'm going back to change at about seven but after that I'll be on the satellite number.'

'Seven it is then. Bye.'

Peter put the telephone down and returned to the kitchen. His post was piled up neatly on the kitchen table. There were a couple of bills which he put aside without opening, together with two magazines and a scientific journal. Only at the bottom were two items of 'real' post.

One was a jiffy bag the size of a book, postmarked Cambridge, and the other was a letter from Liverpool.

Peter looked at the handwriting on the letter from Liverpool and decided to open it first.

Dear Peter

I am glad this is a letter and not a phone call. I have tried to get you several times at the department and the college but nobody seemed to know quite when you would be back from Atlanta and I wanted you to have this news as soon as possible. It is good news and bad news. First the bad.

There is no way of dressing this up. Basically the tracking satellite data we downloaded for you is corrupted.

There are two bio-tracking channels and you have bought time on one of them. I know you have been working on locust movements which is a bit outside our normal patterns and so we would have no way of knowing if you are getting what you are expecting. To us, your data is simply a binary stream and I sign off all the data and put it onto your disk stack here in Liverpool for you to take off as and when you are ready. I occasionally check the bandwidth in terms of gigabytes but that is about it.

My records show that you took time on our Biostat 80 as it passed over Northern Nigeria on eight separate occasions between February and May this year. The other people who used Biostat 80 are all further to the east of you between the Rift Valley and the Pacific. They are tracking everything from baboons to dolphins, as far as I can remember without looking it up. I think it fair to say that only about half the tracking

175

experiments work at the best of times. People tend to put it down to 'biological variation' but, if you ask me, poor experimental design is to blame as often as not.

You may be aware that when Biostat 80 is not being used for tracking experiments it is used for following civil-engineering projects such as bridge building and road construction. It is also an open secret that our most profitable customer is the US government who probably use it to monitor Central Asian troop movements although they would never admit it!

Anyway, Peter, all this is scarcely news to you, but what I am trying to explain is that, with so many 'customers', Biostat 80 has to go wrong in quite a few of its sub-routines for people to press the panic button and contact us.

I say 'sub-routines' because it is usually software that is faulty but, in your case, it is a hardware problem and that is much harder to put right.

Essentially, one of the chips in the cache RAM array has failed. We might be able to isolate it and right a patch but frankly I don't think so. The best I can suggest is to run the data again from your end and to disregard any bad streams we can identify.

As you read this, I can hear you saying that because you work on such a narrow bandwidth you would have to disregard up to eighty percent of your data. Not much use to you, I am afraid.

The fault is definitely ours and, of course, your Institute in Kano will be refunded for your satellite time. No bills.

The good news, such as it is, is that we will grant you free of charge an equivalent time on the new Biostat 90 which launches from the Shuttle some time in November. I appreciate this will be cold comfort to you because you told me that the combination of weather and locust concentrations this year was particularly unusual and may never be repeated.

Please ring me when you return to Cambridge.

Regards to Aurelia,

Yours sincerely

Martin Glynne

Peter looked at the date on the envelope before folding it away. Monday. The day before the Atlanta bomb.

Thank you for nothing, Martin, he thought. 'Particularly unusual'?

The first time in about four hundred years – if that counts as 'unusual'.

He fetched a bottle of milk and opened his briefcase.

He picked out the copy of the paper he had been going to present in Atlanta to see what his data might look like if he disregarded the eighty percent of it that would be wrong. He looked at the title page and then put it back in the case without opening it. What was the point? He knew his own files well enough. If eighty percent of them were unusable then the whole thing was a waste of time. The remaining twenty percent, even if he could decide *which* twenty percent, wouldn't be worth more than a letter to *Science Today*.

The gift-wrapped pen he had been going to give to Jaygo fell out. He looked at it ruefully. What had she said? 'Not exactly a normal sort of week'?

He walked out of the open back door, taking the bottle of milk with him. He drank from it and looked out towards Cambridge in the distance. There was a mile of fields between him and the ugly hospital chimney and, beyond that, another mile before the city itself. The University Library, Kings and John's Chapel. Familiar landmarks all. I have spent about half of my life here, he thought. Most of the important things that have ever happened to me were here.

Until this week. Atlanta. The bomb. The warehouse on the Isle of Dogs.

Jaygo again.

Or the expression in the guard's eyes as he had been shot. The dead girl's red eyes at the lecture theatre. Margaret.

'Unusual sort of week'? Nightmare bloody week more like.

He heard a car on the gravel behind and turned around to see Aurelia driving up.

'Hello, darling. Welcome home,' she called as the car came to a halt.

Maybe the rest of the week would be better. 'Hello, little one,' he said. 'It's good to see you.'

Just as Peter was greeting Aurelia, Laurie Miller was being welcomed by a white-coated doctor at the Special Clinic of the West London Hospital.

'Hello, Laurie. It's good to see you,' he said showing Laurie into a consulting room.

'I've asked a colleague to join us today,' he went on. 'This is Dr Windsor.'

Laurie shook hands with a grey-haired man of about fifty in an expensive suit.

'Call me Miles,' said the man in the suit.

Laurie smiled politely and sat down.

The doctor in the white coat opened a file and laid it on the desk in front of him. 'Well,' he began. 'I've got the results of the blood tests we ran last week.'

Get on with it, thought Laurie.

'We run a lot of tests of course,' the doctor continued. 'Some of them tell us more than others.'

The count, said Laurie to himself. Tell me the count.

'The viral count is the one we really look at the most,' said the doctor, looking up at Laurie. 'It's risen, I'm afraid.'

Laurie did not say anything.

'The thing is,' Windsor said, 'it's the best indication we have of how you are responding to all the pills we are asking you to take.'

Yes, thought Laurie. Go on.

'Dr James tells me you're something of a biologist yourself and so I'm sure you know all of this,' Windsor continued.

There was an awkward silence

'Tell me what it is,' said Laurie at last.

'Of course, it's only one indicator,' said Dr James. 'We have to look at them all.'

'Tell me what it is,' repeated Laurie.

James looked down at the notes again and ran his finger lightly over a row of numbers.

'Eighty-seven,' he said. 'Perhaps eighty-eight.'

'Thank you,' said Laurie quietly.

There was another silence before Windsor began again. 'I think we need to try something else for you now,' he said looking at Laurie. 'Another regime.'

He held out a hand and rocked it back and forth. 'It's a question of balance. Different concentrations, you know.'

'Yes, I do know,' said Laurie. 'Quite a lot actually.'

'Essentially,' Windsor went on, picking up a pen and tapping his hand with it, 'we need to up the dose of the Tri-X and the Beta-Five. I think you've done pretty well on the combinations Dr James has been giving you but we don't want things running away from us at this stage, do we?'

No, thought Laurie, we don't want that.

'There's a new thing I want to try,' said Windsor.

178

Laurie looked up at him. 'New?'

'It's been around for a bit but hasn't been used on HIV before,' explained Windsor.

'Who's it from?' asked Laurie.

'A Swiss outfit. Geneva Pharmaceuticals. They're pretty big and maybe you've heard of them.'

'Yes,' said Laurie, smiling to himself. 'I have heard of them.'

'It's one of their older drugs,' said James. 'It didn't do frightfully well first time around but we ran it though our own testing screen and it looks pretty good.'

'Of course,' said Windsor, 'the advantage to us is that it's passed all its registrations and has a full licence. We can use it straight away.'

'Good,' said Laurie. 'Tell me more.'

'It was used against Hepatitis-C originally but it had some problems and they more or less withdrew it about a year ago.'

'Oh?' said Laurie. 'What problems?'

'Well,' said Windsor and paused. 'It had some side effects, I'm afraid.'

'Ah,' said Laurie again. 'I thought there might be a catch.'

'But we think we can get around them,' said Windsor quickly. 'They were only long-term ones and we think we can balance them out. We hope we can.'

Laurie looked at the two men opposite him. It's not easy for them either, he thought.

'You see,' began James, 'your count is up, Laurie. And it's rising. The Tri-X and Beta Five are not holding you any more and so we have to look at the whole thing another way.'

'Yes,' said Windsor quietly.

'There's a very good chance this treatment will reduce your count,' continued James. 'I won't pretend we know all about it but we want you to try it.'

Laurie looked down at his hands.

Guinea pig, he thought. I'm a guinea pig.

He looked up at the two men and managed a thin smile.

'OK,' he said, 'I think I get the drift. The count's going up and I'm going down. This is all you've got left in the cupboard.'

'I wouldn't put it like that,' said Windsor. 'Not at all.'

Laurie paused. 'Is it a trial?' he asked.

'Not exactly,' said Windsor uneasily. 'The drug is registered so, strictly speaking, we don't need a trial.

'We think it might be right for you. I think it will hold your

179

count until we have an opportunity to look at your therapy in more depth.'

'But you're not sure, are you?' said Laurie.

James leant forwards. 'I wouldn't offer it to you unless I was pretty positive.'

'How many other people are going to try it?' asked Laurie.

'There's going to be quite a few of you, I hope,' said Dr James. '"Going to be"?'

'Yes, I'll square with you, Laurie,' said James, sitting up. 'I don't have to tell you what a terrific job the combination therapy has done. It's changed the lives of literally thousands of people both here and in the States. But it's essentially just a holding procedure and we always knew that. It doesn't eliminate the virus.'

He paused and looked across at Windsor.

Laurie held up a hand. 'OK,' he said. 'When do I start?'

Windsor looked relieved. 'Straight away,' he said. 'I can get the new one put into the pack for you to pick up at the pharmacy as you go out.'

Laurie smiled and stood up.

'Thank you,' said James. 'I hoped you'd understand.'

'Oh, yes,' said Laurie, leaning forward and tapping his notes. 'I think we all understand.'

Aurelia had made a pot of tea and was cutting sandwiches. 'Why don't you have a sleep after these,' she was saying. 'I can wake you up at about five and that will give us plenty of time to be at college for half past six.'

'That's a good idea,' said Peter. 'I'm very tired.'

'Good,' she said. 'You go on up and run the bath and I'll bring this lot up for you.'

'Actually,' he said, 'on second thoughts I'll have them in the orchard and go up later.'

'OK,' she said, putting the plate of sandwiches on a tray. 'You carry these and I'll come along with the tea.

'Do you want to go through your post?' she added.

'No,' he said. 'I've seen the only letter. The rest is just stuff I can look at tomorrow.'

'Ah,' she began and picked up the jiffy bag, 'but it's not just "stuff". This one is from John Lorrington.'

'The solicitor?'

'You remember him, don't you?'

'Of course. Why do you think it's from him?'

'I got one from him in the same post.'

'A book?'

'No, silly. Mine was just a letter about Dad's will, but John said he was sending you something too.'

'Your father's will?' asked Peter. 'I thought that was all sorted out ages ago.'

'Of course it was,' said Aurelia, 'come on.'

They walked out into the garden and turned down the path by the side of the house leading to the small orchard.

'You know solicitors,' she said. 'They love details and apparently a couple of people, servants at the house in Kano, can't be traced from here. He's asked me to look them up when we go out this week.'

'We?' said Peter uneasily.

'Yes,' she said, 'I thought I told you I was coming with you for this trip. Dad's ashes.'

'I don't remember that,' said Peter, thinking immediately of Jaygo's visit to Kano.

'Of course you do,' she said easily. 'I told you just before you went off last week so perhaps you've forgotten. You know Dad always wanted us to take his ashes to Kano after he died. His "bones" he used to call them.'

Peter nodded.

'Yes, you remember he always said that there was no point going to work in Africa unless you were prepared to "leave your bones" there. Anyway, I said I would do this for him.'

They had reached the orchard and Peter walked over the rough grass to a hammock strung between two apple trees. Aurelia set the tray down on an open-sided box. 'Of course, I remember now,' said Peter. 'But you don't have to go. I can do it.'

'I know you can,' she said pleasantly, holding the side of the hammock as he swung his legs up. 'But I'd feel I was letting him down if I didn't do it myself.'

Peter lay back and put his hands behind his head. 'I don't think so,' he said. 'I'll have plenty of time and it's not exactly a cheap flight you know.'

'Don't be silly,' she said, giving the hammock a playful push. 'It's not *that* much and, besides, because I've booked so late I got a special deal from British Airways.'

Peter looked at her, trying to think of something to say.

She began pouring his tea and appeared not to notice his hesitation. 'This box,' she said. 'It's my old guinea pig hutch. I came across it in the garage when I was clearing it out at the week-end.'

She passed him his tea and smiled at him. 'I'd better go and look at Dad's bees,' she said. 'You go ahead and have your doze and I'll be back later.'

Peter watched her go up the path to the house. When she reached the door, she turned to blow him a kiss before going in.

Aurelia. Jaygo. Kano. Not a terribly good combination, he reflected.

Peter had never thought of his life as being divided up into compartments but here were three things that deserved to be kept separate.

He knew Aurelia had only been to Kano twice since she was little. She had not liked it at all.

Her first visit coincided with a particularly hot dry season. A series of power cuts and an unreliable air-conditioning system had not helped. The idea had been for her to travel with Peter and her father to Gombe but she contracted food poisoning and had been too sick to travel. She had been well enough looked after by the servants, and people had visited from the Institute but, when Peter and Tom came back, it was to a very miserable Aurelia who just wanted to go back to England.

Tom thought that perhaps a visit in the slightly cooler wet season might be better and so they tried again the following year but it proved equally disastrous. The sight of open drains overflowing in the middle of Kano had been bad enough but the smell when their own street's sewer broke was enough to convince Aurelia that Kano was not for her. When she left for England a day later, it was on the clear understanding that she would not return to Nigeria again.

Peter and she planned for her to stay in England after they were married. He would only go to Kano for as long on each visit as was necessary and he would start thinking about work nearer home.

They had discussed this quite openly with Tom before he died and Aurelia was relieved when she learnt from the two men that there were probably only five years' life left in the Institute before it went completely downhill. Five years of living mainly apart did not seem such a daunting prospect to her if it meant they would be together afterwards. Many marriages started out that way, she told herself, and they succeeded.

Peter secretly thought that eight to ten years might be nearer the mark but he imagined a compromise might be reached. Perhaps she could try Kano again and come out to visit him sometimes.

But, whatever their plans, he certainly did not expect her to go out again so soon.

He lay on his hammock and told himself he would definitely have not agreed to the Jaygo thing if he had known Aurelia would be there at the same time. But, he thought, he hadn't really 'agreed' to the Jaygo thing anyway. She had just steamrollered him into it – as usual.

That was the difference between the two women, he concluded. Jaygo charged ahead and expected everyone else to fit in with her while Aurelia – well, whatever Aurelia decided to do, it never involved 'steamrollering' people, did it?

And yet, here was Aurelia suddenly deciding to go to Kano and expecting Peter to go along with her. But perhaps that wasn't so unreasonable. They *were* engaged and she had told him about it last week even if he had forgotten in the meantime.

Perhaps he could work it so the two women never actually *met* in Kano.

He immediately dismissed the idea as ridiculous. Unless he could persuade Aurelia *not* to come to Kano, she was bound to come face to face with Jaygo.

And, if *that* happened, he had better know what to do in advance. But what *could* he do about Jaygo?

What did he want to do?

He was reminded, as he lay on the hammock, of an interview he had heard the week before on the radio between two politicians. He had forgotten what they had been discussing but one was being cautious about whatever it was and had said, 'Let's just wait and see how history unfolds on this one.'

'I've got news for you,' the other man had said. 'History unfolded yesterday. It's today now, not tomorrow.'

Yes, thought Peter, sitting up and putting his legs over the side of the hammock to reach for his tea, the Jaygo and Aurelia thing had definitely come unfolded.

'Unstitched, more like,' he said out loud. 'Unstitched, wheels off and heading for the wall.'

He picked up one of the sandwiches Aurelia had made him. Jaygo probably didn't even know how to make a sandwich.

He sat for a while, swinging his legs backwards and forwards.

Well, he decided, there wasn't any *real* need to make his mind up what to do just yet. He hadn't cancelled his plane ticket. There was plenty of time.

*   *   *

In Kano, John Etherington was standing in front of the church of Santa Maria in Sabon Gari, looking at the statue.

If there had ever been a churchyard it was long gone and the rather dilapidated building stood alone in the middle of a square. He looked closely at the depth of the niche the statue was standing in. He decided it was about a foot deeper than the figure itself. Plenty of room to get a rope behind the stone figure.

The statue seemed to have been crudely painted at some stage in the past and so it was difficult to see what stone it had been carved from. He took a small penknife from his pocket and scraped away some of the paint on one of the feet. Several layers of paint came away but he still could not see the stone beneath clearly. He jabbed firmly at the foot to check how hard it was. Harder than sandstone but not as hard as marble, he decided. He folded the penknife shut and put it back in his pocket as he stood back to get a better look at the figure as a whole.

I could put the rope at around the height of the waist, he thought. Then run it down about ten yards to the back of the car, tie it to the chassis and pull. He thought the statue would probably break when it hit the ground but he had better get a sledge-hammer just in case.

He had deliberately been quite open in what he was doing to see if he attracted any attention. He looked nonchalantly around him to see if anyone was watching. A small crowd of children had gathered at the corner of the church but that was about all.

There were no telephone wires or power lines crossing the square to prevent the helicopter from landing so, all in all, it looked as though things might go pretty well. It would be different afterwards of course, he knew. It would not take nosy Jack Ngale long to find out what was happening but that did not really matter.

Etherington knew that if he timed the operation well, he and the torque would be gone from Kano inside twenty minutes. After that things could look after themselves.

He also knew that, whatever Jack Ngale found out about him and the statue, he would never admit that the real torque had been found. In any case, Jack had his new one to play with.

Etherington walked back to his car. Ridiculous, Jack with his pathetic vanity and O'Leary with his obsession to own things. He, John Etherington, would finish up with the only thing that actually mattered. The money. A very great deal of it.

It was all a matter of timing and, even if he did say so himself, his timing this week had been pretty spot on. New York, Atlanta, Kano, setting up O'Leary. All that remained was to sell the torque and head off to Goa.

Stuff you, Jack Ngale, he said to himself as he reached the car.

The driver was holding the back door open for him. 'She's beautiful, isn't she, sah?'

'What?'

'Our Lady, sah. The Sunday Lady.'

'Very impressive,' said Etherington unconvincingly as he slid into the car. 'I'm hot now. Take me to the house.'

'But the market, sah. You have not been to the market.'

'I will come back when it is cooler. I presume it will still be open?'

'Oh, yes, sah. Sabon Gari open very late.'

'Good,' said Etherington quietly. 'That is just what I want to hear.'

If John Etherington was having a good week, Laurie Miller was not.

At the same time that Etherington was congratulating himself on the way back to the rest house, Laurie Miller was returning exhausted to his hotel room. Jaygo had been pretty good about it really, he thought. She seemed to have sensed that he didn't have anywhere proper to stay and had 'insisted' that he stay at the hotel before they went to Kano together.

'And I'll ask around at the studio today,' she had said at breakfast. 'Someone's bound to have a room in a flat somewhere for you. Leave it to me.'

Laurie smiled as he remembered. Of all the people who might lend him a hand, Jaygo was the last one he would have thought of. Perhaps he had misjudged her.

As he put his briefcase down on the bed, he noticed a little red light blinking on the telephone. He sat down heavily next to his case and picked up the receiver. A polite voice on the other end told him there was a message for him. He lit a cigarette as Jaygo's voice came on the line.

'Laurie, darling, it's me. I don't know what time you'll get this but it's twelve o'clock now and we've hardly started here so I'm not going to get back until God knows when. Hugo the Bubo has fixed up for us to meet some record people tonight so dinner's off but I'll drop in on you at about seven. OK?'

'Have a dinner on me in the restaurant if you want to stay

in and there's a swimming pool in the basement if you fancy a dip.

'If I don't catch you tonight, we'll meet up for breakfast about nine which will give us plenty of time to drive out to City, meet up with Pete, and fly out at about eleven.

'Oh yes, I nearly forgot, I'm afraid I told the man in the hotel shop that your clothes are an absolute fright so he's expecting you some time this afternoon to try a few things on. I can't have you turning up as my Press Agent if you look like a scruff pot so get something decent. It's all on me, so don't get anything too outrageous. More Cannes than Hawaii, I think.

'And before you say you can't, remember you're working for me for the next few days and you're going to write something really nice about my African adventure. A proper job won't do you any harm, even if it is for only a few days. Oh God! Now Hugo's banging at me from behind the glass so I've got to go. See you at seven. Byee.'

He put the telephone down and rubbed the side of his neck. He had walked all the way back from the clinic and felt very tired. Perhaps a cup of tea was called for. He rang room service and, yes, he would like a selection of cakes too, thank you very much.

He looked at his watch. Three. Time for another set of pills already. He flipped open the case next to him and took out the new set he had collected from the clinic.

The pills came already sorted and set out in compartments inside a plastic container that looked like a fisherman's bait box. The clinic were always telling him to take them dead on time and in order and after food or before food or whatever.

I do what I can, he thought, and I don't do badly. But, if I was a perfect human being, I wouldn't need to take them in the first place.

Each time he collected a fresh set from the clinic, there seemed to be even more pills of more colours than the time before. At first he had wanted to know what each of them was and what they all did. So he learnt which the main ones were, which ones countered the main side effects, which balanced out which minerals and so on. He had once asked them lightly which ones he absolutely *had* to take.

'All of them,' they said.

He had stopped asking them things after that and began simply scooping them up like peanuts and scrunching them up without water.

Lots of people have to take pills all the time, he told himself. Astronauts, sports people. It's part of everyday life for them.

Part of normal life really. Sort of.

There was a bitter, metallic taste in his mouth after he had taken the pills so he walked into the bathroom to rinse his mouth. He caught sight of himself in the mirror. A pale, pudgy face stared back at him with heavy bags under the eyes. The stubble on his chin looked distinctly grey.

He splashed some water onto his face and smiled at his reflection. 'If you look like this now,' he said out loud, 'fuck knows what you'll look like in six months' time.'

Walking back into the main room, he decided that something a little stronger than water was required and took a can of beer from the mini-bar.

He looked at his watch again. Five past three. And Jaygo said she would be here about seven.

He sat down with his briefcase on his knee. This time he ignored the box of pills and took out a slim manila folder.

He put the case on the floor at his feet before opening the folder and surveying the fifty or so typed pages it contained.

It had been an exaggeration to tell Peter and Jaygo that his book on Jack Ngale was 'all but finished'. Because, in truth, this was all there was of it. A fiction writer could get away with fifty pages and call it a 'novella' but a journalistic exposé was supposed to be a considerably bulkier item.

And better researched, he thought as he looked at his notes. And better backed up. And with enough time to write it all properly.

Jaygo had asked him if he wasn't just tilting at windmills. She might have been right, but if he wasn't going to do this, what was he going to do?

He wasn't very optimistic about his medical treatment. Right at the beginning they had explained to him that he would be 'all right' if his viral count remained below one hundred. Below that he could expect to remain largely symptom free. There might be 'problems', they explained, but these were known about and could be dealt with. Above a hundred, it would be more difficult. Several things might happen at once and the drugs they would need would be too strong for him to cope with.

He read that a lot of people had lived on the combination therapy he took for five or even ten years and had continued to lead quite normal lives. But he noticed that 'normal' for them seemed to involve living in California, having plenty of money and a network of encouraging and supportive friends.

'Normal' for Laurie meant living in assorted bed-sits in London, fighting for stories with other journalists who all seemed younger and more energetic than him. His friends were quite happy to be encouraging and supportive only so often as he could afford to stand his round of drinks.

At around the time his viral count had started to rise, his doctor had told him about the buddy system. This 'buddy' would agree to act as an emotional long-stop. Someone who would always 'be there' whatever happened. And still be there when 'whatever' actually happened.

Laurie did not have a buddy. The nearest he had come to such a person after Peter had gone to Africa was Chris Iltan in Belfast. For those few brief months he found out first hand about having, loving and sharing.

Everyday activities with Chris like shopping in supermarkets or simply driving from one place to another were occasions to look forward to, enjoy and even talk about afterwards. Laurie and Chris had always known that the book about the Belfast drug scene was 'dangerous' but it had been simply one more thing for them to share.

Then, when Chris had been shot, everything stopped. Laurie was quite unprepared for the grief that engulfed him. So often he went over that last day in his mind to see if there was any way he could have prevented the killing. He found himself doing it again as he sat in the hotel looking over his new notes.

It had been an ordinary, happy day. Chris had gone to a pub to meet a contact, as he had done on numerous other occasions.

They had been planning an evening in together and Laurie was going to cook a complicated Chinese dish they had seen on the television the night before. Chris had laughed on the way out and told Laurie to be sure to go to the bank that afternoon and take some money out because they were bound to need it for a proper Chinese meal when Laurie's disaster revealed itself. More laughter.

Well, thought Laurie, finishing his beer, that had been five years ago. He should be more or less over it by now. He lobbed the empty can into a bin and sat back to wait for the tea and cakes to arrive.

But he hadn't 'got over' the Chris business. You didn't 'get over' a thing like that. The best that could be said was that it might get further away with time. He looked forward to that. To be able to look over his shoulder and see it as a small point so far away it didn't hurt any more.

But it didn't look as though that would ever happen. He had no way of knowing how long he had left but he knew it would not be long enough. The memory was still as fresh in his mind as if it had happened yesterday and that wasn't very far away at all.

And the real yesterday? That business in the warehouse or the day before when he had been confronted with all those bodies in the lecture hall in Atlanta? Compared to how he felt when Chris had been shot, they simply did not register. He smiled when he remembered how impressed Peter had been with his ability to cope but really it was not in the same league as Belfast at all.

When you had already had lunch with the devil, you didn't much care who came for tea.

Laurie looked at his watch again. Perhaps he could ring Peter now.

'Hi, Laurie!' said the familiar voice. 'How's things?'

'OK. I'm still in the hotel.'

'Good. I understand from Jay that she's found a way to persuade you to come to Kano after all?'

'Yes. I was being silly. I'm sure it'll be fine. She's spoken to Jack about it and he said it was a good idea for us all to be there at the same time.'

'Oh.'

'Apparently the only reason he wasn't keen in the first place is that he wanted his people to do the press but when she said I could get coverage in London he went along with it.'

'And can you?'

'I can try.'

'And Belfast?'

'That's what put me off at first, of course,' said Laurie. 'But I don't think he connects me with the Iltan book at all.'

'But he must have known you were there.'

'Possibly. But no more than that.'

'If you say so,' said Peter with some doubt in his voice.

'I've got to go for it. I can't go on for ever wondering if he knew I was there, can I?'

'OK,' said Peter, still only partly convinced.

'Anyway,' said Laurie, 'Jay says you're meeting up with us at City and flying out with us.'

'Ah,' said Peter. 'Bit of a prob there, I'm afraid.'

'Prob?'

'Yes, Aurelia. She wants to come too.'

'With Jaygo! Are you out of your head?'

'Well,' said Peter, 'Aurelia doesn't exactly know about Jay going.'

'Are you mad?'

'I haven't told her yet. I will.'

'Peter, in case you haven't noticed, we're going tomorrow. That's less than twenty-four hours away. Don't you think you'd better tell her one or two things pretty damn quickly?'

'What things?'

'Christ, man, Jay's in full flight mode. She thinks that you and her are going off into the sunset, with me recording everything in my junior reporter's ring-bound.'

'It's not like that and you know it. She just wants me to meet Jack with her. That was fixed before you were going at all. You'd be just as good. He knows you.'

'Piss off! You know damn well there's a whole lot more to it than that.'

'Such as?'

'Such as last night for a start.'

'The warehouse?' said Peter.

'No,' said Laurie. 'The hotel.'

'That was different,'

'No, it wasn't,' returned Laurie. 'It was you. It was Jaygo. It was last night.'

'What has she told you then?'

'I had breakfast with her. She told me you were still asleep.'

'What was I supposed to do? Send her back to her room?'

'I don't know what you were supposed to do, Peter. But whatever you did, I'm pretty sure it was the wrong thing.'

Peter paused.

'Are you still there?' Laurie asked.

'Yes,' said Peter. 'It was . . . It just happened. Hell, Laurie, it wasn't planned or anything.'

'Not by you maybe. I could see what was going to happen as we went up in the lift.'

'Look, Lol, you'll just have to tell her that Aurelia's coming. You and Jay will stay in the hotel and I'll come round when it's time to go to Jack.'

'Me tell her? Why the hell can't you tell her yourself?'

'Because I can't get in touch with her,' said Peter crossly. 'And I've got to go to a reception tonight. It's no big deal.'

'You can ring her now,' said Laurie. 'I've just spoken to her at the studio and you can ring her on her satellite thing.'

'Oh, yes? Me and whose phone bill?' replied Peter. 'Do you know how much it costs to ring that thing?'

'No, I don't,' sighed Laurie. 'Peter, she'll go ballistic when she finds out and I don't see why I should take the flack.'

'Well, she can bugger off then. I'm not going to be pushed into anything.'

'Oh, yes?' said Laurie. 'Such as being pushed into making your mind up about something for the first time in your life? Is that what you mean?'

'Yes. Just that. I won't be pushed.'

'Peter, you bloody fool. You've just spent the best part of two days and two nights with her. You can't just turn round and say "Sorry".'

'Laurie. Just tell her. And, anyway, I did not spend two nights with her.'

'One then.'

'Thank you. Look, I'll fly to Kano with Aurelia and I'll ring you as soon as I get there to see what's going on, OK? I just need a bit of time to sort things out.'

'No, Peter. This isn't much of a week for "taking a bit of time". There's quite a lot going on in case you haven't noticed.'

'I've got to go now,' said Peter. 'Aurelia's only upstairs. Everything will work out fine. I'll talk to both of you when we get there, OK?'

Laurie was about to speak again when he heard Peter put the phone down.

Aurelia was coming downstairs with a basket of ironing. 'Who was that, darling?' she asked. 'The college?'

'No,' said Peter. 'That was Laurie Miller. He's going to be in Kano too.'

'Laurie? What's he going to Kano for?'

'I spoke to him in Atlanta and he said he wants to go.'

'Yes, but what for?' she asked, slightly uneasily.

'He was in Atlanta covering the conference but while he was there he ran into Jocasta Manhattan and she set it up for him.'

'Jocasta Manhattan?' asked Aurelia evenly as she went past Peter into the kitchen.

'Yes. She was there at the end of a tour or something.'

Aurelia turned around to face Peter. 'Jaygo?' she said.

'Yes. She was a friend of ours at university. Jack too.'

'"Friend", was it?' said Aurelia, going to a cupboard and taking out an iron.

'I told you about her. I went out with her for a bit.'

Aurelia put the iron on the table and returned to the cupboard for the ironing board. 'Yes,' she said, 'you did tell me. But I thought it was more than just "a bit".'

'Well,' said Peter, coming into the kitchen. 'I suppose, yes. But it's a long time ago. Student days and all that. You know.'

Aurelia began to arrange a white shirt for ironing. 'And didn't she break it off and go to New York?'

'Not really. We sort of came to the end of our student days and all went our separate ways. Jack, me, Laurie. Her.'

He leant back against the sink, watching her iron.

'Laurie and I stayed in touch, of course,' he said. 'And I see Jack a good deal, but Jaygo?' He shrugged. 'She was lost to sight.'

'She did pretty well though, didn't she?'

'I should say so. I mean, she's made a bomb, hasn't she? Mega.'

Aurelia continued ironing.

'I thought she knew you pretty well when she came to college,' she said.

'She's just showbiz now. All air kisses and hello darling. I'm afraid she's changed a lot. Seems to live on a different planet now.'

'And she was in Atlanta this week? You didn't say,' continued Aurelia.

'There was no reason why I should. I didn't know she was going to be there until Laurie said he'd seen her. In fact, if it hadn't been for Laurie, I wouldn't have known she was going to Kano at all.'

'Kano?' said Aurelia suddenly. 'Jocasta Manhattan's going to Kano?'

'On business apparently, with Jack. She'll be there with Laurie doing a record launch.'

Aurelia stopped ironing and looked up. 'Jocasta Manhattan? A record launch in Kano?'

'Yes,' continued Peter. 'She's done some African music or other and Jack's record company is going to launch it for her.'

'African music?' said Aurelia, clearly confused. 'I thought she was classical?'

'She does all sorts. African. American. Pop. She's up for whatever will sell. I think she's turned her hands to most things.'

'Oh,' said Aurelia, turning back to her ironing again. 'I knew she did classical but I didn't know she did African music too.'

'Ladysmith Black Mambazo. You remember, they came to the Corn Exchange in January. We nearly went.'

'Did you know then she was going to do it? You never said.'

'I didn't know about it at all till Laurie told me. Apparently he's going to do a feature on her for one of the London glossies. Laurie says they want to make something of Jack and her knowing each other at university and here they are, ten years later, in business together. Jack owns a couple of radio stations. I know it's a pretty tenuous link but they'll make something of nothing, won't they? You know that.'

'Who?'

'Journalists. Laurie and his lot. He knew them both so it was natural for him to set up a story. Any excuse for a few column inches, he says.'

'And you too?' she asked. 'Are they going to make something of you too – the old flame?'

'Hardly. I'll just be there at the same time.'

'Will we have to see them?'

'Not if you don't want to,' said Peter. 'But it'd be a bit rude if I didn't go and say hello, wouldn't it? I have to keep on the right side of Jack and he's bound to ask us to some do or other while he's showing her off.'

'And me?'

'Why not? Only if you want to. Laurie's OK and you've met Jack a couple of times. I think they'll be pretty busy. Jaygo's only going to be there for a few days and I'm not sure that it's even going to all be in Kano. There will be a bit of socialising but not all that much.'

'She was a bit rude to people at college when she came to Cambridge. Lizzie said she drifted about as if she owned the place. Made car marks in the Great Court and then just went off without even thanking the Master.'

'Lizzie would say that, wouldn't she? She's very college.'

'And she says she asked you about her,' Aurelia went on, 'and you told her you had quite a thing when you were students.'

'Hardly. But I did go out with her. I just told you, didn't I? Look, Aurelia, don't be a silly about it.'

'She sounds rather a destructive sort of person to me,' said Aurelia, unplugging the iron and winding the cord around it.

'Who? Jaygo?'

'Yes.'

'What makes you say that?'

'The way she pushed people about to get what she wanted in college. Like a steamroller, Lizzie said. She upset quite a few people, you know.'

'I didn't know that Lizzie ever met her. Did she?'

'No. But she made all sorts of arrangements for her and Jaygo never even thanked her.'.

Peter did not say anything.

'And what sort of name is "Jaygo" anyway?' Aurelia went on.

'I don't know,' said Peter. 'She's just always been called that.'

'Is it meant to be short for Jocasta? I don't think so.'

'No. Jocasta is just her stage name. Her real name is Jackie.'

'Then why "Jaygo"?'

'I don't know,' said Peter. 'Why not ask her when you meet her?'

Aurelia put the iron in the cupboard. 'I don't think she'll have much time for the likes of us from what you say. If she's doing a public-relations thing we'll probably only get a wave and an "air kiss" across the room.'

'Maybe,' said Peter, picking up the shirt. 'But she's all right really. Or used to be. I don't know her at all now.'

Aurelia glanced up at the clock on the kitchen wall. 'Half past three already,' she said. 'I want to get to college at about six but you can come along a bit later if you like. Nothing happens until the reception.'

Peter smiled, feeling he was on safer ground. 'You make it sound as if it was going to be some huge event,' he said. 'They're just going to open a library and hand around a few drinks you know.'

'It's a big event for Lizzie,' said Aurelia. 'Her husband was very well thought of and it's a great honour to have a library named after him.'

'Even if no one knows who put up the cash,' finished Peter.

'I think it's very nice that it's anonymous,' Aurelia said as she put the basket of ironing on the counter next to the cupboard. 'It keeps the attention on Bell Lessing instead of the donor.'

'Maybe,' said Peter. 'But whoever it is probably decided it would be cheaper to buy a library for the old bugger than pay off his tab at Lawyers.'

'What lawyers?'

'The pub on the corner.'

'That's not a very nice thing to say, is it? You can make light of it if you like. But I think it's an important day for the whole college, as well as for Lizzie.'

'I think it's a bit odd that no one at all knows where the money has come from. Not even Lizzie.'

'Not at all,' said Aurelia. 'And I'm going up for my bath now.

Why don't you finish going through your mail and have one after me?'

'I'll do that. And I'm sorry if I'm a bit scratchy.'

'That's all right,' she said, kissing him lightly on the cheek. 'You're tired, that's all. You and Laurie probably had far too much to drink last night.'

Peter stood looking at the table for a few minutes after she had left the room.

What was I supposed to tell her? he asked himself. Last night with Jaygo had been a one-off. And all the other things of the past couple of days hardly seemed real now he was back at home.

Where he was now was what mattered, he told himself. Cambridge, the house, Aurelia. These were the real things. And even if there was a part of him that wanted Jaygo, none of it would ever come to any good. He was always going to be what he was and Jay was always going to be what she was. He was never going to have the sort of money she had and she wouldn't want a parasite. Perhaps if he had had more money he could have done something.

But he was what he was and that was an end to it. Maybe if they'd gone to New York together he could have done something to make loads of money and then he could have kept up with her.

He smiled at himself. It hadn't happened, had it? And that was it. In his world he didn't even know how much a call to a satellite telephone cost and, in her world, she didn't care.

He picked up his pile of post and walked through to the sitting room.

He sat down on the sofa and gave his post another sort. The magazines and bills he put down again without opening them, together with the letter from Liverpool.

This left the jiffy bag which, as expected, contained a book. It immediately struck him as very old, hand-bound in flaking leather with crude stitching down the spine. On the cover was a faded circle of an inscription in broken gold lettering.

Intrigued, he opened it carefully and found it was all in a close and neatly written hand. It seemed to be a diary of some kind because there were dated sections, some much longer than others. He turned over several of the pages with a puzzled expression on his face. It was all in a language he did not immediately recognise. Spanish? Italian perhaps?

He turned to inside the front cover for more clues and found a modern envelope with his name carefully written on it in Tom Collis's handwriting.

He smiled as he took out the letter and began to read.

Dear Peter,

I have asked John Lorrington to send this to you six months after my 'demise'. I am not sure exactly when that will be but I went to Addenbrooke's today to see my specialist. A rule of thumb for you – when your usual doctor introduces you to a senior colleague who wears a suit rather than a white coat, the news will not be good. Much humming and hahing and veiled references to me putting my 'affairs in order'. Basically they cannot do much more for me. 'Your treatment is complete' is how they put it.

My affairs are pretty simple really. You will have long since seen my will and it will have been no surprise to you that I am giving Aurelia the house and what little money is in my account. The college library will get my books. I would have left them to you but they are mainly work-related and not valuable. In any case, they will be in college if you want to use them. Most of them are only duplicates of your own more careful collection. But the one in front of you now is a little different and when you have read this letter you will understand why I have never shown it to anyone.

The six month moratorium on your reading this letter is easy to explain and needs to be dealt with first. The letter and the book are my wedding present to you and Aurelia. It is the only one you will ever need.

Your engagement to Aurelia was announced to me three months ago now and of course I was delighted. To know she will be looked after by someone as kind and reliable as you was very important to me but I wondered if you were both doing it to please me and whether it was a 'real' engagement. Perhaps I am being over-cautious but she is my only daughter and her future is everything to me.

I have known you for the best part of ten years and saw the happiness you shared with Margaret in your early Kano days. I think you were happy with her and I know she was very much in love with you. But I also sensed you were not so much in love with her. I think you were still getting over the woman with the funny name who went to live in New York and Margaret was some kind of substitute. You never talked about it but that is how it looked to me. Perhaps to Margaret also.

And so I cannot accurately tell the true extent of your feelings towards Aurelia. I still have a nagging feeling that, after my death, the two of you will drift apart and you will decide not to marry her. But if the two of you are still together after this last six months then I think I am safe in assuming that your affection for her has outlived any favours you might have been doing me.

If you are still planning to marry, John will send you this letter. If not, he has my instructions to destroy it and the book with it. I have to trust him on this but have no reason to doubt his professionalism and integrity.

So, congratulations on your continued engagement and I hope you will be given many more years together than Anna and I were allowed.

Anna's malaria was short and cruel. It is ironic that she should have died from Africa's Bane of thousands of years and that I should die of its more recent curse. A curse I fear that will break the very back of Africa and destroy it, or at least set aside for a hundred years or more the progress it is at last beginning to make.

You are a much better epidemiologist than I ever was but the mathematics are not, as you would say, 'rocket science'. Nearly half the people in Africa will die of Aids over the next twenty years. In your more optimistic moments, you used to say the figure could be as low as twenty percent. But, as you pointed out to me, those who die will be the working generation and the social fabric of the poorer countries will be burnt through by such losses. There is no model to predict what will happen but we are already beginning to see things go seriously wrong in East Africa and our own beloved West Africa is sure to follow. If a cure is found they will not be able to afford it. You say the best that can be hoped for is that the virus will attenuate over time. Let us hope so.

Whatever the eventual outcome, the next ten years will not be good ones to be in Africa and it will certainly be no place to bring up a young family. Aurelia has never liked Africa, probably because she blames it for her mother's death and my subsequent isolation. She will not agree to live in Kano.

But that makes me sad because my best memories are all set in Africa. The laughter of Anna as she tried to learn Ngalese from the house-girls. Anna's parties on the lawn behind the house. You and I driving out early in the morning under a scarlet sky to visit the field stations. But these are 'old men's things' as the ever-practical Anna would have said and not at all the subject of this letter. (But they are nevertheless a comfort to me as I go this last mile. Perhaps she would forgive me!)

To go to Africa as young men, as we did, needs ambition and dreams. But to leave it, as you must now, requires money and that is what I am going to leave you and Aurelia.

In short, I am telling you where to find the torque of the Ngale. The Idona Zaki as you correctly call it. The Eyes of the Lion.

I have lost count of the evenings you and I sat outside the house in Kano to watch the sunset, drink beer and speculate where the torque might be. Rome? London? Or perhaps it was lost by the priests as they fled, fallen into some swamp and hidden forever in the mud.

No. The book with this letter tells a different story and I have no reason to doubt it. The book is the journal of one of the original priests and later continued by one of the others. It is in Spanish, and old-fashioned Spanish at that. I do not have to tell you that I neither speak nor read Spanish but I have translated it word by word with the help of a dictionary. I have not kept any notes I made along the way and there are gaps where the paper or my patience was worn away but the bare bones are clear and I am sure I am right.

It seems the priests at the mission did indeed bury the torque near the site of the original mission before fleeing east to what is now Toga. They rightly thought that they could never hope to escape carrying it with them in such a populated area but thought they would one day be able to come back and retrieve it. Perhaps to take it to Rome.

It was to be nearly ten years before they returned and they only found it with considerable difficulty. They had marked the spot with a map that used trees as distance markers. I can see you smiling because you know how long ten years is in rain forest and they were very lucky to be able to recognise the place at all. Actually I think their finding it is the only instance of good fortune ever associated with the torque!

Never mind, they found it at last but were uncertain as to what to do with it. They knew that technically it belonged to John Etherington since he had kept to his side of the bargain by beating off the Bentobe on the day of the beach skirmish. But they could hardly give something so valuable to a slaver they regarded as a murderer and beyond redemption of even their normally forgiving God. They also thought that if they took the torque to Rome it would still be possible for Etherington or his heirs to wheedle it out of the Vatican.

After much debate they decided they should hand it back to the Ngale and began to travel north to Kano, or Ngakano as they refer to it

The bulk of the journal is concerned with this journey. It is an epic in its own right and one that deserves more careful translation than I have been able to give it.

Ngakano is of course to the north of the forest belt and in those days was still a walled city ruled, as it was until the British took over, by the Emir of Kano, a Muslim. The priests were surprised by this. They had expected the Ngale and his people to be the dominant inhabitants instead of merely one of a number of local tribes, albeit an important one. The then Ngale was by the priest's account a most unpleasant character. If anything, he was even more of a brutal slave trader than his predecessor who had developed the selling of people to a fine and profitable art. The priests were shocked. Perhaps they thought the earlier venture into slave trading was a forgivable one-off, I don't know. But it left them with a dilemma. If they could not give the torque to Etherington because he was a slaver, why then should they give it to the Ngale who was little better? Should they head south with it again and thence to Rome or even continue north?

There was much soul-searching and not a little praying. In the end they decided to hide it somehow in Kano until a more Christian attitude prevailed. They really did think they could work as evangelists and convert the people to Christianity. If Islam, a religion they considered inferior, could prevail, would not the people of Kano be glad to hear the word of the true God? Such is faith.

The Emir of Kano, a Muslim as I have explained, did not quite see it that way and did not care for the priests. But they were apparently peaceful and harmless and so he allowed them to build a small chapel outside the city walls in the area that was then, as it is now, the market of Sabon Gari.

Rome approved of the wandering priests even less and the Pope refused point blank to support the mission. He sent word in no uncertain terms that their original brief had been to take their mission to the people of the coastal region where their message would probably receive a more sympathetic hearing than among the 'Ifedelo' Muslims of the north. The priests were told to return south immediately and resume their work.

This, rather rashly, they decided not to do. They felt they had been 'sent' to Ngakano and had suffered considerable difficulties just getting there. They interpreted this as God telling them they were doing a fine job and so remained where they were.

Relations were severed by default with Rome and our maverick priests set up the mission of Santa Maria and began to preach forgiveness of sins to the people of Sabon Gari, the 'Place of Strangers'. The Emir heard of these shenanigans and must have been impressed by their diligence for he eventually allowed them to build four more small churches within the walls of the old city.

You will be surprised to hear the order the chapels were built in. You and I have always understood the four inside the city predated the one by the market. Not so. Santa Maria was definitely the first and it is there you will find the Idona Zaki.

Rome, under a new pope, and perhaps hearing of the four new churches, forgave the priests and began to send them money but never went so far as to send new and younger priests which is what was really needed. The original priests were old men by now and the mission was in danger of dying out for lack of ordained successors. Rome was giving with one hand and taking away with the other. The old priests saw through this and decided to recruit their own priests locally. Technically they could not do this but they could not bear to see ten years' work destroyed.

Within limitations, the churches flourished. Few Muslims were converted but in Sabon Gari things were more promising. To the 'strangers' of Sabon Gari, dealers and market-stall people then as now, the Christian message with its promise of everlasting life was a more attractive proposition than a restrictive Muslim alternative where success seemed to be based on an impossibly expensive pilgrimage to Mecca. It also probably looked a good deal safer than the alternative offered by the Ngale, whose better life awaiting them further south was less than convincing. Wiser perhaps to choose the middle way offered by the 'Sunday Men' of Santa Maria. One day a week was quite enough to spare from their main occupation of wheeling and dealing, it seems.

The priests were practical men and, I think, rather brave. They knew that their complicated Catholic rituals would die with them but hoped their charity work, and particularly the small school they set up, would survive them. We know that this was the case and even when I arrived in Kano in 1957 there were people who remembered the school which the British had thoughtfully closed down because it was vaguely Catholic in outlook.

Such books as the priests had with them were in Latin, of course – their Bibles, some prayer books and some confusing *Lives of the Saints* much favoured by our RC brethren. No one could use the books after the priests died but the new 'priests' revered them as relics and built a small vault for them under the nave of the original chapel.

It was there I came across them in 1958. This book was with them. All were in a poor state of repair and I bought them from the then-owner of the chapel which had long since been taken over by the dye-pit families. I am ashamed to say I paid for them with pots and pans and a sewing machine. But I did not think the books would survive many more years in Kano's climate and hoped they would one day be of historical interest.

I sent them to Cambridge for safer storage and later perusal. But that summer Anna died. And what with that blow and the exhausting business of building up the Institute I hardly thought of them again.

No one in Cambridge was interested in them at the time and Lacrima Christi College, bless its Protestant heart, stored them in the wine cellars under Great Court, still in the original wooden crates I sent them home in.

They were still there when I found them again last year. You will smile when I tell you I could actually smell Africa in the wood when I finally prised the lids off.

Now, I am no Latin scholar of course but I could see the book you have in front of you now was not in Latin but in Spanish. I set about translating enough of it to see what it was. A transcription of one of the other books? Something on St Francis? St Catherine even? I thought the study would do me good and keep me occupied while I was convalescing after one bout of treatment or another.

As soon as I began I could see what it was, the history of the torque leading up to the point it was finally hidden in Kano.

After some debate the priests decided to hide it actually inside the statue of the Virgin on the outside wall at the east end of the chapel.

As soon as you read that, you will see the statue in front of your eyes. She stands about six feet tall in her niche with her arms held slightly forwards and away from her body. (Margaret once said that she looked as though she was waiting for someone to pass her a bundle of sticks but I think she is really welcoming sinners!)

You will see how the arms of the statue, being slightly bowed, could easily conceal the Idona Zaki. It would run all the way from one hand to the other by way of the shoulders. Three feet across at least.

For the torque to be in the arms, the statue would have to made from a number of stones fitted together. This must be true for the upper body at least and, in that case, the torque may even have a structural function, acting as a key to hold the upper body sections together. I am at a loss to understand how the arms were hollowed out to accommodate the torque but perhaps our priests were more practical than me!

The inscription above the niche you probably remember, *Descansa seguro en los brazos de la madre de Dios* – 'Rest safe in the arms of the mother of God.'

At first I thought it was a clue the priest had planted to help someone, one day, find the torque.

Sadly not. The statute is a copy, and not a very good one at that, of a much larger one in Toledo Cathedral near Madrid. That one, carved it is said by Carlos de Angelos, is known as *The Arms of the Mother* and has a similar inscription above it.

It is just possible that the torque is in the plinth or a simple ring hollowed out between the body blocks. But this would make it only about a foot across and weighing perhaps twenty pounds. Most of the book indicates it is bigger than this but is tantalisingly imprecise on that one detail. Because the torque was such a familiar item to the priests, maybe they never felt the need to describe it closely. For this reason I do not know how big the emeralds are, probably not as large as in the stylised pictures we have seen but they will still be valuable. It is even possible that the emeralds were removed before the torque was placed in the statue but I doubt it. You and I might have been tempted but we are not Roman Catholic priests!

The torque is a valuable item, worth up to a million pounds as far as I can estimate. Perhaps more if the emeralds are good ones. More than enough for you and A. to start a new life wherever you choose.

If I seem a little vague as to the exact placing of the torque in the statue it is because a number of pages of the journal have been torn out and are missing from the critical part dealing with the building of the chapel and the placing of the statue. The tear marks are not recent and I think the pages were removed soon after the book was written. They may contain additional information but enough remains for me to be convinced that the torque is where I say it is.

There has been a slight worry in my mind that the missing pages might still be in existence and that they would be enough for someone else to find the torque. I suppose it is unlikely but it remains a possibility. They would probably not be enough on their own but only of use if the reader knew which church was being referred to and where it was. Our Santa Maria has many hundreds of churches named after her all over the world.

You may wonder how the priests hid the torque before they placed it in the statue. The answer lies in the early part of the journal but I will save your translation efforts by telling you they concealed it between two wooden procession icons placed back to back and it is between these two icons that they carried it from the coast to Kano. Procession icons were widely used in Spain at that time and are still seen on high days and holidays. Being made of wood, these icons have not survived and there is no trace of them at any of the Kano churches though they are referred to several times. They would have been about three feet square which fits in with the overall size of the arms of the statue. I think it is a miracle that the torque was not taken from them on the long journey north and the priests interpreted that fact as further evidence from God that they were doing the right thing. People who suffer hardships often justify their efforts in such a way and I am afraid you and I may sometimes be guilty of a similar justification when we look at the Institute. Is it possible that all our efforts have really come to nothing?

203

It only remains for you to decide what to do with the torque now you know where it is.

You could of course return it either to the present Etherington family, if you can find them, or to the Ngalese. But somehow I do not think you will do either of those things. Jack Ngale is a troublesome and unpleasant man and he would only use the Idona Zaki to further promote his parochial political ambitions and reinforce his claim to be the father of his people. Neither Nigeria nor Kano needs that sort of divisive attitude. And the Etheringtons? I hardly think they deserve it. Dozens of shiploads of slaves paid for at well below price was reward enough for the original contract with the Ngalese.

I think you will sell it. It is probably too well-known to be placed on the open market and to do so would open up too many old difficulties and emotions that are best left sleeping. A private buyer is the best option, though how you contact them I do not know. There are many Afro-American collectors' auctions of so-called Ethnic Artifacts in the USA – it might even finish up with a descendant of one of the Bentobese!

You will not get its full value by selling privately but, even allowing for that, the money will be more than enough for you and Aurelia.

Your last option is to leave the torque where it is for someone else to find. That might be the moral high ground, because for you to take it would be stealing. Whoever it 'belongs' to now, it is certainly not you and you have to accept that. But someone will find it one day if you leave it in the statue. I want that someone to be you. Perhaps in some sense I am the current guardian of it and I pass possession, if not ownership, to you and Aurelia.

I have given most of my life to Africa and you ten years of yours. In return we have only a scattering of scientific papers and a deteriorating Institute. Let us even up the score a little.

Finally, Peter, I am very tired. My last bout of treatment left me completely drained and next week I must go round again. We Englishmen do not speak easily of affections or emotions and maybe the dozens of pills I have to take every day have made me a bit feeble-minded but I love my daughter very much and I am trusting you to look after her. I am sure you will not fail me.

That is all. Good luck with everything. Or, as the Ngalese would say, 'Bless now, Sunday Man. Bless now.'

Tom.

* * *

Peter stood up slowly and folded the letter back into the envelope.

He looked around the room and its familiar objects. Ornaments collected by Tom from Africa, a photograph of him with his pretty wife, standing in front of the house in Kano with a row of smiling servants. A blue-and-white Delft vase Peter had bought for Aurelia their first summer together.

Peter put the envelope into his pocket and walked back into the garden. He absently rubbed the side of his face with his hand and gazed out towards Cambridge.

What if this letter had come a week ago before seeing Jaygo again? Would he have felt differently about seeing her? Or even agreed to meet her in the first pace?

He looked up at the sky. The high white line of a passing jet trail caught his eye. Perhaps it was a military jet from one of the American bases. Or a Lear jet like Jaygo's?

It seemed to be very high. Almost a whole world away.

But maybe not quite that far any more.

At exactly six fifteen Peter and Aurelia were turning off Regents Street through the tall black wrought-iron gates of Lacrima Christi college.

'You see,' said Aurelia, 'it's quite obvious where the car parking is. There's even a sign so she didn't have to park on the grass at all.'

'Who?'

'Your friend, Jaygo.'

'Are you still thinking about that? I'm sure it was a mistake,' said Peter. 'Anyway, a college that can polyurethane a perfectly good Georgian table deserved to have their grass parked on.'

'What table?'

'The one in the Senior Combination Room,' continued Peter, choosing a parking space.

'I didn't know it was Georgian.'

'Nor, I hope, did the bursar,' said Peter, looking over his shoulder and reversing into the space. 'Will this be all right, do you think?'

'You're not at all straight,' said Aurelia, looking out of her window. 'But I'm sure it will do.'

Peter switched off the engine.

Through the front he could see the large figure of the Head Porter approaching.

'If he tells me to park straight, I'll tell him to piss off.'

'Peter!' exclaimed Aurelia. 'There's no need to be like that!'

'Ah, Dr Wilson,' said the porter as Peter opened his door. 'I'm glad I caught you, sir. There's an urgent fax for you in the lodge.'

'Oh?' said Peter, going around the car and opening Aurelia's door. 'Who from?'

'A Dr Glynne in Liverpool, sir. He telephoned after sending it to make sure it all came through.'

'Thanks, Charlie. I'll pick it up after dinner.'

'You'll do no such thing,' interrupted Aurelia. 'It might be important, so I'll go to your room and get your gown while you go with Mr Loynes to the lodge so you can see the fax. I'll meet you and we can go straight over to the library.'

Peter looked at the porter. 'OK, Charlie,' he said. 'It looks as though I'm under orders.' To Aurelia, he added, 'I'll see you in about five minutes then.'

The fax from Martin Glynne turned out to be two blurred pages of a letter, followed by four pages of photographs that had come out mainly black.

Peter began to read:

> You're a hard man to run to ground, Peter, but if you read this on Thursday evening at your college, then I'll presume you've already read my letter of Monday.
>
> I hope you don't think I'm being presumptive, but I've been following up our problem with the satellite files by comparing our images with some I managed to 'borrow' from an American military satellite that uses the same orbit but eight hundred miles above ours. (And don't even *think* of asking where I got the decryption from!)
>
> The point is, they don't have to rely on crap, out-of-date computers like ours and the attached photos are the real McCoy. I don't know the exact part of the spectrum they use but the first two pages look like Infra Reds and show pretty normal weather pattern anti-cyclone cloud concentrations. They aren't actually *so* very much better than ours before the array broke down but the second two pages will make you prick your ears up. As far as I can work out, they are taken in the near Ultra Violet (i.e. too expensive for us!) and so there shouldn't be any clouds visible and are probably targeted at ground level. Two scans or more will give a stereo topography to die for, accurate to a meter or so difference in

height a meter apart. (I *told* you not to ask where I got the decryption from!)

But look closely at the second two images. There is a clear ground pattern that matches the central anti-cyclone clouds seen on the Infra Red shots. Sod's Law (and you) will tell me I've mixed the frequencies up and they are just slightly different IR drops. But I don't think so because there are no other clouds visible (hence my supposition that they are UV runs).

So if they're not 'clouds' on the ground under the anti-cyclone, what are they? You told me that a really big locust swarm should be visible from satellite. Is that what we are seeing here?

I've taken the liberty of going over some of your old IR images but I can find nothing that matches these pictures. What do you think?

Reference beacons are few and far between in West Africa and I think the Americans probably use the same geostationary broadcasting satellites that we do. One above Lagos and one above Ibaden. That has to be guesswork but I'm pretty confident.

If I'm right about the positioning, the central point on the four scans, marked by their white crosses, places the sequence about a hundred miles north-east of Kano.

I'm not sure if all this is useful to you but thought you would want to see the scans anyway. If these are your locusts, Peter, you certainly have a lot of them! Because something is sitting bang in the middle of the scans that I calculate to be about a mile high and six miles in diameter. If it's *not* your locusts then a small Ultra Violet-reflecting version of the Milky Way has come to earth!

I don't know how the scans will fax so I'm sending the originals to you and they should be with you by Friday.

Give me a ring,

Regards,

Martin

Peter looked again at the four photographs and screwed up his eyes tying to see more detail but they were nearly solid black broken up by patches of dark grey. He could see none of the patterns Glynne had described.

He was still trying to make sense of them when Aurelia came

into the porter's lodge. 'Come on, darling,' she said. 'I can see people going in and we don't want to be late.'

He tapped the pages of the fax. 'I have to do this. I was right,' he said. 'The locusts *are* heading for Kano. Millions of them. I must get the originals.'

'Later,' she said, holding out his black gown with its long scarlet front panels. 'Lizzie will be waiting for us.'

Peter looked around at the porter. 'Did Glynne leave you a number?'

'Yes, sir. He said for you to ring him if the fax hadn't arrived.'

'OK,' said Peter. 'Ring him back, leave a message on his machine if necessary. Tell him I've got the fax but the scans didn't come out. Tell him to fax them again with a lower contrast setting. Oh yes, and tell him to fax them to me at the Kano Institute if he doesn't get your message until tomorrow.'

'Yes, sir, but does he know the fax number of the Institute in Kano?'

'No, but you do. It's in the list of contact numbers you have for me.'

The porter was about to speak.

'Be a good chap and just do it will you, Charlie,' said Peter, putting on his gown.

'Very good, sir.'

When they were outside, Aurelia turned to Peter. 'I think you were jolly rude to Loynes. You shouldn't be rude to people who can't be rude back you know.'

'I wasn't rude to him. I just asked him to do something.'

'Not very nicely.'

'Look, don't bloody tell me what to do all the time, all right?'

'Really, Peter! There's no need to speak to me like that!'

'God Almighty!' said Peter under his breath.

'What? What was that?'

'Nothing, dear. Oh good, here we are. And there's Lizzie. She looks half-cut already.'

'Peter!' hissed Aurelia.

'Hello, Lizzie,' said Peter, going up to a short woman wearing a tight, pale green dress. He kissed her lightly on the cheek. 'Marvellous dress.'

'Thank you for coming, Peter. Aurelia says you didn't get back until today.'

'Well, I'm here now,' he said, giving her hand a squeeze.

The three of them walked together down a gravel path to a new building in the same classical style as the rest of the college. Two tall columns stood either side of a large pair of double doors and the imposing figure of the Master could be seen inside, greeting the guests as they arrived and asking them to sign a red visitors' book. Beyond him, all around the walls, hung a series of huge, very modern, abstract paintings.

'Good evening, Master,' said Peter, picking up the pen. 'Name and number be all right?'

'I'm sorry?'

'Wonderful turn out for Bell, I said,' continued Peter, passing the pen to Aurelia.

'Good evening, Aurelia.' The Master turned to the two women with a wide smile. 'And Elizabeth. You must be so proud.'

Peter walked ahead into the open body of the library, still empty of shelves. He returned with two glasses of wine for Aurelia and Lizzie. The two women had been joined by a tall, broad-shouldered young man with fair hair and a ring in his eyebrow.

'This is Lewes Northcott,' said Aurelia. 'Simon's son.'

'I thought I recognised you,' said Peter, passing a glass to Aurelia and shaking the young man's hand. 'How are you?'

'Very well, thank you, sir. I don't think we've met since I was at Oundle.'

'Maybe,' said Peter. 'You look a lot like your father. Have you got a drink?'

'Not yet, sir.'

'Well, nor have I. Lizzie, Aurelia, Lewes here and I are going to get a drink. I'll be back in a couple of minutes.'

'Don't be long, darling,' said Aurelia to Peter's departing back.

'Did you know Bell Lessing?' said Peter as they queued for drinks.

'Not very well,' said Lewes. 'Mrs Lessing invited me this evening.'

'Because he was a friend of your father?'

'Yes,' said Lewes, picking up an orange juice. 'He and Dr Lessing were very good friends, I believe.'

'That's right,' said Peter, choosing a glass of wine. 'I'm afraid I didn't know your father well but Bell talked about him a lot. I'm very sorry for what happened. Did you ever hear any more?'

'No,' said Lewes, looking down at his drink. 'We had an apologetic letter from the American police. They never found any trace of my father so they were halting the investigation. They said that the case would remain technically open.'

'And what do you think?' said Peter, finishing his drink in one and selecting another.

'It's a terrible thing to say,' went on Lewes, 'but I'm afraid I think he *was* murdered and the body disposed of. It happens quite a lot in places like Washington. I mean, he wouldn't just "disappear" without leaving some sort of clue.'

'But does that really happen?' said Peter, looking around to see who else was at the reception.

'In America it does, apparently. Someone is mugged, maybe even murdered by mistake, everything of value taken and the body just put in the river. The policeman I rang up said that one in eight of disappearances are thought to be murders over there.'

Peter looked at the young man. 'I'm really very sorry. It must have made it very difficult for you.'

Lewes looked down at his glass again and turned it in his fingers. 'Yes,' he said, 'it was pretty difficult at the time. But you find a way around things. Sometimes I like to think that if he *did* disappear and wasn't just murdered, then there must have been a good enough reason. One I wouldn't know about. And I tell myself that if it was good enough reason for him, then it should be good enough for me.'

Peter smiled kindly at the young man and was about to speak when Lizzie Lessing came up. 'Lewes, darling, there's a beautiful woman here who's simply dying to meet you. She's come all the way from America.'

Lewes looked up to see a tall woman with fair hair and striking blue eyes approaching. She extended her hand towards him. 'Hello,' she said, 'I'm Catherine Felix.'

Lewes looked slightly nonplussed. 'How do you do? I don't think we've met before, have we?'

'No,' she said with a very wide smile. 'I worked in Washington with Bell Lessing on several occasions and he introduced me to your father. I hoped you would be here this evening and, when Lizzie pointed you out, I felt I really must come and say hello.'

She put her hand down and became more serious. 'I liked your father a lot. He was a fine man and I'm very sorry for your loss.'

Lewes smiled politely. 'Thank you, Mrs Felix.'

'Oh! "Mrs Felix"?' she said, smiling again. 'Very English. Please call me Kay, everyone does.

'I'm here,' she added, 'as a representative of Dr Lessing's many friends in Washington. He used to talk about the college often and it seemed too good an opportunity to miss.'

Peter picked up interest. 'You might know who the benefactor is then. Do you think it's someone from the States?'

She laughed. 'No, no! I didn't even know it was built by anonymous donation until Lizzie told me a minute ago. It must be quite an honour for the family.'

'Lewes was telling me about his father,' said Peter. 'He and Bell had known each other for quite a few years. Two good friends, both died in the same week. And while one gets a library named after him, the other gets nothing at all.'

Kay Felix put down her glass and folded her arms. 'Yes, I heard what happened to Simon. I'm afraid Washington isn't always a very nice place off the beaten track. I can't apologise on its behalf of course, but I'm still very sorry for what happened.'

Lewes looked uncomfortable. 'Thank you,' he said awkwardly and paused. 'But it's Dr Lessing's night tonight. I wonder if you'll excuse me, I think I see someone I know talking to Aurelia Collis.'

He put down his glass and set off to the other side of the room.

'Oh dear,' said Kay Felix. 'Did I say the wrong thing?'

'Probably,' replied Peter, putting his second glass down and taking up a third. 'But I shouldn't worry. All he wanted to hear was that his father isn't dead after all and you could hardly tell him that, could you?'

'No,' she said, looking over towards Lewes. 'I'm afraid I couldn't tell him that.'

'Never mind,' said Peter more brightly. 'What do you think of our new library?'

She smiled again. 'Very impressive. But at the moment it looks more like an art gallery. Where are all the books?'

Peter laughed. 'The books will come later. I think you Americans have an expression for it, "Build it and they will come." Isn't that what you say?'

She laughed back. 'That was baseball players. How is it supposed to work for books?'

'Same principle. From now on, Fellows of the college will leave all their books to this place in their wills. Sooner or later it will fill up.'

'But couldn't that take some time?' she asked, puzzled.

'Only two or three hundred years.' He smiled at her. 'And what's that in the life of a college?'

She picked her glass up again. 'And meanwhile you get some-where to show these paintings, is that it? I mean, they're pretty large. There can't be many places you can hang them.'

211

'They're Blacklocks. I think they are always this big.'

'Are they valuable?' she asked.

'Oh, yes. The college doesn't make mistakes about paintings. We've got two Picassos, you know.'

'Really? Where are they?'

'In the Master's Lodge, of course,' said Peter, putting his glass down. 'That's three reds now,' he went on. 'I think that should tide me over till dinner, don't you?'

She looked at the little row of glasses in front of them.

'It was Bell's idea,' he said in explanation. 'He always said college looked better after three reds inside you. And as tonight's meant to be in his memory, I thought at least someone should remember him in the way he would have wanted.'

Kay Felix put her head on one side. 'Mmm. But, if the woman you came in with is your partner, I think I should tell you she's giving you one or two worried glances.'

Peter looked over to Aurelia and gave her a little wave. 'Oh, don't worry about her. She doesn't have to approve. We're engaged, you see.'

Kay Felix laughed and picked up another glass for herself and raised it to Peter. 'OK, here's to Belle and Simon then.'

Evening drinks were not such a light-hearted affair for Jaygo and Laurie Miller in his hotel room in London.

'What the hell do you mean he's not coming?' she was asking angrily.

'He *is* coming,' said Laurie, defensively. 'But he says he wants to go on the normal flight.'

'Why?' she snapped. 'Sven's meat balls not good enough for him?'

'It appears he has to travel out with someone else.'

'Why didn't you say they could both come with us? You know there's bags of room.'

'He's going with Aurelia Collis, his partner.'

'Her!' exploded Jaygo. 'What the hell does she want in Kano?'

'Her father ran the Institute Peter's in charge of. Perhaps it's something to do with that. I'm afraid more than that and you'll have to ask Peter.'

'Well, I think I might just do that,' she said, striding over to the telephone.

'Switchboard? Jocasta Manhattan. Get me Lacrima Christi College in Cambridge. I want to speak to someone called Peter Wilson.'

She put the phone down again without waiting for a reply.

'Huh.' She sat in one of the chairs by the window opposite Laurie and began drumming her fingers on the arm.

'Look, Jay,' tried Laurie, leaning forwards. 'I know Peter. You can't just rush him, you know. He takes his time about things and, if you push him, you'll just frighten him off.'

She stopped drumming and looked at him. 'What? Who's pushing?'

'You are,' he said. 'You know you are. I don't know, but you seem to have made your mind up about Peter in some sort of way and are just going hell for leather. I don't think it's the best method. Anyway, are you sure it's what you want?'

She did not reply immediately but sat with her lips pursed, looking at Laurie.

'Yes,' she said at last. 'And it's not something I have to think about. I just know.'

'It's not a very good week to "just know" about things, is it? More has happened to Pete this week than for a long time and it might not be a very good time for Jocasta Manhattan just to blow in and set up camp.'

'I didn't choose this week,' she said. 'Or, rather, I did but I didn't know what was going to happen in Atlanta, still less what was going to happen last night at the warehouse. God, I just thought Pete and I could go to Kano for a few days and get to know each other again.'

'But you did know you were going to see Jack, didn't you?' continued Laurie. 'And that was never going to be an exactly restful experience.'

'Of course I knew we were going to see Jack,' she said. 'But I didn't think it was going to be such a big deal. Just something Peter and I could do together. Don't forget, it's only since Tuesday that you and Peter have promoted Jack to some sort of monster.'

'We haven't "promoted" him at all,' said Laurie. 'It's just that you didn't know much about him before.'

Jaygo shrugged. 'So what if it has all gone a bit pear-shaped?' she said. 'Despite what happened I still thought I might get Peter to myself for a few days to work things out. Now he's going to bring that other woman with him.'

'No,' said Laurie, with irritation creeping into his voice, 'Aurelia's not the "other woman". You are.'

Jaygo was about to reply when the telephone rang.

She picked it up. 'Peter? Oh. Then when will he be out of the dinner?' She looked at her watch as she listened. 'Don't bother then,' she said, putting the receiver down. 'Apparently His Lordship is at some huge dinner and can't be disturbed.'

When Laurie did not reply, she walked to the door. 'I've got to go and change,' she announced. 'Are you sure you won't come?'

'No, thanks,' said Laurie. 'I think I'll stay in. Give me a ring about nine tomorrow and we'll have breakfast together before we go.'

'OK,' she said, and then added, 'Sorry if I shouted a bit back there. You know.'

'Yes,' he smiled at her. 'Don't worry. It's turning out to be a bit of a week all round, isn't it?'

After Jaygo had left, Laurie went to his briefcase and took out the big plastic box of pills.

He carefully opened it and looked at his watch. Half past seven. Only half an hour late. He scooped up the dose of pills from the appropriate compartment and put them in his mouth. He swallowed them down and then went to the refrigerator to choose a beer. This metallic taste was definitely bad news, he thought, as he pulled the ring on the can and drank.

While Laurie and Jaygo had been discussing the best time to conduct a relationship, the young man cleaning the insects and leaves from the surface of the Ngale's swimming pool in Kano had a more practical problem to deal with.

Each evening he swept the pool with his net until he was satisfied the Ngale would be pleased. He allowed himself half an hour for this before going home to supper with his mother.

This particular evening there were far more insects than he could deal with.

A gentle evening breeze had blown most of them down to one end of the pool where they formed a yellow and brown mat about six feet in diameter.

He gathered a handful of them to examine. They were all locusts. He was familiar with them because they were a common visitor to the pool but he had never seen so many of them at one time.

He also knew that the locusts, or faras as he called them, could swarm but he had heard that was always later in the year. His mother had told him about them. How they would suddenly appear in huge numbers out of the north and eat all the grass and vegetables in the gardens. She said they would fly and swirl as dense as smoke from any fire and they would fall like sand from a tree they were feeding on if you shook it.

He picked up his net again and began patiently to scoop the insects up again. After another half hour he had filled and emptied eight buckets but there seemed just as many as when he had started. It was quite dark by now and he could hardly see what he was doing.

He knew the pool was equipped with underwater lights and he made his way up to the house to ask his mother if she knew how to turn them on.

The Ngale had been silently watching the young man for some time from the terrace at the top of the garden.

'Dabo,' called the Ngale. 'Why are you still here?'

'It's the faras, our father,' said Dabo, stooping and touching his knee. 'There are too many for me and I will need the lights to see them.'

'Show me,' said the Ngale, stepping down onto the lawn and walking to the pool.

'It is dark, sah, you cannot see them.'

The Ngale continued walking towards the pool. 'Then go running to the house and tell your mother to turn on the lights. Then come back to the pool.'

By the time Dabo had returned, the Ngale was squatting down by the pool and was scooping up a handful of dead insects.

'Faras,' said the Ngale.

'Yes, our father, many many.'

The Ngale dropped the insects back into the water and stood up.

'Is it a swarm, Ngale?' asked the young man

The Ngale smiled. 'Not yet, Dabo. But one is coming. These are just a few.'

'But there are many, sah. Too many for me.'

The Ngale thought for a moment. 'Very well,' he said, 'go back to your house and bring your family. You will all work here tonight until the pool is cleaned. Then tell Gwadabe to put the chemical in the water and help him put the cover on the pool. Do you understand?'

'Yes, our father. But when is the swarm coming? Will it be safe?'

'Saturday. Maybe Sunday. But it is safe. Faras are many but they are not dangerous.'

'Yes, Ngale. Thank you.'

'Go and get your family now,' said the Ngale, turning back to the house.

As the Ngale entered the room, Habu was just showing John Etherington in from the hall.

'Good evening, John,' said the Ngale, without offering to shake hands. 'Come in and sit down.' He turned to Habu. 'Two Stars, please.'

'Yes, Ngale,' said the old man, touching his knee.

'So, John. What can I do for you? I thought you were going to telephone.'

'Yes, Jack. The thing is, as you know, I wanted to stay on in Kano for a few days but I had a call from a business associate. It means I may have to leave tomorrow evening and I thought I should say goodbye in person'

'"An associate",' said the Ngale, smiling. 'Yesterday he was a diplomat and today he has business associates.'

Etherington smiled politely back. 'Perhaps I used the wrong words. Maybe "Investment Advisor" would be more accurate.'

'Tell me more,' said the Ngale, continuing to smile.

'Nothing on your scale, Jack, but some land has come up in Cape Town and I want to have a look at it.'

'Cape Town?' said the Ngale, suddenly more serious. 'That's no place to be buying land this year.'

'That's what I thought,' said Etherington, 'but my man tells me it is a good opportunity to get in while the prices are still low. He is very experienced.'

'Experience and money, John. You know what they say about that combination, don't you?'

'I'm sure it is all right.'

'Well,' said the Ngale, 'when the man with money meets the man with experience, the man with experience gets the money and the man with money gets the experience.'

Etherington smiled politely. 'I have heard that but I don't think that will happen in this instance.'

'I hope not,' said the Ngale as Habu came in with the drinks.

As they went through the little ritual of opening their own beer and waiting for Habu to pour them, Etherington said, 'I don't remember the grasshoppers, Jack. I must have been here at a different time of year before but I've never seen so many as I did when I went into the garden this morning.'

'Ah,' said the Ngale, 'they are not grasshoppers. They are faras, aren't they, Habu?'

'Yes, sah,' said Habu as he poured Etherington's drink. 'Many faras are coming now, sah.'

'Fara is the local word for locust, John. What you are seeing is the build-up to a swarm of locusts. And, if you don't go tomorrow, you might get to see the swarm itself. Quite an impressive sight I can assure you.'

'A locust swarm?' said Etherington, raising his eyebrows. 'Isn't that serious?'

'Not really.' The Ngale took an appreciative sip of his cold beer. 'The numbers build up over time and every now and then we get a swarm. Maybe a big one every ten years or so but usually it's just out in the country somewhere. This one, I hear, is actually coming to Kano.'

'But I thought they were dangerous,' said Etherington. 'Don't they do tremendous damage?'

The Ngale chuckled. 'European myth, John. Yes, they will do some local damage to the crops but so will a big storm. And the crops will recover in much the same way after both. And we can spray them these days. We are a modern country.'

'Even so,' said Etherington, 'don't you have to take some precautions?'

'Well,' said the Ngale holding his big hands wide in an expansive gesture, 'I'm putting the cover on my swimming pool!

'No,' he went on, 'you worry too much, John. Tell me, have you a flight arranged for Cape Town? I can ask my office to do it for you if you like.'

'I arranged it all this afternoon on that excellent telephone you lent me. Besides, I want to stop off in Kenya on the way.'

'Kenya? Cape Town?' smiled the Ngale again. 'Deserting the West Coast already?'

Etherington smiled in return. 'Too many locusts here, Jack. What did you call them? Faras? Too many faras for me.'

The two men laughed together. Almost like old friends.

'Jack?' said Etherington after a while. 'Your new torque. When do you expect to announce it?'

The Ngale put his glass carefully down and wiped his lips. 'It depends. I've got what you might call some "popular publicity" lined up for this weekend and I thought I might produce it then. But I'm not sure if a more formal occasion might not be more appropriate.

'I want the first public airing to be a "Ngale" occasion and not a "pop" occasion.'

Etherington looked curious.

'Yes, the Ngale has a "pop" side too! Tell me, have you heard of a woman called Jocasta Manhattan?'

'The musician?' said Etherington 'Plays the violin, doesn't she?'

'Cello,' said the Ngale. 'She and I produced a record a few months ago and now we are following it up with another and a small promotional tour.'

'Jocasta Manhattan? I wouldn't have thought that her sort of music was very popular here.'

'You'd be wrong then,' said the Ngale with a slight edge. 'Don't be condescending.'

He walked over to his hi-fi stack. 'Jocasta has a great feel for African music. Listen to this.'

He placed one of Jaygo's CDs in the system. 'Recognise this, John?'

Etherington listened as the Belle Epoque went through the first few bars of 'The Star and the Wisemen'.

'Can't say I do,' said Etherington. 'Is that Jocasta Manhattan?'

'Oh, yes,' said the Ngale, sitting down again. 'She adapted some music from a South African group called Ladysmith Black Mambazo. What do you think?'

Etherington listened for a few moments again before answering. 'It's different, Jack, I'll give you that. But I'm afraid I'm no musician.'

'Nor am I,' confessed the Ngale. 'I leave that end of it to Jocasta. The first record was something of an experiment but it proved popular with a little help from my radio stations. And this one? Well, I think she and I are going to do very well out of it.

'And if they like it here,' he continued, 'they might like it in America too. Europe even. I'll have a better idea after she's been out here for the promotion.'

'Promotion?' asked Etherington. 'Is this the popular publicity you were talking about?'

'Partly.' The Ngale handed Etherington the CD case. 'Tell me, John, what do you make of this?'

Etherington looked at the picture of Jaygo standing in the torque. He moved his head to one side to read the title. 'The Music of the Lion,' he read.

He looked up at the Ngale. 'I can see the torque, Jack. But what has it to do with Jocasta Manhattan?'

The Ngale took the case from Etherington. 'I've gone to a lot of trouble to have a new torque made,' he said. 'You probably think it has become an obsession with me.'

John Etherington waved a hand noncommittally. 'I'm sure it's not for me to say.'

The Ngale shook his head. 'You're too polite, John. But the

torque, or rather the lack of it, has caused my family a great deal of trouble over the years. I think it would have been better to admit it was lost forever right from the beginning and to set about making another one then. Instead we have had the unedifying spectacle of Ngale after Ngale searching for it and not finding it.'

'And is that why you finally made yourself another?' asked Etherington.

'Yes, but I've gone one better than to just "make another". The new one will directly replace the old one. To all intents and purposes it *is* the original one.'

'I understand that, Jack. Or rather I guessed as much. But I still don't understand how you will tell your people you have "found" it. Or, come to that, what you will actually *do* with it now you have it.'

'I don't think you understand about the torque, John,' said the Ngale. 'I don't have to "do" anything with it. I simply have to *possess* it. I am still the Ngale without it but *with* it I am more. More complete. I have to ask a lot of my people over the next year or two when the Federation breaks up and the more I can be a complete leader, the better it will be for us.'

'You are not talking about your "army" again, are you, Jack?'

The Ngale did not answer but walked towards the window.

'Come here, John,' he said. 'I have something to show you that will explain what I mean.'

The Ngale slid back one of the tall glass doors and Etherington followed him into the darkness of the garden.

Down by the swimming pool, Dabo and his family had begun removing the rest of the locusts from the surface of the pool. Beside them at the pool's edge was a pile of dead locusts about a foot high and more were being added by the net load.

As the men from the house approached, Dabo and his family stepped back from the water, touched their knees and waited.

The Ngale ignored them and bent down to gather a handful of dead insects from the pile. He squeezed the water out of them and opened his hand towards Etherington.

'Your grasshoppers, John. The faras. How many would you say I have here? Ten? A dozen even?'

Etherington looked down. 'About that.'

The Ngale tossed them back onto the heap. 'And in this pile here? A thousand, shall we say?'

'Perhaps,' said Etherington.

'And in the pool? Ten times that? Fifteen?'

The Ngale waved his arm around him. 'And in the garden altogether? In all of Kano?'

'I couldn't begin to imagine,' said Etherington as the two men turned and began to walk back to the house.

'And this isn't the swarm,' said the Ngale, pointing to Etherington. 'That doesn't get here for about another two days. A pretty impressive build-up, wouldn't you say? A force for destruction, wouldn't you say?'

Etherington did not answer immediately.

'But, John,' said the Ngale, pointing at Etherington again, 'I just told you not ten minutes ago that they were no threat at all, didn't I? So which is right do you think?'

John Etherington looked perplexed. 'What you said in the house just now was pretty convincing. But now you actually show them to me I'm not so sure. And more coming, you say? Frankly, Jack, I'm not sure at all.'

'But *I* am sure, you see. There *are* a lot of faras. There will be many times this number. And they *will* do damage. But in less than a week they will be gone. I will tell people what will happen and I will be right. The Ngale will be right.'

They had reached the house by now and the Ngale slid the tall door closed behind them as they went into the sitting room.

'It's the same every time,' said the Ngale. 'People are frightened of the swarms in the same way people are frightened of hurricanes or tornadoes. They are all forces of nature. But no worse. The Ngale just has to tell his people to sit tight and let them pass. It happens. They just need reassurance and I give it to them.

'You, John, even you, were not so sure they would pass without catastrophe when you saw them for yourself. And we are in a comfortable house with doors that close tight and windows with glass. How do you think people will feel in poorer houses without these things when the real swarm comes? It will be thick as smoke, John.

'Despite themselves, they will be frightened. Their children will be frightened. And when it is over they will remember the voice that told them they would be safe. They need someone to tell them that, no matter what damage is done, he will be there afterwards to help set things to normal again. The Ngale.'

John Etherington took up his glass again and looked less than convinced.

'No, John? You don't think so?'

'I didn't say that, Jack.'

'Take your people and what happened to them in the Second World War. The London Blitz. Given rational thought it would have been obvious that a city made largely of bricks and stone would never simply be burnt to the ground. But when the bombs were raining down and whole blocks of buildings were being destroyed it was no time for careful and rational thought. People needed a calming voice to tell them they would be safe. Your Winston Churchill was that voice. He knew perfectly well that London would not be destroyed. The losses on the worst nights were actually never more than a few hundred people killed. All he had to do was say, "Trust me." And, sure enough, in the morning, most of them were still alive.'

'But cites have been destroyed, Jack. Tokyo was burnt to the ground. Hiroshima, for goodness sake.'

The Ngale put up his hands. 'There you go again, John. You exaggerate. This week in Kano we are simply facing a locust swarm. Millions upon millions of them. But hardly a fire storm in a wooden city, hardly an atomic bomb.'

The Ngale smiled. 'Trust me, John. Trust the Ngale.'

'I suppose so,' said Etherington after a moment's more thought. 'Perhaps it's just a trick.'

'Maybe it is a trick,' said the Ngale. 'But I prefer to think of it as leadership. Is there any harm in that?'

'I suppose not, Jack. You know your people better than me.'

'I do.'

'And Jocasta Manhattan? Where does she fit in?'

The Ngale smiled. 'Dear Jocasta, or Jaygo, to give her her real name. She's just a bit of icing on the cake. She is famous. She is coming to Kano to see the Ngale. She appears at his side. Look, they are like old friends. Now, you can't tell me that will do me any harm?'

Etherington smiled back and put down his empty glass. 'No,' he said, 'no harm at all. I must say, you seem pretty confident about the whole thing.'

'I am, John. And one more thing. I will be the Ngale who found the torque. Quite "when" I find it and "how" I am not sure, but you can rely on me to find it. I will tell them I will find it. I *will* find it. The Ngale is right. He is always right.'

Etherington leant forwards. 'But what if you were wrong? Say things didn't always work out as you tell people they are going to?'

The Ngale leaned back in his chair. 'You make it sound as if

I'm taking some sort of risk. I'm not. I know the locusts. I already have the torque. And Jocasta Manhattan will be sitting next to me in this very house this time tomorrow evening. There are no risks involved. I just have to stand at one side and let events unfold to my advantage. I keep telling you, John. I am the Ngale. I am right.'

He stood up. 'But I mustn't keep you, John. I am sure we both have things to do. Come and see me tomorrow if you decide to stay.'

The meeting was over.

'Yes,' said Etherington as he too stood. 'I must be going. Thank you.'

As they walked to the door, the Ngale said, 'You see, John. You are altogether too hesitant. Not confident enough in yourself. That is why you have been working for me and not the other way around. I am in charge. You are on my team now.'

The two men shook hands outside the front door as Etherington's driver opened a car door.

He's a fool, thought Etherington as he settled comfortably into his seat. An arrogant fool. Working for him? No. John Etherington never worked for anyone but himself. I am not one of 'your people', Jack, I am not on your 'team'. I am on a team of one. Soon you will find out exactly what that means.

He smiled as he thought of the Semtex Seven sitting quietly in the freezer. And unless I'm very much mistaken, he added to himself, that 'soon' is coming up fast.

'To the house, sah?' asked the driver.

'No. To Sabon Gari.'

'Sabon Gari, sah? What at Sabon Gari, sah?'

'I want to buy some rope,' said Etherington. 'A long length of nylon rope.'

'Sah?' queried the driver.

But John Etherington did not reply. He merely settled further down in his seat and closed his eyes.

Chapter Five

FRIDAY

The telephone woke Laurie Miller on Friday morning.

'Am I coming to you for breakfast?' asked Jaygo without introduction. 'Or are we eating in the coffee shop?'

'I'm still asleep, Jay. What time is it?'

'Nine on the dot. Chop chop.'

'Oh, Christ,' he said. 'I'm sorry. I didn't set an alarm.'

'Well, you've missed your early morning swim then, haven't you? I'll go downstairs and wait for you but don't be long because I want to get out to City and see they load the right cello.'

'Ok,' said Laurie. 'Ten minutes.'

He swung his feet over the side of the bed to sit up.

Headache, he thought, but not much worse than usual.

He opened the curtains. It seemed awfully bright outside so he half closed them again before collecting his allocation of pills and putting them in his mouth.

They taste like ball bearings, he thought. I'm surprised I don't bloody rattle.

By the time Laurie was ready to join Jaygo for breakfast, Peter and Aurelia were already checking in at Heathrow.

'Just two cases,' Aurelia was saying. 'We are only going for a few days.'

What does that man care how long we are going for? thought Peter, lifting the cases onto the weighing machine at the counter.

Peter started to walk towards the departure gate as soon as he was handed the boarding passes.

'Do you know where to go next?' Aurelia asked.

'Yes,' he said. 'I live here.'

She linked her arm in his and smiled up at him. 'Of course,' she said, 'I forgot. You're an old hand at this, aren't you?'

He looked at her and smiled back, despite himself. 'Most of the time I do it with my eyes shut,' he said.

When they had passed through passport control and were sitting with plastic cups of coffee in the departure lounge, Peter noticed that Aurelia was fidgeting.

'Are you nervous?' he asked.

'No,' she replied immediately. Then, after a pause, 'Well, just a bit.'

Peter thought no more about flying than he did about catching a bus. He took her hand. 'Don't worry. Think of it as sitting down in the sitting room at home. They'll even show you a film you've seen before to make it more realistic.'

She squeezed his hand and let go. 'You're right,' she said. 'I'm being a silly, aren't I? But I'm glad you're here.'

He smiled again.

'It's not the going along bit I mind,' she went on. 'It's the going up at the beginning. I always seem to leave my tummy behind.'

'Just pretend you are in a lift,' he said. And then added to himself, And be grateful you're not flying Air Jaygo.

'It's going to be funny back at the Kano house without Dad,' she said. 'He lived there longer than anywhere else, you know.'

'I never thought of it like that,' said Peter. 'I suppose he did, now you come to mention it. In that sense, his ashes going there is a bit like him going home, isn't it?'

'That's what I think too,' she said. 'I told Lizzie and she said I was being ghoulish taking the ashes all this way but you don't think so, do you?'

'Not at all,' said Peter. 'If Tom wanted it, it's fine by me.'

She went quiet for a moment and then asked, 'Have you decided what you want done with your ashes?'

'Now, that *is* ghoulish,' he said. 'I think I've got a few years yet before I have to make up my mind. Come on, old thing,' he said, standing up. 'They're calling us. Time to get into the lift.'

As Peter and Aurelia were boarding their aeroplane, a very different flight was being planned by John Etherington and Frank O'Leary.

'Yes,' he said. 'I do want you to repeat it back to me word for word. There is absolutely no room for errors of any kind and the deal's not done until I land in Abejan so you'd better not screw

224

it up. You just remember that up until then the torque belongs to me.'

'John, John, John,' said the voice at the other end of the telephone.

'Go over it then,' said Etherington.

'OK, OK. Ten o'clock the helicopter lands at Santa Maria.'

'With who on board?'

'The pilot and me.'

'Are you *sure* he can find it?'

'Yes,' came back O'Leary, 'and I can too.'

'At night?'

'At night.'

'How can you be sure?' asked Etherington.

'John, I have been dealing in Kano for ten years now. It's a small city. I can find it.'

'Go on then.'

'We collect you and the torque. Take off for the airport. Ten forty, you and the torque take off from there on my jet for Abejan. I return to my house in the helicopter.'

'And?'

'About midnight you land at Abejan. Hand it to Mitchell and you fly on to Kenya by schedule.'

'Good.'

'I still don't see why we have to collect it from Santa Maria. Why there?'

'Because that's where I'll be with the bloody thing. Anywhere else will not be safe. Believe me.'

'And how can you be so sure the Ngale won't follow. He'll hear about the helicopter flight at night even if he doesn't know what's happening at first. That bastard's got people everywhere.'

'Don't you worry about the Ngale. He'll have plenty else to worry about tomorrow night.'

'Are you sure?'

'Take it from me. Tomorrow night he's going to be very busy indeed.'

'If you say so.'

'I do. Now, that's it. You have to be at Santa Maria at exactly ten o'clock. Five minutes either side and the deal's off. Is that clear?'

'Clear, John.'

'Good. See you at ten o'clock.'

Etherington switched off the telephone and lowered the lid.

Next he took a small black automatic pistol from his suitcase.

225

He held it with both hands out in front of him and worked the action backwards and forwards several times.

Not fully satisfied, he took a white cloth from the suitcase and spread it carefully on the table next to the satellite telephone. He dismantled the pistol into its component parts and laid them out neatly on the cloth. Next, he took a small bottle of oil and a rag from a wooden box in the suitcase. He cleaned and wiped all the gun parts before reassembling the pistol and checking the action again.

This time he was pleased with the result and filled the magazine with rounds from the wooden box. Finally he double-checked that the safety catch was on and only then put the pistol into the inside breast pocket of his jacket. Today was not the day for an automatic pistol to jam.

He looked at his watch. Ten o'clock. Twelve hours to go.

Peter fell asleep before the flight took off from Heathrow. Aurelia had planned to hold his hand but she did not want to wake him and settled for gripping the armrests of her seat instead.

When the aeroplane eventually levelled out, she took a magazine from the seat and tried to read but she found the engine noise prevented her from concentrating properly.

Peter did not stir until they were an hour from Kano.

The bumping and rocking of the plane as it descended through the tropical turbulence greatly alarmed her but Peter did not acknowledge it with more than an occasional reassuring smile.

She took his hand and held it tightly until they safely touched down at three o'clock local time.

Locusts, like most insects, have a characteristic smell when gathered in large numbers. Theirs is a dry, almost bookish odour like the closed wing of an old library. Peter thought he could recognise this smell almost as soon as the exit doors of the aeroplane were opened.

When he stood at the top of the steps down to the tarmac, he immediately looked around him, expecting to see at least an occasional swirl of insects but there was none.

He noticed a few adult insects hopping and making short flights as he descended the steps with Aurelia holding onto his arm. There were more on the ground as they walked to the airport terminal building but hardly enough to be responsible for the pervasive background scent.

'What's that funny smell?' she asked.

'It's locusts,' he said. 'It's nothing to worry about.'

'I didn't know they smelt.'

'You don't notice it unless there's a lot of them. I told you there was a big swarm to the north. Because the wind is blowing south, we can smell them.'

'Will the wind blow them too?'

'Yes, eventually. But you don't have to worry. You know they don't bite even if they do hop about a lot. You'll stop noticing the smell in a few minutes.'

Tijja, Peter's driver, was waiting for them when they had negotiated customs and immigration.

'You remember Miss Aurelia?' Peter said to him. 'Dr Tom's daughter.'

'Oh, yes, sah. It is good to see you in Kano again, Miss Aurelia.' Tijja effortlessly lifted the cases up and put them in the boot of the Peugeot.

About twenty locusts were sitting on the roof of the car with as many again on the bonnet.

'Many faras, Tijja,' said Peter.

'Yes, Dr Peter, many faras. I never see so many.'

Peter opened the back door of the car for Aurelia and brushed a couple of locusts off her seat before she climbed in and sat down.

'And more is coming all day,' said Tijja. 'Swarm is coming I think, sah.'

'I think so too, Tijja,' said Peter, getting in the front of the car next to him. 'But if you want to know for sure, you will have to ask in Sabon Gari.'

Tijja threw his head back and laughed. 'Oh, yes, sah! They will know it at Sabon Gari!'

'Certainly will!' Peter laughed back.

'Sabon Gari?' asked Aurelia from the back of the car. 'Is that where those smelly drains were?'

Tijja laughed again. 'Oh yes, Miss Aurelia, Sabon Gari very smelly.'

'Why will they know about the locusts there?' asked Aurelia again.

'Well,' said Peter, putting his arm on the back of Tijja's seat and turning round to her. 'They won't really, but we have a saying in Kano. If you want something, you can find it at Sabon Gari. And that probably includes the latest opinion on the locusts.'

Aurelia smiled politely.

*   *   *

227

The house Peter had taken over from Tom Collis as Director of the Crops Institute was large by Kano standards. It had six bedrooms and was situated in an expensive residential district on the east side of Kano.

Tom Collis had planned and built the house in 1957 when land and building costs were low. Newly married and ambitious, he had chosen to build such a large house because he had looked forward to the life style of a senior ex-patriot. Big parties, dances even, were common and frequently reciprocated between families. Entertaining was not expensive in those days and, in truth, there was little else to do in a largely Muslim or Ngalese city hundreds of miles from the next European community.

The early death of his wife and the ending of the colonial period curtailed Tom's plans. He continued to live in the big house, perhaps because it reminded him of his wife, but he seldom entertained at much above a dinner-party level. But he kept most of the servants on and the house maintained a rather grand air.

One by one the big houses in the acacia-lined streets were taken over by Nigerians as the Europeans gradually departed. The new owners liked the area as much as their predecessors – it was still one of the most exclusive parts of Kano to live in. The roadside stall-holders and street-traders so common everywhere else were not welcome and the quiet, suburban atmosphere was preserved.

One of the little vanities of the closing colonial era was the hiring of day and night watchmen for the houses. These were men whose job it was to sit on the porch in front of the house to deter burglars and turn away beggars and other undesirables.

The modern approach to security was to simply erect a barbed-wire fence, sometimes electrified and to turn a couple of large dogs loose in the garden.

Tom Collis had never favoured this option because he said it turned the area into a 'Mercedes-mentality fortress'. His gate was never closed and, twenty-four hours a day, a man sat on the porch 'guarding' the house.

When Peter had taken over the house, he too preferred a watchman to an electric fence and had kept on the original men. So it was that, as Peter and Aurelia turned off the road into the driveway of the house, they were greeted by an ancient day-watch who rose awkwardly to his feet to greet the master and lady of the house. In his youth, he had been a member of the King's Own West African Rifles. Though his uniform had been replaced by more traditional clothes, he still kept an ancient Lee Enfield rifle by his side.

Peter had once asked Tom where the rifle came from and if it was such a good idea. Tom had laughed and said it was purely decorative and completely useless as its bolt had been removed. The gun was a status symbol among watchmen, he explained. Though it could never be used, it made the guard feel more important and might even deter the more persistent and less observant door-to-door traders.

Half an hour later Aurelia had unpacked the cases and had decided upon a shower.

Peter had elected for a Star beer and a walk in the garden. As he pushed open the mesh door from the sitting room onto the back terrace he immediately found himself walking on a scattering of locusts that had found their way under the shadow of the house.

Meandering down the garden he brushed his hand over several small bushes and dislodged a small cloud of locusts from each bush that he passed.

The vegetable garden lay beyond the flat area of grass that had once been a croquet lawn. Among the rows of vegetables, Peter could see the figure of a woman picking sweetcorn and brushing insects from each cob as she placed them into a basket perched on her hip.

'The faras are very bad, Halima,' he said as he approached her.

'Yes, sah, what is not under the ground, we will lose. The yams and sweet potatoes will be safe but all the corn and the beans will be eaten now.'

'I'm afraid so,' he said, reaching out and shaking one of the plants free of locusts. 'When did they come?'

'Some few yesterday, sah. More this morning. But no fara dango, only faras.'

Peter looked puzzled. Fara dango was the term for the immature, wingless locusts and, even if most of the insects had flown in, there should be some immature ones among the locusts always present in the garden.

He squatted down to look more closely at the locusts he had dislodged from the plant. He brushed his hand to look for the fara dangos.

'No,' he said, straightening up again. 'But we always have some fara dangos, don't we?'

'Yes, sah, always some. But I do not see them this year. Is it bad luck, sah?'

229

Peter squatted down again and brushed his hand backwards and forwards over a group of insects. Only adults.

'These have flown from the north, Halima. There are many more coming but when they fly the dangos cannot follow.'

Peter dug his hands into the soil by his feet and sifted it through his fingers. He repeated the action in several place about six inches apart before brushing the dry soil from his hands and standing up again.

'What are you doing, Sunday Man, sah?'

'Looking for fara eggs, Halima,' he said, taking out a handkerchief and wiping his hands.

'Why, sah?'

'The faras will lay eggs where they feed to make fara dangos. But I can't find any eggs here.'

'But there is food, sah,' she said, waving her free arm. 'All food.'

'Now there is,' he said, squatting down and beginning to dig again between the plants. 'But if many many faras come they will eat all the food and there will not be any for the fara dangos to eat. They know that and so will not lay eggs.'

Halima looked puzzled. 'How can they know it? They are faras.'

Peter smiled at her kindly. 'Dr Tom told me,' he said. 'He said that when there was a big swarm of faras they do not lay eggs. They just feed and fly. He said the faras in a very big swarm are different from usual swarm faras and do many strange things.'

'But what can a fara know, sah? They are very small,' she insisted.

'I don't know, Halima. There is much still to learn about faras.'

'Maybe the zaki tell them.'

'The zaki? The lion?' said Peter with interest.

'Yes, sah. Zaki fara. The old people say that when you can smell the faras before they are here then a zaki fara is coming every time. You can smell the faras, sah.'

Peter looked at her thoughtfully and then back at the insects on the ground. 'Yes,' he said, 'I could smell them at the airport. Too strong for the faras we have now.'

'And if zaki fara come, sah,' she went on, 'they say he will be very hungry and eat all the people like when he come before, sah.'

He looked suddenly up at her. 'Before? They say a zaki fara has been here before?'

'Yes, sah. Long time. In old times. Before the Sunday Men come, sah. They say zaki is frightened of the Sunday Men and not come when he is here. But now most of the Sunday Men are gone, sah, and so the zaki fara will come back to eat the people.'

'No,' he said. 'That is not true. No faras can eat a person, no matter how many come. Did you ever see a fara that could eat a person?'

'No, sah, but zaki fara maybe is different. Very big.'

Peter smiled. 'No, Halima. Even if a Lion Swarm is going to come, and I don't really think it will, it will only be many many ordinary faras. It will be safe.'

'Thank you, sah,' she said, looking only partly reassured.

'A zaki fara is only a very big swarm,' he added. 'They may come and eat all the trees and the plants but they cannot even eat each other. They are only faras.'

'Yes, sah. But they are saying it. I don't believe them.'

'Good for you,' he said. 'But if a swarm comes they will get into the water pipes. Do you have a water tank at your house?'

'Yes, from Dr Tom. But it is empty.'

'Fill it then, Halima. Just in case.'

He turned to walk back to the house. 'Don't worry, Halima. I will see you tomorrow.'

'Yes, Sunday Man. Thank you.'

Aurelia was in the sitting room when Peter came in from the garden.

'The telephone isn't working,' she said.

'I'm not surprised,' he said. 'I'm afraid it doesn't work very often. Who were you going to ring?'

'Lizzie,' she said. 'I promised to tell her we had arrived safely.'

'Never mind,' he said. 'I'm sure she won't worry. I'm going to have a shower now after all. Why don't you ask them to make some tea for you?'

'Oh,' she said, 'I can make the tea. Would you like me to bring some up for you?'

'No thanks,' he said, putting his now-empty beer bottle down on a table, 'I've already had some.'

Peter was in the shower and Aurelia was just wondering if her tea tasted peculiar because of the milk, when Jaygo and Laurie arrived.

Jaygo breezed straight into the sitting room wearing a long chiffon scarf with her red hair trailing behind her.

'My God!' she announced. 'That hotel!'

'Hello,' said Aurelia, standing up.

'I'm Jaygo,' said Jaygo, stretching out her hand. 'You must be Aurelia. Sorry but the door was open and we came straight in.'

'How do you do?' said Aurelia, shaking her hand. 'Peter didn't say we were expecting you.'

'No one expects the Spanish Inquisition,' said Jaygo. 'But I left a message for Peter saying we'd drop by. Didn't he get it?'

'I don't think so,' said Aurelia. 'I'm afraid he's in the shower.'

'Never mind,' said Jaygo, waving her arm behind her. 'You know Laurie Miller, don't you?'

Laurie shrugged apologetically at Aurelia. 'I think we met a couple of years ago in London,' he said, and then added, 'I'm most frightfully sorry. I didn't know you weren't expecting us.'

Aurelia gave a polite smile and shook Laurie's hand.

'The thing is,' said Jaygo, sitting down expansively on a sofa, 'the hotel is simply frightful and Peter said we could stay here if we didn't like it.'

'Oh,' said Aurelia, taken completely aback.

'There was no electricity and hardly any water,' said Jaygo. 'And the manager said he didn't know when the power would come back on. So some idiot had opened the windows and the place was literally filling up with flying cockroaches.'

'They are locusts, Jay,' said Laurie. 'Jack's driver told us that.'

'Anyway,' went on Jaygo. 'We simply couldn't stay there another minute. I hope it's OK to drop in on you like this but Peter did say.'

'He'll be down in a minute,' said Aurelia. 'Perhaps I can offer you a cup of tea?'

Jaygo did not reply but put her head back and closed her eyes.

'Well,' said Aurelia after a minute. 'I'll go and get it then.'

'I'll come and help you,' said Laurie, following Aurelia to the kitchen.

When they were safely in the kitchen, he said to Aurelia, 'Look, I really am most frightfully sorry. This had nothing to do with me.'

'It's all right,' said Aurelia, beginning to fuss with the kettle. 'It's just that Peter didn't say anything.'

'Well, that's just it,' said Laurie. 'I don't think she told him.'

'What!' said Aurelia, looking suddenly up. 'Do you mean she just turned up here expecting to stay without a word of warning?'

'Well, your telephone isn't working,' said Laurie lamely.

*   *   *

Peter came down the stairs expecting to see Aurelia sipping her tea quietly but was greeted with the sight of Jaygo lying back on the sofa with her arms out sideways and her eyes closed.

'What!' he exclaimed.

'Hello, Peter, darling,' said Jaygo, opening her eyes. 'Guess who?'

'What the hell are you doing here?' he demanded.

'That's no way to greet me. Aren't you supposed to say "Dr Manhattan, I presume?"'

'I said,' he repeated evenly, 'what the hell are you doing here?'

'You sound almost as pissed off as she does,' said Jaygo.

'Aurelia? What did you say to her?'

'Nothing much,' replied Jaygo. 'Just that Laurie and I have decided to take you up on your kind offer to have us to stay.'

'Laurie!! Is he here too?'

'Of course he is, darling.'

'Where is he then?'

'In the kitchen, counting out tea bags with Goldilocks.'

'And you haven't come to stay,' said Peter. 'You're booked into the hotel.'

'I am *not* staying in that flea pit,' said Jaygo. 'Problem?'

'Yes,' he said. 'Problem.'

'What?'

'What the hell do you think?'

'Oh dear,' said Jaygo. 'Didn't you tell her you'd been just a teeny bit unfaithful to her on Wednesday night?'

Peter looked toward the kitchen door and was relieved to see it was shut. 'For Christ's sake, Jaygo.'

'Well? Did you tell her or didn't you?'

'Of course I didn't,' he snapped

'Oh dear. Do you want me to then?'

'Jesus!'

'No, Peter, Jesus doesn't have to know. Only Aurelia.'

'If you say anything, I'll kill you,' said Peter, pointing a finger at Jaygo.

'Can't we make up our mind then?' said Jaygo.

'What?'

'It's like this, Peter darling,' said Jaygo, holding up her two index fingers and pointing them from side to side like windscreen wipers. 'Aurelia,' she began, pointing one way. 'Or Jaygo,' she went on, pointing the other way. 'Aurelia, Jaygo, Aurelia, Jaygo. You get the idea.'

233

'You're ridiculous,' he said, walking past her towards the kitchen.

The Ngale sat at his desk, on the satellite telephone to England.

'Is everything prepared in Manchester?' he asked.

'Yes, Ngale. I bought one reagent set and one drum of alcohol from the Swiss.'

'That won't be enough.'

'No, our father, but that is all that is here. The Swiss man is sending for more and it will come in on Sunday night. We will have enough to begin work on Monday.'

'It will have to do then. Have you made arrangements for the shipment to go to Manchester?'

'Yes, Ngale. Abale will take charge. The flight is to come to Speke Airport in Liverpool and the container to go direct into bonded store. Over the night we take out the cotton bales, cut out the packages and repack them in English containers for taking to Manchester in the morning.'

'Good,' said the Ngale. 'Now, tell me about London. What have you found out?'

'It was not the people you said, Ngale.'

'How do you know?'

'We asked them very hard, our father. They could not tell us.'

The Ngale paused. 'Are you completely sure?' he asked.

'Yes, Ngale. At the end they would have told us but they did not know, sah.'

'Are they gone?'

'Yes, Ngale.'

'Who is it then? I will know.'

'I don't know, sah. Maybe it was electrical.'

'I have already told you it was not that,' said the Ngale. 'Go to the policeman I talked to in London and ask him. I want to know what they found in the warehouse after the fire.'

'He will not know me.'

'He will see you all the same,' said the Ngale, confidently. 'Tell him I will pay him when I come to London at the end of next week.'

The Ngale picked up his pen and began to write.

There was a gentle knock at the door and Habu came in quietly.

'Is he here?' said the Ngale, without looking up.

'Yes, Ngale.'

'Tell him to wait. Stay with him until I come.'

Five minutes later, the Ngale had placed his work in an envelope file and locked the file in his desk. He picked up the satellite telephone and walked into the sitting room.

John Etherington's driver was standing very upright in the middle of the room. When he saw the Ngale he touched his knee briefly and stood to attention again.

'Well?' said the Ngale, sitting down on one of the low sofas. 'Where has he been since last night?'

'Back to Sabon Gari, sah.'

The Ngale raised his eyebrows. 'To buy what?'

'A rope, sah. Very strong rope.'

'A rope?'

'Yes, Ngale, like this one, sah,' said the driver, proudly reaching into his pocket and producing a six-inch length of blue nylon rope.

The Ngale smiled with amusement. 'Very good, Bawa. Anything else?'

'A big hammer, Ngale. For posts.'

The Ngale furrowed his brow. 'Did he say what he wanted them for?'

'No, sah. He just put them in the car himself.'

'Curious. And has he been anywhere today?'

'No, Ngale. He is in his room all day. He say for me to be ready at nine o'clock tonight to go for dinner.'

'Did he say where?'

'No, sah.'

'Very well, Bawa. Go now. But when he is home from dinner tonight, come here and tell me where he went. Habu will stay up for you. If it is important he will wake me.'

The Ngale returned to his study.

Back at Peter's house, Laurie had returned to the sitting room, leaving Peter and Aurelia alone in the kitchen.

'Did you really ask them to stay?' Aurelia asked Peter as she set cups and saucers out on a tray.

'I think it would have been rude not to. But when I heard you were coming here with Tom's ashes, I rang Laurie and suggested they stay in the hotel.'

'What? It's all right for her to stay when I'm not here but not when I am?'

'That's not it at all, Aurelia. It's not to do with her. It's to do with you.'

'Well, if she's working with Jack Ngale, why can't she stay at his place?'

'No one stays at Jack's place.'

'Why not?'

'I don't know. They just don't. But it'll be all right. They'll probably be out all day and we'll hardly see them.'

'What about tonight then? Dinner?' Aurelia went on. 'It's a bit late to tell Halima there will be two more, isn't it?'

'We'll go out then. And where is Halima anyway?'

'She was here when I came in but I said I wanted to make the tea and she said could she carry some water down to her house or something so I let her go. She'll be back in a minute if you want to see her.'

'It's all right. I can book us into the French Club. You'll like that.'

'Oh, no, don't let's go out,' she said. 'It's been a very long day and there's a lot I want to do tomorrow. Why don't you and I eat in and Laurie and Jaygo can go out?'

Peter smiled. 'We can try that,' he said.

Aurelia took the tea tray into the sitting room. Peter followed.

'Peter says you're here to launch a record, Jaygo. That must be exciting,' she said politely, passing a cup to Jaygo.

'It will be if they like it,' said Jaygo. 'Bit of a bummer if they don't.'

'I'm sure they will like it,' said Aurelia, passing another cup to Laurie.

'I expect you'll be wanting to contact Jack now you're here,' continued Aurelia. 'We can send a driver with a message if you like.'

'Technology to the rescue,' said Jaygo, putting her tea down and reaching into her bag for the satellite telephone.

'I didn't know they had mobiles here,' said Aurelia. 'Look, Peter, what a good idea.'

Jaygo held the telephone out in front of her and began to key in a number.

'Mobile numbers always seem so long,' continued Aurelia. 'I don't know how people remember them.'

'Jack, hi,' said Jaygo into the phone. 'We came in about half an hour ago. We went to the hotel but Peter said we have to stay with him at his house. So, if you want me, I'm here.'

Peter looked at Aurelia and shrugged.

'What time shall I come round then?' Jaygo continued. 'Oh. I thought we were going to meet up this evening? Tomorrow will be all right of course. At ten. Yes. Hello? Jack? Are you still there?'

Jaygo switched off the telephone and put it back in her bag.

'That's a short call,' she announced. 'Bloody rude actually.'

'Perhaps you were cut off?' said Laurie helpfully.

'I'm going to see him tomorrow at ten. So we can all have a nice lie-in in the morning. That'll be nice, won't it, Peter?'

'Marvellous,' said Peter flatly. 'Where are your cases?'

'Piled up next to that funny little man outside on the porch,' said Jaygo. 'Does that mean you're going to let us stay after all?'

Peter looked at Aurelia. 'I'll put Laurie and Jay in the two rooms at the end,' he said. 'I'll go and find Halima. She can make the beds and get someone to take the cases up.'

'He's such a sweetie, isn't he?' said Jaygo, when Peter had gone.

Aurelia smiled awkwardly at Jaygo.

'Lots of locusts everywhere, aren't there?' said Laurie, conversationally.

'Oh, yes,' said Aurelia, glad to have something to talk about. 'But Peter says there will be even more tomorrow. I must say I absolutely hate them. I can't imagine what it will be like when there are even more.'

'Is it a proper swarm?' asked Laurie.

'It might be tomorrow,' said Aurelia. 'Peter has worked on them for years so I've learned a lot about them secondhand. They are frightfully unpredictable. Peter sometimes jokes that he could spend his whole life studying them and still barely scratch the surface.'

Jaygo appeared not to be listening; she was making another call.

'Hugo, darling,' she began. 'Yes, I know I said I would ring before but we must have been in a dead zone or something. Look, there is a simply dreadful delay here in Rome and so we're not going to get to Kano till after midnight. I'll ring you first thing tomorrow and give you simply all the news.'

She paused, reached down for her tea and took a sip.

'What's that?' she went on. 'Tell him no. He has to record it again. If that's his idea of backing us up, I'm a Dutchman. Yes. Even if it means a delay before release.'

There was another pause. More tea.

'No. Yes. No. You too.'

Jaygo turned the phone off and dropped it back into her bag.

'Sorry,' she said to Aurelia. 'I had to call Hugo before I forgot.'

'Who is Hugo?' asked Aurelia.

'One of the band,' said Jaygo, crisply.

Laurie was about to intervene when Peter returned. 'I've got to go up to the Institute,' he said. 'I want to get the proper story on the swarm from the people there if the satellite link is up. Laurie, you might like to come and see how it all works.'

'I'm a bit whacked, old man. Could I make it tomorrow?'

'Of course,' said Peter. 'Anyway, everything is fixed up with Halima and I should be back at about six.'

'We can't have you going off by yourself, Peter,' said Jaygo. 'Aurelia and I will come with you.'

'Oh,' said Aurelia, startled. 'I think I ought to stay and arrange things for dinner here.'

'OK,' said Peter, going towards the door. 'Six o'clock then.'

'Hold on,' said Jaygo, 'I'm still coming,' and she stood up to follow him.

Outside, Tijja was brushing locusts off the car.

'I never see so many, sah,' he said. 'Where shall we go?'

'I'll drive,' said Peter, opening the front passenger door for Jaygo. 'You go and help your mother fetch water. I won't need you again today.'

'Thank you, sah. She is very busy.'

Peter walked around to his side of the car and climbed in.

He paused for a moment before driving off and shook his head.

'What's up?' said Jaygo. 'Are you cross at me for coming with you?'

'It's not that,' he said, pulling out of the drive onto the road. 'It's the locusts. There are too many for a swarm precursor and all the wrong sort. But at least they are alive.'

'What?'

'It's a bit technical,' he said. 'Probably very boring.'

'That's never stopped you before,' she replied.

'And that's another thing,' he said.

'Another thing?'

'All this "before" talk of yours.'

'Does this mean you're about to give me another of your "It's a long time ago" lectures?'

'No. I mean, yes. It's just that . . . It's just that it's not a very good *week*, is it?'

'It seems like there's no such thing as "good" weeks for Peter Wilson to make up his mind. As far as I'm concerned there are only "last" weeks which are too late and "next" weeks which are miles away.'

Peter turned left onto the main road out of the city.

'We can talk about it later, if you want,' said Jaygo, when Peter did not reply.

In a few minutes they were clear of Kano and driving through dry scrub country broken up by occasional trees.

After about a mile, Peter pulled the car into the side of the road by a low bridge. 'I have to check something. You wait here,' he said as he climbed out and shut his door.

'I'll just talk to myself then,' she said quietly. 'Which I might just as well have been doing anyway.'

The bridge spanned the dried bed of a ditch about six yards wide. Peter scrambled down to the bed of the ditch and scrutinised a carpet of dead locusts.

'Shit,' he said, brushing some aside with his foot.

He put his hands on his hips and looked up and down the ditch before squatting down to examine the dead insects more closely.

After about a minute he returned to the car.

'What were you doing?' asked Jaygo as he drove off.

'The locusts are not supposed to be dead,' he said almost to himself. 'They only got here yesterday and they are not supposed to be bloody dead yet.'

'Why don't you want them dead? They're not going to eat anything if they are dead, surely?'

Peter looked briefly at her. 'That ditch back there,' he said. 'The only time it's got more than a trickle of water in it is during the rainy season, which is months away but there must still be enough moisture in it to attract locusts.

'They don't drink, of course, but moisture means plants and that is why they go towards it. They can smell damp soil from about a mile away. Now that ditch looked as dry as a bone to me so they must be pretty desperate. I suspect that means they haven't been near food for at least a week so that lot must have been pretty high up and not able to land.'

'I don't understand,' she said. 'Surely if they want to land they can just fold up their wings.'

'Sadly not,' he said. 'If a swarm begins to swirl in an anti-cyclone, the ones near the middle get sucked up by the wind and can't land.

239

'You get a column of locusts, perhaps a mile high. And if the wind is strong enough a mile up, some of the locusts will start to spin off and be carried by the higher winds away from the main anti-cyclone. The locusts that have been separated will be able to land – like the ones in the city and those back there.

'Those that got to Kano are all right because there's plenty to eat but the ones here had nothing to eat and so died. The fact that they died within twenty-four hours means that the main swarm is pretty high and if it's high it's also pretty damn big.'

'Oh,' she said, not really understanding. 'Does that mean the big swarm is somewhere else and the ones we have seen are just a few off the top then?'

'Something like that.'

He stopped the car again. 'But look around here,' he said. 'No locusts at all.'

He got out of the car and walked towards a row of low bushes about a hundred yards away. She could see him brushing the foliage with his hands and squatting down to look at the soil.

Next he stood up and, sheltering his eyes with cupped hands, he looked back towards Kano and then forwards in the direction the car was pointing.

He walked slowly back to the car and waited before closing the car door after him.

'Can you hear anything?' he asked.

She put her head on one side and listened. 'No,' she said. 'Am I supposed to?'

'Not a hum? Very faint?'

After listening again he shut the car door and drove off again. 'No,' he said. 'I thought I could hear it when I was out by the bushes but perhaps I was imagining it.'

'Peter, I couldn't hear anything at all.'

'The thing is,' he said as much to himself as to her, 'there aren't any locusts out here at all. Not even any dead ones. And that means they must have flown over here before coming down, so wherever they came from they must have been pretty high up.'

'Well, we wouldn't have heard them if they were high up, would we?'

'Any humming will come from the main swarm and, if we can't hear it, it's still a good few miles away.'

Back at the house, Aurelia was showing Laurie his room. 'I don't think it has been used for quite a while,' she was saying, 'but

240

Peter says Halima keeps all the rooms fresh so it should be all right.'

'It looks absolutely fine,' he said. 'Did I see a bathroom across the corridor?'

'Yes,' she said, 'and there's a loo and a hand basin of your own through that door over there but no bath, I'm afraid.'

'Don't worry,' he said, smiling. 'It's fine.'

She smiled back. 'You must have thought Peter was a bit rude not to invite you in the first place, mustn't you?'

'Not at all,' he said. 'But I must admit it's nice to stay in a real house. Even someone like me can get a bit sick of hotels.'

She took some towels from a cupboard and put them on the bed. 'There. All done.'

She walked over to the window and fidgeted with the curtain. 'You've known Peter and Jaygo a long time, haven't you?' she said.

'Oh, yes,' said Laurie. 'We met at university. God, that must be nearly ten years ago now.'

'And Jack?' she said, without turning around. 'Did you meet him at the same time?'

'Not quite,' said Laurie, sitting on the bed and looking at his watch. 'We didn't see much of him at first. At least, not until he started chasing Jaygo.'

Aurelia turned back into the room. 'But she was going out with Peter by then, wasn't she?'

Laurie looked down. 'I don't remember exactly,' he said. 'It's quite a while back, you know.'

Aurelia did not reply.

'Well, yes,' said Laurie after a pause, 'I suppose it would be about then. Yes.'

'She dazzled him a bit, I expect,' said Aurelia. 'She's very beautiful, isn't she?'

'I suppose she is. But I don't think you really notice when you know someone, do you?'

'Everyone else does though,' Aurelia continued. 'When she came to Cambridge a while back, people in college couldn't stop talking about her. She made quite an impression, you know.'

'Jaygo in Jocasta Manhattan-mode you mean?' asked Laurie.

'Jocasta Manhattan-mode?' said Aurelia thoughtfully. 'That about describes it. The Great Jocasta Manhattan.'

Laurie looked up at Aurelia. 'You don't like her much, do you?' he said.

241

'Sorry,' she said. 'I hope she didn't notice.'

'I shouldn't worry. I don't know that Jaygo notices very much except Jaygo.'

Aurelia paused before saying quietly, 'Or Peter.'

'Do you think so?' said Laurie.

'Don't you?'

Laurie thought for a moment before replying. 'I'm not sure what you want me to say to that,' he replied at last.

Aurelia stood up and rubbed her hands together as if they had dust on them from the curtains as she walked towards the door. 'Well, I want you to say I'm being silly, that's it's nothing and that you don't know what I am talking about.'

When she reached the door she turned and added, 'But I don't think you are going to say that, are you?'

Laurie looked at her without speaking.

'Just call downstairs if you want anything,' said Aurelia as she closed the door behind her.

As they approached the Tropical Crops Institute, Peter was surprised not to see the usual row of orange Land Rovers outside the main building.

He parked near the main entrance. As they got out of the car, a red-headed man emerged from the door and locked it behind him.

'Michael?' said Peter, going up to him. 'Where is everyone?'

'Well, well,' said the man, turning round. 'If it isn't the original Sunday Man. Where the hell have you been, Peter? I've been leaving messages all over the place for you in the last twelve hours.' Then, seeing Jaygo, he said, 'Sorry, I'm Michael McKecnie. How do you do?'

'Jaygo,' she said, shaking his hand.

'Where is everyone?' asked Peter. 'Are you shutting up shop?'

'Dead right I am,' said McKecnie. 'Have you had your head in the sand for three days or what?'

'Sorry?' questioned Peter.

'I've sent everyone home,' replied McKecnie. 'That's where I'm going and so will you if you've got any sense. And shut your doors and windows when you get there is my advice.'

'Do you mean the locusts?' said Jaygo.

'I do indeed,' said McKecnie. 'Hold on,' he added, 'don't I know you from somewhere?'

'I don't think so. This is my first visit to Kano.'

'Oh,' he said, starting to walk towards his Land Rover. 'Look, Peter, if you've got your key, go in first and look at the charts on my desk. The power was down all morning but we rigged a generator up to the dish and managed to get a satellite download about two hours ago. I only managed three frame grabs but my guess is that the swarm's about twenty miles across by nine long and a good two miles high. It's going to be here by this time tomorrow.'

'Twenty miles?' said Peter. 'It can't be that big. Martin Glynne sent me a fax yesterday and it was five miles at best.'

'That US picture?' said McKecnie. 'He sent it to me, too but he was wrong about it. He thought it was an Ultra Violet scan but it was a heavily filtered visible range one so he failed to see anything less than a mile from the surface. Our friend Glynne only saw the top of the cone. I'm afraid it's at *least* twenty miles across at the base.'

'Come and show me,' said Peter, taking out his keys and searching for the right one.

'Sorry, Peter, but I've got Janet and the kids booked on an Accra flight at ten. It's already pretty crowded at the airport so I want to leave plenty of time.'

'Accra? That seems a bit extreme. No matter how bad the swarm is, Ibadan would do.'

McKecnie unlocked his Land Rover and climbed. 'Internals are booked solid. It was Accra or nothing.'

'You're being over-dramatic,' said Peter as McKecnie wound down his window. 'Janet, of all people, too. She's seen enough locusts to know them. Pretty inconvenient, but hardly justifies going as far as Accra.'

'Well,' said McKecnie, starting his engine, 'neither you nor I have ever seen any swarm more than two miles across at the core. Twenty? I think we're looking at something a bit different here, don't you?

'You go and look at the charts for yourself. I'm only staying in Kano because I have to but I don't expect to leave the house for a week, let alone get out here. I'll lay a quid to whatever you offer that we are in for one hell of a bumpy ride over the next five days. See you.'

McKecnie tooted his horn as he pulled out and headed towards Kano.

'He's a funny chap, isn't he?' said Jaygo.

Peter was looking thoughtfully after the disappearing Land Rover. 'Oh, I don't know. He's always a bit like that. But he looked rattled as all hell, didn't he? And that's not like him at all.'

Peter found the charts McKecnie had been talking about scattered on the desk in his office on the first floor. While Peter examined them and made measurements with a plastic ruler, Jaygo wandered around the room like someone browsing in a shop, picking some things up and bending down to peer at others.

'I don't think I've been in a proper laboratory since university,' she said. 'When you see them in films they are always so tidy but really they're like the insides of bathroom cupboards.'

Peter carried a chart to the window to see it in a better light.

'Why doesn't the electricity work?' asked Jaygo.

'It hardly ever does,' he said absently. 'We're ten miles from the city on a quiet road. There's only one power line and it gets stolen every time we put it up again.'

'Who would steal a power line?' she said, picking up a plaster model of a locust's head and trying to work out what it was.

'Anyone who can find a ready market for scrap copper,' said Peter. 'Which happens to be almost anyone in Kano.'

After five minutes without talking he finally looked up at her. She was leaning against the window, looking at him with her arms folded.

'He's right,' said Peter. 'I make it twenty-one miles by six at the base. But he's wrong about the speed. We won't see it in Kano until Sunday.'

Jaygo came over to look at the chart and leaned over him, putting her hand on his shoulder.

'Very pretty,' she said. 'But as far as I can see it's just a load of smudges and you've made it all up.'

'I wish I had,' he said. 'I think we'd better go and see Jack about this.'

'Why don't we phone him? I've got the phone with me.'

'I would rather see him,' said Peter, holding the laboratory door open for Jaygo. 'McKecnie will have already spoken to him but Jack doesn't have much time for him and may not have taken much notice.'

'What notice is he supposed to take then?'

'He can tell the people to get ready. You see, most people will know what a swarm is like but this one is going to be a lot worse than usual. A lot worse. He has to tell them not to panic and sit very tight until the locusts have gone.'

Peter and Jaygo went down to the car and Peter double-checked the lock on the main door as they went out.

'What about my CD launch?' she said. 'Do you think that can still go ahead all right?'

'Ah,' he said as she slid into her seat, 'I hadn't thought about that. It rather depends what Jack has in mind for you and whether it's indoors or out.'

'He sent me a list,' she said as Peter started the engine and drove off. 'There are a few radio interviews, a couple of receptions in Kano and then we're going to visit some other towns round and about. Record shops and that sort of thing, I expect.'

'Record shops?' said Peter, surprised. 'Always one for expansive ideas, our Jack.'

'It wasn't supposed to be all that time-consuming,' she said. 'You and I were meant to be able to spend some time together too.'

He looked at her. 'At least that was the general idea,' she went on, 'but then Goldilocks turned up.'

He laughed. 'I'm not sure Aurelia would see it quite like that.'

'Well, she wasn't going to let me near you in England, was she? This seemed to be a good opportunity. I told you.'

'Opportunity for what?'

'Us, you fool,' she said. 'Was that such a terrible prospect?'

Peter did not reply but drove on for five minutes. Then he stopped the car and pointed to an uneven row of trees about a hundred yards away.

'That's part of a dry river bed,' he said. 'I want to see if there are any locusts in it. I won't be long.'

'Can I come?' she said brightly.

He looked at her, slightly surprised. 'Sure,' he said. 'Why not?'

As they walked away from the car to the row of trees, she slipped her hand into his and gave it a slight squeeze.

'It all looks pretty much the same to me around here,' she said. 'How do you know where the river beds are?'

'Easy,' he said. 'You just have to drive up and down this road every day for a few years.'

'Has Aurelia been here with you?'

'She hates it in Kano. This is only her second or third time as an adult. She was born here.'

'Born here? Does that make her a real African then?'

'I suppose so,' he laughed. 'But don't tell her!'

When they reached the river bed, Peter helped Jaygo down the bank onto the flat area in the middle. They could only see a light scattering of locusts on the dry red mud.

'You see?' he said. 'Not nearly as many as in that ditch near the town.'

Jaygo picked up a dead locust and examined it closely. 'Didn't people round here used to eat these?' she asked.

'They still do,' he said. 'It would be a waste not to.'

'What do they taste like?' she asked.

'Not bad. It depends a bit what they've been eating. Why don't you try one?'

'What! Are you serious?'

He shrugged.

'All right,' she said, breaking the locust in half. 'Which end?'

'Oh, the head I think. It's always the best part.'

She looked at him uncertainly. 'Are you kidding me?'

'Would I do a thing like that?' he smiled.

She looked at him suspiciously before closing her eyes, opening her mouth and popping in the locust head. She grimaced as she chewed and swallowed.

Then she opened her mouth for inspection. 'All gone! That was totally disgusting! They don't really eat them at all, do they?'

'Of course they do,' he said, taking her hand. 'But they tend to cook them first.'

'You bastard!' she laughed back at him. 'You total bastard.'

Laughing easily together, they scrambled up the bank of the river.

'Does this place have a name?' she said, brushing some dust off.

'Yes. Ker-Odi – last water. When the river dries up, this is the last part to stay muddy. I suppose when there was grazing here, it was quite important.'

'Grazing?' she said. 'It doesn't look as if there's anything to eat around here. There's no proper grass or anything.'

'Oh, not now,' he said, starting to walk back to the car. 'But a couple of hundred years ago, before over-grazing, this was quite an important cattle area. That's all gone now, of course, and in about another fifty years this will be proper desert.'

'That sounds rather gloomy. Can't they stop it?'

'No,' he said. 'The Sahara's getting bigger by about twenty miles in all directions every year. The desert proper is still a few hundred miles to the north of here but that's only ten years or so.'

'What will happen to the Institute? Or even Kano?'

'The Institute will be pretty much redundant by then so it won't matter and Kano has some pretty deep wells so it'll tick over for quite a while. But there are going to be so many changes over the next hundred years that running out of water will be the least of their worries.'

They had reached the car and Peter opened the car door for her.

'Hold on!' she said, holding up her hand. 'I think I can hear it. Listen.'

She cupped her hands behind her ears. 'Yes, there it is. That's it again. It's a low noise like bees. Humming.'

Peter turned to face north and held his ears forward.

'I can't hear anything,' he said after about twenty seconds.

She dropped her hands. 'It's gone now, but I definitely heard it.'

Peter climbed into the car. 'Perhaps we'd better phone Jack after all to tell him we're coming.'

'OK,' she said. 'You drive and I'll call him.'

After a minute with the telephone to her ear, she said, 'He's not answering. Wonderful, isn't it? Zillions of pounds of techno and it's no good if they don't pick it up.'

'Never mind. At least you don't have to worry any more about which phone to use.'

She held the telephone in her lap and looked at it. 'Yes,' she said, 'I'm down to one now.'

She put the telephone into the bag at her feet.

'The other one,' she said thoughtfully. 'Do you think they'll find it?'

Peter considered for a moment. 'Perhaps,' he said. 'They're bound to sift through everything.'

'They can't trace it,' she said, looking straight ahead. 'It hasn't got a number on it or anything.'

He looked across at her. 'How do you mean?'

'Hugo told me when he gave it to me. I mean, they're totally illegal even in America and the people you get them from aren't much into serial numbers.'

'Weren't you taking a bit of a risk carting it about then? What if someone had to search your bag. Security somewhere, say?'

'Nobody searches my bag,' she said firmly. 'Never. And even if they did,' she added brightly, 'I'd say I had a quick call to make while they did it!'

He smiled. 'We haven't talked much about it yet, have we?'

'The warehouse, you mean?'

'Yes.'

'Do you want to?'

He thought for a moment. 'Not today,' he said. 'Do you?'

'I'm not sure that I can yet,' she said quietly. 'I think we will have to one day.'

'Do you think Laurie's all right with it?' he asked.

'I think so. He wasn't there when . . . you know.'

'When we shot the man, you mean.'

'Yes.'

Neither of them spoke again until the car was on the outskirts of the city.

'He's a funny fellow, isn't he?' said Peter.

'Laurie? Yes. I've always liked him.'

'One way and another he's been a pretty good friend to me over the years. In fact, I've probably known him as long as I've known you. I think we all met in the same week, didn't we?'

'Yes,' she said. 'The same day.'

'But he doesn't look well, does he? I mean he's always been pretty fat looking but somehow things seem to be catching up with him now.'

'Has he said anything to you?' she asked.

'Oh no, I don't think it's anything much. Perhaps he's just looking older. He probably thinks we're looking older too.'

'We do,' she said. 'But ask me in ten years and I'll say I looked great now.'

He drove on for a moment. 'Let's not go to Jack just now. There's something I want to show you.'

'What is it?'

'You'll have to guess,' he said. 'You have to look at it and tell me what you think it is.'

'That sounds mysterious.'

'It is,' he said. 'Very.'

Peter turned off the main road and headed down increasingly narrow and bumpy side roads. Modern buildings gave way to old broken-down housing. Soon they were in what Jaygo might have called a shanty town. Crowds of people were pushing and shouting. The sides of the roads were lined with stall-holders selling an amazing variety of wares. Here were people selling yams. Here a colourfully-dressed group selling chickens in small wicker baskets, then a row of people in covered stalls selling rugs, belts, light bulbs, tins of food, car tyres. And still more with boxes full of sweet potatoes, children's clothes, cloth.

Jaygo held on to the dashboard as the car bucked slowly over ruts and potholes. Everywhere she looked were people, shouting laughing.

The afternoon sun was beginning to fall and the red dust from the road clouded up behind them almost scarlet, but nobody seemed to mind. This was the heart of the city. Anything went.

'Welcome to Sabon Gari,' announced Peter.

'Sabon what?' she asked above the clamour.

'Sabon Gari. It means the place of strangers although the people who live here have always lived here. They like to think they are special.'

At the end of an uneven track the road suddenly opened up into a square about a hundred yards wide, with a row of low wells along one side and a small church in the middle.

'Those are the dye pits,' said Peter, pointing to the wells. 'They've been here even longer than the market.'

'Do stop, Peter, I want to have a look.'

Peter pulled over.

Jaygo ran towards the nearest dye pit and leaned over it.

'Don't touch it!' Peter called over. He was too late.

'What?' she called back. 'I can't hear you!'

'Look at your hands,' he said, walking over to her.

She held her hands out in front of her. They were stained a deep blue from the wetness on the edge of the pit. 'Oh my God!' she shouted. 'I'm covered in it!'

'Don't worry,' he said, passing her a handkerchief. 'It'll wash out in about a week.'

A man's voice called over from behind the dye pits. 'Hey! Sunday Man!'

A young African wearing a T-shirt the same colour as Jaygo's hands appeared.

'Oladi!' said Peter. 'Good to see you. You've got very tall all of a sudden.'

'Yes, sah, very tall, sah. I am working,' he said, holding up two very blue hands, 'I won't shake you.'

Peter turned to Jaygo. 'This is Oladi, a very old friend of mine.' He waved at the row of pits. 'These belong to his family.'

'Yes, Sunday,' Oladi said proudly. 'You want dye cloth today? I have very good for you.'

'Well, I can shake your hand,' said Jaygo, holding one out nearly as blue as Oladi's.

Oladi laughed as he shook it. 'Oh, yes, you are a Tuareg Lady today.'

'Tuareg?' said Jaygo, looking at Peter.

'It's the colour,' he said. 'Tuareg blue.'

'Oh,' she said. 'Has he got something to get it off?'

Peter looked up at the young man and smiled. 'What do you think, Oladi?'

'No, sah!' he laughed. 'It won't come out!'

'Bugger,' she said.

'How is your father?' said Peter to Oladi.

'Ah, no, sah,' he said, suddenly more serious. 'He is gone now. The dye pits are for me.'

'I'm sorry,' said Peter. 'I knew him a long time.'

'Yes, Sunday Man. Thank you,' said Oladi. 'But,' he went on, 'if you don't want dye cloth today what are you here for?'

'To show my friend,' he said.

'Is she fara lady too, sah?'

'No. No,' said Peter. 'She is just a Tuareg!'

The two men laughed again while Jaygo peered into one of the pits.

'Is it deep?' she asked.

'Quite,' said Peter, 'between ten and twenty feet, depending on how old it is.'

'Is this what we came to see, Peter? Do I get anything for guessing?'

'No, we came to see this,' he said, turning and pointing to the church. 'Our Lady of Santa Maria.'

She looked at the small church with its chipped plaster walls and the statue in its niche on the end wall.

'I didn't expect to see a church here,' she said. 'Is it a real one?'

'No,' he said, turning and walking towards it with Jaygo and Oladi.

'These days it's only used by Oladi and his family for storing things. But it's quite famous because of the statue.'

'Yes, Tuareg,' said Oladi. 'She is very famous. A man came yesterday to see Our Lady. But he was a bad man and hit her with a knife. Very bad.'

'What do you mean?' said Peter, puzzled.

'I will show it to you,' said Oladi, pointing to the marks on the statue that John Etherington had made with his penknife.

Oladi put his finger in the hole Etherington had made. 'Very bad man, sah.'

Peter looked at it curiously.

'Did he say what he was doing?'

'No, sah, he not say. But he is from Ngale.'

'The Ngale?' said Peter with surprise.

'Yes. I know the driver, sah. Ngale man.'

'Does he mean Jack?' said Jaygo, standing back and looking up at the statue.

'Yes,' Peter said absently to her.

He turned to Oladi. 'What sort of man was he? Did you know him?'

'No. He is white man. And he is very tall, sah. Very bad man, not smiling.'

'Tall?' Peter asked with interest.

'Oh, yes. Very tall.' Oladi held his hand high above his head. 'This tall, sah!'

'Is he now?' said Peter, almost to himself, as he turned to look at the mark again.

'Tell you what, Oladi,' said Peter, taking his wallet out of his pocket and passing a twenty Naira note to the young man, 'Do you think you could lay your hands on a couple of Star beers for me and Tuareg here?'

'Oh, yes, Sunday Man. But is not cold beer.'

'Never mind,' said Peter. 'Sabon style will be just fine.'

'Why does everyone call you Sunday Man?' asked Jaygo when Oladi had gone.

'It's a bit of a nickname,' he said. 'It just means white man really.'

'But the man at the Institute called you Sunday Man too. Isn't he a Sunday Man himself?'

Peter laughed. 'McKecnie? I shouldn't think so. McKecnie works at the Institute, drives home with the window up and the air conditioning on, goes into his house with an electric fence around it and doesn't come out till it's time to go to the Institute again. I shouldn't think anyone in Kano knows him well enough to call him a Sunday Man.'

'Doesn't McKecnie like it here then?'

'No. He hates it. Can't wait to move on, in fact.'

'Why did he come in the first place then?'

'Good question, said Peter, brushing a couple of locusts from the base of the statue. 'Look,' he said, 'they're everywhere.'

'Go on about McKecnie. Tell me why he came.'

Peter looked at her and sighed slightly. 'Michael's actually a very mediocre academic and wouldn't get a job at most Institutes. So Jack, just before he went completely local, picked up Michael pretty cheaply. He shouldn't really be here at all. I should have kicked up more of a fuss but Tom was ill at the time and Michael sort of slipped in under the net.'

He smiled at her. 'I should think you've seen more of Kano in an hour than he has in two years.'

She smiled back at him. 'Does that make me a Sunday Lady then?'

'Possibly. But you will always be number two in that line, I'm afraid.'

'Goldilocks! I'm not going to be Sunday Lady Two if she's Sunday Lady One!'

'No. No,' said Peter, pointing upwards. 'This is the real Sunday Lady for me.'

'The statue?'

'Yes. Do you like her?'

Jaygo stood back again and looked up.

'What's the matter with her arms?' said Jaygo, holding her arms out like the statue. 'She doesn't have any proper elbows. Look, she's all bendy. She looks as though she should be holding something.'

'Perhaps she is,' said Peter. 'You have to guess.'

'This is it? Have I got to guess what the statue is meant to be holding in her arms?'

'Yes,' said Peter. 'What do you think?'

Jaygo put her hands on her hips. 'Well, she's dropped it whatever it is, hasn't she?'

'No clues.'

'I don't know,' said Jaygo. 'But she's a big girl.'

Peter smiled.

'Up top, I mean,' she went on. 'I bet old Joseph couldn't wait to get his hands on her.'

'Jaygo!'

'Well,' said Jaygo, 'I give up.' She held her arms bowed out and down in front of her again. 'Ooh, bugger me! I've just dropped the baby Jesus on His head!'

Peter threw back his head and laughed.

She laughed too and the two of them were still laughing when Oladi came back with the beer.

He held out a bottle and an opener to Jaygo. 'For Tuareg Lady!'

Jaygo opened her bottle and passed the opener to Peter.

'Sah?' said Oladi hesitantly.

'Yes?' said Peter, sipping carefully from his bottle.

Jaygo, who was not at all careful, tipped her bottle straight up to her mouth and was immediately sprayed by an explosion of foam. 'God!' she shouted. 'It's *warm*! Hot beer!'

Peter laughed and Oladi looked embarrassed. 'Sorry, lady,' he said. 'No cold fridging in Sabon Gari.'

'Don't worry about her,' laughed Peter. 'Did you want to ask me something, Oladi?'

'Yes, sah,' said Oladi seriously, turning to Peter. 'They say zaki fara is coming. You talk to the Ngale, is it true?'

'I'm all beer down the front, Peter!' cried Jaygo. 'Blue hands, covered in beer. I'll be lucky if Goldilocks lets me into the house!'

Peter put a hand on Oladi's arm. 'I'm afraid I don't know. Maybe. Just maybe.'

'But if zaki fara come, it is very bad. Very dangerous.'

'No,' said Peter firmly. 'Not dangerous. The fara in a zaki fara are only ordinary fara. Just many more of them. If a zaki fara comes it will be very messy and cause a lot of trouble but it will not be dangerous for people. Trust me.'

'Yes, I do, sah. But one come in the old time and many people die.'

'I know what the stories are. But that was in the old time. It is different now. If a zaki fara comes there will be help. People will come from outside to help us.'

'How do we know? They not come in the war.'

'The civil war? No. They did not come then but they will come to help this time.'

'Thank you, Sunday. I will tell my family.'

'You do that,' said Peter.

Oladi turned to Jaygo. 'Bye, lady. Come back to Sabon Gari. Bless now.'

'Thank you, Oladi. I will,' she said, holding out her hand to him.

The short sunset was already half over as Peter and Jaygo walked back to the car. Scattered locusts hopped away from them across the square, scattering little puffs of terracotta red dust as they jumped.

'What was that about a "zaki fara"?' Jaygo asked. 'Is it a special sort of locust?'

'No, it's what they call a very big swarm,' he said. 'It means a Lion Swarm.'

'Why did Oladi think it was going to be dangerous, and why is it called a Lion Swarm?'

'I don't know the real answer to either of those questions,' said

Peter as they got into the car. 'No one has ever seen one but I'm beginning to think there was one here once. Myths and stories will have exaggerated what happened but I should think it would be pretty horrific.'

'One of your stories again?' she asked.

'The only Lion Swarm I ever read about was the Locust Plague in the Old Testament. But, for God's sake, this is the twentieth century; we would be able to handle one if it happened.'

Peter drank the last of his beer. 'Besides,' he said, 'from what I've seen of the satellite scans, there's certainly a hell of a swarm coming, but a lion? I doubt it.'

'But you still haven't told me why it's called a lion?'

'Well that,' he said, 'I really don't know at all. If one comes, perhaps we'll find out.'

He smiled across at her. 'Come on, drink up and we'll go back to the house.'

'In a minute,' she said. 'Give me a minute.'

Oladi was pulling sheets of corrugated iron across the top of his dye pits helped by several small children dressed in T-shirts even more stained than Oladi's. Further along, another man was covering the next set of pits in clothes stained a deep crimson, accompanied by another set of laughing children. The two families called out to each other and the children ran back and forth as the men pulled the heavy sheets over the low walls.

In front of Jaygo and Peter, the evening sun was just catching the statue of Santa Maria as she leaned forward in her gesture of apparent mercy.

A little girl of about eight in a white cotton dress ran in front of them chasing a piglet.

Some of the stall-holders were beginning to light cooking fires and the sweet smell of the wood smoke curled up in wisps into the dusty air above Sabon Gari.

'Your friend McKecnie misses a lot if he doesn't come here,' said Jaygo. 'It's magic.'

'I've always liked it,' said Peter. 'I know Tom did too. He brought me here on some pretext my very first day in Kano to judge my reaction. I think we were looking for light bulbs, stayed three hours and went home with a Berber rug and three chickens. I've been coming here ever since, but I still hardly ever end up with what I came for.'

'And today?' she said, reaching out for his hand, still looking out of the front of the car.

'I was bringing you to see the statue,' he said.

'So I could guess its secret?'

'Oh yes, but I think we're going away without that this time. We can always come again.'

She squeezed his hand and let go to point towards a row of small huts behind the dye pits where Oladi and his children were heading.

'Do they live there?' she asked.

'Some of them.'

'They look like bike sheds,' she said, 'not houses.'

'Nope,' said Peter. 'Houses.'

'They don't have much, do they?' she reflected quietly.

'It's not so bad,' said Peter. 'Oladi owns the pits, his children look healthy enough and, when it rains, he can put his drying racks in the church.'

He looked at her. 'You're right,' he said, 'Oladi is poor. Yes, he would like a proper house with water and electricity and doors but he knows he's not going to get it so he just gets on with his life. He's a bit better off than his father and maybe his children will be a bit better off than him. But it's a slow thing.'

She watched Oladi and his family go about their evening business for a moment before speaking again.

'Does Aurelia like it here?' she asked quietly.

Peter smiled at himself. 'I think we both know the answer to that, don't we?'

'But I like it here, Peter,' she said.

'I know you do.'

'And it's more fun coming here with someone else, isn't it?' she went on.

'Yes, Jay, I know that too.'

'Well,' she went on, 'our trouble is that we like doing things together better than with other people.'

He did not answer her.

'So what do we do about it?' she continued. 'Just have an hour or so here and there every few years until we're too old and tired to do anything about it?'

He still did not say anything.

'Because I think that's silly,' she added. 'I want to see you a lot more than that.'

He turned to her and brushed her hair from across her forehead. 'You make it sound easy,' he said. 'This is not just about what you and I want.'

'I know it's not easy,' she said. 'If getting things right were easy, more people would be able to do it, wouldn't they?'

He smiled again. 'It's not just a question of "getting it right", is it? It's what to do about everything else. Everyone else – isn't it?'

'That's not to do with it. That's separate.'

'Sorry, I think it is to do with it. Very much,' he replied.

'You're talking about Aurelia, aren't you?'

'Of course I am.'

'Well,' said Jaygo, drawing in her breath, 'ask yourself – do you love her.'

'What?'

'It's a simple enough question,' she went on. 'Do you love her?'

'That's a ridiculous question to ask.'

'Put it another way,' said Jaygo. 'Do you *like* her enough to spend God knows how many really boring years with her.'

'Hey! Aurelia's not boring.'

'Oh no?'

'No.'

'Well, I think she's pretty boring and I've only met her once.'

'Exactly.'

'OK, then,' she went on, 'how many times did you have to meet her before you found she was *not* boring. Actually not boring to the point of being fascinating. And then, *so* fascinating that you simply *had* to spend the rest of your life with her? Five minutes? Ten?'

'That really is being ridiculous.'

'OK again. How long after you met me did you feel that way?'

He looked at her without answering.

'You see, Peter darling,' she said, 'I think if it doesn't fall out of the sky on top of you, it doesn't count.'

He took her hand in both of his. 'Jaygo, darling, you still left me. And that's the real point here, isn't it?'

'Big mistake,' she said, smiling at him. 'Everyone is allowed one.'

He smiled back at her. 'And mine? What was my big mistake in life?'

'I'm trying to stop you making it, Pete.'

He put his hands on top of the steering wheel.

'I couldn't just get up and leave her,' he said.

'You might have to one day.'

'What?'

'If it's not me that comes along, then it might be someone else.'

256

'Oh, no,' he said. 'It would never be anyone . . .' His voice trailed off. 'Anyone else,' he said finally.

She waited for a moment before replying. 'Well, I didn't get a secret out of Our Lady but I think I've just squeezed one out of you.'

'I'll think of something,' he said, starting the car. 'Just give me a bit of time.'

It was quite dark before Peter and Jaygo arrived back at the house.

'Where have you been?' asked Aurelia. 'I was beginning to get worried.'

'Sorry,' said Peter. 'I needed to get a couple of things for the Institute and so we stopped off at the market on the way back.'

'That market,' said Aurelia to Jaygo. 'It's too awful, isn't it!'

'Yes,' said Jaygo, dropping her bag on the sofa. 'Simply frightful.'

'I expect you would like a drink,' said Aurelia, then, noticing Jaygo's hands, 'Good heavens. What happened to you?'

Jaygo help up her blue hands. 'Dye,' she said, without further explanation. 'Yes, I'd simply love a drink. Do you have any hot beer?'

'What?'

'I'll get them,' said Peter. 'One for Laurie and you too?'

'I'm afraid Laurie's gone to bed,' said Aurelia. 'He said he wasn't feeling very well.'

'One for you then?'

'No, thank you darling, I had another tea just a while ago.'

Peter shrugged and disappeared towards the kitchen, leaving Aurelia and Jaygo to sit down opposite each other.

After a slightly awkward pause, Aurelia said, 'I was listening to the World Service in our room while you were out.'

'Really,' said Jaygo.

'Yes,' Aurelia went on. 'They have a special programme for this part of Africa and they were talking about the locusts.'

'The faras,' said Jaygo, leaning back.

'Yes,' said Aurelia, slightly surprised. 'That's what the locals call them. Did Peter tell you?'

'No,' Jaygo replied. 'Oladi did.'

'Oladi? Is that someone at the Institute?'

'Yes,' said Jaygo, standing up. 'I think I'll go and look in on Laurie. He's in the room opposite mine, isn't he?'

'I think he's asleep.'

'What's he been doing? Listening to the World Service?'

'What?'

'Never mind,' Jaygo said.

Peter returned with the beers and sat down next to Aurelia.

'Where's Jay?' he asked.

'Upstairs with Laurie. I told her he was asleep.'

'I see Halima's got supper all sorted out.'

'She's marvellous, isn't she?'

'Umm, look,' he said, 'Jaygo wants me to go over and see Jack about her record this evening. Do you want to come?'

'Tonight?'

'Yes, she's a bit worried about the launch.'

'She doesn't look as if she worries about anything very much.'

'It's the locusts,' Peter went on. 'If they get bad it might make getting about difficult and she wants to know how much Jack's got planned.'

Aurelia thought for a moment. 'From what they said on the radio, it's going to be pretty bad. I was listening to the BBC and they had a feature on them. There was that Dr McKecnie from the Institute.'

'McKecnie?' said Peter with surprise.

'Yes, by telephone from Kano. It was an awful line though. It's silly, isn't it? He has to telephone to London and then they have to relay it all the way back here by radio just so we can find out what is happening up the road.'

'You could have asked me, of course.'

'I know that, but this was the BBC. Anyway, I think a lot more have come. I could hear them hitting the back windows. Laurie and I thought it was hailstones at first. I didn't go out of course, but the back porch is absolutely thick with them now.'

'Really?' said Peter, standing up. 'How long ago?'

'They've stopped now. They came in a sort of wave about half an hour ago.'

Peter went over to the glass door to the porch. 'Christ! It's like a snow drift! I think I'll go out and take a look.'

He collected a torch from the kitchen and went out of the back door. Immediately he was walking on a soft carpet of locusts, about four inches deep. He shone the torch down at them. They were barely moving and many of them appeared to be dead.

In the main part of the garden the insects lay six or seven inches deep.

He crunched over the insects and walked down to the vegetable garden where he had talked to Halima earlier in the afternoon.

Here, most of the locusts were still alive and, as he shone his torch, he could see that all the plants were stripped completely of leaves and were standing up like a row of sticks.

He looked at his watch by the light of the torch. Seven o'clock exactly.

In the Ngale's guest house, John Etherington was just finishing a light supper in his room. He always preferred his own company to that of other people and was pleased with the day that he had spent alone. And now that it was seven o'clock he had things to do.

He wiped his mouth with a linen napkin before he went downstairs to collect the Semtex Seven and its timing device from the freezer.

He knew the explosive was temperature sensitive and would not ignite properly if it was too cold. He guessed that three hours in the heat of a Kano night should bring it to within its optimum range.

By five past seven he had returned to his room and, after locking the door behind him, placed the black briefcase containing the Semtex and the timing device on his bed.

He noticed that a film of condensation had formed over the surface of the case. He wiped it away with a handkerchief before carefully lifting out the timing device.

The mechanism was in a small red plastic case about the size of a pack of cards. On the front was a dial like a kitchen timer, marked out in minutes up to three hours. Below the dial were the terminals for attaching the double cable that led to the detonator buried inside the Semtex.

The cable was coiled up at one end of the case and the ends due to be attached to the timer were enclosed in an orange plastic cap.

More condensation was forming on the surface of the Semtex and he went to his bathroom to fetch a towel to dry it. He did not think the condensation was anything to worry about but it would be better not to take any chances.

Never mind, he thought, it will be up to temperature in an hour or so and then the condensation will stop.

Before that, he could wipe it away. But he was not to know that condensation was also forming on the two-inch-square printed circuit-board inside the timer, underneath the dial. This was the condensation that mattered.

Peter returned to find Aurelia sitting by herself in the sitting room.

'They're very uneven,' he said. 'There were only a few at Sabon Gari but here they are inches deep all over the garden. I don't understand it. Perhaps they are going to be here sooner than I thought.'

'Peter?' Aurelia began.

'Perhaps there's more than one group,' he went on. 'Maybe the main one will come later. But if this *is* the main one, it should be solid without any breaks. If these are just the early ones there shouldn't be so many.'

'Peter, I want to ask you something.'

He walked over to the window. 'About half an hour ago you said?'

'Peter, please. It's important.'

He turned to her.

'Sorry,' he said, 'talking to myself. What did you say?'

Aurelia took a breath and began. 'It's Jaygo.'

'What about her?'

'Well, you and Jaygo really. I don't know what's going on.'

Peter sat down opposite her

'I mean, she's got everything. She's used to getting her own way, you can see that. I don't know what to do.'

Peter did not reply immediately.

Aurelia waited a moment and then took another deep breath. 'Has she come back for you, Peter? Is that it?'

Peter looked down and said, 'I haven't seen her for a long time.'

'This is our home, Peter,' Aurelia continued. 'Daddy's house. And she's just treating it as her house. I don't like the way she speaks about things. Or people.'

Peter looked up at Aurelia. 'She's just got here. You can't say that.'

'You know what I mean. Everything she says is a put down of someone or other.'

'Aurelia, I don't want to talk about this now. I'm sorry if you don't like her. I didn't think you would but . . .'

'But what, Peter? But you do? You like her, don't you?'

'I don't know what you mean,' he said, standing up.

'Yes you do,' she said. 'She talks as if I was in the way. Don't just walk away from me.'

'I'm not walking away,' he said. 'She's just a bit different, that's all.'

'Different from what? You and me? Or just me?'

'I have to talk to Jack about the locusts,' he said. 'I can use Jaygo's phone.'

'You're not listening to me, are you?' said Aurelia. 'Peter, this is important to me.'

'Yes,' he said, 'but the locusts are important too. We may have to go.'

'Go? Go where?'

'We may have to go home,' he said. 'Now, I have to make that call. Where's Jaygo?'

'She's upstairs,' said Aurelia. 'With Laurie.'

Peter turned back to Aurelia. 'Look,' he said, 'let's just do one thing at a time, shall we? We can talk later.'

Peter met Jaygo coming down the stairs.

'Hello,' she said, 'I hope I'm not interrupting anything.'

'No, of course not. Look, can I borrow your phone? I need to call Jack.'

Jaygo came down into the room and slipped her bag from her shoulder. 'Of course,' she said. 'Why do you need to talk to him all of a sudden?'

Peter walked back towards the window and pointed. 'The locusts,' he said. 'They may be more of a problem than I thought. I just want to find out if Jack knows anything I don't.'

Jaygo passed him the phone. 'His number is on the little menu when you press the star thing.'

Peter took the handset.

'How's Laurie?' he said as he waited for the number to pick up.

'He's all right,' she said. 'He's just a bit tired but he says he should be down for supper.'

'Jack?' said Peter, turning his attention to the handset. 'Peter here. I tried to ring you earlier. I think we need to meet. Can I come over? Yes, about the swarm. I gather McKecnie has spoken to you so you know what's happening, but if it's going to be bad, we may need to make some plans.'

He paused and smiled at Aurelia and Jaygo before turning back to the telephone.

'Yes, I know,' he went on, 'it's just a swarm, Jack. But there are a whole lot more coming. Or there might be. I think the two of us should go to the Emir and draw up some contingency plans.'

Peter waited a moment.

'Yes, Jack, I do know what you think of the Emir. But he's important and we need to involve him. No, tomorrow won't be any good. Look, Jack, I'm going to see him anyway but I want to talk to you first. Now? Yes, I can come now. Thank you.'

Peter took the phone from his ear and passed it back to Jaygo. 'Thank you,' he said, turning back to Aurelia. 'Sorry. I have to go out.'

'Oh,' said Aurelia. 'What about supper?'

'I shouldn't be more than half an hour,' he said, turning to go.

Jaygo sat opposite Aurelia and picked up her beer.

'Old Peter must be in a hurry if he didn't drink his beer first,' she said.

'I think he's really worried about the locusts,' said Aurelia. 'A lot more came while you were out but he said you didn't see so many where you were.'

Jaygo shrugged.

'I wonder if eight o'clock is all right for supper,' Aurelia went on. 'I'll go and ask Halima to make it a bit later. Peter says he's going to be half an hour but he might be longer. When he gets involved with his locusts he tends to be a bit vague about time.'

'Really,' said Jaygo,

Aurelia watched her. 'It must be funny seeing him after all this time,' she said at last.

'Why?' replied Jaygo.

'I expect he's changed. I mean, I've only known him for four years but I'm sure he's changed quite a lot.'

'No,' said Jaygo, standing up. 'I don't think he's changed at all actually.'

'Oh,' said Aurelia. And then, as casually as she could: 'He tells me you went out together for a while when you were students.'

Jaygo turned from the window and looked at Aurelia for a moment before speaking. 'We lived together for three years,' she said. 'If that counts as "going out".'

'Oh,' said Aurelia, clearly taken aback. 'I didn't know it was that long.'

'Yes,' said Jaygo, sitting down again. 'Night and day.'

'I see,' said Aurelia awkwardly.

'And in case you're wondering what happened at the end, I made a mistake. Left him and went to live in New York.'

'Oh,' said Aurelia, beginning to flounder.

'Did he tell you?' asked Jaygo.

'He said you did go to New York.'

'If you must know, I won a cello competition and was offered a job.'

'I didn't mean to pry,' said Aurelia.

'You're not. But you must have wondered why I left him.'

'I'm sure it's none of my business,' said Aurelia.

'Isn't it?' returned Jaygo. 'Didn't you ever wonder why? I mean, you wouldn't up and leave him, would you?'

'Of course not!' said Aurelia, shocked. 'We're engaged.'

'So why do you think I did it?'

'Well I . . . I don't know. I couldn't imagine leaving Peter. He's . . . We're part of each other's lives now. Perhaps it was different for you. Maybe it didn't mean as much.'

'Ah,' said Jaygo. '"Didn't mean as much"? You have a better relationship with him, do you? The love of your life, you mean?'

'Yes,' said Aurelia quite firmly. 'Yes, I think he is, now you ask. Maybe it was different for you.'

'I don't know if it was different or not,' said Jaygo, standing up again. 'But I'll tell you one thing,' she added, pointing a finger at Aurelia. 'I'm the love of *his* life.'

Jaygo hitched her bag up on her shoulder and headed for the stairs.

Aurelia was left with her mouth open, trying to think of something to say.

Jaygo spoke over her shoulder when she reached the foot of the stairs. 'And don't bother trying to think up an answer to that,' she said, 'because there isn't one. And the sooner you realise it the better.'

'How dare you!' shouted Aurelia, getting to her feet. 'You come back here and apologise for that this instant!'

Jaygo turned slowly around to face Aurelia.

'What did you just say to me?' she said.

'I asked you to apologise.'

'What for?'

'For what you said.'

'I don't have anything to apologise for.'

Aurelia was lost for a suitable reply.

'Don't keep opening and closing your mouth at me like that,' said Jaygo. 'You look like a bloody goldfish.'

'Well really!' said Aurelia. 'Don't speak to me like that!'

'Look,' said Jaygo firmly, 'in case you haven't noticed, I say what I want when I want. I'm not going to change the habits of a lifetime just for you.'

She stared at Aurelia angrily before turning with a flick of her hair and heading upstairs.

Aurelia sat down and clenched her hands between her knees.

Peter and the Ngale sat on the long white sofas in the main room of the Ngale's house.

'What exactly did Michael McKecnie tell you?' Peter was asking.

'He told me he had taken it upon himself to close the Institute. If you ask me, I think he is panicking. He should have asked me, or at least you, first.'

'The line is down again. I don't think he could get through.'

'Well, he should have sent a driver with a message. He knows where I am and presumably he knew you were coming to Kano.'

'I think he was acting for the best, Jack.'

The Ngale waved his hand dismissively. 'He is a little man. He has no experience and doesn't know what he is talking about.'

'Jack, I've seen the satellite images. There is a hell of a swarm coming.'

'Yes,' went on the Ngale patiently. 'But what is he comparing them to? He may know all about looking at pieces of paper but he has never seen a swarm for himself. He has no background knowledge of what to do.'

'I don't think experience would have helped him much. I've seen plenty of swarms but this one is something different.'

'It's not different,' said the Ngale. 'It's bigger than usual from what he tells me. That is all.'

'Yes, Jack, but a big swarm will behave differently. I've only been in Kano a few hours but I can see already. There are locusts six inches deep at my house and I've never seen that before.'

'Come, come, Peter. There are always a few dehydrated individuals blown off the top of an approaching swarm. Tom Collis could have told you as much.'

'This many?'

'Yes, this many. I keep telling you it is just an ordinary swarm. The only kind. People here have been dealing with them for thousands of years.'

'I don't think they are all the same, Jack.'

The Ngale waved his hand again. 'You have been listening to local stories. Next you'll be telling me a zaki fara is coming to eat up all the bad children who won't go to bed on time. Stories. Myths.'

'There have been Lion Swarms before.'

'Let me put it another way,' said the Ngale, standing up. 'When I first went to England it was at the beginning of that long freeze. There was two feet of snow and it lasted for four weeks. Everyone told me there hadn't been anything like it in living memory. The lowest temperature ever recorded, they said. And so on. And so on. But people coped. Life went on. There was a lot of expensive cleaning up to do when the thaw came, and people complained a lot, but in six weeks everything was back to normal again.

'And it will be the same here,' he said, picking up one of Jaygo's CDs and returning to his seat. 'The locusts always make a mess. They get into the drains, they eat the vegetables and they stink. But we clear the drains, the vegetables grow all the year so we don't have to wait for spring. And as for the smell? It soon goes. I have already been on my radio stations telling people to take sensible precautions and not to worry. That is an end to it.'

Peter sighed. 'Jack, I really think . . .'

'Now, now, Peter,' interrupted the Ngale. 'You do what you have to do but my advice is to sit tight and leave it to the experts. You can go and talk to the Emir if you want to but he will tell you much the same as I have. He has already been on the television saying more or less word for word the same as I did on the radio. Relax, Peter.'

'Perhaps you're right,' said Peter. 'I don't know.'

'So. To more interesting things then,' said the Ngale holding up the CD case. 'What do you think of this?'

'*The Music of the Lion*? I'm afraid I haven't heard it yet.'

'No?' said the Ngale with surprise. 'I thought you were her number one fan.'

Peter smiled. 'I was once. She showed me the new CD but I haven't been able to play it yet.'

'Wait no longer then,' said the Ngale, taking the CD over to his hi-fi.

'Tell me,' he said as he switched the unit on. 'What do you think of the cover picture?'

'I like it, Jack. It's very clever.'

The music began. ' "The Star And The Wiseman",' he announced.

The Ngale returned to his sofa and passed Peter the CD case. 'You recognise it, of course?'

'The Idona Zaki? Oh yes. I like the picture but I'm not sure why you put it on the case.'

The Ngale smiled as much to himself as to Peter. 'We have been without it for a long time. Do you think I am raking up old memories?'

'Something like that.'

'The thing is, it's not that my forefathers were looking in the wrong places, more they were the wrong people to do the looking.'

'What do you mean?'

'I'll tell you in a few days. Meanwhile I'm afraid we may have to delay the launch of this in Nigeria until public attention switches away from the locusts. I don't think she will mind if we hold things up for a week or so, will she? It would give us a clearer run.'

'She's come out here specially, you know.'

'It's all right. She's on holiday after her American tour. She'll be here for a couple of weeks.'

'Are you sure?' said Peter doubtfully. 'She told me she had a programme worked out with your people here.'

'Oh, no,' said the Ngale, adjusting the volume. 'That was nothing and I told her as much. I'm sure she won't mind sitting the swarm out with the rest of us. Your house is pretty comfortable and she might even enjoy the experience of a real locust swarm. It's not everyone who gets to see one at first hand, you know.'

'That's as may be, Jack,' said Peter, 'but you really ought to discuss it with her. I didn't think she was planning to be here for more than a few days.'

The Ngale shrugged. 'Sorry, but I'm not in such awe of Jocasta Manhattan as everyone else. She must adjust her schedule to fit in with mine if she wants to do business with me.'

Peter smiled to himself at the thought of Jaygo 'adjusting her schedule' to fit in with anyone.

'Do you want me to tell her when I get back to the house?'

'If you like. I was going to see her this evening but I can't now. Tell her I'll ring her tomorrow about noon.'

'You can expect a call from her as soon as I tell her.'

'No problem, Peter. Now, I have one or two things I must do.'

'Of course,' said Peter, standing up. 'I have to get back anyway.'

'By the way,' said the Ngale as he walked Peter to the front door. 'I hope she understands that I never have house guests. I would have offered her my rest house but a business friend of mine is staying there this month.'

'No problem. The Institute house is just about big enough for her and all her suitcases.'

'Good. Perhaps you and Aurelia can join us for drinks tomorrow and the three of us can try to placate Jaygo about the delayed launch.'

'That would be very nice. And Laurie?'

'Ah, yes. I'd forgotten about him. You can bring him if you like. I remember him as a rather annoying little man. I think he was a bit of a "hanger on" when we were students. I'll get McKecnie to come along and the two of them can "hang on" together.'

'Good. Tomorrow then. Twelve o'clock.'

It was half past eight before Peter arrived back at the house and Laurie and Jaygo were standing in the sitting room, looking out of the window.

'Hi, Laurie,' said Peter. 'Feeling better?'

'Yes, thanks. We didn't think you would be back so soon, so Aurelia put off supper till nine.'

'Is she in the kitchen?'

'No,' said Jaygo. 'I think you'll find she's upstairs. Maybe you can persuade her to come down and join the party.'

'Is she all right?'

'Sort of,' said Jaygo. 'I haven't seen her since I went for my shower.'

'Laurie?' said Peter.

'Nothing to do with me, old boy,' said Laurie, putting his hands up.

'Jay,' said Peter sharply. 'What have you said to her?'

'Nothing, Peter. She's just gone upstairs to get ready.'

Peter headed upstairs.

When he was out of earshot, Jaygo added quietly 'Well, I didn't say all that much.'

As soon as he entered the bedroom, Peter could see that Aurelia had been crying.

'Little one,' he said. 'What's up?'

'Don't you "little one" me, Peter. What do you think is up?'

'What did she say?'

'She doesn't have to say anything. She just has to *be* here.'

'What?'

'She made a fool of me, that's what. You told me you went out with her and she said she lived with you properly all along.'

'Well, it's the same thing.'

'No, it isn't. And you know it isn't. Why didn't you tell me about her right at the beginning?'

'When?'

'When I met you.'

'What? It was done. I told you that.'

'I told you things,' said Aurelia reproachfully.

'There wasn't anything for me *to* say.'

'She said leaving you was a mistake. She said she was sorry she ever did.'

Aurelia looked as though she was about to start to cry again.

Peter put his arm around her but she shook herself free. 'Don't *touch* me. Leave me alone.'

'For goodness sake, Aurelia.'

'I didn't want to come to this horrid place but I came for Daddy. Because he wanted me to and because I thought you wanted me to as well. And when I get here, she turns up. It's as if she's come to get you like some suitcase she's left behind or something. So what if it's my house? It's her suitcase. Well, it *is* my house, Peter.'

'Look,' said Peter, sitting down on the bed. 'Calm *down*, Aurelia. Anyway it's not your house. Or mine. It belongs to the Institute now.'

'You know what I mean. Don't pick on my words.'

Peter paused. 'Yes,' he said heavily. 'I do know what you mean.'

Aurelia sat down at the dressing table. 'Four years, Peter. We've been together for four years. And then one day she comes along and knocks it all aside.'

Peter did not reply.

'What am I supposed to do, Peter?'

'I don't know,' he said. 'We can talk about it when we get home.'

'And then what?'

'We'll work something out,' he said slowly.

'Can we?' she said. 'I don't think so. All of a sudden there doesn't seem to be much *to* talk about, does there?'

The two of them sat in silence for a while.

Eventually Peter stood up. 'I'm going downstairs,' he said. 'Are you coming?'

When she did not reply he walked over to the door and turned back to her as he opened it. 'Look,' he said. 'I'm very sorry about this. But I'm not sure what you want me to say.'

She wiped a finger underneath her eye. 'No,' she said. 'It's all right. Four years. Puff. Gone.'

He stood with his hand on the door knob.

'Just go,' she said. 'I'll come down in a minute.'

When he had gone she turned to look at herself in the dressing-table mirror. 'I won't cry,' she said. 'That's what she wants. I won't cry.'

She put her hands to her face and rubbed her eyes.

Downstairs Jaygo was sitting by herself on the sofa.

'Where's Laurie?' asked Peter.

'He's gone to get his camera.'

'It's dark.'

'I know. But he wants to take some flash pictures of the locusts. Um. Look, Peter . . .'

'Yes?' he said, sitting down next to her.

'She's upset, isn't she?'

'You could say that.'

'I didn't mean to say the things I did. They just came out. She provoked me.'

'I can't think what she can have said to provoke you. Aurelia's never provoked anyone in her life.'

'Maybe it would be better for her if she did from time to time.'

'Jaygo, she's not like you. She doesn't go round sticking pins into people all day. And she hasn't got your defences. She's completely different.'

'I'm sorry if I hurt her but she was going to get hurt sooner or later and you would never have got around to telling her things.'

'What things?'

'About us, of course.'

'You seem to think it's all cut and dried,' he said.

Jaygo took his hand. 'Peter, darling. The thing is, you can't have us both. Not even for a day.'

'There isn't a hurry,' he said. 'I could have worked something out.'

'But you never do work things out, do you? You just wait until it's too late and things happen anyway.'

'I don't.'

'Yes, you do.'

Further discussion was halted by Laurie coming downstairs with his camera around his neck. 'I'm going out into the garden to take some flash, Peter. Come and give me some expert photographic advice.'

'You don't need any advice from me,' said Peter. 'You go ahead.'

'OK,' said Laurie. 'If I'm not back in ten minutes then I've been eaten.'

Peter and Jaygo sat without talking after Laurie had gone.

'Perhaps I'd better go with him,' said Peter eventually. 'He'll only go and fall over or something.'

269

'Fine,' said Jaygo. 'I'll watch from here.'

He patted her hand as he stood up. 'Bugger of a week, isn't it?'

'Never mind,' she said. 'You're the Sunday Man, remember. I'm sure everything will work out by then.'

'They stink, don't they?' said Laurie as they pushed open the back door and walked out onto a carpet of locusts.

'I'm afraid so,' said Peter. 'And it'll get worse.'

Laurie began to take photographs.

'Come down to the vegetable garden,' said Peter. 'There are even more there.'

'I don't see how they can ever get enough to eat,' said Laurie. 'There's bloody millions of them.'

'This lot haven't eaten for a long time,' said Peter. 'If you look closely you will see most of them are dead.'

Peter picked up a handful and looked at them in the light of his torch as he and Laurie walked along. 'And they don't all start out together,' he said. 'A long way north-east of here is a big scrub area on the edge of the desert. When it rains, which it does sometimes even there, you get a green flush over a few hundred square miles. The locusts don't have any natural enemies there because there's not usually enough locusts to make it worth a predator's while. Anyway, the locusts have a feeding-and-breeding frenzy over a couple of months or so. The numbers really build up but as soon as all the food is gone they take off and the wind concentrates them and the end result is what you see here. Too many in one place.'

'But the sheer numbers,' said Laurie, taking a photograph of Peter. 'I just can't begin to imagine how many there are.'

'This is the vegetable garden,' said Peter, pointing to where the beans had stood. 'But there isn't much to see, is there? Shall we get back?'

'I suppose so,' said Laurie. 'One part of a garden covered in locusts looks very much like another. Anyway, I don't think we should leave our two lady friends together for too long before dinner, do you?'

'No,' said Peter as they approached the back of the house. 'I'm sorry you have to see it. Perhaps I could have handled it differently.'

'Maybe. Hold on, what's that over there? It looks like a whole bank of them.'

'It's the hedge. I'll shake it and you watch what happens.'

270

Peter walked over to the hedge, lifted his foot and pushed against it.

Immediately a cloud of locusts flew up and the two men were engulfed by insects flying in all directions.

'God almighty!' called Laurie. 'What the hell are you doing!'

Peter laughed. 'Welcome to Africa, Laurie!'

'Hell's teeth!' said Laurie as the insects settled down again.

'No harm done,' smiled Peter. 'It's an old trick and I couldn't resist it.'

The two men laughed and went back into the house.

Dinner was turning out to be a rather strained affair and Laurie was valiantly trying to make polite conversation.

'Where are the Lear crew staying, Jay?' he said. 'I didn't see them turn up at the hotel.'

'No,' she said. 'They stay with the aircraft. It stops the wheels getting pinched and it means I don't have to round them up if I want to go somewhere in a hurry.'

'It's a bit like Removals men then, isn't it?' said Laurie. 'They always stay with the vehicle. Must be an ancient tradition.'

The meal was chicken, sweet corn and sweet potatoes but no one seemed to have much appetite.

'You see,' tried Laurie again, pointing at his food. 'You might think this was a traditional meal but, in fact, none of these three things is African at all. Chicken comes from China and the sweet corn and sweet potato are South American.'

'Are you sure that's true?' said Peter. 'I am pretty sure that sweet potatoes are African.'

'No,' said Laurie, 'you're thinking of yams. Or millet.'

'Millet?' chipped in Jaygo. 'Isn't that what they feed to budgies?'

'Yes,' said Peter. 'But people eat it here. They grow it if they don't think it's going to rain much. It's very drought-resistant.'

'What does it taste like?' asked Jaygo.

'A bit like sand,' said Peter. 'But it makes quite good beer.'

'Like locusts then,' said Jaygo. 'They taste a bit like sand too.'

'Oh,' said Aurelia, 'you've eaten a locust, have you?'

'One flew into my mouth and I bit its head off.'

'I see,' said Aurelia, smiling. 'Maybe you should keep your mouth shut more often.'

Jaygo threw her head back and laughed along with Peter and Laurie.

Aurelia went quite pink and continued her meal.

'I nearly forgot, Jaygo,' said Peter. 'Jack says he wants to delay the CD launch.'

'Why?' she said sharply.

'The locusts, of course,' he replied. 'He wants to go ahead in seven days' time, if that's all right with you.'

'I can't do that,' snapped Jaygo. 'I'm due back for a session on Thursday.'

'I thought you were having a holiday after your American tour?' said Laurie.

'I am,' she said. 'But the Belle still have to practise even if there aren't any concerts. Besides, the Lear is in for a refit starting on Friday. So, no way.'

'I said you might want to ring him about it,' said Peter.

'Of course I want to bloody ring him! He's signed a contract and now he can stick to it.'

'But can't he claim *force majeure*?' said Laurie. 'Act of God and all that?'

'No, he can't. Anyway, whose side are you on?'

'It's not a question of sides, Jaygo,' said Peter. 'If the locusts stop people getting about, there isn't much anyone can do, is there?'

'How bad does he think it's going to be then?' asked Laurie.

'He doesn't know any more than anyone else,' said Peter. 'I told him what I thought, what I *know* actually. He admitted it might be worse than usual but that everything would be back to normal in a week.'

'I take it he doesn't subscribe to your Lion Swarm theory then?' said Laurie.

'No, he doesn't,' said Peter. 'He thinks that more locusts just means more of the same but I think it will all go to pieces when normal clearing up isn't enough.'

'What do you mean?' asked Aurelia.

'Take the garden,' said Peter. 'You can think of it as being full of locusts if you want but it's really just bio-mass.'

'Bio-what?' said Jaygo.

'Bio-mass,' said Peter. 'Say it was meat. Dog food. Now, if the garden was six inches deep in rotting dog food, then in this heat it would be pretty dreadful after a few days, wouldn't it? But say it was a foot deep. Or two feet? So, two foot of rotting dog food over the whole city with all services broken down and you get the general idea.'

'Surely it won't be like that,' said Aurelia.

Peter pointed towards the garden. 'This time tomorrow, this lot, the dead ones anyway, will have started to go off and there are more coming. At the moment it's a nice dry carpet but in two days, take it from me, it will be one big sticky mess.'

'Christ, Peter! Hello?' said Jaygo angrily. 'Why the hell aren't we on our way to the airport right now then?'

'Don't look at me like that,' said Peter, raising his voice. 'You can see out of the window as well as I can. You can see what is going to happen.'

'God almighty!' said Jaygo. 'Of course we don't know. You're supposed to be the expert. Why didn't you tell us all this before?'

'I didn't think I had to,' said Peter. 'What did you think it was going to be like?'

'I don't know what the hell I thought it was going to be like,' rounded Jago. 'But I'm pretty sure I didn't think I'd be walking around in six inches of dog shit!'

'Dog *food*,' he said.

'Whatever,' said Jaygo.

'I haven't been in a big swarm any more than anyone else,' said Peter. 'But it's not all going to vanish overnight.'

'Wait on,' said Laurie more calmly. 'You said the other night that a big swarm, a Lion Swarm you called it, would really put a stop to things. Plague of Egypt, you said. "Hell on Earth" you said. Now, I'm with Jay on this. If you think one is coming then I think we should get the hell out of here. Now, tell us, should we stay or not?'

'I just don't know,' said Peter. 'That's why I went to see Jack. To see what he thought.'

'What did he actually *say* to you then?' said Laurie exasperated.

'I told you. He didn't think it would be so bad. Not much worse than usual. Look, he's not leaving, most of Kano *can't* leave. Even bloody McKecnie isn't leaving. And anyway I thought we all had things we wanted to do here. He said it was just like the snow in England. It would go away.'

'Snow?' said Jaygo. 'What has snow got to do with it?'

'Peter,' said Aurelia, 'what *are* you talking about?'

'Right!' said Peter, standing up and banging his hand on the table. 'Yes, there are locusts. Yes, they will rot and stink. And if a lot more come it will stink a lot more. But it's not fucking Berkshire or South Ken, is it? It's Africa. Kano. You're not watching TV so you can change to some other channel if you don't like what's on. This is as real as it gets. Locusts? Bad drains? Yes, for God's sake! Aurelia, you of all people should know what it's like here. And I told you

273

and Laurie on the plane,' he said, pointing at Jaygo, 'I told you it wasn't like other places you've been, but you didn't hear me. So don't all turn to me if it isn't some English garden party. You all wanted to come here so don't blame me if you don't like it. I just work here. Grow up, the lot of you! You can all piss off home if you want to but I'm staying!'

He looked around at each of them in turn before pushing back his chair and leaving the room.

The three of them were silent after Peter had gone.

'Well,' said Jaygo eventually. 'I think that counts as a little outburst, don't you?'

She stood up quietly and went out to find Peter.

He was standing in the sitting room with his back to her looking vacantly out into the darkened garden.

She put her arms around him. 'Don't be a cross patch,' she said. 'How were we supposed to know what it was going to be like? Don't be cross with us.'

'None of us should have come,' he said, without turning around. 'At least, I'm the only one who should have. I should have made the rest of you stay behind.'

'And wait in a little row for you to come home?' she said. 'No, Peter, we all wanted to be here. Jack didn't decide to cancel the launch until today so I'd have come and Laurie's here because I'm here. Perhaps the only one who didn't have to come was Goldilocks and, as you say, she should have known what it was going to be like.'

'Perhaps,' he said, turning around. 'But I shouldn't have shouted, I'm sorry.'

She squeezed him gently and let go. 'You just gave us all a bit of a fright, that's all.

'And before you say anything else,' she said, putting a finger to his lips, 'I'm not sorry I came. If you stay, I'll stay. Jack or no Jack.'

'No,' he said, 'I don't think that's a good idea. You take Laurie back in the morning and I'll see about getting Aurelia a flight.'

She shook her head.

'You could come back in a week,' he said. 'I'll still be here.'

'Do you promise?' she said.

'Yes,' he said. 'It might be for the best.'

'So I can go away and change my mind about you?'

'You might.'

'And then again I might not. And if that's the case I'd rather be here not changing my mind than somewhere else.'

'And Laurie?' he said.

'If I stay, he'll stay too. He likes it with us. You know that.'

'It hasn't been much fun so far for him, has it? We shoot off the minute we get here leaving him in bed and, when I get back, I shout at him.'

'Never mind,' she said. 'He knows you. So that just leaves Goldilocks. I don't know why she came here at all.'

'It's silly really. She was the only one who knew in advance she wasn't going to like it. Besides, what she came to do, she can't do now anyway.'

'Oh?'

'She promised her father that she would bring his ashes here. He's the only one who really did like it here.'

'You like it here, don't you?' she said.

He thought for a moment. 'I honestly don't know. I've never thought about it. You find yourself working somewhere and you get used to it. The next thing you know it's become your home.'

'I thought people were supposed to be important,' she said, 'not places.'

'Maybe. But if there aren't people in your life, places have to do.'

'I know my favourite place,' she said.

'Oh?'

'Santa Maria,' she said quietly. 'Come on, I think we'd better get back to the others.'

John Etherington's plans to leave Kano were well advanced. He was down to deciding what items he should take and what he should leave behind.

Lined up on his bed were the briefcase containing the Semtex, his own briefcase and the one containing his satellite telephone.

Clearly too much, he thought. Who goes to dinner with so much?

His large satellite telephone was the first to go. It had been very expensive a year ago but he would soon be able to afford a better one and in the meantime he could use the one lent to him by Jack Ngale. Etherington did not think the Ngale would cancel the number for a day or so and that would be more than enough to see him as far as Goa.

It would have been nice to take some fresh clothes but he could always buy some as he went along.

That just left the Semtex and his own briefcase.

275

He opened the Semtex case to see how its temperature was going. It still felt very cold to the touch but it would have to do. It was now nine o'clock and there was still another hour or more before he would need it to explode.

He took the case over to the table and sat down to arm the bomb.

First he picked up the timing mechanism and worked the dial backwards and forwards several times. He put it to his ear and listened for the little click as he wound the dial to zero and the contacts inside closed.

Then he switched on the electronics from the slider switch to the left of the dial and watched the small green LED light. He noted with satisfaction that it changed to red when he wound the dial to its zero position, taking its cue from the closing of the mechanical contacts.

It seemed the spell in the freezer had not affected the circuit.

Next, he pulled the two plastic plugs out of the base of the unit, pushed the two multicore leads from the detonator buried inside the Semtex itself into the sockets. He set the dial for two hours and, finally, pulled out the locking safety pin and broke it off at the point it joined the case.

It was now armed. Breaking the safety pin meant that there was now no fail safe. Whatever was done to the unit it would set off the Semtex in two hours. Or less if an attempt was made to cut the multicore cables.

The fact that he would now be carrying a live bomb around with him did not worry him in the slightest. He smiled as he closed the case. What would the Ngale do when it arrived at his house? Open it? Try to dismantle it? Put it in the swimming pool even? It did not matter, because it would go off whatever was done to it.

It might kill and it might not. That was not the point. What mattered was that it should occupy the Ngale's attention long enough for Etherington to make good his escape. It would take someone a great deal more level-headed than the Ngale to ignore the little green light. Even if he had never seen a bomb before, he would see immediately what it was and what it was going to do.

Etherington smiled to himself again as he shut the case. Good enough for Atlanta. Good enough for the Ngale.

Perhaps a more domesticated man than John Etherington would have known that something of the Semtex's bulk would need at least six hours out of a freezer to thaw properly, even in the heat of a tropical evening.

He picked up the two briefcases, looked around the room once and then went out without bothering to switch off the light or close the door.

Bawa was waiting by the car and opened the rear passenger door as Etherington emerged. But Etherington went to the boot first, to check the rope and sledgehammer were still in place before he took his seat.

'Dinner, sah?' said Bawa. 'Where are you going to?'

'Later,' said Etherington. 'First take me to Santa Maria.'

'In Sabon Gari, sah?' said the driver with surprise.

'You heard,' said Etherington, settling down into his seat after placing the two cases on the seat next to him.

As Bawa took the car out of the short driveway onto the road, the wheels slipped on the locusts and slid sideways.

'Watch out!' snapped Etherington. 'What do you think you are doing!'

'Sorry, sah. The faras are on the road.'

'I can see that,' said Etherington. 'Just take a bit more care.'

'Yes, sah. But it is difficult, sah.'

Etherington sighed and put his hand onto the Semtex case next to him to steady it. It was still cool, but there was little trace of condensation left.

Inside the case and the timing mechanism box, the vibrations of the car and the slipping had caused a number of condensation droplets to run together on the printed circuit board. But they were still small enough and far apart enough not to cause any problem.

Etherington had timed his journey that morning from the house to Sabon Gari and had allowed half an hour for his evening journey.

The poor driving conditions meant he was running late. It was nearly nine forty by the time they arrived in the short road leading from the main market up to the square of Santa Maria.

Etherington was annoyed. Now time was tight and he would have to hurry.

'Stop here,' he said. 'Now listen. This is what I want you to do. I am only going to tell you once so you listen to me. Understood?'

He leaned forward over the front seat and pointed at the square ahead of them.

'You will wait here while I go to the church and get ready for you. In exactly five minutes, drive into the square and stop the car where I show you. You will remain in the car and do exactly what I tell you to. When I am finished, you will drive to the Ngale's house and give him this briefcase. It contains some very important documents he needs. Tell him it is from me. Do you understand?'

'Yes, sah. But you can tell him yourself.'

'No, you fool. I am not going to the Ngale's house. You are.'

'But you can't stay here, sah. It is not safe.'

'Shut up and do what I say. I am going to the square now. Come in exactly five minutes.'

Without waiting for an answer, Etherington stepped out of the car with his briefcase and collected the rope and the hammer from the boot.

There were fewer locusts in this part of town but quite enough to fill the potholes in the track. He slipped and lost his footing twice as he made his way to the square.

It was reassuringly dark when he got there but enough light came from the lamps and cooking fires of the nearby stalls and houses for him to see his way about.

He placed the case and the sledgehammer on the ground and slipped the coil of rope from his shoulder.

Reaching up, he tied a loop of rope around the waist of the statue. He ran the rope back from his loop into the square and prepared another loop to tie to the chassis of the car when it arrived. He checked his watch. Eleven minutes to ten. Close enough.

Bawa started the car and began to drive the last few yards into the square. He could see the potholes no better than Etherington and the car dipped and bucked over the uneven surface. The briefcase with the Semtex slid off the back seat and jolted onto the floor. The jolting forced some of the water droplets on the circuit board to run together and they shorted out the mechanism. Unseen by anyone, the green light went out. The red one blinked once and the bomb went off.

About half of the Semtex was still too cold to explode properly but enough ignited immediately to fill the car with an orange blast of flame. Bawa was thrown forwards. The steering wheel snapped off and his neck broke as it hit the dashboard. All the doors and windows of the car were blown outwards and the Semtex that had not exploded began to burn fiercely as it came up to temperature. Within seconds the car was a blazing wreck.

Etherington looked back horrified. His plan for pulling the statue down and, more importantly, his means of occupying Jack Ngale were gone in one. It did not occur to him to wonder what had happened to the driver.

He turned back to the statue and ran towards it. He did not think he would be strong enough to pull the statue down with the rope around the waist but there might be enough of an angle if he could move the loop up as far as the neck.

He climbed up into the niche and began to work his loop up the figure. He went as far as the arms and then passed a loop over the head. It would have to do.

He jumped back to the ground and ran the rope out to its full length again before winding it around his waist and beginning to pull.

He need not have worried about not being able to dislodge the statue. At the fourth jerk on the rope he could feel it begin to move. Two more and it began to topple. Suddenly the rope went slack as the statue fell forwards and crashed down into the square.

The head had broken off with the impact but he could see that the rest of the body and legs were still in one piece. He took the rope from his waist and ran forwards to collect the sledgehammer.

He swung it above his head and brought it down on the statute as hard as he could. He hit it on the shoulder. The body and arms broke into a dozen pieces. He rested the hammer and looked down. There were pieces of broken stone everywhere but no traces of a torque or anything resembling one.

Perhaps the legs, he thought. Or the base. He raised the hammer and brought it down again and again on the remaining parts of the figure.

Nothing.

Out of breath and suddenly very frightened he stood holding the hammer and looking down with a sick feeling at the pieces of broken stone in front of him. No torque. No gold. Nothing to offer O'Leary and no car to get away in.

Further thoughts were interrupted by the clattering approach of the helicopter and soon its landing light picked him out as he stood in the square.

He dropped the sledgehammer, picked up his briefcase and waved the helicopter to land over on the far side of the church.

He raced towards it and as the side door opened, Etherington recognised the familiar bulk of O'Leary leaning out and extending a hand towards him.

'Hell of a night for a flight!' shouted O'Leary above the noise of the rotors. 'Where's the torque?'

'It's not here,' shouted back Etherington.

'Come again?' yelled O'Leary.

'It's not here but I'm still coming with you!'

'Get back!' bawled O'Leary. 'If you don't have it, you don't come. No torque, no deal.'

Etherington reached into his jacket, pulled out his automatic pistol and pointed it in O'Leary's face. 'There's no torque but I've got this. Now move over and let me on,' he grated. 'I'm still coming with you!'

'The hell you are!' shouted O'Leary, lunging out with his foot and sending Etherington falling backwards.

The pistol went off but the shot went wild. Before Etherington could pick himself up to fire again, the helicopter was wheeling up over the roof of the church and out of sight. Etherington was alone in the square.

He looked out to the road he had come in by. The still-burning remains of the car were now surrounded by a circle of people waving and shouting.

He looked back at the broken remains of his statue and the briefcase next to it. Not much of a chance, he thought, but it's one I have to take.

He took out the Ngale's telephone and keyed in the number.

'Jack,' he said as the call was answered. 'Something has happened. You have to come and pick me up.'

'John?' the Ngale said. 'Is that you? Where are you?'

'It's O'Leary, Jack. He's gone crazy.'

'I don't know any O'Leary. What are you ringing me for, John?'

'I'm in the market square, Jack. O'Leary has just tried to blow up the church.'

'What church? What are you talking about?'

'Santa Maria, Jack. O'Leary asked to meet me here. He turned up with some of the Emir's men. He said he knew the torque was here and I should meet him here.'

'The Emir? John, what are you saying? What has the Emir to do with whatever it is? You're not making any sense at all. Are you drunk?'

'No. I am not drunk. O'Leary tricked me into coming to the square tonight because he said he had a deal for me. He said there was something he wanted me to take to Kenya for him. Then he turned up with half a dozen of the Emir's men and said he'd found the torque.'

'Torque? The Idona Zaki?'

'Yes, Jack. He said the Emir has found out about your new one and wanted to produce the real one before you could announce yours. He said it was in the church and he was coming to collect it. I can tell you the rest when I see you but you have to send a car here to collect me.'

'You have Bawa and your own car. What do you mean?'

'No, Jack. There is no car here. Please do what I ask you.'

'You are making no sense at all to me. Ring me when you do.'

'It will make sense Jack, I promise you, but I have to come to the house.'

'Very well,' said the Ngale. 'You may come but I want to know exactly what is going on.'

'Thank you. Believe me, you will want to hear what I say. You can't trust the Emir but I can help you. Send your man to Santa Maria as fast as you can.'

'He will be with you in fifteen minutes.'

Etherington switched off the phone.

I had to think of something, he told himself. I have from now until I get to the house to complete it. If I can blame O'Leary and work out how to involve the Emir I should be all right. I have done the best I could in the time I had, he thought.

He looked down at the broken statue and kicked at it angrily with his foot. If it's not in your arms, he said to himself, where the hell is it?

He slowly wound up the rope and coiled it around his arm. He carried it over to the nearest dye pit and dropped it in before returning for the sledgehammer which he also dropped in. No need to make things more complicated than they are already, he told himself as he walked slowly back to the church and sat down on the steps to wait for the car.

Aurelia and Jaygo had gone up to their rooms, leaving Peter and Laurie alone.

'Aurelia needs to go home,' said Laurie.

'Yes,' agreed Peter. 'Kano isn't very lucky for her, is it? You can have my ticket and go with her if you like.'

'No,' said Laurie with a sigh. 'I'll stay. I'll wait until you and Jaygo go back if that's all right.'

Peter looked at his old friend and thought before speaking. 'Do you think I'm doing the right thing?' he said at last.

'I don't know,' said Laurie. 'You have to be the judge of that. I've known you and Jay a long time. I know what you are like together and I'm probably not the best person to say.'

'What about Aurelia?'

'Very nice,' said Laurie. 'Not bad-looking in an English rose sort of way. But I can tell you there is one thing she will never be.'

'What's that?'

Laurie smiled. 'She'll never be a Jaygo for you.'

Peter smiled back. 'I think that's safe to say. Thank you.'

Laurie leant forwards. 'That's not the point, is it, Pete? Jaygo may be special and she may be the one for you but that's not the same thing as you being the one for her, is it?'

Peter shrugged. 'I don't know. She came back for me, not the other way around.'

'And what will you do on a day-to-day basis?' went on Laurie. 'Are you going to follow her around on tour? Is she going to come here to Kano with you? Have you thought?'

'No,' said Peter, shaking his head. 'I don't know what we'll "do" as you put it. That's all secondary. Things will work out because we want them to and not just because they are convenient.'

'And Aurelia?' Laurie persisted. 'How are things going to "work out" for her.'

'I don't know,' said Peter. 'It's a complete mess and I'm sorry.'

'I think she's pretty dependent on you for a lot of things, Peter. Perhaps everything. She's going to find it pretty hard on her own.'

'Maybe. But she wasn't always with me. There was a before and she was fine then.

'Anyway,' said Peter, standing up. 'Why are you giving me the third degree on all this?'

'Because,' said Laurie, standing up too, 'I want you to know exactly what it is you are letting yourself in for.'

'With Jaygo? What did you say to me once before? Being married to her would be like being married to a bonfire? Deciding on her is the best decision I've made in a long time. It's the right thing for me and I know I won't regret it.'

Laurie smiled and turned to go. 'I'll quote that back to you.'

'Do you fancy a brandy?'

'Hate to refuse a drink, old boy, but I'm pretty much all in. I think I'll go up.'

'I'll see you in the morning then. Thank you.'

The Ngale was walking up and down the length of the windows onto his terrace when Habu showed John Etherington in.

'Well, John,' he began, without interrupting his pacing, 'I think you have some explaining to do.'

'Yes, Jack. I have.'

'You see,' continued the Ngale, 'I have done a little checking up since you telephoned me. It seems I do know this Mr O'Leary after all. I didn't recognise the name but he is involved in the buying and selling of printing machinery, is he not?'

'As a front, yes,' said Etherington. 'But only as a front. Artifacts are his main thing. He is a dealer.'

'Yes, that too. So tell me your connection to him.'

'He approached me about a year ago,' said Etherington. 'He had heard about me apparently.'

'And your interest in the torque? Your so-called claim to it?'

'I suppose so, yes. But I don't think he was aware I knew you at the time.'

'And you didn't tell him?'

'No. I wanted to see what he knew. Jack, if he had come to you, would you have told me?'

The Ngale smiled. 'No. But that is in the past. I want to know what happened tonight.'

'He said he had found it but I didn't believe him.'

'But you went anyway?'

'Yes,' Etherington replied, 'I did. And I think you would have too.'

'No, John. I would not have gone,' said the Ngale sharply. 'I have the new torque. It is not in my interest that the old one ever be found. But you went even knowing about the new one. Did you tell him I had the new one? Did you think that between you, you could spirit the old one away without me finding out?'

'Of course not, Jack. I told you I didn't believe he had found it. You and I agreed yesterday that if it was anywhere to be found then you or I would have found it by now. But he was convinced it was in the statue on the church at Santa Maria. In the arms or in the base. He was determined to break open the statue and check.'

The Ngale looked sharply at Etherington. 'When exactly did he tell you this?'

'This afternoon.'

'You didn't mention it to me. You should have.'

'I didn't know how you would react, Jack. I thought I could convince him not to go ahead and that is why I went to the square. But when I arrived, his men were already pulling the statue down and breaking it up. They found nothing, of course.'

'And?'

'He went wild. He said it *had* been in the statue but that someone had got there before him.'

'And taken it without damaging the statue?' said the Ngale incredulously. 'Come, come. That hardly seems possible.'

'Not recently. But fifty years ago perhaps. And the present statue was a copy. He was very angry.'

The Ngale held up his hand. 'Wait,' he said. 'Do you think it could have happened? That it *was* in there before?'

'I don't know, Jack. But the statue they broke tonight was *not* new and the torque was *not* in it. That much I do know.'

'And the car? The driver? What happened to them?'

'You've heard already then?'

'Oh, yes, John. I told you that not much happens in Kano that I don't hear about pretty fast. And when one of my own men is murdered I hear about it *very* fast, I can tell you.'

'It was O'Leary,' said Etherington. 'I told you he went wild.'

'And he just happened to have some explosive with him?' mocked the Ngale. 'And just happened to set it off in your car?'

'It wasn't like that at all. He had planned to use the explosive on the church after he had taken the torque so that no one would know he had broken the statue.'

'And blame who, for pity's sake? Act of God?'

Etherington paused. 'No, Jack. He wanted to blame me. That is why he wanted me in the square tonight. He wanted to make it look as though I had blown it up and he put the bomb in my car to make it look as though it had gone off early.'

'And then?'

'As soon as I heard the explosion, I naturally ran to the car to see if the driver was hurt. But it was hopeless, of course. I went back to the square but by then the helicopter had arrived and he was leaving.'

The Ngale paced silently before speaking again. 'It seems I am right not to trust white men, aren't I, John?' he said at last. 'You are a fool and O'Leary is a thief.'

He stopped and looked at Etherington. 'Would you agree?'

'No, Jack. I called you as soon as it happened. You know that already.'

'Afterwards, yes. But not before. You should have told me what was going on this afternoon.'

'Yes, Jack,' said Etherington, looking down. 'I'm sorry.'

'Quite,' said the Ngale, beginning his walking again. 'But it is done now. You are leaving tomorrow. Good. And I think, torque or no torque, that you will not be coming back again, will you?'

Etherington did not reply.

'I asked whether you will be coming back,' said the Ngale.

'No,' said Etherington quietly. 'I will not.'

'And as for Mr O'Leary,' continued the Ngale. 'He will not be looking for any torques either.'

The Ngale looked at his watch and went on, 'In fact, round about now, several of my men should be arriving at his house to remind him in no uncertain terms. I hope his passing will be a lesson to you and everyone else.'

'Passing?' questioned Etherington.

'Yes,' said the Ngale. 'Crossing me is something people only do once. Now go.'

Etherington paused for a moment and then turned for the door.

'Oh, and by the way,' the Ngale called after him. 'I will suppress what happened in the square tonight and replace the statue. No one will speak of it if I tell them not to and nor will you. If I hear you have ever discussed it with anyone I will take it that you "have crossed" me. You don't want to do that, do you?'

Etherington turned as he reached the door. 'No,' he said. 'Good night, Jack. Call on me if you come to Goa.'

'Maybe,' said the Ngale. 'Maybe not.'

Chapter Six

―――――

SATURDAY

Kano, Nigeria

Laurie woke up at eight o'clock on Saturday morning. His headache was worse than usual and so he treated himself to three paracetamols with his early morning set of pills.

Looking at the compartments of multi-coloured tablets, he realised he had missed one of yesterday's batches. I'll double up later, he thought. Not a good idea to take too many on an empty stomach.

He dressed and went downstairs to see about making himself some coffee.

He could not find the coffee in the kitchen so settled for a glass of water from a plastic jug in the refrigerator and went out to the front terrace for a cigarette to take away the metallic taste of the pills.

On the terrace, he found the elderly night-watchman slowly sweeping locusts off the paving and onto the drive.

'Faras,' said Laurie, pointing.

The old man looked up and smiled.

'Dr Peter says more will be coming,' added Laurie.

The night-watch smiled and nodded again.

'What is your name?' asked Laurie.

The man smiled again.

Laurie put his hand to his chest and said, 'Laurie.' Then he pointed at the man. 'What is your name?'

The old man shook his head.

Laurie pointed at himself again. 'Laurie,' he said before pointing back.

'Ah!' said the man, understanding. He pointed to himself. 'Robert!'

287

'Robert?' said Laurie, rather surprised.

The man smiled and pointed at Laurie. 'Laurie!' he said before pointing back to himself. 'Robert!'

The two men smiled and felt properly introduced.

Laurie offered Robert a cigarette which was gratefully accepted into the folds of his robe.

'Good idea,' said Laurie, lighting his own.

Robert resumed his sweeping and Laurie looked out over the garden. The locusts from the day before appeared like patchy snow over the front lawn. Most of them were dead as far as he could see.

Laurie stepped off the terrace and kicked some aside with his foot. No locusts flew up but there was a buzz of flies that rose and settled again a few feet away.

He was about to go out further when he felt a hand on his shoulder.

'No, sah, Laurie.'

Laurie turned to Robert. 'What?'

'No, sah,' said Robert, who pointed at the garden and made a weaving motion from side to side with his hand. 'Macijai.'

'Macijai?'

Robert waved his hand again and this time accompanied it with a loud hissing noise.

'Snakes?' said Laurie, imitating the hand movement.

'Macijai,' confirmed Robert.

'I think I'll stay on the terrace after all,' said Laurie, stepping back.

Robert nodded his approval and stood watching Laurie.

'Snakes. Locusts. Flies. A good start to the day, wouldn't you say, Robert?' said Laurie.

Robert nodded, clearly not understanding.

Laurie noticed Robert's rifle propped up against the wall. 'Rifle,' he said, pointing.

'Yes. Rifle. Lee Rifle,' said Robert enthusiastically.

'Lee?' said Laurie, looking at the gun again. 'I think you're right, old boy. Unless I'm much mistaken that's a Lee Enfield Mark V Three Oh Three.'

'Lee, Three Oh Three,' said Robert, nodding again.

'We had these at school in the cadets,' said Laurie. 'I had to shoot one of these. Yes, a Lee Three Oh Three.'

'Three Oh Three,' repeated Robert, picking up the rifle and passing it to Laurie.

Laurie took the rifle and examined it. The wood of the stock and along the barrel were black with oil and there was an oil-stained cloth wrapped around the middle of the weapon.

'May I?' said Laurie, pointing at the cloth.

Robert nodded vigorously and Laurie removed the cloth to reveal a spotlessly clean and oiled breech and trigger mechanism.

Laurie looked up surprised and, sensing the anxious expression on Robert's face said, 'Very good, Robert. Very clean.'

Robert stood to his full height and smiled proudly, indicating Laurie should continue his inspection of the rifle.

Laurie raised the rifle and looked into the breech and down the inside of the barrel. It was perfectly clean and the twisting of the rifling in the barrel gleamed with freshly applied oil.

Laurie regarded it with admiration. 'That's pretty good, Robert. Much cleaner than I ever kept mine.'

Robert raised himself smartly to attention again.

Laurie hefted the weight of the rifle and smiled down at it. 'A Three Oh Three eh? We had to learn drill with these and everything. I'm afraid I didn't like the cadets thing much. We had to do it every Tuesday afternoon.'

Robert smiled politely.

'Do you know the English poet, Henry Reed, Robert?' Laurie asked absently. 'No. Probably not. He wrote a poem I used to like at school – "The Naming of Parts" I think it was called.

'Let me see,' he continued to himself, 'how did it go?

'This is the lower sling swivel. And this
Is the upper sling swivel, whose use you will see, when you are
    given your slings.
And this is the piling swivel,
Which in your case you have not got.'

Laurie tapped the different parts of the rifle as he recited.

' "Today we have naming of parts". I'm afraid I don't remember any more,' he said, looking up at Robert. 'Upper sling swivel, eh? God, that takes me back. Must be fifteen years or more.'

He looked down at the rifle again and smiled as he pointed at the open breech mechanism. 'You seem to have lost your bolt and magazine, Cadet Robert. I'm afraid you'll have to go on extra parade with that useless Miller boy. You two are a complete shower, do you know that?'

Laurie looked up at Robert. 'No bolt,' he repeated.

Robert smiled in sudden understanding 'Yes, bolt, sah.'

He turned to hurry along the terrace and beckoned Laurie to follow him.

Laurie made to put the rifle down against the wall but Robert waved for Laurie to bring it with him.

The two of them went through a door at the end of the terrace that led into the garage at the side of the house.

Robert carefully shut the door behind them and skirted a Land Rover, pointing to the floor on the far side. There, placed neatly next to each other, were a carefully folded khaki blanket and a military haversack.

Even in the gloom of the garage, Laurie could see the brass buckles of the haversack were polished and gleaming.

Robert stood to attention beside his possessions.

Laurie was unsure what was expected of him but Robert did not notice the hesitation and knelt down to unfold the top of the blanket and pointed for Laurie to look.

There, in the fold of the blanket, was the missing bolt and magazine from the Lee Enfield rifle. Robert looked up at Laurie and put his finger to his lips. 'Shh,' he went, 'No say. No say.'

'Ok,' said Laurie uncertainly.

Then Robert stood up again and put his hand on Laurie's shoulder encouraging him to take a step backwards and hand over the rifle.

Next, Robert stood at attention in front of Laurie again and theatrically screwed his eyes shut and put his free hand over them.

He took his hand away and, still with eyes tight shut stood still again for a moment before kneeling down next to the blanket; then, very quickly and smoothly, he picked up the bolt and magazine and clicked them into the breech of the rifle before standing up to attention again.

Finally, Robert opened his eyes and grinned widely at Laurie.

'Very good, Cadet!' laughed Laurie and raised his hand in a correct salute.

Robert stiffened himself and returned the salute. 'Sah!'

'Well, well, you certainly know your rifle drill old boy, don't you? That was pretty quick.'

Robert appeared to hesitate a moment and then said again, 'No say. No say.'

'Yes, I get it,' said Laurie. 'No say, old chap. Laurie no say.'

Robert knelt down again and folded back another layer of

the blanket. Underneath were two small and very old-looking cardboard boxes and something wrapped in a clean white cloth.

He looked up. 'No say?' he questioned.

'Absolutely, old boy,' Laurie replied. 'Laurie no say.'

Robert carefully took the lids off the boxes and unwrapped the white cloth. Inside the cloth was a gleaming clean .45 Browning British Army service revolver and the boxes contained neat rows of ammunition. One box for the rifle and one box for the revolver.

'Jesus, Robert! It's a fucking armoury!' exclaimed Laurie.

The old man looked suddenly anxious that he had gone too far and quickly covered the items with the blanket. 'No say! No say!' he said quickly.

'No,' said Laurie. 'It's OK, Robert. Laurie no say. No say.'

Robert looked relieved and turned back to the blanket again to put the lids back on the boxes and to wrap up the revolver in its cloth once more.

When he had finished, he stood up and pointed to the door for them to go out again.

Jaygo was standing on the terrace looking into the garden when Laurie and Robert came out.

'Oh, there you are,' she said. 'I was beginning to think you'd done a runner.'

'It's all right, Peter,' she called back into the house. 'He's here.

'Come on, Laurie,' she added going in. 'Peter says we have to eat something called Faw-Faws for breakfast which he says is posh Hausa for Paw-Paws.'

Laurie turned to Robert. 'Very well done, Cadet. We'll make a Lance Corporal of you yet. Now I must join the ladies.'

Robert came to attention again.

'Good,' said Laurie, going up the terrace to the front door. 'Carry on as you were.'

Laurie and Jaygo walked through to the dining room where Peter was already sitting down to his breakfast.

'Were you talking to old Robert?' asked Peter. 'He's quite a character though I'm afraid he's a bit light on vocabulary.'

'We got as far as names,' said Laurie. 'Why is he called Robert? It doesn't sound very Nigerian to me.'

'No,' said Peter, offering Jaygo and Laurie the fruit bowl. 'His real name is something unpronounceable so Tom called him Robert and the old boy seems to like it because it sounds British.'

'Oh?'

'Yes,' continued Peter. 'In those days, the 1950s, quite a few

Africans took up English names and his sort of stuck. He made out to Tom that he used to be in the West African Rifle Brigade when there was one. He wasn't, of course, but I suppose in those days he cut quite an imposing figure so Tom hired him and he's been here ever since. He won't retire and I haven't the heart to get rid of him. He comes under the heading of "faithful retainer". Actually, I don't think he's got anywhere else to go.'

'What does he do then?' asked Laurie. 'A bit old to be a night-watch I would have thought.'

'He doesn't do anything really. He used to help out in the garden a bit before he got past it and so now he just sits there.

'If someone comes up the drive he doesn't like the look of, he stands up and shakes his rifle at them if he remembers.'

'His rifle?' said Laurie, helping himself to another paw-paw.

'Yes,' Peter went on. 'Frightful old thing. He wipes the outside of it with cooking oil every now and again but I think you'll find the innards are rusted solid. It hasn't even got all its bits but he seems to like it and so I let him keep it.'

'It looked real enough to me,' said Jaygo.

'That's the idea,' said Peter. 'He waves it at people like you and they go away.'

'Well, there's a thing,' said Laurie quietly as Peter and Jaygo laughed at each other.

They stopped laughing abruptly and Laurie looked up to see Aurelia at the door holding a small wooden box in front of her.

'Peter,' she said, walking into the room without looking at anyone. 'I have decided to go home so you will have to deal with this.'

She went to the table and placed the box in front of Peter.

'Is that what I think it is?' he asked.

'Yes,' she said. 'Daddy's urn is inside. You said you wanted to deal with it and now you can. I've looked at the flight times and I'm going to see if I can get on the twelve o'clock.'

No one answered her and so she continued, 'I know it's only an open ticket but obviously I can't ring them so I'll just have to go and see.'

'This isn't necessary, Aurelia,' said Peter. 'It really isn't.'

'Don't insult me, Peter,' she said. 'It's what I want to do.'

She looked briefly at the three of them before leaving the room.

There was an awkward pause before Peter said, 'I'll take her to the airport.'

'It's only getting on a plane,' said Jaygo. 'I think you'll find she can manage that on her own.'

'It won't be easy,' said Peter. 'You heard what McKecnie said about flights out. Kano Airport is pretty chaotic at the best of times so God knows what it will be like now. There's only one direct flight to London every day and someone will have to push pretty hard if she's to stand any chance of getting on it.'

'Pushing not being her strong point?' said Jaygo.

'I can go to the airport with her,' said Laurie. 'I can be rude and pushy with the best of them if I have to. I could get her on that flight as well as you could.'

Peter looked at him thoughtfully.

'And if it's a question of getting her on an indirect, I could do that too,' added Laurie.

Jaygo looked at Peter. 'Well?'

'I suppose so,' said Peter. 'You'd do it for me, would you?'

'No problem,' said Laurie. 'In fact I could, er, I could actually go to London with her, couldn't I?'

'What?' said Peter. 'Go?'

'No way!' said Jaygo. 'You're here to do a job.'

'Hardly,' said Laurie. 'Your launch thing is off for at least a week and it doesn't look as if we'll be able to get around much so I might as well be getting on with things at home.'

'You haven't got a ticket,' said Peter.

'No. But you have,' replied Laurie. 'You'll be going back with Jay, so you can give yours to me and I can switch it.'

Peter thought for a moment. 'Are you sure?'

'Positive, old man. I'll go and pack.'

'Well,' said Jaygo after Laurie had left. 'Goldilocks didn't put up much of a fight, did she?'

'What was she supposed to do – pull your hair and scream?'

'She could have tried.'

Peter smiled down at his plate. 'If you'd been her, would you have?'

'Bloody right!'

Peter sighed heavily. 'Hell. There isn't much practice in life for things like this. I don't even know what I'm supposed to feel.'

'Look at me, Peter,' she said, raising her fingers like windscreen wipers again and rocking them back and forth. 'You can't have absolutely everything in life you want. It's about choices and you made one.'

'I know,' he said. 'But there's a bit of a complicating factor I haven't told you about, I'm afraid.'

'Oh?' she said. 'And what's that?'

'It's difficult,' he said, 'very difficult. It's not something that makes much difference to you but I'm afraid it does to her. Or would have done. To me and her anyway.'

He looked at her and leaned back in his chair. 'It's to do with money. Quite a lot of money actually. And to do with her father.'

'Well, if he left her money, then it's one less thing for you to worry about, isn't it? You don't need it now so I don't see what's so complicated about that.'

He smiled. 'You will when I tell you about it. Look, there's something I want you to read. I'll go and get it. You wait here.'

Laurie knocked at Aurelia's door and put his head round. 'Can I come in?' he said.

Aurelia was putting the last of her things in her case on the bed.

'I'm going to come with you,' said Laurie.

'Thank you, but that isn't necessary,' she said.

'No. To London. I'm coming back to England with you.'

'I thought you had things to do here with Jaygo.'

'That's all out of the window now,' he said. 'The CD isn't going to happen and I don't fancy sitting in the house and watching it rain locusts for a week. I can use Peter's ticket and we can be home by tonight.'

She smiled tiredly. 'Home? That sounds nice.'

'Look,' he said. 'I'm really sorry things didn't work out for you here. I'm afraid they don't always.'

'No,' she said, locking her case. 'And I don't think things will work out for Peter either but he won't listen to me.'

She sat down next to her case. 'It's funny, but of all the things I thought could go wrong in my life, this wasn't one of them. Peter doing this was something that never even occurred to me. Perhaps I was stupid. I mean, do you think he planned it this way?'

'No,' said Laurie. 'I'm sure it's not that. She may have planned it but I'm sure *he* didn't.'

'Oh, yes. I'm sure she planned it. I expect her whole life is a series of plans. And she's pretty used to getting her own way too. I don't know what it takes to be like that, but whatever it is, I don't have it.'

'Perhaps it was just chance,' he said.

'No,' said Aurelia, standing up and lifting her case onto the floor. 'Not just chance. Everyone gets what they want sometimes but some people do it more of the time than others.'

'Here, let me take that,' said Laurie reaching for the case. 'Let's just you and I go home.'

'You don't have to come.'

'I do,' he said. 'I want to. Truth is, I don't like it here much. Give me London any day.'

'Thank you,' she said. 'Let's go down and see about the car, shall we?'

Peter had returned to the dining room with Tom Collis's letter for Jaygo to read. 'Take this upstairs and read it,' he said. 'I can see to Laurie and Aurelia.'

'Don't you think I should at least say goodbye to her?' she said.

'No, I don't. Now just go and read this.'

She took the envelope from him. 'It feels quite bulky. Are you sure my attention span is up to it?'

'Just read it.'

'But I want to say goodbye to Laurie.'

'You'll see him again in a few days. Off you go.'

Jaygo shrugged.

As she was going out of the door she saw Laurie and Aurelia coming down the stairs.

'Oh,' she said. 'I . . . umm. I'll say goodbye then.'

'Yes,' said Aurelia without looking at her. 'Goodbye.'

'Don't you think you should at least telephone the airport first?' said Jaygo. 'You can use my phone. Or Peter can.'

'There isn't much point if the phone isn't working at the other end,' said Aurelia crisply.

'I didn't think of that,' said Jaygo. 'I'll . . . I'll go upstairs then.'

'Perhaps we'll meet again sometime,' she added as she passed Aurelia.

Laurie put the cases by the front door and came back just as Peter emerged from the dining room. 'Can we use the car and the driver, Peter? You can always use the Land Rover if you and Jaygo have to go out. You know, the one in the garage.'

'Of course,' said Peter. 'But how did you know there was a Land Rover in the garage?'

'I know all sorts of things,' said Laurie. 'You always forget I'm a journalist.'

295

'OK,' said Peter. 'I'll see you back in London then, Lol. And Aurelia . . . Cambridge then?'

'I'll send your things to Lacrima Christi if that is what you are worried about,' she said. 'Now, if you don't mind, Laurie and I really should be going.'

Peter was standing in the sitting room, looking out at the locusts, when Jaygo joined him half an hour later with the letter in her hand.

'Wow,' she said. 'Quite a thing, Peter.'

'It is,' he said, taking it from her. 'What do you think I should do?'

'I'll tell you one thing. And that is that I don't think it's hers.'

'The torque?'

'Of course. I don't think it was Tom Collis's to give away and I don't think it's hers or yours *and* hers to keep.'

Peter held up the envelope. 'But he's not giving it away, is he? He's just saying where it is and what he wants to happen to it.'

'Possibly,' she said, sitting down. 'But what gives him the right to decide what happens to it?'

'Somebody has to.'

'No, they don't,' she said. 'If it's where he says it is, it can stay there. No one has found it yet.'

'It's a lot of money just to be sitting there. So who do you think should have it then?'

'From what you said the other night, it's between the Ngale and any Etheringtons who are still around.'

'The Ngale? But that means Jack.'

'Yes,' she said. 'He doesn't need it. But you do.'

'Me?' he said. 'I don't want it.'

'If you *really* don't want to leave it where it is, why not take it?'

'Are you serious?'

'Why not? We know where it is. We just have to go and get it.'

'Hold on a minute. If it's not Aurelia's, it's certainly not ours either.'

'Millions,' she said. 'The best part of a Lear Jet I expect. But, actually, I've already got one of those.'

'And you couldn't use another? Or a yacht?'

She smiled. 'Nice idea, but I don't think so. Take it from me, Peter, great wealth really does not bring great happiness.'

'That's easy for you to say.'

'Maybe. But becoming rich is just like getting a new job, or getting married. You think things will be different, but they're not. The sun comes up and goes down just the same and you have to deal with every day regardless of what you start the day with.'

'You don't know about being married.'

'I can guess.'

'Or having a proper job come to that,' he added.

'Being Jocasta Manhattan may not be ordinary but it's still a job. The bar the other evening in Atlanta, remember?'

'I do,' he said with a smile. 'God. Was that really only this week?'

'Yes. And as far as the torque goes, I don't think the Etheringtons should have it either. I should think that particular family has wrung enough out of Africa, don't you?'

'Yes,' he said.

'Well, then. Let's just leave it where it is. If it's going to belong to anyone it can belong to the person who finds it. Finders Keepers.'

'And not us?'

'I don't need it and now you don't. I come with a dowry in case you hadn't noticed, Peter.'

'I suppose you do,' he said. 'But I haven't got much to bring to the table. A flat in Cambridge and an I-Spy book of locusts isn't a lot for the girl who has everything, is it?'

'You'll do,' she said. 'It's a come-as-you-are life.'

'I can't even compete in the engagement ring department,' he said. 'Look at the thing Hugo gave you. And what about Hugo anyway? God, I haven't thought this thing through at all. What will the Belle Epoque think? Or do?'

'Don't worry about the ring,' she said, turning it with her thumb as she spoke. 'Don't forget he gave me that gun on the same day. Somehow I don't think I'll miss either of them. And don't worry about the Belle either. They won't miss Hugo any more than I will. There's nothing like a string trio, I always say.'

'Are you really sure about all this, Jay? I mean, have *you* thought things through?'

'No,' she replied. 'I haven't. I'm a doer, not a planner. Sorry.'

She stood up and put her arms forwards and downwards like the statue again. 'And if *you* change your mind, you can always come back for Big Mary, can't you? Deal?'

'Deal,' he laughed.

'Good,' she said. 'That's settled then. Now, why don't we go and do something with that box of fertiliser before it starts raining locusts again.'

'Tom's ashes? I suppose we could. I think he would have liked them to go somewhere near Santa Maria. We could have a look at the market as well if you like. The locusts might not be so bad there and it would be better than hanging around the house all day.'

'I'd love that,' she said. 'I promised the people at the studio that I'd bring them presents. What's the best thing to buy?'

'I don't know,' he smiled, 'but whatever it is, I know you'll find it in Sabon Gari. Come on, Tuareg. I'll get the Land Rover out.'

The traffic heading towards the airport was heavy as soon as Aurelia and Laurie's car joined the main road. Five minutes later it had slowed to a walking pace and in another ten it had stopped altogether,

'How much further is it?' Laurie asked the driver.

'It is far, sah. Four mile.'

Laurie turned to Aurelia. 'Do you want to go back?' he asked.

'Perhaps it will clear in a minute.'

'I'm not so sure,' said Laurie. 'You wait here while I see how it is further ahead.'

Five minutes later he was back. 'Sorry, old thing,' he said 'It's solid as far as I can see. If we want to go we'll have to leg it unless Tijja here knows of another road.'

'No, sah. Not from here.'

'OK,' said Laurie. 'Walking, it is.'

'You cannot walk, sah. The faras are on the ground and you will have to walk on them.'

'What about the cases?' said Aurelia. 'We can't carry them all that way.'

'Can you come, Tijja?' Laurie asked. 'Bring the cases?'

'No, sah. I must be with the car. It will not be safe if I leave it.'

'Can you get someone to carry the cases for us then?'

'Oh, yes, sah. I can find a man but you will have to pay him much money.'

'All right,' said Laurie. 'You go and find someone. Miss Aurelia and I will wait here.'

'Have you got any other shoes with you, Aurelia?' Laurie asked. 'Trainers or something? Those sandals you've got on won't be much use.'

'In my case,' she said. 'And a sun hat. I'll get them now.'

'It won't be much fun,' he said. 'Are you sure you want to do it?'

'It wasn't much fun back at the house for me, was it? Maybe

it will only take an hour or so and I think we will still have time.'

'OK,' he said, 'I'm up for it if you are.'

Aurelia and Laurie had only been waiting a couple of minutes when Tijja returned with a boy of about eighteen, wearing just a pair of shorts.

'This is Biram. I know him from my brother,' Tijja announced. 'He is very strong.'

'OK,' said Laurie, 'you stay with the car, Tijja, and catch us up if the road clears. If it's still not clear by the middle of the day, go back to the house and tell Mr Peter what has happened.'

'Yes, sah. But the faras. There will be more of them.'

'If Biram here can manage on bare feet, I'm sure we will be all right.'

'Yes,' said Aurelia, sounding not at all convinced. 'Shall we go then.'

Before they had walked even a hundred yards, Laurie realised it would take them much longer than an hour. Aurelia clearly hated walking on the locusts. In places, cars had worn a furrow but their crushed bodies made the surface slippery. Aurelia looked very unhappy about the whole thing.

'Take my arm,' Laurie said to her. 'Just keep walking and try not to think about it. I'm afraid we will have to go a bit faster. It's still a long way.'

'I know,' she said, holding on to his elbow. 'But they are awful. And they smell so awful. Everything is going to smell.'

Biram had no problems with the locusts. He strode well ahead of them and stopped every few yards for Aurelia and Laurie to catch him up.

A mile down the road they came to a petrol tanker that had jack-knifed completely across the road, blocking it in both directions. It was surrounded by a crowd of people who were all shouting and gesticulating but who didn't seem to know how to clear the obstruction. At least it meant that the road beyond the tanker was clear. Laurie hoped for a taxi or even a lift from another car but none came.

An hour later they were in sight of the airport terminal. They could see the comforting tail of the British Airways 747, sticking up like a sail beyond the main building.

'There you are,' said Laurie. 'Practically there. What say we rest up for a minute while we send old Biram off to see if he can get us a drink or something?'

Biram ran off and shortly returned with six very large bright green oranges.

'Don't worry about the colour,' said Aurelia, beginning to peel one. 'Nigerian oranges are always green.'

'I didn't know that,' said Laurie. 'Something new every day. Probably taste pretty good too.'

'They do,' said Aurelia. 'But don't you think we should try to eat them going along? There isn't that much time left, you know.'

Laurie had needed the rest far more than Aurelia. The heat and her leaning on him had completely drained him of what little energy he had had when they set out. He was blinking from the pain in his head and the last few hundred yards to the terminal building were very difficult for him.

His heart sank even more when he saw the large crowd gathered around the British Airways desk in main hall.

'There was always bound to be a bit of a crush,' he said. 'You sit back here with the cases and I'll go up front and see what I can sort out.'

Aurelia sank gratefully onto her case. Laurie braced himself and began to push though the crowd.

'I'm sorry, sir,' a clearly exasperated young woman was explaining to someone else when Laurie reached the front. 'There are no available seats at all on today's London flight. I am holding two reservations for passengers who have confirmed their bookings and there are no more available. I am sorry, sir, but I simply cannot help you.'

'How come they confirmed?' shouted a very angry man. 'Your effing phone has been out for three days.'

'They confirmed in person, sir,' she said in as even a voice as she could manage. 'I am sorry, but those are the regulations.'

Laurie pushed past and began to climb over the weighing machine into the space behind her,

'Please get back, sir,' she said angrily. 'Passengers have to remain the other side.'

'That's absolutely right,' said Laurie. 'But I'm this side now.'

'Please, sir. These people were all in front of you.'

'Wrong,' he said. 'I've been waiting a hundred years and it's my turn now.'

'I will have to call security, sir. Please get back.'

'Go on, then,' he said. 'But you'll have to shout pretty loudly because your phone isn't working.'

'I must insist.'

'Look,' said Laurie, leaning forwards and beckoning her towards him. 'You just listen to what I've got to say and then I'll get back to the other side like a good boy. All right?'

'No, sir. Please get back now.'

Laurie was suddenly angry too and shouted at her, 'Are you on that fucking flight? Are you?'

'Sir! Please!'

'Look at it this way,' he said in a normal voice again and waving his hand at the counter. 'Do this lot look as if they want to stay in Kano to you?'

'What?'

'They don't, do they? They want to get out of here as fast as possible and so would you if you had any sense.'

'I'll have to call security,' she said, turning around and trying to see over the crowd.

'Fine,' said Laurie. 'Do that, but *listen* to me first, will you?'

The woman could not see anyone useful over the crowd and turned back to Laurie.

He produced the two airline tickets from his pocket and held them up in front of her.

'Right,' he said. 'Two tickets. Open. Valid London today.'

She looked over at the crowd behind her and back again at Laurie.

'There are no seats left on that flight.'

'No,' he said, holding up the tickets again. 'You just said there were two that hadn't been taken up yet. Now I don't see anyone else getting to this airport, so that makes two seats not taken up, doesn't it?'

'I have to hold them open,' she said.

'Until when? Until the bloody plane's gone?'

'It's regulations. If the seats are confirmed, I have to hold them.'

'Let me try again,' said Laurie. 'Are *you* on that flight?'

'What?'

'You,' Laurie repeated. 'Are *you* on that flight? I didn't think so. Well, I've got two tickets here and one of them is yours. Now I don't care what you have to write on the back, or how you do it, but unless you get your finger out you'll be stuck here with the rest of them. Now, you know as well as I do that a swarm of locusts the size of Manchester is going to be here tomorrow. And a penny to a pound says that just about everyone who is anything to do with British Airways in Kano is on that flight. Right? I thought so.

Look,' he said, peering forward at her name tag, 'Anita, you can be in London tonight or you can be in Kano. What's it going to be?'

She hesitated and looked back at the crowd.

'That's right,' said Laurie more quietly. 'I've been here long enough to know I don't like it and I'm guessing you don't like it much either. Now, the rest of your lot are already out there with nice cold glasses of gin in their hands and you are left here holding the baby, right?'

She hesitated again but before she could speak a tall African in uniform came up behind her. 'What is going on here?' he demanded. 'Passengers are not permitted in this area.'

Laurie glanced up at the man and then back at Anita before holding the tickets up one last time.

'It's all right, Colin. I said he could sit here.'

She reached out and took the tickets from Laurie. 'He was feeling unwell and so I told him he could sit here while I sorted out a problem with his wife's ticket.'

'He is not permitted here. He has to be behind the barrier.'

'Yes,' she said sharply. 'I am well aware of that. But he is unwell and has to sit down. Now go to the aircraft and tell them that the two remaining passengers have arrived and will be ready to board in two minutes.'

She walked the two steps to the counter and opened the tickets. The man showed no sign of moving.

Anita glared up at him. 'Did you hear what I said? Stop wasting time and do what I say or I will report you.'

Colin turned reluctantly to go. 'Bitch,' he said audibly.

Laurie and Anita pretended not to hear. After writing on the tickets and ticking a list next to her she turned and walked back to Laurie to the protests of those still on the other side of the desk.

'All right,' she said quickly. 'But there's no time to put your cases on. You will have to leave them here and they can be sent on. But you are going to have to hurry. Go to the far end of the hall and wait by the door marked "Apron – Authorised Staff Only" – the red one. I have to go around the back and stamp the boarding passes. Now hurry, before I change my mind.'

'Thank you,' said Laurie. 'But it won't be me. It will be a woman with fair hair in a blue dress.'

'What?' said the woman, suddenly alarmed. 'There really are only two seats. The flight is completely full.'

'I know,' said Laurie. 'You and her.'

'But I thought . . . ?'

'Two minutes, you say. She'll be there.' He climbed back over the weighing machine. 'Have a boiled sweet for me.'

Anita picked up the tickets and list and disappeared through a door, ignoring the angry shouts from the people as Laurie pushed through them.

He joined an anxious looking Aurelia who was sitting on the cases with her hands clasped on her knees in front of her.

'I had to work a bit of a wangle,' he said.

'What? Is everything all right? Can we get on the flight?'

'Oh, yes,' he said. 'No real problem. The flight was nearly full but they always keep a few seats back for people like you and me. I persuaded them to let us have them but I'm afraid we won't be able to sit together. Now I've got to go and get the cases weighed in and we're too late to go to the departure lounge so the ground girl will take you to the plane herself. OK? She says you have to go and wait by that red door down there and she will come and get you. Now, have you got your passport ready?'

'Yes. But won't I need a boarding pass or something? You have to have one of those I think or they don't let you on.'

'I've got them,' he said. 'I need them to get the cases on. Now, quickly, you go down to the door and I'll go round the normal way to see the cases don't get left behind.'

'I think we should stay together,' she said. 'I'll come with you if that's all right.'

'No,' he said, looking surreptitiously at his watch. 'Just go and meet the girl by the door. We can sort everything out when we are in the air.'

'But I have to put my own case to be weighed,' she said. 'It's got my name on it.'

'Just go to the door,' he said with all the control he could find.

'If you are sure.'

'Just go, will you!'

Laurie picked the cases up as Aurelia walked slowly down the hall. He stopped on the far side of the crowd from Aurelia and stepped carefully back, just in time to see her being taken by the hand through the red door.

He gave them a minute before picking up the cases and returning slowly to the entrance door.

Once out in the sun again, he carried them to the corner of the building and sat down.

One of the side doors to the Boeing was open. A man was

303

standing at the top of the steps and waving at two figures hurrying over the tarmac towards him.

Laurie could see Aurelia stop and protest about something. Anita practically had to push her up the steps and into the open door.

The door closed and engines began to whine into life almost before the steps were wheeled away.

Laurie lit a cigarette as he watched the large aeroplane taxi away down to the far end of the runway for take-off.

He heard the engines come to full power, saw the Boeing start forward and gradually gather speed as the engines became louder and louder. When it was almost opposite the terminal building it seemed to sit up for a moment on its rear wheels before taking off with a roar and climbing quickly into the hot afternoon sky.

He did not think Aurelia would be looking out of a window or could see him if she were, but Laurie stood up and waved anyway.

At one o'clock the Ngale was relaxing in his cool sitting room, drinking a glass of freshly squeezed orange juice and crushed ice. He wiped his lips with his forefinger before picking up his satellite telephone and keying in the number for John Etherington.

It answered on the second ring.

'Good afternoon, John. I am sorry to hear your flight has been cancelled,' he began. 'Fortunately I have something to occupy you while you wait for another. I have sent a car for you and I wonder if you would care to join me to discuss it. Immediately. There is an old friend of mine I want you to go and see. A journalist. Thank you.'

He switched off the telephone and placed it next to the glass of orange juice.

Peter and Jaygo were standing in front of the church of Santa Maria staring at where the statue had been.

'That's the end of your little dilemma then,' Jaygo said. 'I may not have been able to guess her secret but it looks as though someone else has.'

'It can't just have been taken,' said Peter. 'It was huge. Let's go and see if Oladi knows anything.'

As they walked over to the dye pits, Oladi himself walked out to meet them.

'Ah, Sunday Man,' he called. 'Our Lady is gone.'

'I can see that,' said Peter. 'What the hell happened?'

'Hello, Oladi,' said Jaygo.

'Tuareg,' said Oladi, reaching down to his knee in greeting. 'It is very bad.'

'Did someone take it?' asked Peter.

'No, sah. She is broken up in many parts on the ground.'

'What? She fell and broke? Surely not.'

'No, sah. He pull her with the rope and then he strike at her and she break. The tall man. The one I say come before and hit her with the knife. He is a very bad man, sah.'

'Whoa, Oladi! Let's start right at the beginning, shall we? Start by telling me when it happened.'

'It was four in the night, sah.'

'Four in the morning?' said Jaygo. 'Today?'

'No,' said Peter, 'he means four after sunset. This was at ten o'clock last night, was it?'

'Yes, sah. Ten clock time. Come with me and I will show it all to you.'

Oladi led Peter and Jaygo over to the side road to the square and began his account. As he talked, he directed to them to all the places in the square where the night's bizarre events had taken place. He acted the part of Etherington himself in detail, even to the point of falling backwards as the rope went slack when the statue fell. He enacted the whole sequence with great relish and imitated the helicopter as it landed and took off. He ended his scenario by pointing to the direction Etherington had taken in the Ngale's car at the end.

'A Ngale car?' said Peter sceptically. 'Are you sure?'

'Oh, yes, sah. I know the man who was driving it.'

'And the car that was burnt out? Where is it now? It wasn't in the road as we came in.'

'No, Sunday, sah. The Ngale men come and take it away before it is morning. It is gone now.'

'I can't believe it,' said Peter to Jaygo. 'I don't understand it at all.'

'But it is true, sah,' said Oladi in a slightly hurt tone. 'I am only saying what has occurred.'

'No,' said Peter quickly. 'I didn't mean I didn't believe *you*. It's just that I don't understand what it all means.'

'I don't know it, sah. But the tall man is very bad.'

'It seems so,' said Peter thoughtfully, picking up a scrap of stone from among the scattering of dead locusts. 'But what happened to the statue after it was broken up? Did he take any part of it with him? Any part at all? Or did the Ngale's men come back for it?'

'No. He does not touch it after it is broken by him and the Ngale men do not take her so I put her to be safe.'

'You have the parts?'

'Oh, no, sah,' said Oladi, putting his hand flat on his chest. 'I would not do that. She is broken very badly so I take all the pieces and put them for the other lady in the church. But the wooden lady is not strong and she was beginning to break and so I put the stone lady by her on the ground.'

'Other lady? Do you mean there is more than one statue?'

'No. The wooden painting. Come with me and I will show her to you.'

Peter and Jaygo followed him into the nearly dark interior of the church. All the windows, long broken, were covered by Oladi's blue cloths hung up to dry on wooden poles. It was hard to see clearly after coming in from the brightness outside.

Their eyes became accustomed to the gloom, as they followed Oladi up the nave.

At the end was a single step leading up to the stone altar about four feet square and three feet high. It had once been covered in plaster stucco but most of this was broken away and they could make out that the block was made of the same stone as the walls of the church itself.

In front of the altar, laid out on one of Oladi's long pieces of cloth, were the broken pieces of the statue. He had tried to put them in order, giving the broken statue the appearance of bones laid out in a tomb.

Peter knelt down and ran his hand over the broken surface of the pieces.

'Did I do right, sah?' said Oladi. 'If I leave her outside, people will take the stones and she is not for them.'

'You did the right thing, Oladi,' said Peter, standing up again. 'She is not for them.'

He looked carefully down at the parts, trying to see if any of them were obviously missing.

'Can I go, sah? I have to go to my dye pit because I am doing a colouring and I cannot leave it in there too long.'

'Of course,' said Peter. 'We have taken too much of your time already. Thank you very much.'

'I am by my dye pit if you are needing me.'

'Thank you very much, Oladi,' said Jaygo. 'You are very kind.'

'One more thing,' said Peter. 'You said "the wooden lady". I don't know where she is.'

'She is the painting lady,' said Oladi, pointing towards the altar. 'You can see her on top of the table but she is breaking now.'

Oladi walked down the nave as Peter stepped over the broken statue to the altar. Sure enough, on a three-foot wooden panel set into the centre of the altar fixed at each corner with rusting bolts, was a painting. He brushed his hand over it to clear it of dust and pieces of chipped statue. There was a large, fresh-looking crack across the centre of the painting and it was nearly worn away in places down to the bare wood.

He brushed his hand over it again and, in the gloom, could make out a life-size painting of the top half of the statue. There was Mary's head in its hood and her two bowed arms running out and around the edge of the picture in their curious bent shape.

'I've been in this church dozens of times,' said Peter. 'But I've never seen this before.'

'Perhaps it was covered up,' said Jago. 'You said they use the church to store things.'

'It looks as old as the church,' he said, running his hand over the face and along the crack.

He stood up and raked his fingers through his hair. 'But why is there a painting on top of the altar where no one can see it? Why isn't it on the wall at the end?'

'I don't know,' said Jaygo. 'Perhaps they did things differently then.

'Wait!' she said, suddenly gripping his arm. 'I think I know what it is!'

She leaned over the painting and tapped in the middle with her knuckle. 'It's hollow,' she said. 'It's the icon! The one the priests brought from the south.'

'What?'

'Yes. It's here. "Safe in the arms of the mother of God"! It's in here, Peter! It's in here!'

She hit the side of the painting with her fist. The wood she struck broke away and fell inwards. She quickly unclenched her fist and put her hand through the hole.

Suddenly she froze. 'Oh, my God, Peter. It's here. It's huge. Big as a man's arm!'

Peter pulled out her hand and pushed his own through the hole. About four inches below the surface he touched something metal.

He worked his hand back and forth along it as far as he could. It was curved.

'Am I right?' she said. 'Can you feel it?'

He slowly took out his hand and looked at her. 'Yes,' he said, stunned. 'It's the torque – Idona Zaki. We've found the Idona Zaki.'

The Ngale was standing with his back to the large table when Habu showed John Etherington in.

'Good afternoon, Jack,' began Etherington.

'I told you I don't like to be crossed,' said the Ngale flatly.

Etherington was about to reply when the Ngale put his hand up. 'You should have known by now.'

'I do know that, Jack,' replied Etherington immediately.

'Anderson, the man in Atlanta, crossed me.'

'Yes.'

'He had been interfering with my business.'

'You said.'

'And I didn't like it. He should have learned from reports that I have my own way of dealing with things.'

The Ngale leaned back against the table.

'He was American,' he went on. 'Do you imagine he thought that would be an excuse?'

'Excuse?'

'Yes. You see, John, everyone in life thinks they are a special case. Perhaps he thought I would not act against someone in his position. But I don't have time for special cases or exceptions. In politics and in business you have to have plans and follow them through. Yes?'

'I'm sure,' said Etherington uneasily.

'And I have to be sure of the people who work for me,' said the Ngale. 'People have to prove themselves, wouldn't you say?'

'If you don't know them, yes.'

'And you?' continued the Ngale. 'How well do I know you? You are white. Why should any African trust a white man?'

'Jack, you know you can trust me.'

'Because of Atlanta. Can I take that as proof?'

'If you like.'

'Maybe. But there is a slight doubt in my head,' said the Ngale, lifting a hand and tapping with a finger on his forehead. 'Last night.'

'I told you what happened as soon as I could.'

'Sabon Gari,' said the Ngale. 'Do you know what that means?'

'The place of strangers.'

'And it is just that. New people. Strangers. Immigrants. Tell me, John, how do you fare with the immigrants in your own country? Are they welcome? Do you treat them as your own? Are black and white people equal in London?'

'We have laws. People have to be fair.'

'Ah! "Laws". I remember them in England. You have one called "The Race Relations Act" as I recall. So do you know what the black people call that law in England? What I learned to call it when I was a student?'

Etherington did not reply and so the Ngale went on.

'The Shut-Up-Or-Go-Home Act. It didn't matter to the English people where you came from or what it was like there. People, strangers, could either shut up or go back.'

'New people find it difficult wherever they go, Jack.'

'Yes,' said the Ngale. 'They do if they don't want to shut up.'

'I hope not, Jack.'

'Well, we can agree to differ about England, John. We are talking about our own immigrants in Kano. The "strangers" in Sabon Gari.'

Etherington looked puzzled.

'I'll be frank with you, John. They are scum. Hangers-on. Parasites. They live little better than animals and I don't like them.'

He stood up from leaning on the table and walked over to his hi-fi.

'So when they tell my people something, I don't know whether to believe them or not.'

The Ngale picked up Jaygo's CD and looked at the case absently.

'So should I believe them or you about what happened last night?'

He took the CD from its case and put it into the unit.

'I told you what happened,' said Etherington. 'You can believe what I told you.'

'Good.' said the Ngale, pressing a button to turn on the music and going over to his sofa to sit down. 'Because what they tell me is very different from what you tell me. I am very glad to hear that what you told me is what actually happened. After all, they're only scum, aren't they?'

'I'm no stranger to you, Jack.'

The Ngale leaned back and rubbed the side of his face thoughtfully.

'We can let it go then, can't we, John? You and I are not strangers to each other after all. But I am afraid a real stranger has come to town. A short, fat, white one. A journalist.'

'The one you mentioned on the telephone?'

'Yes,' said the Ngale, sitting up again. 'You don't need to know the details but I have reason to believe that he is planning to cross me in no uncertain way.'

'Oh?'

'He was in Atlanta on Monday at the same time as you. Laurie Miller. Do you know him?'

Etherington thought for a moment.

'I don't think I know that name. Should I?'

'No reason,' said the Ngale innocently. 'But these things are always easier if you don't know the person, I think.'

Etherington furrowed his brow slightly. 'And he is here in Kano?'

'The thing is,' said the Ngale, 'I know him from a long time ago. I never liked him. He's a pathetic little man, always going around sticking his nose into other people's business. Not long after I last saw him, I thought he was sticking his nose into my affairs. But I left him alone because he was friendly with some friends of mine. People I do trust.

'I should have trusted my instincts,' he continued after a pause. 'But now I think he's up to his old tricks and I want him dealt with once and for all.'

'Dealt with?' said Etherington.

'Yes,' said the Ngale, staring directly at Etherington. 'And I want you to do it for me.'

'I'm sorry?' said Etherington.

'Yes. Is that a problem for you? You managed to dispose of a whole roomful of people in Atlanta. I don't think one man on his own should present you with too much difficulty.'

'You want me to kill him?' said Etherington. 'Here in Kano?'

'For goodness sake,' said the Ngale impatiently. 'Do I have to spell it out for you? You have a gun, don't you?'

'A gun?'

'Yes, a gun. A point three seven automatic pistol. Oh? Didn't I tell you? I had your cases checked while you were out of the house. And you have a satellite telephone which you also failed to tell me about. Come, come, John, I think even in your own house you check the guests' cases, don't you? And I do too. Now, are you going to do what I ask you or not?'

'But . . .' began Etherington.

'No buts,' said the Ngale, standing up. 'You work for me now and this man Miller is in my way just as Anderson was in Atlanta. It's your job to deal with him.'

'But in Kano?' said Etherington. 'You have your own people here. Atlanta was different.'

'Yes, I do have my own people in Kano and you are one of them. I'll be honest with you, John. I like you and you have done very well but I do have my doubts. If you can do this for me, I am prepared to set those doubts aside and we can continue as friends. All right?'

Etherington opened his mouth to say something but the Ngale suddenly put his hand up and spoke with an edge to his voice. 'I am not offering you an alternative. I have already dealt with O'Leary on your behalf and you should be grateful to me for that. Do this for me and we will say no more about last night. I myself will be leaving Kano tomorrow morning for at least a week and I can set you on your way to Nairobi, if you do what I ask.'

'Nairobi?' began Etherington.

'Yes. That is where you want to go, is it not? You can take it from me that Kano will be no place to be for the next seven days and I have no intention of staying. Here is what I require you to do.

'At seven o'clock exactly you will go to the man's house and do what you have to do. You will then come here to confirm it and we shall leave together in the morning. Do you have any objections to that?'

'No, of course not,' said Etherington, trying to think quickly. 'But I need to plan.'

'No, you don't,' said the Ngale. 'I have done the planning for you. He will be alone in the house, probably sitting down to a large meal if I know him. A car will take you to the end of his road, you will then walk to his house and the car will wait for you.'

'But if I just arrive at his house,' questioned Etherington, 'will he let me in if he does not know who I am?'

'John, John, John,' said the Ngale impatiently. 'Of course he will let you in. Any white man arriving on foot at a white man's house at night will be let in, believe me.'

'But what shall I say?'

'You don't have to engage him in conversation, do you? Now, if you don't mind, I have a great deal to do before this evening. Not the least of which is to make sure Miller is in the house on his own at seven o'clock. So, if you will excuse me, I have to get on.'

* * *

After Aurelia's flight had left, Laurie sat on the cases for a quarter of an hour to gather his strength. One home, three to go, he thought as he stood up at last and walked slowly over to the car park to look for a taxi.

He was soon surrounded by a crowd of small boys all trying to carry his cases. 'Taxi,' he explained. 'I want a taxi.'

'Yes, taxi! Very good taxi!' they all seemed to be saying as he followed them towards a row of ancient blue-and-yellow taxis at the far side of the terminal building.

'Sah! Mister, sah!' he heard someone shout and he looked up to see Biram running towards him.

'You no go, sah. Why you no go?'

'No, Biram. No go. No seats.'

'But lady? Where is lady?'

'Lady go,' said Laurie. 'One seat.'

Biram looked surprised at this apparent precedence.

'And now I need a taxi to go back to Kano,' said Laurie, pointing after the cases.

'I will do it,' said Biram, hurrying after the boys. 'Biram can do it.'

Laurie was relieved to leave the travel arrangements to Biram. By the time he had reached the row of cars, Biram had selected one and was putting the cases into the boot.

Biram enthusiastically accepted Laurie's offer of a lift and one minute later Laurie was sinking down onto the threadbare back seat and Biram was sitting proudly in the front with the driver.

He was not at all daunted to learn that Laurie did not have the first idea where the house was. From sign language and broken English, Biram assured Laurie that he had a brother who lived near the broken-down petrol-tanker who knew Tijja and would be able to find the house.

Well, thought Laurie, closing his eyes, if I can't have a G and T with Aurelia, at least I can have a cold beer with Dr Peter.

Meanwhile, Peter and Jaygo were still sitting on the steps of Santa Maria, trying to decide what to do about their discovery.

'It's not like before,' Jaygo was saying. 'When you thought it was in the statue, we could leave it where it was, but you saw the wood on that altar. It's cracked and someone will find it very soon.'

'They will now you've made a bloody great hole in it,' said Peter. 'What did you go and do that for?'

'It was cracked already from where Oladi put the statue on it.

He'd have found it himself if he'd put his hand in. Or the next person would.'

'It's still not ours,' said Peter. 'I thought we agreed this morning that we couldn't just take it.'

'Yes,' she said. 'And I also said it was Finders Keepers and I've found it now.'

'What would you do with it?'

'Give it to a museum. Sell it or something.'

'It's ridiculous anyway,' he said. 'Even if we did want it, we could never get it out of the church without being seen. You saw how big it is.'

'That wouldn't be a problem,' she said. 'We can wrap it up in one of those cloths. Come at night and back the car up to the door.'

'No,' said Peter. 'We could not. You heard Oladi. He and everyone else saw what happened last night.'

'Yes, but that was different,' she said, 'A helicopter, someone pulling a statue down, a car blowing up and God knows what. Of course they saw all that. But we're just talking about you and me coming here, parking for a minute and driving off again. We could do it, Peter. We really could.'

He thought for a moment, moving his foot back and forth in the dust. 'And then getting it out of the country,' he said. 'What do we do about customs?'

'Oh, for God's sake! If it was up to you, you'd say we should roll it like a hoop all the way to the airport. No. We put it in the cello case and just load it into the Lear.'

'They might want to look inside,' he said.

'God Almighty!' she said. 'They will *not* look inside. Now, I don't care what you want, but I am *not* leaving that thing in there. It's coming home with me and that's all there is to it. We can decide what to do with it when it's sitting in a nice cool bank vault in London.'

'If Laurie were here, he would know what to do,' said Peter.

'Well, he's *not* here. He's up there emptying the drinks trolley. And, for all the help you're being, you might as well be up there with him.

'This is Peter and Jaygo day one,' she went on, 'and you're dragging your feet already. Make your mind up, Sunday Man. Are you going to help me or not?'

'I suppose so,' he said. 'All right.'

She leaned over and kissed him on the cheek. 'There,' she said, 'that wasn't so difficult, was it? Come on,' she said standing up, 'let's go back to the house and get ready before you change your mind.'

As they walked back to the car, Peter looked up at the sky. 'You're forgetting the locusts,' he said.

'What about them?'

'They will be here tomorrow. I don't know what it will be like, but the airport's bound to be closed. We can't just sit with it in the house for a week.'

'Well, we'll go tonight,' she said. 'Dump it and come back for the CD launch next week. You said yourself there wouldn't be much to do here for the next few days.'

'We can't go at night,' he said. 'The airport usually only operates during the day.'

'They've got lights, haven't they? Aeroplanes *can* fly at night, you know. They don't need sunlight to hold them up.'

'Yes, there are lights,' he said, 'but they don't work all the time and British Airways say they will only land and take off during the day.'

'I'm glad I'm not flying British Airways then,' she said as they reached the Land Rover. 'Sven will take off and land when I tell him.'

'If you're sure?'

'I'm sure.'

'All right. But I thought you wanted to look around the market.'

'I can look around tonight then, can't I?' she said. 'We're coming back later in case you've forgotten already.'

'I don't like it,' he said.

She rolled her eyes upwards. 'Shut up and get in.'

Biram was taking the cases out of the boot of the taxi when Peter and Jaygo arrived back at the house.

'What's happened?' said Peter. 'Where's Aurelia?'

'Gone. Gone. Gone,' said Laurie. 'I blinked and she was gone.'

'What?'

'Gone,' said Laurie, putting his hands on his hips. 'But Biram here persuaded me to stay.'

Peter turned to Biram. 'And who are you?'

'Biram. Taxi. Very good taxi, sah.'

'I don't know what sort of Kano day you've had, Peter, old boy,' said Laurie, going towards the front door, 'but I need a beer.'

314

Laurie turned to give Robert a casual salute and went into the house.

The Ngale was sitting in his study admiring the new torque on its black velvet.

He was pleased with himself. Had that idiot Etherington really thought his activities in the square had gone unobserved? Was it likely that such a place did not contain people only too keen to pass interesting information to the Ngale?

Perhaps the best part was that Etherington had now saved him the trouble of looking in the last possible place the old torque could possibly be. No, perhaps the best part was that now he had an opportunity of getting rid of both Etherington and Miller in the same evening.

The only cloud on the horizon was that he had had no word from England on the origin of the warehouse fire. It appeared that the police there thought the fire really had started of its own accord. His man in London had told him that the police had found nothing suspicious so far. How different, he thought, from the police in Nigeria, who would find whatever they were paid to find.

He was just speculating as to which style of policing he preferred when there was a soft knock at the door and Habu came in quietly.

'Akinkobi is here, Ngale.'

'Good,' said the Ngale, standing up and closing the box. 'I will see him in the sitting room.'

'Shall I bring beer, Ngale?'

'No, thank you. He will only be here a moment.'

'Yes, Ngale.'

The Ngale locked the box before going through to the main room to greet his guest.

'Akinkobi. Good afternoon. Thank you for coming.'

'The road is very bad, Ngale. I am sorry I am so slow.'

The Ngale waved the apology aside. 'The faras, yes, I know all about them. But I have not asked you here to talk about them.'

The Ngale sat on one of his sofas but did not offer for Akinkobi to sit down.

'You heard what happened to Akin in London?'

'Yes, our father. Very bad.'

'He was a good man. You grew up together, I believe.'

'Yes, sah. I am very sad.'

'Quite so. I want the man responsible punished.'

'Yes, Ngale.'

'And I want you to do it for me.'

'Thank you, Ngale.'

'Good. The man is in Kano. He is a white man.'

'In Kano, sah?'

'Yes. Now, do you know where the Tropical Crops Institute Rest House is?'

'Dr Peter?' said Akinkobi with some alarm. 'I know him.'

'No, no. Not Dr Peter, of course. But the man who killed Akin will be at Dr Peter's house this evening. He is at my rest house now.'

'The Ngale rest house, sah?'

'Yes,' said the Ngale, drumming his fingers on his knee. 'He does not know I suspect him.'

'But I can go to your rest house now, sah,' said Akinkobi. 'I want to go now.'

The Ngale smiled. 'Maybe,' he said. 'But I want you to do it this evening. Now, listen. At a quarter to seven tonight, the man will be driven from my rest house to Dr Peter's. You are to follow him but he must *not* see you. Is that clear?'

'He will not see me, Ngale.'

'Good. When he is near Dr Peter's, he will get out of his car and walk to the house. Again he is not to see you so you must not go into the side road until his car has been in there for two minutes. Do you understand?'

'Yes, two minutes, Ngale.'

'Right. Then you are to drive into the side road. When the man's driver sees you, he will leave and you will park opposite the gate of Dr Peter's house. You will wait there for the white man to come out and, when he does, you will shoot him. Do you understand?'

'Yes, Ngale.'

'Good. Now repeat what I have told you.'

Akinkobi did so, word for word.

'Fine,' said the Ngale when Akinkobi had finished. 'You will do this for Akin.'

'I want to do it, Ngale.'

'You may go now.'

'Thank you, Ngale.'

One cold Star beer and the prospect of several more had improved Laurie's mood. His head still ached and his feet hurt but at least he was out of the heat and feeling reasonably satisfied with what he had done. He had even remembered to take his pills and now he was only one or two compartments behind.

'Was that the last flight out?' Jaygo asked.

'I should think so,' said Laurie. 'I didn't see any other planes. And, come to think of it, I didn't see yours either. Are you sure it's still there?'

'Oh yes,' she said. 'Sven rang last night and they found space for it in Jack Ngale's shed thing on the far side of the airport.'

'Is he really called Sven?' asked Peter.

'One of them is,' said Jaygo. 'But I don't know which one.'

'And what do they do all day while you're gallivanting around? Just sit there and play cards?'

'I don't know what they do,' she said. 'They can play with each other as far as I'm concerned.'

'Well,' said Laurie, 'I hope you told them to lay in plenty of supplies. If Peter is right about the locusts, they won't be able to get about much in the next few days.'

'Ah,' said Jaygo. 'Actually, we may not be staying after all.'

'What?' said Laurie, surprised. 'I thought you two were set for the duration?'

Jaygo looked at Peter. 'Are you going to tell him?' she said.

'Tell me what?' said Laurie. 'Have I missed something?'

'I think Jay had better tell you,' said Peter. 'It will save her interrupting me.'

So Jaygo began to tell her story from the point when she had read Tom Collis's letter. But it was Peter who did the interrupting, mainly at the point where she was missing out parts of Oladi's account and where she skated over what they had decided to do with her find.

'Hold on,' said Laurie. 'If you touched it but didn't actually *see* it, how do you know it's what you think it is?'

'Of course it's the torque,' said Jaygo. 'It was where it said it was in the book and it's as big as it's supposed to be.'

'No,' corrected Peter. 'We haven't actually read the book. There are some pages missing and apparently it doesn't actually say how big it is.'

'We could hardly have taken it to the door to check, could we?' said Jaygo. '"Oh, sorry Oladi. Just checking to see if this is the Idona Zaki. You carry on at the dye pit."'

'I'm sure it's the real thing,' said Peter. 'I ran my hand right along it to the end. It's the torque all right.'

'Could you tell how big the emeralds were?'

317

Peter held up his forefinger and thumb in a circle. 'Like golf balls.'

'Oh, my God,' said Laurie.

'Don't get all excited,' said Jaygo. 'Peter says they won't be cut properly and may not be worth all that much.'

'What do you mean, "not cut properly"?'

'Don't ask me,' said Jaygo. 'Apparently Peter is a gem-stone expert which is something I didn't know.'

'No,' said Peter patiently. 'I'm not an expert but the stones must be at least three hundred years old and there was no tradition of gem-cutting here in those days, so they will only be crudely chipped into shape.'

'I don't know why we are sitting here talking about what they might or might not look like,' said Jaygo. 'In an hour it will be dark and we can go and get the bloody thing and look at it. I'm going up to pack. Laurie?'

'I'm packed already, aren't I?' said Laurie waving to his case. 'And that's Aurelia's, by the way.'

'She actually got on the plane without it, did she?' asked Peter. 'She won't be very pleased.'

'Mea culpa again,' said Laurie. 'But you can give it to her, can't you?'

'Mmm,' went Jaygo. 'I think we may have to settle for posting it on. Look, are we going straight from the church to the airport or are we coming back here first?'

'Coming back here first,' said Peter. 'I'll drive the Land Rover to the church and you two can do the heavy lifting. Then we come back here, put it in the cello case, pop it in the car and drive to the plane.'

'My cases won't all fit in one car,' said Jaygo. 'Not with the cello case as well.'

'Leave the cases then, 'said Peter. 'They'll still be here at the end of next week.'

'Ah,' said Jaygo after a slight pause.

'What is that supposed to mean?' asked Peter.

'Are we actually *coming* back?'

'Of course we are.'

'Yes, but do we actually *need* to?'

'Yes,' said Peter. 'The CD launch. The Institute. Laurie's book, for God's sake. Of course we "*need*" to come back.'

'Oh,' she said vaguely. 'Mmmm.'

'Laurie?' said Peter, turning to him.

'Don't look at me, old boy. I just do what I'm told.'

Peter turned back to Jaygo. 'Are you serious?' he said.

'No,' she said defensively. 'It's just a possibility, that's all. All sorts of things are possible.'

'OK,' said Peter, finally. 'One case each it is then and a small one at that.'

'But that's two for you,' said Jaygo. 'Aurelia's counts as yours.'

'Well, you want to bring the torque, don't you? I think that counts as one too.'

She was about to answer when there was a loud thump and a rattling noise from the window.

'What the hell was that?' said Peter jumping up.

'It's the locusts,' said Laurie quickly. 'Like last night.'

'Christ, look at them!' Peter said, suddenly pointing at the window.

Wave after wave of locusts were banging against the window, as if someone were playing a dozen fire hoses, loaded with pebbles, onto the back of the house.

'Get back, Peter!' shouted Jaygo. 'The glass will break!'

A few seconds later the hail of locusts stopped as suddenly as it had begun.

The three of them ran to the window and looked out into the garden.

'That was a hell of a shower,' said Peter. 'I've never seen anything like it! More over there, look. They must be two foot deep by that tree. And look over there,' he said excitedly, pointing at the sky. 'Another lot is coming down beyond those houses! Get the camera quickly, Laurie!'

'Oh no!' said Laurie. 'I'm not going out. Walking on them all day is enough locusts for me. You help yourself if you want, old boy.'

'Is this the beginning of the swarm, Peter?' said Jaygo, taking his arm.

'No,' he said, leaning forwards to see more clearly. 'They're not flying. These are still mostly dead ones.'

'They're not dead,' she said. 'I can see them moving from here. It's beginning to be like you said. Two feet of yellow dog food.'

'No,' said Peter, pointing upwards. 'This lot that just came down must still be blowing off the top of the swarm and coming ahead. They're alive but too weak to fly properly because they haven't been able to get down and feed.'

He turned back into the room and looked at Laurie and Jaygo in turn.

'The ones in the lower swarm will all be alive and they will come in a solid wall and not in waves like this.'

'But, Peter, 'she said, tugging his arm. 'You said it wouldn't be two feet deep until the big swarm got here and it's more than that in places already.'

'It's not even,' he said. 'They won't be this deep everywhere.'

'What about the airport?' she asked. 'Could a plane take off if they were this deep?'

He looked at her. 'We just have to hope so,' he said. 'It will depend on how high off the ground the engines are.'

'The Lear's engines are on the tail,' she said. 'That's quite high up, isn't it? But I was thinking of the wheels. Won't they get stuck?'

'The wheels won't be a problem,' he said. 'The locusts aren't very solid and they won't stop the plane going along. But if they get into the engines, it could be a different story.'

'But do you actually know that?' said Laurie.

'It's a reasonable guess,' said Peter. 'If they are mainly dead and on the ground I don't think it will be a problem.'

Jago tugged at his arm again. 'Come on,' she said. 'I think we had better get on and get the toothbrushes packed.'

There was some debate in the bedroom as to which of Jaygo's suitcases counted as 'small'. Eventually she decided on the second largest one and proceeded to pack it as tightly as she could.

When she was sitting on it to try to close it, she said, 'Do you think we should call Jack and tell him we're going?'

'Probably,' said Peter. 'Do you want me to do it?'

'No,' she said, going over to collect the telephone from her bag. 'My idea. And I might be able to sweet-talk him a bit about the launch.'

'He won't mind,' said Peter. 'We'll only be gone a few days.'

'Possibly,' she said, beginning to key in the number. 'But he might not think we're coming back.'

'But we are coming back, Jay.'

'Jack, hello,' she said. 'Fine. If you count a foot and a half of locusts as fine.'

Peter lay down on the bed and put his hands behind his head.

Jaygo began to screw her face up with concentration. 'It's not a terribly good line, Jack. Can you hear me all right? What? At seven? But we are getting packed to go back to London for a few days. Can't it wait until we get back next week? What's that? But not before seven?'

Jaygo put her other hand up to the telephone and held it tightly to the side of her head. 'Peter's here now if you want to talk to him. No, not Aurelia. She went on the London flight. But Laurie's still here. Shall we bring him with us?'

She listened again for a while as Peter watched her.

'Why not?' she said. 'What do you mean it's not to do with him? He's my Press agent.'

Another pause.

'Oh, all right then, if you insist. Just me and Peter. Yes, Jack, seven on the dot.'

She took the telephone from her ear and switched it off.

'He says he wants to see us this evening but doesn't want Laurie there. What shall I tell him?'

'Did Jack say why?'

'Not really. Except that he just wanted it to be between the three of us.'

'Curious.'

'And he sounded a bit too friendly,' she went on. 'Oily.'

'He always sounds a bit oily to me.'

'Patronising then.'

'That sounds like him too,' said Peter, getting up from the bed. 'I'll go and put the cases in the car for later.'

'And he says we can't go just yet,' she added. 'He wants us there on the stroke of seven because there is something he has to get ready first.'

Peter looked at his watch. 'We'll have to set off now anyway,' he said. 'We don't know what the roads will be like.'

At exactly twenty to seven, Peter brought the Land Rover round to the front of the house and parked it against Robert's carefully swept terrace.

'They really do smell, Peter. I think I'll remember it for the rest of my life,' said Jaygo, climbing up and taking her seat next to him

'I thought you didn't mind them,' he said. 'Why don't you bring a few along for a snack on the way?'

'Don't!' she said. 'I can't believe I did that.'

He smiled and started the engine.

'How far is it to Jack's?' said Jaygo as she took her seat.

'It's the other side of Sabon Gari, about twenty minutes if the roads aren't too bad.'

321

'Can we go to Sabon Gari on the way back then?'

'Could do. Fancy a bit of last-minute shopping?'

'Not exactly,' she said.

'Ah.'

'It won't be so easy without Laurie to help us but it would mean not having to come back again later.'

'I suppose so.'

'You don't sound very enthusiastic.'

'I'm not,' he said. 'I still think we should leave it where it is.'

'Well, we're not going to and that's that.'

After Peter and Jaygo had left, Laurie finished his beer at leisure before taking his camera from his suitcase.

I ought to take some more photographs, he thought. It might look very different next week so I had better get on with it.

He took another roll of film from his briefcase and caught up on a compartment of pills while he was at it.

Come back here? he thought. I must be mad. And if the headache gets any worse I won't be able to anyway. But what would I say to Peter and Jay? 'Sorry folks, my travelling days are done?'

Perhaps that's being a bit defeatist, he concluded as he carefully loaded the film. I ought to go on being as normal as possible for as long as possible. That's what Chris would have done, isn't it? At least he was spared all this. The endless pills. The loathsome clinic. The 'count'.

I could have been his Buddy if the worst had happened to him, he told himself as he went into the kitchen to collect a torch. Done something useful with my life. But that's all finished now, isn't it? And here I am, miles from bloody anywhere, ferrying women to the airport and taking pictures of dead insects while my friends go out for a few drinks.

He waved a greeting to Halima, who was sitting at the kitchen table peeling beans, and went out into the garden.

Thoughts of a more menacing nature occupied John Etherington twenty yards down the road. He checked his automatic pistol. Click open, click shut. Safety off. Into his right-side pocket where he could reach it most easily. Bugger you, Jack, he thought. What the hell am I doing this for? Because you didn't leave me much alternative, that's why.

He looked at the Ngale's satellite telephone in the open briefcase

322

on the seat next to him. He picked it up and put it in his other jacket pocket.

I might need it in case something goes wrong, he thought. But nothing was going to go wrong. There was only one man alone in a house. And that man was his ticket to Nairobi.

'Now, look,' he said, leaning over the front seat to the driver. 'I might be ten minutes. You wait here, keep the engine running and don't move one inch.'

From his position sitting at the front of the house, the night-watch could see Etherington come into the drive.

Robert raised himself awkwardly to his feet, using the rifle as a support. It looked like a Sunday Man coming but why was he on foot? He held the rifle in front of him just to be sure. It was dark and Sunday Men never came without a car.

Etherington saw the old man raise the rifle and panicked. Christ, he thought, it's a trap! He pulled the pistol from his pocket and fired.

Etherington missed but immediately Robert raised his rifle to his shoulder and began shouting.

Etherington steadied his hand and fired two more shots, hitting the old man in the shoulder and the stomach.

Robert shrieked and fell back against the wall, dropping the rifle.

Etherington ran the few remaining yards to the house. When he reached the terrace he pushed Robert's rifle away and kicked him as he lay there holding his stomach.

Etherington inched his way carefully towards the front door. He tried the handle and was relieved to find the door unlocked. He slowly opened it a few inches before taking his pistol in both hands, pushing the door further open with his foot and carefully going into the house.

Laurie had heard the shouting and the shots from the back garden. He thought he recognised the voice as Robert's but did not know what the cracking noises had been. More curious than anxious, he walked around the side of the house past the garage and around to the front terrace.

By now, Robert had raised himself to his knees and was beginning to crawl along to the garage door.

'Christ, man! What's happened?' cried Laurie as soon as he saw him. 'What have you done?'

'No, sah. Relver, sah,' said Robert through clenched teeth.

'Was it a shot? Are you hurt?' said Laurie, getting down on one knee. 'Blood! You've been hit?'

'Hit, sah. Get relver in garage, sah.'

'What relver? Is it your shoulder?'

'No, sah, Laurie. You get relver. Officer relver from blanket.'

'Oh, shit,' said Laurie, suddenly understanding. 'You want the revolver from the blanket?'

Robert shut his eyes and nodded towards the garage door. 'In there, sah. You, sah.'

Laurie looked towards the garage door and back to Robert.

Robert's eyes were tight shut and he was moving his head from side to side in pain.

'You mean me?' said Laurie with rising panic in his voice.

Robert nodded vigorously with his eyes still shut.

'But I can't,' said Laurie. 'I don't know what to do.'

Robert's body went slack and he collapsed forwards onto the terrace.

From inside the house came the sound of a woman screaming followed by a man shouting, a single shot and then silence.

Laurie saw the open front door and then looked back at Robert by his feet.

Laurie quickly knelt down to turn Robert over. The old man's eyes and mouth were open and he was not moving at all. He looked dead.

Laurie slowly stood up. He rubbed the side of his face with his hands. 'Don't worry, old chap,' he said out loud. 'Leave this next bit to me.'

Inside the garage he hurried over to the neatly folded blanket and haversack by the far wall.

He had never used a pistol before but thought it should be reasonably straightforward. He quickly unfolded the blanket, unwrapped the Browning and began loading the cylinder with rounds from the little box.

It should be just like a rifle, he thought. Put the bullets in, flick off the safety, point it in the general direction of whatever and shoot.

But at a person? And who the hell was in the house anyway?

After Etherington had shot Halima, he made his way back into the sitting room. The place is empty, he thought. Or maybe he's upstairs? But if he's up there, he's not going anywhere and I've got some time to think. And time to reload.

He sat down on the sofa and put the pistol next to him. He took the telephone from his pocket and placed it on the table in front of him, reaching into his pocket for the automatic pistol rounds.

While he was doing this, Laurie came into the room with the service revolver held out in front of him in both hands. 'Don't move!' he shouted. 'Not a bloody inch!'

Etherington's head shot up and he began reaching for his pistol.

'I said "Don't move"!' shouted Laurie again. 'You move at all and I'll shoot you.'

Etherington slowly raised his hands above his head. 'No,' he said. 'Please don't shoot.'

'Stand up and come away from that gun.'

Etherington stood up slowly with his hands above his head.

As he reached his full height, Laurie suddenly recognised him. 'I know you,' he said, 'John Etherington. What the hell are you doing here?'

'Please don't shoot me!'

'I said tell me what you are doing here,' said Laurie, feeling suddenly very uncertain. 'Are you John Etherington or not?'

'Yes, I am,' said Etherington. 'But I can explain. Please put the gun down.'

'I will not!' said Laurie, gripping the revolver more tightly.

Laurie's sudden movement was enough. His fingers squeezed the fine trigger mechanism and the gun fired.

The round hit Etherington in the chest and he was thrown back by the force of the shot, over the top of the sofa and out of Laurie's sight.

Laurie stepped forward slowly, the pistol still held out in front of him, his arms beginning to shake. He brought the Browning down slowly as he looked at Etherington.

He reached out gingerly with his foot and pushed the motionless body.

Etherington seemed to be dead. Laurie lowered the pistol to his side and knelt down.

Etherington had landed on his side and, as Laurie turned him onto his back, the head rolled limply over and banged onto the floor.

Laurie stood up and looked down at the body.

I've shot a man, he thought. Someone with his hands up. But what's John Etherington doing here? And why did he shoot the night-watch?

And how did he get here? he went on to himself. There's no car in the drive. Did he walk? Surely not. It's night.

Laurie walked to the front door and looked out cautiously. Robert's body was still lying where he had fallen and outside the gates, up the drive, Laurie could see the headlights of a parked car.

He brought the Browning around in front of him again and held it pointing down in both hands as he walked slowly towards the gate.

Akinkobi had been sitting in the dark and his eyes were more accustomed to the gloom. He saw Laurie before Laurie saw him.

It was a simple matter for Akinkobi to bring the hunting rifle up to his shoulder and shoot. He was one of the Ngale's best men and at that range he could hardly miss.

The single shot hit Laurie in the middle of his chest and the man knew he would not need to fire again as Laurie spun around and went down.

Evening activities at the Ngale's house were much more civilised.

He was elegantly dressed in a white dinner-jacket complete with wing collar as he invited Peter and Jaygo to sit down.

'Really, Jack,' said Jaygo. 'You didn't tell us this was to be formal. I'd have put on a special frock for you if I'd known.'

'Not at all, my dear,' he said smiling. 'I'm afraid I am due to dine with the Emir at ten and he loves the formal touch. Tell me, what do I call you now you have come to Kano to launch your African career, Jocasta or Jaygo?'

'Jocasta,' she replied.

'The Emir?' questioned Peter. 'I thought you didn't want to have anything to do with him.'

'I wouldn't usually,' said the Ngale. 'But he seems to think this locust business calls for a meeting and he has invited me to dinner. But where are my manners? Let me offer you a drink. Jocasta? Some wine? Perhaps some juice?'

'G and T, please Jack,' said Jaygo.

'And for you, Peter?'

'The same, please Jack. That would be very nice.'

The Ngale waved at a hovering Habu before sitting down on a sofa opposite Peter and Jaygo. 'Now,' he began, 'I expect you are wondering why I asked you to join me at such short notice.'

'We're going to London until the launch, Jack. It was tonight or not at all.'

The Ngale raised his eyebrows a little.

'I see. However, before I come to the point, I want to talk to Peter a little about the swarm.'

'Oh, yes?' said Peter.

'Unfortunately it seems I was a shade optimistic. As you rightly point out, I don't like the Emir. But I have to admit he knows more about what happens a hundred miles north of here than I do.'

'Isn't that where the swarm is now?' asked Jaygo.

'There or thereabouts,' replied the Ngale. 'But it seems it's a much bigger swarm than even our friend McKecnie thought.'

They paused while Habu came in with the drinks on a silver tray. Habu touched his knee and went out.

'Yes, much bigger,' the Ngale continued. 'And it's moving much faster than we were led to believe. It really has done a lot of damage to the north and I am afraid Kano will be next.'

'I told you it was a Lion Swarm, Jack. You wouldn't listen.'

'No,' said the Ngale firmly. 'It's not a Lion Swarm. There's no such thing but it is nevertheless a very big swarm and we are going to need some outside help in dealing with it.'

'What sort of help?' said Jaygo, picking up her drink and pressing the slice of lemon against the inside of her glass with her finger before licking it.

Peter frowned at her and she briefly stuck her tongue out at him.

The Ngale was picking up his glass and so did not notice this little exchange. 'Well,' he continued, 'the aid agencies are standing by. The Red Cross, MSF, the usual ones. And who knows, we may even get the Americans to chip in but somehow I doubt it.'

'They must think it's going to be pretty bad if they're ready to come in even before it's happened,' said Peter.

'That's one way of looking at it,' said the Ngale. 'In a curious way, the worse the locusts are, the better it will be for my people in the long run.'

'I'm sorry, but I don't see how any good can come of it,' said Peter.

'Don't be so parochial, Peter,' said the Ngale, smiling. 'Look at the wider picture. Let us suppose for a moment that it was some sort of raging forest fire rather than locusts. Ultimately that could be cleansing, don't you think? An opportunity for regeneration.'

'Cleansing?' said Jaygo. 'Peter says they're going to leave a horrid sticky mess.'

'In the city, that may be true,' said the Ngale. 'But in the

327

country it will disperse rather more quickly. Perhaps in just a few days.'

'Leaving nothing at all growing in the way of crops,' said Peter. 'And if it's a really big swarm, hardly any of the crops will recover. Planting will have to begin again if you can call that "regeneration".'

'I wasn't thinking so much of agricultural regeneration,' said the Ngale. 'More financial.'

He smiled at his guests as if he knew something they did not.

'I can see you don't know what I mean,' he said.

'I'm afraid not, Jack,' said Peter. 'I think it will be a disaster, however you play it.'

'Not so,' said the Ngale, walking over to his hi-fi. 'Jocasta, my dear, may I play some of your excellent music for us?'

Jaygo smiled politely but perhaps a little too sweetly at him. 'That would be nice, Jack. The new CD?'

'Of course,' he said, pressing a button and listening to the music begin for a moment before returning to his seat.

'Quite wonderful. I think you have captured the feel of the music exactly,' he said.

'Thank you,' said Jaygo, 'I like it too. But you were just about to tell us something more about the swarm.'

'I was.' The Ngale put the tips of his fingers together. 'You see, I am afraid the farming people, my people many of them, share the same burden of agricultural debt that so many do in what I think you call "the developing countries". Some people think of it as a colonial legacy but that is not important. What matters, and I am sure you will correct me if I am wrong, Peter, is that they do not stand a cat in hell's chance of ever paying it off. Isn't that so?'

'Yes,' said Peter. 'But it's not a new problem and a failed growing season can only make it worse.'

The Ngale smiled again. 'But what if the aid agencies persuaded the World Bank to pool the debts into one and nullified them?'

Peter shook his head. 'We have talked about that before. They never do it, even after major disasters. They simply cannot afford to set a precedent. Help one country out after a natural disaster and you have to help them all.'

'That may be true of storms or floods, Peter, but locusts such as we experience, only happen here in West Africa. They are not going to strike with such severity anywhere else and so there would be no danger of a precedent being set.'

'They still won't do it,' said Peter. 'You know they won't.'

'Peter, in the long run, there is no alternative to cancelling the debts. We all know that even if not everyone is prepared to come out and say it. I think the time is right, and so does the Emir, for the Bank to practise its humanity on a small scale to see how it works out. They will have to do it one day and they won't find a better opportunity than our present little problem to experiment with.'

'Cancel the debt?' said Peter, shaking his head again. 'I don't think you're serious, Jack.'

'I am very serious about it, Peter. If the Emir, myself and the big aid agencies combine our efforts in Washington, we have a very good chance of succeeding.'

Peter swirled the ice in his glass thoughtfully before speaking. 'Washington? You and the Emir?'

'Well, not myself,' said the Ngale. 'He will go with the head of the Red Cross and MSF. I think my place is at home at a time like this. I am much more closely in touch with my people than he is with his. They will need me here in the coming days.'

Peter thought again and looked over at Jaygo before replying. 'A fresh start? Do you really think it's possible?'

The Ngale folded his arms. 'I do. And with the debt gone, along with the endless stream of "expert monitors" that comes with it, we can be free to make our own investment. I have considerable resources waiting to be utilised. I can use them for my own people to develop the crops and markets *they* choose and not those decided for us on the other side of the world.'

Peter looked at the Ngale and thought of what they had seen in the warehouse in London. Of what Laurie had told him about the Ngale's 'markets' in Eastern Europe and South Africa. I wonder just what 'crops and markets' you have in mind, Jack, he thought to himself.

'It all sounds a bit complicated to me,' said Jaygo.

The Ngale smiled patronisingly at her. 'I'm afraid international politics *are* a bit complicated, Jocasta. And that is why so few people succeed at them. I just try to stay focused on what opportunities present themselves and to utilise them for the benefit of my people.'

The Ngale looked from Jaygo to Peter. 'My people are very important to me and I am to them.

'And that brings me to what I have asked you here to see,' he continued. 'Because, as of today, Jocasta, yours are not the only beautiful green eyes here in Kano.

'If you will follow me,' he said, standing up, 'I will show you something that is as important to my people as I am myself.'

Peter and Jaygo exchanged a rapid glance that the Ngale did not see and Peter shook his head briefly at her.

'There is something in that room,' he said, pointing to the study, 'that has been missing for a very long time.'

He turned to them as he unlocked the door.

'I can tell from your expression, Peter, that you have already guessed what it is. And perhaps Jocasta will recognise it when she sees it.'

'The Idona Zaki?' said Peter. 'Surely you don't mean it?'

'Precisely,' said the Ngale, switching on a single overhead light. 'Are you ready?'

Without waiting for them to reply he opened the wooden box to reveal the gold torque resting on its black velvet. The overhead light showed it to its maximum advantage. The gold shone with a deep and even sheen. The brightness caught the green of the stones and cast little points of light on the darkened wall of the study.

'Home at last,' said the Ngale quietly.

Jaygo gripped Peter's hand very tightly as they looked down on the spectacular imitation.

The Ngale rubbed his hand over the torque as if to free it from a speck of dust.

'Where was it?' said Peter at last.

The Ngale ran a finger absently over the torque again. 'In Rome,' he said, almost to himself. 'Think of all the searching that has gone on here in Nigeria and it was safe in Rome all along.'

'Rome?' said Jaygo, leaning over to get a better look at it. 'What was it doing in Rome?'

'Ah,' said the Ngale. 'That is a long story, Jocasta, and I am sure Peter knows it nearly as well as I do myself. Perhaps he will tell it to you. But for now what matters is that it is back where it belongs. With me.'

Jaygo reached out a hand to touch it but the Ngale took her arm and gently pulled it back. 'Forgive me,' he said, 'but I am a little superstitious about people touching it. The last Ngale who let that happen paid a very high price. I'm sorry.'

He closed the lid of the box and waved a hand back toward the sitting room.

'I don't think I have ever seen anything so beautiful,' said Jaygo.

'I agree,' said Peter as they went back into the main room.

330

'It is simply magnificent. You must feel a tremendous sense of achievement having it here again.'

The Ngale smiled modestly. 'I confess I do allow myself a little pride on that score, Peter.'

'But what will you do with it now?' asked Jaygo.

'What people normally do with such a national treasure,' said the Ngale as he locked the study door. 'Put it in a museum for people to come and see. It is the torque of the Ngales but it belongs to my people as much as it does to me.'

'When will you tell them you have it?'

'Tomorrow,' said the Ngale. 'The best day, I think.'

'But that's when the locusts might be here,' said Jaygo. 'Surely there couldn't be a *worse* day?'

'Not so, Jocasta. If the locusts are only half as bad as Peter here predicts then my people will be much in need of something to lift their flagging spirits.

'I wanted you to see it,' he said. 'But I must insist on your discretion until tomorrow's announcement. I know I can trust you because you are two of my oldest friends but I think you can understand now why I did not ask Mr Miller to attend.'

'You should have showed it to him,' said Jaygo, picking up her drink. 'He could have taken a picture of it and taken it to London for release.'

'Ah, well,' said the Ngale. 'Perhaps I know one or two things about Laurie Miller and his activities that you do not. I prefer to leave him out of things.'

'Hang on,' said Jaygo, 'Laurie's an old friend of mine. What do you mean?'

'I don't say he's not a friend but some things are better handled by my own publicity people. You deal with journalists every day, Jocasta, and I am sure you would agree that some things are best done by your own people.'

Jaygo was about to reply when Peter put a hand on her arm. 'Let Jack's people handle it.'

'Thank you, Peter,' said the Ngale. 'It's wonderful to see you two here in Kano and thank you very much for coming this evening. I look forward to more time together next week-end. I am sorry if the new CD has been rather overshadowed by events but, launching it next week-end will make an excellent addition to the beginning of what I hope will be a very good time for us all.'

'No, Jack,' said Peter, 'it is for us to thank you for sharing the finding of the torque with us. We're very privileged, aren't we, Jocasta?' he added, squeezing her arm.

'Oh, yes,' she said. 'Thank you, Jack. We'll keep our fingers crossed for you the entire time we are away.'

The Ngale looked at his watch. 'Now, if you don't mind, there are one or two calls I have to make before I go for my dinner with the Emir.'

'Of course, Jack,' said Peter.

Jaygo put her empty glass down and the three of them walked to the door.

'And don't forget, Peter,' said the Ngale, smiling as he held the door open for them, 'there are no lions these days in Nigeria.'

As soon as they were in the Land Rover and safely out of earshot, Jaygo began. 'Honestly, Peter, did you ever see such a loathsome, slimy, vain, puffed up, oily . . . well I don't know what he is.'

Peter laughed as he pulled out of the gate. 'Gone off him a bit, have you?'

'What was all that about anyway?' she said. 'Negotiating with the World Bank. Who does he think he is, for God's sake?'

'It's not as crazy as you think,' said Peter. 'Laurie knows much more about it than I do. You should ask him.'

'And talking of Laurie,' she went on, 'why on earth *not* let him see the torque? Jack can't seriously think we're not going to tell him, can he?'

'I think you're right,' he said. 'There is something distinctly odd about not asking him. Perhaps Laurie will have a better idea about that than us.'

They drove in silence for a few minutes before Jaygo spoke again. 'Ours is bigger,' she said. 'Much.'

He laughed. 'The beautiful thing is, now he's got that thing back there, and God knows where he cooked it up from, then he can hardly kick up a fuss if someone makes off with a different one, can he?'

'I hadn't thought of that,' she said, impressed. 'He's handed it to us on a plate, the silly bugger.'

'Let's just get it home before we get too excited,' said Peter.

'I think the one back there is a complete fake,' she said. 'Did you see those stones? They look as if they'd fallen off some Victorian chandelier.'

'I wouldn't know,' said Peter. 'Don't forget, as Laurie pointed out, we haven't actually *seen* our one yet.'

*   *   *

There had been a fresh fall of locusts at Sabon Gari and the square had an eerie, almost wintry look to it as they drove over the carpet of locusts. Peter parked with the back of the Land Rover up against the church steps.

'What about Oladi?' said Jaygo. 'What if he comes?'

'Let's just get on with it,' said Peter. 'With any luck, he'll be in his house with all hatches battened down.'

'OK. Have you got a torch?'

'Under the seat.'

'That's lucky.'

'Not lucky,' he said. 'There's always one there.'

'Practical as well as clever.'

'Shut up. Just don't turn it on until we are in the church, and keep it pointed down.'

'I'm not a complete fool, you know. What if the church is locked at night?'

'You are beginning to sound like me,' he said. 'Come on.'

'Yes, sir.'

The door was not locked and, as they made their way up the aisle, Peter took the torch and shone it down with his fingers held half over the front.

'It's nice not to be walking on locusts for a change,' she whispered.

'You don't have to whisper,' he said.

'It's a church. You whisper in churches.'

'It was a church this afternoon and you didn't whisper then.'

She ignored him. 'We didn't bring anything to carry it in,' she said.

'You said we could take one of Oladi's pieces of cloth.'

'Won't he mind?'

'Well, we can pay him next week, can't we? Help me get the wooden thing off.'

'Wooden icon,' she corrected him as she put her hand into the long central crack and pulled.

The wood was even more fragile than Peter had expected and it soon broke away. A minute later Peter was training the torch down on the torque. It was certainly bigger than the one in the Ngale's house but not frightfully impressive.

The metal was dark, not gold. Peter rubbed at the surface with his free hand but it remained stubbornly black.

'It's not made of gold,' he announced. 'Even if it was old, it would

333

still shine if it was gold. Look,' he said. 'Not even a sheen.'

'Let me see.' She reached down. 'It's just a coating. Varnish or glue or something.'

She scratched with her nail and a flake came away. She quickly shone the torch at the mark and was greeted by the sight of a deep golden colour from the metal beneath.

Peter scratched some more of the coating away in another place.

'Gold,' he said. 'All of it.'

'Told you,' she said. 'Now let's look at the stones.'

She rubbed at the two shapes at either end of the torque. They felt like broken flints to her but, when she took her hands away, they could both see the deep green colour of West African emeralds glinting in the torchlight.

'I can hardly believe it,' said Peter. 'All those years and it was here all along.'

'Never mind the history lesson. Let's just get it out of here. You go round to that side and we'll see how heavy it is.'

It was much heavier than they had expected and the two of them could only just lift it from the top of the altar onto the floor.

'We'll never manage it,' he said. 'Perhaps we can drag it somehow.'

'We'll do it in stages,' she said. 'Now, lift again.'

Once they were past the broken statue and down the altar steps, they made better progress. Soon they were carrying it sideways, flat between them like some grotesque crab.

'Keep going,' he grunted. 'If they brought it all the way from the coast, we can get it to the door.'

'There were more of them,' she said between breaths.

Two minutes later the torque was lying on the ground just inside the door as they rested and caught their breath.

'We'll need one of those cloths now,' said Peter after a minute. 'We can't take it down the steps like this.'

'Give me the torch while I go and get one,' she said. 'You go down and open up the back of the Land Rover.'

As Peter went out of the door, he heard a familiar voice call to him from across the square. 'Sunday Man? Is that you, sah?'

'Yes, Oladi,' said Peter in a voice he hoped was loud enough for Jaygo to hear. 'Hello.'

'What are you here for?' asked Oladi with uncertainty in his voice.

334

'It's Tuareg,' said Peter. 'She has lost a ring and thinks it may have fallen off here.'

'I can look for you, sah. I have a torch.'

'Uh? No, that's all right, Oladi,' said Peter.

Jaygo appeared at the door of the church holding up her hand. 'Hello, Oladi.'

'You are losing a ring, Tuareg?' asked Oladi.

'Yes, but I've found it now, thank you. It was on the wooden lady.'

'Well, OK. But you should not be here, sah. Sabon Gari at night is a bad place.'

'I know,' said Peter. 'But we are not going to be very long.'

'You cannot be safe, sah. I will stay with you.'

'It's all right, Oladi,' said Jaygo. 'Sunday Man and I have to pray.'

'Pray, Tuareg?'

'Yes,' she said. 'To the Sunday Lady. About the faras.'

Oladi looked nonplussed.

'Yes,' went on Jaygo. 'To pray for them not to be bad.'

'I can wait by your Land car if you are inside.'

'No, it's all right,' said Jaygo firmly. 'We will come and see you to tell you when we have finished if you like. Please. We want to be alone. It is our way.'

'Oh,' said Oladi in a hurt voice. 'I want to help but I will go to my house if you say.'

'Yes, Oladi. I do say. Thank you.'

When Oladi had gone, Peter turned to Jaygo and said, 'Pray?'

'Well, I didn't see you come up with a better idea.'

'I said you'd lost your ring.'

She ignored him. 'I've got a cloth,' she said. 'Now open the back of the Land Rover and get it in before Oladi changes his mind.'

Wrapping the torque in the long, heavy cloth and manoeuvring it down the steps proved to be the most difficult part of the enterprise. They were both completely out of breath by the time Peter finally shut and locked the back of the Land Rover.

'I'll tell you another thing we forgot,' said Peter, rubbing his back.

'What now?' she said impatiently.

'Tom Collis's ashes. They are still at the house.'

'Then that's just another thing for next week, isn't it? Drive over to Oladi's place and I'll tell him we're going.'

Peter parked by the dye pits, which resembled little more than a series of locust-covered mounds. Jaygo carefully picked her way between them to meet Oladi who was standing outside his small house.

'What are you taking?' he said suspiciously. 'You are bringing something from the church.'

'One of your lovely big pieces of cloth, Oladi. How much will it be?'

'You can't take it,' he said. 'It is not finished in the church. I have to put it in the pit again. I can have a better one for you. A good one.'

'No, I'm sure that one will be fine. Now, how much is it?'

'They are big ones in the church. Very much. Why do you need a big one?'

'Wait, Oladi,' she said, holding up her hand. 'We can talk about it when the faras have gone. In the meantime, take this. It will be enough.' She took his hand and held his palm flat while she placed something in the middle of it and wrapped his fingers around it. 'Good luck, Oladi.'

Before he could answer or take what she had given him into the light to properly see what it was, Jaygo had hurried past the dye pits and was getting into the Land Rover.

'What was that about?' said Peter, driving off.

She held out her left hand in front of his face to show him that her engagement ring from Hugo was gone.

'Christ, Jay! That's a hell of a lot of money. For Oladi. For anyone, come to that.'

'Well, you said he didn't have much and now he has. And so do we.'

'If you say so.'

'Besides,' she said as they took the bumpy track out of the square, 'I want a nice new one. I fancy a big Amsterdam-cut emerald.'

Peter laughed. 'An emerald ring. That's not very lucky, you know. And it's the colour of jealousy.'

'Too right!' she said. 'If anyone so much as looks at you, I'll have her eyes out.'

The two of them laughed and they bumped past the point where Etherington's car had exploded the night before.

'I have to say,' said Jaygo, 'much as I like Santa Maria, it feels good to be going home. Just another few hours and we'll be out of here.'

*   *   *

The headlights picked out the hump of Laurie's body as soon as they turned into the drive of the house.

'What the hell is that?' said Peter. 'It looks like a body!'

'It can't be,' she said. 'It must be a pile of locusts.'

'No,' he said, climbing out with the torch. 'It looks like a person.'

'Get back in, Peter.'

But Peter was already shining the torch beyond the back of the Land Rover. 'No!' he cried.

'What is it?' said Jaygo in alarm, climbing across the front seat.

'Oh, my God, it's Laurie. Look at him!' she cried, kneeling down next to the body. 'His chest, Peter! It's all gone!' She put her hand up to cover her mouth.

Peter helped Jaygo to her feet.

'What's happened?' said Peter. 'What is he doing here?'

'The house, Peter. There must be someone there! The others!'

She slipped out of Peter's arm and started running through the locusts towards the house.

'No, Jaygo! Stop!' he shouted and ran after her.

Jaygo had already reached the terrace and was standing in front of the slumped body of Robert by the time he caught up with her.

'He's dead too,' she said. 'They're both dead.'

'But Laurie was shot by the gate,' said Peter looking back. 'He must have been chasing someone.'

'What do we do, Peter?' said Jaygo.

'We don't go in,' he said. 'There may be someone still inside.'

'But if Laurie was chasing someone, they must have gone,' she said.

'Or come back,' said Peter.

'Looters?' she said. 'Do you think they were waiting and saw us go out?'

'No. The night-watch was here. He's always here.'

'Then I say we go into the house,' she said.

'No, Jay. If they've come back, they'll still have a gun. We can't go in.'

'But we can't stay outside all night. And there was no car outside. We have to go in, Peter.'

'I'll go round to the back then. I'll call you if it's clear.'

He went around to the back door but came back a minute later to find Jago crouched down at the corner of the house.

'It's locked,' he said. 'The curtains in the kitchen are closed. I could see into the sitting room and the lights are on but there's no one inside.

'I say we go in,' he added. 'I'll go first and you follow.'

'Please be careful, Peter,' she said as he went down on all fours and began to crawl to the still open front door.

'I will be,' he said. 'You can be sure of that.'

He saw Etherington's feet sticking out from behind the sofa as soon as he entered into the sitting room.

He crawled over as quietly as he could and did not stand up until he saw that whoever it was lying behind the sofa, was dead too.

'Jaygo,' he called, 'it's all right. You can come in now.'

'Who's that?' she said, taking Peter's arm. 'He's white.'

'I've never seen him before in my life. But he doesn't look like a looter to me.'

'Who is he then? And Halima, where is she?'

She let go of Peter's arm and went into the kitchen.

'I'll see if he's got a wallet or something,' said Peter, getting down on one knee and peeling back Etherington's blood-soaked jacket. He took a long wallet from the inside pocket.

'Peter!' called Jaygo. 'Come in here!'

In the kitchen, Jaygo was turning Halima onto her back.

Halima's face was unmarked apart from a splattering of blood but her mouth hung open and her staring eyes told them she too was dead.

'This is carnage,' said Peter flatly.

He peeled open the wallet, which was sticky with blood, and pulled out a maroon passport with gold lettering.

'Four people, Peter,' Jaygo was saying. 'Three people we know.'

'It's Nigerian,' said Peter. 'It's a Nigerian Diplomatic. Oh, my God, you know who I think this is? John Etherington!'

'Etherington!' exclaimed Jaygo. 'Then Laurie knew him. That's why he let him in. But why has he been shot too? Do you think it was by the same person? The one who ran away?'

'It doesn't make any sense otherwise. And yet Laurie said that John Etherington was working for the Ngale.'

'Jack?' she said, with horror. 'Do you think this could be some-thing to do with him?'

'I can't think it is,' said Peter. 'Let me see if this man has got anything else on him.'

Peter knelt down again and peeled back the other side of Etherington's jacket.

Jaygo put a hand on Peter's shoulder. 'If this man is John

Etherington and he works for Jack, then Jack has must have something to do with it.'

'That can't be true,' said Peter, finding nothing. 'We were with Jack not half an hour ago.'

'Yes and what for?'

'He wanted to show us the torque,' said Peter.

'Not Laurie,' she said, 'specifically not Laurie. Jack wanted *us* out of the house but not Laurie.'

'But this man has been shot too. And Laurie's over by the gate.'

'Perhaps Laurie shot him.'

'No,' said Peter. 'That's not possible. Laurie didn't have a gun. He would have told me if he had.'

Jaygo took Peter's arm in both hands and squeezed it. 'I think we should just go, Peter.'

'We will as soon as I find out what's happened. Someone's shot Laurie and we have to find out why.'

'Does it really matter,' she said, beginning to plead. 'Can't we just get out of here?'

'I'm not going anywhere until I've worked out what has happened,' he said firmly.

'Please, Peter,' she said, almost shouting at him. 'I'm very frightened and I want to go to the airport now. Please!'

Peter looked back down at Etherington's body.

Suddenly there was a crash and a roar at the back of the house and a fresh wave of locusts banged against the windows.

A pane of glass gave way and locusts came pouring in. Many of them were very much alive and soon Peter and Jaygo were surrounded by buzzing locusts flying in all directions and banging into their faces and bodies.

'Peter!' she screamed, pulling him towards the door.

Another pane of glass broke as they turned and started to run for the door. But Jaygo slipped and Peter had to practically carry an hysterical Jaygo out to the front of the house.

She was sobbing uncontrollably as he slammed the door behind them and put his arms fully around her. 'They are here, Peter,' she cried. 'The swarm is here. I know it is.'

'No, no,' he said, trying to calm her. 'It's not the swarm. It's just another fall of locusts. Look. It's stopped now.'

She stopped crying. 'I'm sorry,' she said, taking a hand up to wipe her eyes. 'But I was so scared.'

'It means that the swarm is nearly here. We have to go now.

339

I'll go back in and get the phone and you can call Sven on the way.'

'Peter, I've got the phone in my bag.'

But Peter had already turned and gone back into the house.

'No!' she shouted. 'Don't go back in!'

She ran over to the door and watched as Peter tried to make his way across the locust-filled room to the phone. It seemed that with every step he took, he disturbed even more of them.

'Peter,' she said, when he came out, 'what are you doing? I've got the phone in my bag.'

'What's this then? Another one?'

'It must be that man's. He must have taken it out to use.'

'Who would he call?'

'Jack? Did Laurie find him using the phone and shoot him?' said Jaygo.

'Hell knows what's happened here,' said Peter. 'But we can't find out now. We have to go.'

As Peter turned the Land Rover around, the lights picked out Laurie's body by the side of the drive. He stopped the Land Rover and Peter and Jaygo looked at each other.

'We have to leave him,' said Peter. 'We can't take him to the Lear with us and we can't do anything for him here.'

Jaygo nodded. 'But just to leave him there,' she said quietly.

As they drove away, Jaygo turned and leaned over the seat, across where the torque lay on the floor, and out of the rear window towards Laurie's body. 'What has become of us, Peter?' she said. 'That's Laurie back there.'

Peter patted her shoulder. 'Was,' he said. 'He won't mind now.'

Jaygo turned to the front.

She suddenly seemed to be listening intently. 'Is the engine all right? I can hear something not right.'

'No,' he said. 'That's our friends.'

'What?'

'That humming the other day. That's what they sound like when they are a long way away with a following wind. I guess they are only ten miles off and it's going to get a lot louder yet.'

She pulled open the side window and listened. 'It's like a growling,' she said. 'Or a big cat purring.'

'That's right,' he said. 'A very big cat.'

Jaygo was shutting the window and perhaps did not hear him.

She picked up her bag. 'I'll call the Lear,' she said. 'Tell them to get ready.'

At first the main road to the airport was clear of locusts and they made good progress. But soon the Land Rover was slipping and sliding across the road on the insects and Peter had to struggle with the wheel to keep straight.

'Tell them to taxi over to the terminal and meet us there,' he said.

'It's a terrible line. It's gone all hissy and isn't picking up.'

'Just keep trying,' he said. 'It must mean the locusts are in line with the satellite.'

She tried.

'I'm through!' she said triumphantly.

Pressing the handset close to her ear, she could just make out the voice at the other end.

'What?' Peter heard her ask. 'Can you hear me? He says to meet us at the terminal. Yes, go there now. What? I can't hear you!'

She put the phone down. 'Line's gone. But he was saying something about too many there. Something about taking off.'

The growling noise was much louder now and Peter had to raise his voice for Jaygo to hear him. 'We just have to hope then,' he shouted. 'We're only going to get one shot at it.'

'Do think it will be hard to take off?'

'Maybe. I've got an idea that could help us but we can only do it once. I need to know if he's got radar and how much fuel he's got on board.'

'I'll try,' she shouted back. 'But I think it's hopeless.'

It was a few minutes before she got through.

'Ah!' she called at last. 'Peter says how much fuel have you on board and have you got radar?'

She cupped her hand over the telephone, then put the phone down. 'Gone altogether. But he says he has full fuel and I could hear him say something about the engines again. That's all.'

'Shit!' said Peter, banging a hand on the wheel. 'I wanted him to do something before we got there!'

He held his hand down to look at his watch in the light from the dashboard. 'Five minutes at most now. There will be a lot of locusts in the air when we get there and it's going to be very loud. Do you think you'll be all right?'

'I'll be fine, Peter.'

'I hope so,' he said quietly so she would not hear him.

The terminal building was in darkness as Peter turned in to the car park. He could make out the landing lights of the Lear to one side and drove towards them.

The locusts in the car park flew up as the Land Rover passed and he could see clouds of them around the Lear as he drove up.

One of the crew must have been watching out for them because, as Peter slowed down about ten yards from the aeroplane, the side door opened and steps were lowered into the two-foot deep layer of insects.

The growl of the swarm was much louder here and they had to shout above it to make themselves heard.

'Are we going to leave it, Peter?' she shouted. 'Or try to take it?'

'Jack can have the locusts if he wants; we're going to have the torque,' he shouted back. 'Get the men!'

Almost before the Land Rover came to a halt, Jaygo was opening the door and running towards the Lear.

Peter tried to line up with the lights pointing towards the aircraft before getting out. The locusts came up to his knees as he got out and opened the rear doors.

Jaygo returned with the two crew members and the four of them pulled the torque out of the back of the Land Rover. It practically splashed to the ground through the locusts in its cloth before they could unwrap it and lift it as high as their shoulders.

The men did not question what it was, they were just as keen as Jaygo and Peter to be out of the swirling clouds of locusts that rose denser and denser with every slithering step.

Jaygo's face was tightly screwed up and her eyes shut tight with the effort. She slipped and went down but the men could not stop to help her. She scrabbled to her feet only to slip over again as she tried to catch them up.

The noise of the locusts was so loud that, only when they reached the Lear, could Peter hear the whine of the jets.

He went backwards up the steps as the two men pushed from below.

The torque was too wide to fit through the door flat and they had to lower it into the carpet of locusts to turn it on its side and try again.

It was much more difficult to manoeuvre up the steps in this position but, two minutes later, Peter pulled Jaygo inside. One of the men pushed the door closed as she fell onto the floor into the cabin.

'That noise!' she said, sitting forwards and putting her hand to her head.

'Oh yes.' said Peter, brushing locusts off himself onto the floor. 'And now you know why it's called a lion.'

'Shit!' she cried. 'I never want to do anything like that again! I fell over in them, Peter! I was *in* them!'

'You did pretty well, but that was the easy bit, I'm afraid. I have to go and talk to the pilot.'

'What?'

'I'll tell you later,' he said. 'You three get this thing strapped in somehow and then do the same yourselves. I have to go and see about the fuel.'

Peter went straight through to the flight deck and sat down in the right-hand seat. 'OK,' he said. 'Listen to what we have to do.'

The pilot looked over at him. 'We have to go back to the hangar. They are getting in the engines and I can't take off now. Look.' He pointed out of the cockpit window at the dense cloud of locusts banging blindly into the glass.

'Don't worry about them,' said Peter. 'Just do what I say.'

'If they get to the intakes, they will cut off the air and the engines will fail.'

Peter waved the protest aside. He pointed out of the side window. 'Take us down to the end of the runway,' he said. 'The end away from the take-off point. Line up as straight as you can.'

'But I have to take off into the wind. I may not have full power and I can't risk it.'

'Shut up,' said Peter. 'You have a full load of fuel on board, is that right?'

'Yes, but . . .'

'Shut up, I said,' repeated Peter. 'There's no time to argue.' He pointed behind him. 'Listen to me,' he said angrily. 'There's a million tons of solid insect coming towards you at ten miles an hour.'

The pilot opened his mouth to speak again.

'And if we're still sitting here when they hit us, we'll be crushed like a fucking drinks can! Ten minutes. Tops. Now, am I getting through to you?'

The pilot nodded.

'Good,' said Peter, turning to the front again. 'Now, get going and when you get to where I say, line her up and stop. I'm going back to the others for a moment but when the plane stops I'll come back.'

The pilot shook his head but reached forward for the throttle and the Lear jerked forward. Peter stood up and, steadying himself against the low ceiling of the flight deck, went back to the cabin.

'Where's the torque?' he asked, looking around the cabin.

'In the back cabin. But what are we doing?' cried Jaygo. 'Piers says we may not be able to take off.'

Peter looked at her and at the two young men who had strapped themselves into seats on the other side of the aeroplane.

'I'm afraid it's going to be pretty close but I think we'll be all right.'

She did not look reassured.

He squatted down next to her and took her hands. 'Look,' he said. 'Don't worry. I think I can settle them down long enough for us to take off. We'll have a clear run and in five minutes be out of here.'

He felt the aircraft turn and come to a halt.

'I have to go now,' he said.

'Where are you going? I want you here with me.'

'I can't. I have something to do. Back soon.'

He hurried back to the flight deck.

'OK,' he said, sitting down and doing up his harness.

'But they are worse here,' protested the pilot. 'We'll have to stay on the ground.'

'Go on,' ordered Peter, 'all the way down to the other end. And open the fuel cocks as you go. By the time we get to the other end it will have flattened them enough to give you a clear take-off path.'

'No!' cried the pilot in alarm. 'Are you crazy?'

'Just do it!' shouted Peter. 'We only get one chance!'

'But the fuel! It will be too dangerous!'

Peter reached forward and pushed the throttle levers. 'Come on,' he shouted as the engines picked up. 'Or do I have to do this all by myself? Show me the fuel cocks lever!'

'You're mad!' said the pilot. 'Crazy!'

'Fine!' Peter retorted. 'You come up with a better plan by the time we get to the other end and we'll do it your way! Just open the fuel, will you!'

The pilot took the throttle lever from Peter without another word and threw a switch on the panel in front of him.

'Wing tanks,' he said. 'All right.'

The fuel began to gush from the valves on the wings and splash down onto the locusts below.

Peter rubbed his face with his hands. He had no idea if the fuel

344

would flatten the locusts or not. But he knew they would never be able to take off at all if it did not.

He peered forwards as the Lear came to the end of the runway and turned round into its take-off position.

The lights shone only about fifteen yards into the night and Peter could not see if his plan had worked or not.

'There!' he said. 'Go for it!'

'I can't see!' said the pilot, leaning forwards next to Peter. 'It looks the same!'

'Do it!' shouted Peter, slamming the twin throttle levers forwards. 'It's now or never. Go! Go! GO!'

The engines roared to full power and the pilot pushed Peter's hand aside while he released the wheel brakes with his other hand.

The Lear bucked, as nine feet below the flight deck, the wheels began to move through the slush of aviation fuel and dying locusts.

Peter sat back and closed his eyes.

Behind them, as they gathered speed, the fuel was churned up into the swirls of the jet exhaust.

Peter thought he could hear the roar of the locusts above the engine noise.

As they gathered speed, the swirling fuel mist rose higher. Closer to the engines.

The front of the Lear began to lift, pushing the hot exhaust lower. Suddenly the rich mixture of fuel and air ignited and a blue whoosh of flame streaked out behind them along the runway.

Peter watched with horror as a tongue of flame, twenty feet wide, shot straight ahead of them.

The pilot held the nose wheel off the ground as they raced into an exploding blue curtain of flame.

Behind them, Peter could hear Jaygo screaming as the aeroplane suddenly rocked backwards and left the ground.

The pilot immediately reached forward to retract the wheels as the nose began to rise and the Lear did its trick of going up like a lift.

As the Lear leaned forwards and came to a more comfortable angle, Peter looked across at the pilot. 'Well, done, Sven. I thought you were going to drop us in it for a minute back there.'

'What? Who is Sven?'

'Never mind,' said Peter, unfastening his seat harness and standing up. 'I'll tell you when we get to London.'

345

In the cabin, Jaygo was sitting back with her eyes closed. Peter touched her gently on the shoulder. 'Wake up.'

She reached for his hand.

He squeezed it as he leaned over her and tried to see out of the window.

It was completely black except for the flashing red navigation beacon on the wing tip and he could see nothing.

'Well,' he said. 'That seemed to go off OK, didn't it? Shall we go back and see if our passenger is all right?'

'In a minute, Sunday Man. Just sit down first.'

He smiled at her as he slid into the seat. 'Africa, eh?' he said. 'I told you it would be a bit different.'

'I'm not going back,' she said. 'Not ever.'

He smiled at her again. 'No,' he said. 'Nor me.'

Below them in the blackness, the swarm of locusts was already crushing its way over the airport and rolling towards Kano. The lion was coming home.